Gene Krenz

Back to Never Been

Outskirts Press, Inc.
http://www.outskirtspress.com

ISBN: 978-1-4327-3917-1

Outskirts Press and the "OP" logo are trademarks belonging to Outskirts Press, Inc.

DEDICATION:
To my girls, Pat, Kim, Heidi and Traci who, together have
enriched my life along the way.

Gary

GENE KRANZ

1·15-10

Chapter 1

He stood there in the rain, hardly noticing the puddles at his feet. His head and heart were elsewhere, caught up in a time warp he could neither escape nor comprehend. For the first time in his life he was grappling with the certainty that he had failed. He hadn't yet fully come to grips with why, but somehow he knew that whatever had spurred the sudden dissolution of his marriage and the meltdown of his family, it was largely his own doing.

His son and daughter had never shared with him the excitement of landing a rainbow or speckled trout on the Yellowstone. They had never climbed Granite Peak or hiked in the Bitterroots. Faintly, he remembered camping once or twice with them in Virginia when they were in elementary school, but never since. They could have done so much more together, and it was his fault they hadn't. A guilty conscious told him he had never been there for his teen-aged daughter when she sought his counsel and, apparently, he had never really been there for his wife. All these years, he thought, his head had been off somewhere caught up in himself. He was a mess and a damned poor excuse for a father and husband. That much he did understand.

A career, making money, being somebody, that's where his head had been, and now it was over. An important part of his life had ended, and the road back was blocked with anger, harsh words, guilt and infidelity. It was a road to be avoided. There would certainly be no welcoming committee along the way or at the other end, for he had paved his path through life as an adult with a litany of mistakes and indiscretions. What guarantee was there that in starting over he would not make the same bad choices and decisions? None. Zilch. Nada. Zero. Still, he could not know what the future held. Time was what he needed. He needed to clear his head of mental and emotional cobwebs, faulty connections and squandered linkages. That process had to begin in Montana, close to where his value system and beliefs had been forged. It was the only way, the only place. He had come home to his prairies and mountains, and it was here he hoped to regain his self-confidence and self-esteem.

That is the sorry spectacle I looked upon as I stared at myself through a veil of foggy drizzle and personal despondency. That was me. Jim Pengilly. That's what I saw. A pathetic, forlorn Jim Pengilly. A Jim Pengilly who needed help.

Suddenly, I was back in the real world, divorced from my recent past, confronting more immediate problems. I was soaking wet, cold, and at least a little disoriented. My head and shoulder throbbed with excruciating pain. I had a vague recollection of a roadside tavern, the noisy crowd of regulars, the steak and the drinks. In my mind's eye, I could still see clearly the shapely and flirtatious barmaid, and I remembered leaving her an extravagant tip. But all of that was prologue. Now I was standing in the rain on a lonely back country road, and I was lost. A vague notion of *where* I had touched down, after several days of travel from the east coast, was lodged in my mind, but my perceptions of precisely who I was and where I belonged had changed.

Even my best friends here and in Baltimore would tell you I no longer resembled that naive Montana kid who had headed east some twenty years earlier to make his fortune. I lacked the boundless energy of that youngster; a bright eyed, ambitious, spanking new college graduate who couldn't wait to take aim at the world he damn well planned to conqueror. Now as a man, I was heading home and feeling a little like the old time cowman who bragged that he had cattle in the bank and money on the range. Not one of my fingers was needed to count the number of cattle I ran on my non-existent range, but I did have a fair amount of coin jingling in my pockets. I had been successful financially, but that was about all. My life was shattered, and I felt regret commensurate with my losses and a colossal sense of emptiness. That old cowman, who couldn't say where he kept his cattle or money, was only slightly less screwed up than me.

My truck's front end was lodged in the borrow pit, with its hood crumpled like fabric bunching up in tiny corrugations under the needle of a sewing machine. Its long box and open tailgate were perched on the shoulder of a slippery gravel road. As I stood there swaying in a fair degree of inebriation, I suddenly seized on how I had come by the blood on my forehead and the pain in my shoulder. Images of having cramped the steering wheel sharply to the right, trying not to hit a deer, flashed across my mind. Shaking my head from side to side, thinking of the fix I had gotten myself into, I chuckled as I thought of how my truck, a chunk of steel and rubber and glass with smoke rising from folds in its crumpled hood, shared with me the same level of understanding about our dilemma. It understood nothing, and I knew only slightly more. I had a foggy notion of where I was but absolutely no idea of what I should do next.

My eyes caught a flicker of light in the distance, and I began walking toward it, wishing I had stayed away from the hard stuff. The lights were off the road a couple hundred yards, and the road leading to the low-slung house was in worse condition than the main road. Through the large window at the front of the house, I could see the outlines of two middle-aged people watching TV. Automatically, like Pavlov's canine companion, their hands went to the huge bowl of popcorn occupying the space between them. Like the rest of mankind, when so engaged, their eyes never left the screen.

From far away came the barking of a dog and, as I approached the house, the yippy, sharp bark of the small dog staring at me through the window, alerted the couple to my presence.

The light bulb on the porch was burned out, a fact that helped me not at all in finding a doorbell. Finally, I tapped lightly on the front door and waited. It occurred to me that the image I projected was not one likely to open many doors this time of night. But after what seemed several minutes, the door did open to reveal a tall, slender and attractive gray headed woman, leaning on a cane.

"Ma'am," I said, "I had car trouble back down the road a bit, and I'm hoping I can use your phone to call a wrecker. My truck is in the ditch, and it will take a wrecker to get me out."

"Oh, goodness," she exclaimed, "you certainly picked a bad night to have car trouble. You better come in. You'll catch your death."

"I'm fine, here, Ma'am," I replied. "You don't want me dripping water all over the place. If I could just use your phone...."

"You do as I say, young man," she said again, in a pleasant voice. "Don't worry about the carpet. Carpets can be cleaned."

With that I edged through the doorway, leaving my rain-soaked jacket draped over a chair on the porch. With but one foot across the threshold, I was already feeling guilty over the mess I knew I would make. From the living room a man's voice asked if everything was all right. The lady said that everything was fine, but that a man who had car trouble down the road was asking to use their phone.

"My cell phone battery went dead on me," I said, feeling the need to further justify my being there. "I've a charger, but forgot to plug it in." Then as an afterthought, I added, "My name is Jim...Jim Pengilly."

"Jim," the lady said, "our name is Macintosh. I'm Jenny and my husband is Claire. He says it's a girl's name, but I like it."

She went on to say that it would be hours before anyone could make it out to their place with the road in the shape it was in, and that I couldn't stand there all night wet and waiting. I protested but she ignored me and threw several scatter rugs in a line leading to their bathroom. Then she left and quickly returned with a pair of washed-out Levis, a plaid flannel shirt, stockings, and underwear. She laid them on the sink in the bathroom and told me to change.

"They're Claire's," she said. "You look to be of a size. You change and I'll make us some coffee. When you're dressed, I'll want to take a closer look at your forehead. It's bleeding, you know."

Sensing the futility of arguing with this kind women, I tiptoed into the bathroom, toweled away the wetness and changed into the dry clothing. A few minutes later, I edged out into the hallway, feeling warm and dry...feeling wonderful. She took my arm, led me into the living room and introduced me to her husband.

Claire Macintosh remained seated but extended his hand. He was as gray as her and on the slender side as well. He looked to be quite tall, but it was hard to know for he continued sitting. I could see a pair of crutches leaning against the sofa, which explained why.

"Can't be of much help to anyone these days," he said, as he caught me staring at the crutches. "Mom and I got banged up pretty good in a car accident a couple months ago, and I'm still on the mend. Didn't see that big mule deer until he was part way through our windshield. Wasn't content with smashing my leg when the car hit a post, I waited a few days to fall off one of our trailers.

"Are you from around these parts?" he added, as if to signal that he didn't wish to go into more detail about the accident. I explained that I was originally from Moccasin, that I had attended Montana State in Bozeman, but that I had lived in Maryland for several years.

"Well, you're a fair piece from Moccasin, young man," Claire said. "It's close to 200 miles up there. You headed that way?"

"No, Sir, I'm not," I replied, "at least not yet. Actually, I'm on my way to Deer Lodge. My folks live there now."

"Work at the Prison?" Claire asked.

"No, they're retired. Dad works part time at the truck stop in Garrison. Something to do, I guess."

"I see."

"What's the best way to get back on the Interstate from here," I asked, instantly wishing I hadn't.

He eyed me with a look that told me that my being there was beginning to arouse his suspicions. He was likely thinking that someone born and raised in Montana ought to know how to get around. I knew I was indebted to them for their hospitality, and they deserved the truth. So, I confessed, with considerable embarrassment, that I was lost, that I had made a wrong turn somewhere along the line, and that I had become disoriented in the darkness. My explanation was that it had been a long time since I had visited the state and that I had deliberately followed back roads to help me get a fresh perspective on my roots. I ended my confession by admitting that I might have had a drink or two more than I could handle at the steak house down the road.

"Well, Jim" Claire said, seemingly satisfied with my explanation of how I happened to be sitting across from him, "our place is located about 15 miles southwest of Norris, so if you're looking for back roads, you've found it. The Tobacco Root Mountains are just to the west, the Madison River and the Madison Mountains to the east."

"I remember crossing the river," I replied, "but I must have missed the sign."

"Well then," he said, "as far as the best route out of here goes, point the nose of your truck east and drive 'til you reach 287. You'll know when you get there. It's a good, hard-topped road. Hang a left there and head north. You'll go through Norris in a few miles and, before you know it, you'll reach Interstate 90 near Whitehall. You know the way from there, I'm sure. Is you're truck fit to run?"

Claire had a way of changing the subject abruptly, as if to say that no further discussion about his presence was necessary.

"It is," I answered "At least it was still running after I hit the borrow pit. The hood is crumpled up some, but the truck should make it to Deer Lodge. Which way is east from here?"

I was exhausted when I shut the door of one of their spare bedrooms behind me, but sleep was slow to come. My mind was leap-frogging from one crisis to another, but the self-inflicted turmoil faded gradually and, without knowing just when, I fell asleep. The bed might have been my own, for I slept until the spattering of rain on the windows and the rush of a strong wind battering the house lifted me from my slumber. The ceiling above me was the first thing I noticed. It was unique mostly because it's chandelier-type light fixture had obviously been crafted by a welder with a flair for reshaping horse shoes. I was flat on my back with one of my legs crooked, exactly as I remembered it having been when I first plopped down on the bed the night before.

I chuckled to myself, marveling at how that crooked leg had managed to maintain itself in it's fixed position throughout the night. Amazingly, I dredged up from my past a memory of another time when my exhaustion had been so complete as to lock my leg in that same position throughout a long-ago night. It was my first night in a barracks during boot camp following my spur-of-the-moment enlistment in this man's army during the Korean War or conflict, as the folks in Washington insisted on calling it. Obviously they hadn't been there.

My momentary disorientation vanished like a cloud pushed across the sky by a gale force wind, and it all came back to me as if someone had flicked one of my many internal switches. A picture of last night's events was etched now indelibly in my mind. Mine was now the body of a rested, relaxed, and completely sober man who was soon sitting on the edge of the bed that had enveloped him in warmth throughout the night. That man was ready for whatever might confront him in the days ahead.

"Oh, Jim, you're up," Jennifer Macintosh said, almost in a whisper, as she helped the two eggs in a large, cast-iron frying pan travel the short journey between sunny-side-up and over-easy. "How do you like your bacon?"

"Crisp," I said, as if I were replying to the waitress in the shiny, aluminum-sided diner I had stopped at for years on my way to work.

"Crisp it is, then," she chirped. "There's coffee's on the counter. Help yourself."

Mrs. Macintosh and I were nursing our second cup of strong coffee when Claire shuffled into the room cussing his crutches. I could about imagine what it must be like for a vigorous, active man to suddenly find himself in his present, restrictive state.

"Sorry, I'm runnin' late, Jenny," he said, once he had dropped into one of the kitchen chairs. "Didn't think there was an reason to hurry since it's still pouring out there."

"He's right, you know, Jim," she said, looking straight into my eyes as if she owed me an apology for the weather. "I think you're stuck here for another day at least. The bottom simply drops out of this country with a rain like this."

"It's a chance for us to get better acquainted," Claire added, dryly.

And, that's what we did over the next day and a half. Actually, we covered so many subjects it could easily be argued that our collective conversations qualified as a bonafide bull session. We talked of everything, including Montana's junior senator, foreign affairs, and the Bobcat's football prospects for the coming year. I could tell they were enjoying it, and it occurred to me that they probably spent much of their time alone and hungered for conversations with someone besides each other. They were curious about my life and my family, but they were also careful not to pry.

Jennifer slipped away from our conversation only long enough to answer the phone. In her absence, Claire and I talked about cattle, grass, machinery, fuel prices, and the weather, but we steered away from personal things. When Jenny returned, she was carrying a fresh pot of coffee and some homemade doughnuts. Delicious, both of them. As her and I sat there talking about weather fronts, Claire interrupted to ask about the phone call. She said it was their daughter, Megan, calling from Denver.

"Everything okay?" Claire asked.

"Said she's been feeling tired and lethargic for a couple of weeks, but figured it was probably nothing more than not getting enough sleep."

"I suppose," was Claire's simple response.

"We have a daughter and granddaughter living in Denver," Jenny offered. "We wish we saw them more often."

"I'm sure," I said. "I have a son and daughter back in Maryland. They are both in highschool this year. They live with their mother. We are in the process of getting a divorce, I'm afraid."

"Oh, I'm sorry, Jim," Jennifer said, "so sorry."

"Well, thanks," I said. "Our marriage has been heading in that direction for some time."

With that admission, the flood gates were thrown open and,

from that point on, nothing was deliberately excluded from our conversation.

"We lost our only son several years ago," Claire said out of the blue. "Killed in a plane crash down in Wyoming. Him and another fellow. Ran into a mountain just out of Rawlins. On their way to the Stock Show in Denver. He's the dark-haired man you see in all the pictures around here."

"It's been fifteen years," Jennifer added, "though at times it seems like yesterday."

It was my turn to tell them I was sorry, and I did. We sat there for a while, none of us knowing quite what else to say. I knew immediately I had stumbled into sharing with this good man and woman what must have been a most difficult subject for them to discuss.

"He was such a good boy," Jennifer said after a while. "Kind. Courteous. Loving. A wonderful brother to Megan and everyone's friend. He loved fly fishing. He loved flying and fishing. Soloed when he was 16. Had over 3,000 hours. Fished when he found the time. He was flying with a friend in his friend's plane when they crashed. His own plane is out in the shed. No one, including the two of us, has ever opened the door of that hanger since the day we lost him."

"He was engaged to be married to a girl over in Bozeman," Claire said. "They were both engineering students at Montana State. She has moved away. To Salt Lake, I think. Said she couldn't live here with all the memories."

Once again there was silence but, like before, it ended when I said the words I had never said to anyone else before.

"My own life is in a shambles," I started. "My wife has filed for divorce, and neither of my children has talked to me since she told them. I don't know how it all happened, but I know it was mostly my own fault. We have lived apart for over a year now, but up until she had me served with divorce papers, my kids were still talking to me. Not anymore, though. My son blames me, and my daughter despises me."

"Jim," Jennifer said, trying to console me, "you are being too hard on yourself. I'm sure the fault is not entirely yours. It never is. There are two sides to every story. Don't you know that?"

"I suppose," I said. "We have been drifting apart for a long time as far as that goes, and this is just the culmination of what we could both see coming at us for a long time. She is "with" another man now, probably driven to him by yours truly and, for a time, there was another woman in my life. We are both guilty of having expended too little effort to preserve our marriage. I was engrossed in my job, and I'm afraid I have been a very poor parent."

"I doubt that, Jim," Jennifer responded. "Maybe there is still hope."

"No, Jennifer," I said. "There isn't. It's over between us. Both of us have to begin rebuilding our own lives. No one can do it for us. That's why I'm here, I guess. We certainly can't do it for each other but, maybe, we can help ourselves."

The wrecker came early the next morning, and I left wearing Claire's clothing and one of his old hats.

"That hat will keep the sun out of your eyes, Jim," he said, "but I want it back. And I want it delivered personally, if you get my meaning."

His arm went out to me and I shook his hand hard. Jennifer came up to me and encircled me in her arms. I had come here a stranger. Two days later, I was feeling like a member of the family. I knew I would come back for a visit, and I knew it would be soon.

Highway 287 was smooth and surprisingly straight. It dipped here and there like a bobber in flowing water, only to rise gently and give me fantastic, picture-window views of the Tobacco Root Mountains. I stopped in Whitehall for gas and a highway map. My own had been misplaced somewhere in the shuffle of things, and I knew I would be hitting Montana's back roads again soon. I was gradually remembering how wonderful this place was. Add to that the fact that I had two new friends, that I was borderline euphoric, a state-of-mind I hadn't visited for a long, long time, and you had the beginnings of a new and different person. I firmly believe it to be so.

Interstate 90 and Homestake Pass lifted me over the Continental Divide and gave me the first view of Butte in nearly 20 years. It had changed dramatically during my absence, but the north shoulder of the Berkeley Pit was   still clearly visible until I turned off at Harrison Avenue, looking for a sandwich and a fresh cup of coffee. The sandwich ended up being a Big Mac and the coffee was the hard stuff, large size. My Montana wings were starting to flap. I was glad to be home. I was feeling more and more like the new man I was just beginning to define, the man I knew I wanted to become.

As I sat waiting for my food, I found myself speculating about how many individuals and families had a connection of some kind or other to Butte and the surrounding towns. The mountain sides had been worked for almost a hundred years, and thousands of men had either labored in underground tunnels or had operated a variety of gigantic machines above ground after the company shifted to surface mining.

At one time the Company had been the fourth largest in the world and by far the largest in Montana, controlling or influencing almost everything that happened in the Big Sky Country, including newspapers and politics. Four of my uncles spent their entire working life in the mine, and the oldest died there before he drew a dollar of pension money. My dad worked there for a year before he married my mother, but at her insistence, they left town to work for a rancher east of Great Falls. Moccasin came later when he became a grain buyer for a local elevator.

A beat up '75 GMC pickup had pulled up along side my truck while I was inside. The bumper sticker proclaimed it to be a Cowboy Cadillac. Three mangy, long-haired dogs had a home in the box. One was sleeping, the other was whining about something, and the third was staring off toward the Continental Divide with a forlorn look on his face.

"Cheer up boy," I said to him. "Soon enough you'll be home."

He heard me, turned to me, but quickly looked away as if to say, "What the hell do you know about anything?" As if looking for a response, he turned his head back in my direction, and I said, "Well not much, but I do know I'm home."

Heading west and north, I quickly passed on my left the road leading to Idaho Falls and Salt Lake City. Every minute brought me closer to Deer Lodge and my mother. I began verbalizing aloud how I would explain my presence, but nothing sounded right. By the time I passed Opportunity and Warm Springs, I knew I was going to wing it.

I took a chance that my mom was working at the 4 Bs restaurant on the northeast end of town just off the highway, and stopped there first. She came in two days a week to make pastries, but today was one of her off days.

"Oh, my God," she shouted when she saw me on the doorstep. "What's wrong?"

That was my mom. She knew no other way. Go to the heart of matters. Don't dilly dally around. Go straight at it, particularly when you're dealing with your feckless son.

My approach, given my Mom's temperament and mind set, was to do the same. I told her I would explain but not until I had exacted a genuine squeeze and a peck or two on the cheek. She complied. I knew she was glad to see me when she reached up and pecked me a third time. It took me almost two hours to plead my case, mostly because she kept interrupting me wanting details. "I knew it," she said. "I could see it coming a long time ago."

"You should have let me know, Mom." I commented. "I didn't see it."

She knew I was pulling her leg, but she didn't miss a beat.

"We still talk with Bob and Carmen from time to time, and Carmen told me you and Rebecca were having a rough time of it. Becky had said something over the phone."

"Well, it's true," I said, "and our troubles were larger than Carmen would have guessed. We have separated. I have left my job, and I've come back to Montana to live."

"How are we going to tell your dad?" she asked. "He'll be upset, you know. I liked Rebecca like a daughter. So did he."

"The only thing that upsets him is when the price of barley drops in Seattle or Duluth, and maybe not even that anymore," I said.

"I hope so," she said, "But don't count on it. He has his views."

Her apprehension was genuine, for my father was one of those individuals who was brutally frank in dealing with others, including me or my sisters. He knew no other way, except when he was dealing with my mother. She had worked her magic on him for almost forty years and, while he might not tell her his chronic back problem made even standing painful at times, he would never lie to her about things that mattered or speak in a raised voice. His love for her was boundless, and it was that fact that had me not just a little worried as we parked my car in front of the truck stop café.

"Better let me do the talking, Jim," my mother said.

"Don't worry, Mom," I replied. "We won't be talking about my problems 'til later unless you can't resist telling him now. This is one of those, 'Hi, Dad, bet you're surprised to see me?' visits. I'll talk to him later tonight."

He was the first person I saw as we entered the front door. He looked up from a ledger of sorts flattened out on the counter-top that protected the candy bars, slowly laid his pencil down, and walked out to meet me. He was one of those individuals who never seemed to change. He still had a heavy crop of hair except that it was now a shiny, silver-gray. It looked good on him. Gave him a distinguished look. He still had the narrow hips of a working cowhand and the trophy belt buckle called attention to his flat mid-section. His complexion was clear but weathered after thirty or more years working on a ranch or scouting the county looking to purchase grain.

He was at least two inches taller than me, so I found myself looking up at a face sporting two large dark brown eyes and bushy eyebrows. The only change I could discern in the three years it had been since I last saw him was a pencil-thin, gray mustache above his upper lip. His handshake, as always, was hard enough to make me wince in pain, though I did my best to hide it. He smiled as he watched my facial muscles tighten. Satisfied that his reputation was still intact, he draped his long arm over my shoulder and pulled me to him in an uncharacteristic display of tenderness.

"You could have knocked me over with your pinky," he said, "when I saw you come through that door. Did your mother forget to tell me you were coming?"

"Nope," I answered. "I just happen to be passing through. On my way up to Moccasin to attend to some business up there." My response was not altogether a fabrication. My plan was to drive up there soon to talk to Rebecca's parents. I didn't think it had to actually come to one of those his-side, her-side contests, but I wanted a chance to explain. Rebecca was not the kind to try to lay all of the blame on me, especially since we both acknowledged that we had to share the guilt. Bob and Carmen were good folks. I loved them dearly. I wanted them to know I was sorry. They would understand.

"Well, it's good to see you, Jimmy. I'm glad you thought to stop by and see your old man. How long have you got?"

I told him I'd be seeing my "old man" tonight in Deer Lodge and that I planned to stay around for a few days. He thought that was a great idea. We could talk about the Grizzlies and Bobcats he said, allowing that it was hard for him to choose between them, given that Deer Lodge was roughly half way between Missoula and Bozeman and that I had attended both schools.

That night we drank a few beers while my mother grilled the T-bones and, later, while she was on the phone we talked. He didn't interrupt me even once as I laid out my woeful tale. When I finished, I asked him if he had any questions, and he asked me if I thought I had done everything I could to save my marriage. I told him that I probably hadn't, but that neither of us was sure anymore that we wanted to stay married. I didn't go into details because doing so didn't seem to serve any useful purpose. He seemed satisfied.

"Well," he sighed, "I'm sorry for you. I am not going to scold or lecture you for what has happened, or is in the process of happening. If I thought you were an idiot, I'd tell you. You know that. If it is any comfort to you, I'll say that in this day and age marriages seem to require the strongest possible glue to hold them together."

"The glue just wasn't there for us, Dad," I said. "My brain has been working overtime trying to discover the underlying causes. There are so many that it's impossible to lay the blame on any one thing. We have both been derelict in not making an effort to add more of that glue where it was needed. I think we both quit caring sometime ago. Our careers became too important. Maybe neither of us ever cared enough. I just don't know."

"If I knew what you should do, Jimmy, you know I would tell

you. I have no experience in dealing with the kinds of problems you are facing. So, I'll say nothing. That's probably not what you expected me to say. So, what happens now? What about Michael and Morgan?"

"Wish I could say that they won't be scarred by all of this," I said, "but the truth is I don't know. Neither of them is willing to even talk to me since they learned their mother was filing for divorce. Michael, for now, is ignoring me. I think he is hurt because of the hurt I have brought to his mother and sister. But, he's not blind. He's perceptive enough to know what has been happening. In his case, I am hoping he may come around to at least wanting to listen to me."

"That Mike, he's a good kid," my Dad said.

"They both are," I agreed, "but Morgan despises me I think. I have called the house on several occasions, and as soon as she hears my voice she hangs up. The first time she shouted that she hated me. Since then, never so much as a single word."

"My heart goes out to all of you, Jimmy," the elder Pengilly said in a measured voice. "You are my son, and you know I love you. But I love Rebecca too, and I adore those kids. Would it do any good for your mother and I to call them?"

"In time, maybe, but not just yet. Give them a chance to process all that has happened. They are both bright kids. Maybe in time..."

During my three days in Deer Lodge, we never spoke again about my problems. The closest we came was when dad asked me once again what I was planning to do. Stay in Montana at least for a while, I told him. Could live off my savings for a good while, but I needed to find something to do. I knew I couldn't turn the corner in rebuilding my life until I found work. Work was a part of what I am. My pockets might be bulging with thousand dollar bills, and I would still need work. Immersing myself in a job naturally meant I would be focusing on something other than the mess I had brought down upon myself.   Plainly said, I needed to stop feeling sorry for Jim Pengilly before I could start rebuilding.

My trip to Moccasin was a leisurely one. It took me from Deer Lodge up to Garrison and then on to Missoula on I-90. I stopped and had coffee with dad in Garrison. I had friends in Missoula but was content to just drive over by the University campus to see how it had changed. Like me, it had changed dramatically, with several new buildings and a cracker jack new football stadium. I found Elrod Hall, my old dormitory. It hadn't changed at all and still retained its character as one of the older buildings on campus.

Before I pointed the nose of my truck toward Lincoln and then Great Falls, I stopped at the Big Sky Drive-In on Broadway to feast on the best burger I'd eaten since the last time I was there. As a student, I either ate there or at the Oxford Bar downtown, when I had the money.

The drive up the Blackfoot River road, known to most natives as the Lincoln Highway, brought back memories of float trips I had taken with friends on more than one summer weekend. The Blackfoot Valley and its Canyon lacked the majesty of Glacier's peaks and the Bitterroots Spires, but it was astoundingly beautiful. Its mystique flowed from a melding of its almost flat water pools in its upper reaches to its white water, bouldered reaches downstream. In Lincoln, I purchased a caramel role big enough to cover a dinner plate and filled the small thermos my mother had sent along with coffee.

The stretch of road between Lincoln and Great Falls was one I could have negotiated even today with one eye closed. These were the foothills of the Rocky Mountain Front, and I had followed their ups and downs hundreds of times like I was riding a shiny horse on a merry-go-round. In Great Falls, I drove down by the Missouri River and, for a couple hours, killed time watching people. The bike paths and people paths were something I had never seen before, and they were superb in a park-like setting. A leisurely stroll down river built up my appetite, so I checked in at the Holiday Inn and walked across the street for supper. Supper! Damn it. I was back in Montana, and I was growing more and more comfortable with my roots as the memories of earlier days slipped in on me at every turn. God, this was country!

Moccasin was located due east of Great Falls on Highway 87. The town had been formed in 1908 as a homestead community, but earlier settlers had been ranchers. The Hales fell into the latter category, though much of their land was now devoted to dryland, strip farming. Their ranch was tucked down into a fold in a line of hills 15 miles southwest of town. The Hales were retired now, spending part of each winter in Prescott, Arizona, where one of Becky's two brothers lived.

Before I made the turn onto the gravel road leading to their place, I pulled over to the side and stopped on an approach. I needed a little time to collect my thoughts. It was also almost noon, and I also didn't want to barge in upon them while they were eating.

Our conversation would surely come down to the *why* question, though we might circle around it for a while before tackling it. They were like family to me, but I was not of their blood, and that could make a difference. The burden was on me. So what should I tell them?

They couldn't know why our marriage had unraveled unless Becky had said something to her mother on the phone, so I had some decisions to make. I wanted to respond to them with only as much truth as I thought they could handle, so there were a few realities I would shield them from. What purpose, I asked myself, would be served by telling them that we had both been involved in love affairs with another person? That we had both been unfaithful to each other and our wedding vows? Knowing would only diminish their respect for both of us.

They were from the old school, where such things seldom ever happened...but mattered. They would not hear it from me. Some things belonged to Becky and me alone, not to be shared, either because they were too personal or likely to be hurtful. Rebecca was their oldest daughter; the first of their children to go to college; the first to marry; the first to give them grandchildren; and now, the first to divorce. She was their pride and joy, and I knew I must leave that intact. She was a gem, and I was lucky to have had all the years we had been together. But the love was gone from our marriage, and the past was prologue for both of us.

In a more perfect world, grappling with the *why* questions was best left to the parties themselves. But the world was far from perfect and, because divorce involves families, friends, and even colleagues, certain details much be shared. It wasn't as if everyone was inherently nosey, or that they reveled in possessing knowledge others lacked. It was a matter of coping. Those of us who gave a damn about how they felt, were obligated to be honest with them. Knowing led to understanding, and understanding led to acceptance. I knew as well as anyone what had driven us apart, so there was no confusion there. My only uncertainty lay in not knowing for sure how to tell people I cared for very much.

The truth was that it may have been the shallowness of our love for each other and a rushed marriage that simply could not sustain itself when a host of other factors came into play. In retrospect, it seemed both of us had been negligent. We both saw our careers as transcending all else in importance, and over time we unwittingly became so immersed in them that we lost sight of what really mattered. My guilt was probably greater than hers in that regard, but hers was just as real. After the first few years, she had never expressed even the slightest interest in my career, nor had I for hers. We were simply too caught up in ourselves as individuals to have time for each other. Becky was devoted to our children, and I applauded her for that. Shamefully, I now had to admit that I had largely left the responsibility for their upbringing to her. Her devotion and thoughtful shepherding through their early years was commendable, but her willingness to devote so much time to them, left her with less time for me. Had I pitched in to assist her, our estrangement might not now be an issue.

And then there were the people we worked with. We spent more of our waking hours with them than we did with each other, and we shared many of the same interests. In time, and it took years, our interface with each other was characterized as one of assiduous attention to our work and an almost totally insular view of marriage. How could things have turned out any differently? How could two relatively perceptive people let it happen?

Bob and Carmen were sitting in the shade of their spacious porch when I drove into the yard. Harley was with them. Their oldest son, he now operated a combination cow-calf and small grain operation, on what was left of the Hale holdings. Several quarter sections of land had been sold off over the years to area farmers and newcomers who had come to the Judith Basin to get away from congestion elsewhere, but the Hales were still one of the largest property owners in the county.

Bob raised himself up out of his comfortable recliner to watch me drive up, leaning against one of the several rustic log poles supporting the roof. Carmen and Harley stood as well when I climbed the steps and stood before them.

"Jim," Bob said, as he shook my hand, "good to see you. Becky said you might be stopping by."

So they knew. It was just as well. I shook hands with the men and hugged Carmen. About them was a nervousness that told me they had been, by sheer coincidence, discussing Rebecca and me as I drove into the yard. My feeling was confirmed when Harley excused himself and left. He apologized saying he had to go pick up one of the hired men so they could move a tractor, but it may have been that he didn't want to be around when we got around to talking about Becky. We had always been close, and I am sure he was disenchanted with me.

"What happened, Jim?" Robert inquired. "We'd like to know."

"Of course," I said. "That's why I am here. You two have been like a second mom and dad to me since long before Becky and I were married. I remember coming out here to throw those 65 pound alfalfa bales around, hoping to catch a glance of Rebecca. I wish I had better news, but I don't. I'm assuming Becky has filled you in on most of it, but I wanted to come back and tell you that I am sorry. If I though I could talk her into changing her mind, I'd try. But it wouldn't work. She probably told you that herself."

"She did," Carmen offered, "but we're still not sure what exactly brought this all about."

"A lot of things, none of which couldn't have been fixed," I said, "had we tried. But it was like a cancer diagnosed only after it is too late. Oh, it wasn't as if it just swooped down on us one day, and it was over. We could both see it coming, and we had our heart-to-heart talks. Sometimes at her instigation, sometimes at mine. The funny thing is we never fought. Harsh words and shouting were just never part of it. It was as if we were both biding our time until something came along to alter the status quo.

"What that was, exactly," I continued, "neither of us had a clue. Then, one day, she said she'd had enough and wanted out. Suddenly, one of us got up enough nerve or simply got tired of what had become a loveless marriage. We were both relieved. I had sensed for a long time that Becky had come to believe that I didn't want her anymore. I was thinking the same about her.

"In any case, here I am," I continued. "Beat on me if you must. I am so sorry. I know I've hurt a lot of people, and I'm sure Becky feels exactly the same. Somehow, over several years, we simply fell out of love. The chemistry is caput. Gone. We agree about that. It's about the only thing. I am sorry."

I'll never forget what happened next. Carmen lifted herself out of her chair and came to me with outstretched arms. She slipped them around my waist and squeezed hard. It was she who was comforting me now. I know tears were streaming down my cheeks, and I wanted to cry or die, whichever helped the most.

"The news that you two are breaking up," she said, "ranks right up there with the worst I've ever heard. If I could shake my magic wand and make it all better, I would. But I can't. If it is any comfort to you, though, let me try to tell you what I think about marriages that fail the test of time. For starters, it is almost never the fault of just one of the parties involved. You need to understand that we are not placing the blame solely on you. Somewhere deep inside of relationships there is a kind of malignancy that spreads if untreated. It is probably a matter of too much routine and way too much indifference. I believe the two of you still care for each other, and I know you love your children, but the kind of love that can sustain a relationships in the face of tough times or indifference was probably never there. You are both at fault. Neither of you is at fault. I just hope that each of you find what you are looking for."

I thanked both of them. My reservoir of words was flirting with empty. I didn't know what more to say. It was Bob, normally a man of few words, who bailed me out by asking about Michael and Morgan.

"My instincts tell me," I said, "that at least for the time being, their place is with their mother. There will be no nasty custody battle. The court will probably deal with the children on a joint custody basis but, for now, they will spend more time with their mother than with me. They are fast approaching adulthood and will soon be making up their own minds about their life. With some urging by myself and the two of you and by my parents, I'm hoping they can be lured out here now and again."

"You better stay for supper," Carmen said.

It was then that I told them my first and only outright lie. Had a job interview in Bozeman, I said. Needed to get on the road. There was no job interview, of course, but I felt everything that could be said had been said. Now was the time for all of us to reflect on what had happened and, hopefully, find some comfort in knowing it could have been worse.

They waved at me as I drove down the road toward Moccasin. Three hours later I was knocking on the door of my rancher friends just beyond Norris. It was Claire who came to the door, shuffling along with a crutch under one arm and a cane in the other.

"Brought your hat back, Claire," I said.

He smiled and waved me in.

Chapter 2

Jennifer hugged me like I was one of her own brood, and before I could thank them both for their warm welcome, she had poured me a cup of coffee and placed a dish covered with homemade doughnuts before me. Being here made very little sense to me. I should be in Bozeman or Butte or maybe even Billings looking for work. But it never occurred to me not to stop. A scant week earlier, I had stumbled, half drunk, upon two wonderful people who had instantly made me feel better about my self, by providing a comfortable haven at a time when I sorely needed a soft place to land.

In some ways returning to Montana was like being transported back in time 20 years. Memories of my sitting at Bob and Carmen's kitchen table at noon during the haying season came rushing at me like a soap opera flashback. Picking spuds for pocket change, unloading 90 pound sacks of cement at the lumber yard, swimming in a stock pond with friends, scrubbing the school gymnasium floor Saturday morning so I could shoot baskets Saturday afternoon, and mucking out the box stalls in a horse barn, all flowed back at me now as my mind began to re-connect and embrace what used to be.

In one sense, Jennifer and Claire Macintosh were more than a link to a quieter, less troubling time. They were a work in progress.

They had managed to keep pace with the changes taking place in their lives and the lives of others who wrested a living from their land. They had gradually walked away from the labor-intensive ditch-type irrigation to huge, revolving sprinkler systems that covered 140 acres and applied not only water but fertilizer, herbicides, and pesticides. The new, more productive seed varieties were a part of their cropping plan. The tractors and equipment that took much of the manual labor out of farming and ranching had found a home southwest of Norris.

They had taken trips to Denver, Prescott, Hawaii and Cancun, and their small motor home had made the trip to Alaska and back twice. They had a computer. Electronic mail flew back and forth between Jennifer and her daughter and granddaughter. Claire researched the markets, contracts, and crossbreeding practices in the evenings or when weather trapped him indoors. Even on a cold and blustery day, after he had done his chores, he wiled away his afternoon battling the odds offered by a host of electronic Solitaire programs.

During the few days I had earlier spent with them, I had learned that while they had kept pace with changing times, they hadn't altered their value system or their view of life. They had changed, and they hadn't changed at all. They still struggled to make it all work. The value of their assets was shockingly large, but technology had by no means removed all of the risks. Help was growing increasingly hard to find. They were still at the mercy of the markets. Even with a part of their operation under irrigation, prolonged drought could exact a heavy toll on the vast acres of dryland range they used. Disease could wipe out their profit margin, or grasshoppers could chop down their contract barley in a matter of days. When the optimum combination of conditions prevailed, they reaped healthy profits. With adverse conditions, profits evaporated, and they sometimes made that somber trip to the banker for interim financing. Yet in spite of everything, they persevered and marked time until the following year gave them another chance. For them, life was an adventure. Who could ask for more?

Like golfers and bowlers, who leave every game believing they will do better on the next, Claire and Jennifer were frequently looking ahead not to the next game but to the next year. They were literally bouncing from one high to one low, from one setback to the next, believing there was a chance that what followed would be better. They were next-year or the year-after-people, believing that the rains that didn't fall this year would fall the next year, or that the markets that failed them this year would heal and bounce back.

To my way of thinking, what is important about all of this is that it did not have to be this way. They could sell out and retire with enough money to last them two life times. They both knew it and had admitted as much to me. But they hadn't jumped ship, and they wouldn't. I had met them only very recently, but their words and actions had convinced me they wouldn't even think about it. Why would they? They loved what they were doing.

I admired them because the word quit was not a part of their vocabulary. They were so immersed in their life in the shadow of the Tobacco Root Mountains that no amount of adversity could change them. They were now what I wanted to be. They were resilient, self-reliant, honest, trustworthy, strong believers in the power of the human spirit, and excited about the future. When I was around them, I became excited about my own next year's life. Somewhere in that new life, when I was ready, perhaps I would find love again.

The shadowy vision I had of my future didn't embrace anything remotely resembling the magnitude of what Jennifer and Claire had built for themselves. Thinking along those lines was a huge waste of time. I did not see myself throwing my hat into the ring of large scale farming or ranching. I did not have the resources to do so, and would not even if I could. It wasn't what I wanted, at all. My inclinations were pointed elsewhere. What I was beginning to think I wanted was a place of my own. A few cows, a few horses, maybe even a bunch of chickens, and a modest home up against the mountains where I could begin sculpting the new Jim Pengilly.

I had worked hard for better than 20 years at a job with excellent wages, better than average job security, and a comfortable retirement program. I wanted more. I was vested in the retirement system, and down the road a nice piece of change would flow at me every month. I wasn't knocking that, but that was in my future. Right now, I wanted to live, really live for the first time, and I knew I had to get my hands dirty. I had to face challenges up close and personal, and I had to learn to deal with setbacks and even failure. I felt something like a parachutist about to make his first jump. I was uncertain about the future and I was scared to death, but I knew that one way or another my life would never be the same once I jerked on that cord, once I took the first step toward my future.

My life was suddenly like a *tabula rasa*, a blank slate. What had once been was no more. My suit and tie days were over. For years, that was me, and what had it brought me? Money in the bank? Yes, I had some. Enough to give me the freedom and the wings to fly through life as if I were on a never-ending vacation? No. My financial resources were far from unlimited. In fact, at the moment they were also very much in a state of flux. I would know better once Rebecca and I had tight-roped a path through the divorce proceedings. I knew that a tidy sum was out there with my share of our equity in the house. But no matter. I would have to work because even drifters must occasionally do so. I needed to immerse myself in something uplifting. I needed a project, and I needed to start feeling better about myself. More than anything else, though, I wanted the time and opportunity to define next year's Jim Pengilly. This time it was going to be slow and easy. I wanted to get it right.

Where to begin? A job would be nice. My friend, Jim Madsen, a former classmate in Missoula and Bozeman and now a partner in a small construction firm, seemed like a good place to start. For my entire career, except for the year I shivered and froze in the mountains of Korea, I had been an office engineer. My organizational skills, which I came by without knowing how or why, lifted me out of the field and into an office. What I wanted now was to get back out in the field. Jim's firm was too small to warrant an Office Engineer. If they needed anyone at all it was someone who didn't mind wearing a hard hat and rooting around in the dirt. That was me. I would call him in the morning and set up a lunch date.

Then there was the "place". Twenty, thirty acres, maybe even a 40, was what I had in mind. I was pretty much out of touch with Montana land prices, but I knew they had jumped dramatically with the influx of money from California, Washington, and a few other states. My pocketbook was on the lean side, and I would buy accordingly. I didn't mind stretching my dollars some because, after all, I said I wanted to live and take at least modest chances. I would stop at one of the banks in Bozeman, open an account, and talk with a loan officer about credit.

At lunch my first full day back with the Macintoshes, I unveiled my thinking about looking for a job and starting the hunt for a piece of land. The outcome of that discussion, and that is exactly what is was because I wanted their counsel, was a pleasant surprise for me. I was looking for advice, but and what I got was a proposal from them to sell me some of their land.

"We own a quarter section we think you would like," Claire said. "It's seven and a half miles straight west of here up against the Roots. We would consider selling it to you, Jim."

"Goodness," I said, "I'm thinking a lot smaller than that. More like 40 acres at the most. I don't know as though I can afford a quarter right now. Maybe after my divorce is final. Right now, I'd be nervous about sticking my head out that much."

"Jim, you listen to me," Jennifer said, in a voice that was mildly scolding. "We've talked about this before you ever mentioned wanting a place of your own. We'd like to see you on that place. We'll sell it to you on a contract-for-deed and give you as much time as you need to pay us off. You might find something closer to Bozeman, but you'll die when you hear how much they'll want."

"Tell me more," I said.

"Well," Jennifer continued, "like Claire said, it's a quarter section we bought more than 20 years ago from Benny Tovar. Benny came to work for us after he decided that a quarter section of range was too small to make a living on, unless a good part of it was irrigated. For a while, he lived down by the river in a shack he purchased for next to nothing and patched up. Needed to be close by for the fishing, he said. But when fishing was less important than my cooking, he moved up here and has lived with us for years. He still has his shack. He is a bachelor, a hunter, and a fisherman, and he wasn't much into keeping the place up. Still, it *does* have potential. The run down log cabin on the place should probably be burned where it stands, but it could be salvaged by someone who isn't afraid of work."

"Sounds interesting, guys," I said. "Maybe when I get done with my business in Bozeman, we could go take a look at it. I'll have a better feeling about a job by then, I hope."

"Why wait?" Claire asked in his easy drawl. "Let's jump in the pickup and drive over there. We haven't been over there for a couple of years. I'd like to see it myself."

"Okay," I replied. "Let's do it."

The graveled portion of the road lasted only about four miles, based of my count of section lines, before it became little more than a set of wheel tracks, a prairie trail. Both sides were lined with barbed-wire fences, but I saw few cattle, which led me to think the adjacent acres of rolling prairie were used for winter grazing.

The road dropped then rose again following the lay of the land but, without really noticing it, we were gradually climbing. Most of the low spots had a single 30 inch culvert under the road to keep spring flows from overtopping the modest grade. Small ponds of water on both sides of the culvert, choked with cattails and tall, reed-like grass, were home to small groups of ducks making it their summer home.

I could hear and almost feel the tall grass that grew between the two wheel tracks brush against the underside of Claire's truck as we moved along slowly. The trail pointed generally west, but seldom in a straight line. We threaded our way between a string of low-lying hills, following the contour of the terrain. Surprisingly, the road itself was relatively smooth. In places, the borrow-pits on both sides supported a thick stand of what looked like a mixture of brome and crested wheat. Even on the slight rises, where you would expect gravity to drain away moisture in the soil, it didn't look bad. I could see myself trying to cut hay in those ditches. But a closer look told me that it could be an adventurous undertaking. Too many holes. Too many rocks. Too hard on machinery. Too much trouble. One idea considered. One idea put to rest.

"Never was much of a road, even when Benny was using it," Claire noted. "Gone downhill ever since. Come elk season, it sees a few hunters. We use it when we move cattle to and from our grazing permit twice a year. That's about it.

"I think the Township Board could be persuaded to send a grader in here," he added, "if someone were living at the end of the road."

"That would be you, Jim," Jenny said.

"Got a good ring to it, Jenny," I sighed. "I like what I'm seeing." This was Montana, pure Montana, I thought. But it was "pass through" country for most tourists wanting to immerse themselves for a few days in rushing rivers, mountain peaks, pine trees, alpine lakes and scenery. The Madison River to the east provided all of that plus wonderfully relaxing hours, even days, of floating in rafts and tubes. Stay out of my Roots, I said to myself. I want them for myself.

The road leading south out of Norris carried you to Ennis and Virginia City. The latter was once the State's Capitol, and a veritable treasure chest of Montana history, the gold rush, and the Vigilante phenomenon. My spirits were always elevated when I could perch myself on one of Montana's mountain peaks and survey the far horizons. But prairie born I was and, while I loved and often craved short doses of the mountains, my comfort level was only elevated for a short time as I looked down into the wide valleys and the horizon in ever direction. The allure of the rolling prairies was greater if only because I was born to it.

The trip to the place was a short one. Twenty minutes after we left the Macintosh ranch, with a few stops in between to point out a particular topographic feature or a hazardous spot in the road, we drove up to the gate on the southeast corner of the property. I jumped out, loosened the rope holding the gate in place and pulled it aside. Working properly, it would have wheeled around without touching the ground; sagging as it was, I had to drag it aside. Claire drove through. I hopped into the box, and as we drove the hundred yards or so to the buildings, I surveyed our back trail. There were at least a dozen places on the way I could learn to like. The Madison range stood out in dark blue to the east, and its power and majesty were indisputable, but when I turned again to look at the buildings and surrounding acres, I knew I had just come home.

Run down it might be, after years of neglect, I knew almost instantly that it was just what I was looking for. Why not? We were a perfect match; a run down place, a run down man. Besides, it was probably all I could afford, if that. Buried somewhere within the pile of rubble before me was precisely the therapy I was seeking. If ever there was a project to warm the heart of someone in need of large doses of immersion, this was it. Lurking somewhere within all of the effort needed to transform the place into my place was a challenge quite unlike any I had ever faced.

The cabin was 28 feet long and 16 feet wide. It's roof was absent-without-leave, its rafters and shingles resting, for the most part, comfortably on the floor. All of the four-pane windows were either broken or missing. The front door hung by one hinge, but I noticed that the four starter-round logs were solid and without decay. The foundation was what was called rubble masonry, which meant that forms had been staked for the back side, but the facing portion was made of rocks laid one upon another much like bricks. It was that foundation's strength and durability that held the wall logs in plumb. Much of the chinking had long since disappeared, and sections of the floor were missing. The small fireplace near the one end stood tall and proud, but sections of rock had slipped out of place or had dropped to the floor.

The cabin had two rooms; a combination kitchen and living area and what passed for a bedroom. I loved it. Didn't know where to begin, but I loved it. Couldn't wait to get started.

As if to compensate for the derelict cabin's shortcomings, a nice stand of ponderosa pine, interspersed with aspen and cottonwood, formed a pretty backdrop that would cool and shade the cabin on a hot, sunny afternoon and soften the cold winter winds blowing off the mountains. Off to the south was a power line I could tap into. And in addition to the creek, which I immediately named Macintosh, the place boasted a well. The old pump was rusty and several strokes on the pump handle told me the pipe had rusted out below or the walls had caved in on themselves. I would need someone to come in an re-work the well, and I would have a pit-less unit installed so I could pipe water directly to the house in the middle of winter, knowing the line would not freeze.

"Wait a minute, Jimbo, I said to my self. "Getting a little ahead of yourself here, aren't you?"

"No," I answered, once again to myself, "how could a man in my soon-to-be position as the heavily indebted land owner, cowboy-in-the-making, and potential squire of this magnificent domain be expected to function without running water, electricity and a computer? After all, how could my boss-to-be or my office, if I had one, know, that I was sick or that the roads were blocked between me and the highway and that I couldn't make it to work?"

The now-named creek running between the cabin and a squat, combination barn and chicken coop was three feet wide and less than a foot deep. But, it had a rocky bottom, and the cool, clear water that moved slowly past on its way to the Madison River. It was enough to supply my personal needs, water my garden, and fill a stock tank or two when I got around to purchasing a half dozen crossbred cows and a couple of horses. That would happen only after I repaired the fence and cleaned out the small steel grain bin situated next to the barn.

We spent a couple of hours driving and walking around the place to help me get a feel for it. I learned that off to the south I had a neighbor, a widow, by the name of Michele Lowry. Her husband had died three years earlier, Jennifer said, and she was running the place by herself. From what I gathered, she apparently used another east-west road to reach her ranch, but she moved her cows to the grazing permit she shared with Claire, using a prairie trail that led straight north from her place to mine. There it joined the road that ran on the south side of my buildings. There I was: already calling the place mine. I was hopeless. My analytically disposed engineering mind was suddenly absent-without-leave when it came to matters dealing with Benny Tovar's shack up against the mountains. I wanted it, but couldn't see how I could make it happen.

Jennifer served us lunch on the grass under an elderly cottonwood tree growing in a low spot north of the cabin. We all sat on the ground as we ate and struggled to balance our coffee cups in our hands or on the ground without spilling. Claire's bum leg made it difficult for him to get in and out of chairs and virtually impossible to lower himself to the ground and then get up again. So I played scavenger and brought an old bench I found leaning against the cabin over to him. Claire was tougher than nails no doubt, but his injury was slow to mend. As I watched him struggle to seat himself on the rough, none-to-sturdy bench, I couldn't help but wonder if his old bones would ever recover enough to once again do the multitude of tasks he had been performing for years.

He was a cowman from the top of his soiled Stetson to the underside of his Tony Lama rough-out boots. Through one of his shirt pockets the outline of a tin of chewing tobacco was visible, and in the other was a plastic pencil carrier, advertising the products of a local feed dealer. The two lead pencils showing against the carrier need not beg for something to write on because he carried the small tablet he used to jog his memory in his back pocket.

He was built to be astride a horse. His legs were long, his back was short, and together they gave him a center of balance that made him a good rider. I had never actually watched him ride, but Jennifer mentioned to me one day that he was still regarded as the best older rider in the area. His hair, like his wife's, had turned gradually gray over the years, or so I was told but, in his case, the change bestowed upon him a very distinguished look. His broad shoulders were covered with thin layers of muscle, the product of years of manual labor. His dark eyes still sparkled with a zest for life that a machinery accident could not dispel.

"So, what do you think?" he asked.

"I love it, Claire," I said. "I want it. I want it in the worst way. But can I afford it?"

"You can afford it, Jim," Jennifer interjected. "We'll work out the details after you've returned from Bozeman. You might as well know that we want you to have this place. We like you, Jim Pengilly, and we want you close by."

Those words, spoken by this middle-aged woman I had known for less than two weeks, were like a beautiful rhapsody to my ears. I simply could not fathom why they had take a liking to me but, whatever the reason, I knew I had two people who really cared and that I was about to take a gigantic leap toward healing. I could feel tiny tears at the corners of my eyes, but I didn't care.

"You've got yourself a deal," I said.

"And you've got yourself a deal too," Jennifer announced. Her eyes sparkled like whitecaps on a tiny stream, and I wanted to hug her.

I settled for thanking them for their generosity, and promised to remember their kindness forever. They hemmed and hawed as if it were nothing, but it was a lot more than nothing. It was a new beginning for me and maybe even for them.

"I just thought of something," I said.

"What's that, Jim," Jennifer asked.

"If I find work in Bozeman, and if I live here, my commute will be about 40 miles one-way. That's better than twice the distance I traveled each day in Baltimore. Of course, I'll admit the traffic was a little heavier there."

We all laughed at that, but I can tell you there was one individual sitting there who was already beginning to worry about how he would pull it all off.

When I turned at Four Corners to drive into the west end of Bozeman, my heart was pounding with both excitement and apprehension. Twenty plus years I had spent on a job that involved the overall operation of the Port of Baltimore, Maryland. Now all of a sudden, I was looking for another. In Maryland, I had been Chief of the Port's Operations Department. My marching orders came from a Port Authority Board in the form of policy directives. Once a contract was executed, it became my job to implement it and see to it that all specifications were met. The Authority's projects always took years to build, involved multi-millions of dollars and, at times, three or four of various sizes or kinds were underway at the same time. At one time, segments of the Seagirt, Dundalk, and Fairfield Marine Terminals were underway concurrently.

It would be an understatement to say that my plate had been full back in Baltimore. But I had not done it by myself. A large and capable staff managed everyday affairs on the ground. Still, it was impossible to function without a willingness to become immersed in the responsibility and challenge implicit in every endeavor. Looking back now from a distance, I understood better how I had lost my way in terms of my family.

My background with the Baltimore Port Authority had left me with management skills that ought to be useful to someone. But, in Bozeman, Montana? I wasn't sure, but I consoled myself by thinking that an engineer was an engineer and, surely, somebody could use me. The truth is, I no longer coveted either position or authority. My goal was two-fold. Immersion and a few earned dollars. The latest information I had was that the demand for port managers in and around Bozeman was minuscule. But I was almost certain, someone would need a hard-hat engineer to design and oversee the pouring of concrete for residential streets, driveways and sidewalks. I hoped

I was that man. I was meeting Jim Madsen for lunch. He was a fanatical Bobcat fan and my best friend in times past.

The Yellow Pages said he was part of a local engineering firm, and it was with him I would begin my job search. My hope was that he had something for me or could steer me to another firm that might. His 250 pounds were leaning against the wrought iron railing leading up a few stairs to the rear entrance of the Over Easy café in downtown Bozeman when I drove into a crowded parking lot, nearly overflowing with SUV's Jeeps, trucks and a lonesome Pontiac 4-door. Bicycle carriers, ski racks, kayaks and a canoe adorned the tops of many, which meant some things had not changed.

He still had the same head of curly, red hair, and it was readily apparent that his addiction to tobacco was unabated, as I watched him toss a butt to the ground and rub it out. His hand was on its way to his shirt pocket for another when he caught sight of me walking toward him.

"Jim, boy," he greeted me, his big hand outstretched, ready to make me wince from his powerful grip. "Damn, you're looking good."

"You know what they say," I answered. "Flattery will get you someplace only if you pick up the tab."

"Consider it done, old man," he said. "How in the hell are you doing?"

My response was that I was doing just fine.

'Well, then," he said, "let's get in line."

And get in line we did. Out in the hall, as we waited to be called "in 20 minutes or so", we nursed a cup of self-serve coffee and got most of our reminiscing out of the way. At the sound of the name Madsen, we elbowed our way through the door and were directed to a table in the far corner, our Styrofoam cups still in hand, as if we were unwilling to be without our coffee for even a few seconds.

As was our practice of 20 years earlier, we ordered hearty breakfasts for lunch, loaded with calories and taste. He was in no hurry nor was I, so we sat there for a couple of hours talking about things in general and about my search for a job in particular. I pulled absolutely no punches with him as to how I came to be back in Montana or why I was looking for work. He knew where I had been, and he knew what I had been doing. He subscribed to the Engineers News Journal just as I did.

"This is our busy time," he said, "but things really taper off after freeze-up. We could use you this summer, I'm sure, and throughout the fall, but I couldn't promise anything later. And, I sure as the dickens can't offer you any Baltimore salary. Some years business is pretty good and, when it is, we try to dole out at least a small bonus; other years it's not worth a damn."

My salary expectations were low. In fact, I had none. I wanted work. My need to be some place in the morning was greater right now than my need for money. Still, I hoped to do better than a construction worker, and I told him so. Rebuilding Pengilly Acres was going to cost a bundle.

My divorce hearing was tentatively scheduled in a little more than three weeks. Being there was essential. I needed to see my kids and try to set things straight with them if nothing else. So I asked if I could, should his partners agree to hire me, defer starting until after that. He advised me that he couldn't hire me on his own, that he was one member of a three person firm, and that he would have to touch base with his partners. He said he would be meeting with the other two late the following afternoon, and that he would discuss hiring me, what they could pay, and the delayed start I had requested.

"I'll be honest with you, Jim," he said. "I think they are going to be nervous about the idea of employing someone like you with all of your experience. Intimidation. That might be the right word."

My assurances that they need not worry was enough for him, and he promised to get back to me in a couple of days. I gave him the Macintosh phone number, and drove straight to Ressler Chevrolet and traded my damaged pick-up truck in on a new-to-me, white, 4-wheel drive Silverado with dual wheels on the rear. That's a mouthful, I know, but it was essential to my transition back to being a Montanan.

When I drove it into the Macintosh yard, the box was filled with barbed-wire, steel posts, a post driver, wire hangers, and several treated, wood corner posts. In the passenger seat was a basket of cut flowers for Jennifer and a six pack of beer for Claire and yours truly. Things were looking up for me. I wanted to celebrate, and we did. Jennifer loved the flowers, hugged me, and grabbed two cans of beer for herself. I could tell they had been talking since I left in the morning, and they didn't waste any time letting me know they expected me to bunk with them until my place was ready. My place! Where did I start?

The sky that night was clear and filled with a million stars, and a soft breeze set the leaves in the old cottonwood to thinking they were quaking aspen. We sat there, the three of us, gazing upward, saying very little. Had I special ordered the night it could not have been more perfect. It had been warm in the late afternoon, but now with a breeze, humidity hugging zero, and a hot cup of coffee cradled in my hand, I was totally comfortable. More importantly, I knew I had landed here for a purpose. My mind, even as we discussed weather and grass and cattle prices, everything and nothing, was sifting through the reasons why these people had taken to me in the short time we had been acquainted. Did I remind them of their own son? Did young Patrick and me share certain mannerisms? Did my voice remind them of him? Was it something else totally unrelated to their lost boy? Or was it simply a matter of loneliness?

I knew they went for days without seeing or talking to anyone but their hired men. Claire was on the quiet side, but Jennifer was gregarious and friendly, spending time on the phone everyday with friends or meeting them in Norris or Ennis for lunch. They told me they went back and forth with three couples they had known since grade school. No, loneliness had nothing to do with their generosity. They were simply too occupied with the ranch and plain old living to give in to loneliness. They apparently liked me, wanted to help me, and I'm not sure why. Not one to look what amounted to a gift horse in the mouth, I made up my mind to use them, if they were willing, as a listening post and a fount of ideas on how I should approach the renaissance I hoped to see play out on my 158.8 acres of Heaven.

My expectation was that I would sleep in the same room I had used that first stormy night but, instead, I was led into Patrick's old room. I had glanced in only once looking for something to read, and found it to be, for all intents and purposes, a family shrine commemorating the life of their dear, departed son. Yearbooks were piled neatly on top of the dresser. Several photos of a very pretty young lady were still sticking between a dresser mirror and its trim. Five balsa wood model airplanes, each of a different color and design, hung from the ceiling attached to almost invisible wires.

Three pictures showed him riding saddle broncs at the Livingston rodeo. Another caught him standing at the free throw line during a regional tournament in Three Forks. I quickly flipped through a thick scrapbook tracing his life in the form of news clippings, cards, hand-written poems, photos, valentines, and report cards. Hanging from one wall was a olive colored Boy Scout sash covered with dozens of merit badges. On the back of a captains' chair in one corner was the gray, dirty, sweat-stained hat he had been wearing in the rodeo pictures. Right then and there, before I learned more about this remarkable young man, I decided he was something special.

I had no business sleeping in his room with all his photos and memorabilia, but before I could protest, I was startled to find that, in spite of what remained, much of what I remembered seeing earlier was actually missing. I could think of no other reason for that other than to make room for me and my things. So, I kept my mouth shut and moved in along with my meager possessions. I couldn't help sensing that I had somehow been unofficially adopted as their son. The idea was troubling, of course, but my instincts told me to let matters play out. Wait-and-see made sense.

Claire's other hired hand, Odin Norgaard, joined us for breakfast the next morning. I learned that he was actually returning to work after a two week absence, doing some doctoring in Billings.

He had broken his left leg in two places when he stepped off a loading chute, and needed a bit of minor surgery not offered by area hospitals. Born on a small ranch in the upper end of the Madison Valley, Billings was as far from home as he had ever been...or ever wanted to be. Like Benny, he still had a small place of his own adjacent to the river, but worked for Claire to help pay the bills. He seemed like a personable gentleman, and I knew instantly I was going to like him.

"When you need a loader over on your place, Jim," Claire offered, "I'll have Benny or Odin bring one of ours over. We've got a heavy duty tandem-axle trailer to haul it on. It won't take long. You'll want something to lift those heavy roof stringers up when the time comes, and it will come in mighty handy when you start cleaning up around there. You'll be giving thanks to the Lord or John Deere or someone for hydraulics before you're finished."

He walked out with me to my truck and surveyed what I had piled up in the box. Then, he turned to Odin and asked him to run over to the Quonset and bring back the wire stretcher, some staples, and the 16-pound sledge. I was feeling a mite sheepish, especially about the staples, but you can't expect and engineer to remember everything. Right?

A quick "see you tonight" and the two of them were gone only to be replaced by Jennifer who was struggling to manage a large steel thermos bottle and a cooler holding a couple of roast beef sandwiches and two cans of beer.

"Now, you be careful, Jim," she warned. "Don't get sun stroked your first day on the job. And, supper's ready here at six. If you aren't here, we'll eat without you."

I told her thanks, jumped in the cab and started pulling away from the front of the house. She was too much. She stood on the door step waving to me like a mother whose son was going off to war. I couldn't wait until my own mother came to visit so the two of them could meet. They reminded me of each other in countless ways. Jenny was a comely tall woman. So was my mother. Jenny, with subtlety and suggestion, largely directed and managed the sprawling ranch lands that she and her husband had begun purchasing when they were in their late 20s.

My mother's only management responsibilities focused on my dad, and she did so with just enough subtlety to largely control him without his knowing it...or so she thought. They shared similar backgrounds in that their parents pursued their own dreams as ranchers and stockmen at an earlier time in Montana.

Jennifer and my mother were both looking back at 60-years of age now, yet neither of them devoted any time to thinking about it.   One of the differences between the two of them was the direct result of a physically active life. Mom was fighting her weight while Jennifer, for reasons she didn't bother to analyze or particularly notice, had somehow managed to keep the pounds at bay. Her narrow face and determined countenance lacked the tell-tale wrinkles which were beginning to show on my mother, especially the crow's feet around her eyes. Jennifer   didn't sag where she ought to be sagging, and she was still very attractive. Had gravity had its way with her body, it would not have mattered She was tall and slender with a figure bound to be the envy of ladies 20 years her junior, but looks were not an issue with her.

As near as I had been able to deduce in the short time I had known her, her assessment of herself and others went far beyond mere looks, and it was apparent that her motherly instincts, not only for her daughter and granddaughter but for her husband and virtually everyone else, overshadowed her other characteristics. She was a prize, and everyone knew it. It was partly her charm and hospitality that drew me to the Macintoshes. My own mother shared many of those same attributes, but her efforts were dedicated almost exclusively to keeping my dad in line.

Twenty minutes later, I was sitting in my yard, drinking my first cup of coffee from the thermos, and staring at the collective and jumbled vision of everything I had to do. The clipboard lying beside me on the seat already had a priority list of 11 tasks I saw before me. Repairing the fence that encircled the buildings to keep livestock out headed that list. Later, I would have to drive the entire quarter section and repair that fence as well, before I could even think about purchasing cows. That trip around the yard, which was like a voyage of discovery, sparked several other ideas to be added to my list.

I dropped my load to the ground, except for the treated posts, and backed up to the gate. Two hours later, minus my shirt and what seemed like several quarts of perspiration, I had replaced the taller gate post, and braced it sufficiently to allow the wooden gate to swing freely. Someday, a long time from now, I would build a genuine Montana gate made of heavy logs imbedded in the ground with another large log arching over the top with a heavy iron replication of my very own brand hanging from it. I dropped the end gate on my pickup, reached for the cooler, saved a can of Miller Light from hypothermia, popped the cap, and surveyed my handiwork.

The roar of a muffler-less truck, which I could not yet see, jerked me from my run-away slide into unabashed self-satisfaction. Looking around, I saw a cloud of dust racing at me from the south like a NASA missile gone astray. A minute or two later, out of that cloud of dust, emerged a tall, work-worn, soiled figure, and I mean figure. There were women and then there were women. She definitely fell into the latter category. I knew without being told who it was. I stood and waited. She was tall and pretty, with dark brown hair, dark eyes and a slender face. The soiled green and white cap advertising the John Deere farm implement dealer in Belgrade was pulled down hard on her head, and her jeans were tucked into a pair of rough-out men's high-heeled riding boots. Her figure was superb. Her hair was largely hidden under that green cap, but I could see frizzy samples of it clinging to her head like a wet carpet. She could walk any runway in the world's fashion centers, as far as I was concerned, and she had just the right amount of meat on them there bones.

"Hey, Jim," she said as she stepped forward to shake my hand. "Know your name. Jennifer gave it to me. We are neighbors."

"I-I've heard we were," I stammered, with embarrassment "Also from Jennifer, of course."

"Well, I can see you are busy, so I won't stay long. On my way up to check on a couple of sick calves. Thought I'd stop by and welcome you to paradise."

I told her I appreciated the warm welcome and looked forward to seeing her again. Back in her pickup, her arm resting on the window well, she hollered out, "we trade labor around here. If you need help, let me know. I'll do the same. Say hello to Jennifer and Claire."

With that she was gone. I watched her hang a hard right and head up toward the mountains and her calves. My instincts shouted out to me that here was a woman who could reel me in like a hungry trout if

I wasn't careful. No doubt about it, she had tripped one of my inner switches the second she stepped down from her truck. I found myself thinking this lord of the manor would have put up precious little resistance had she decided to unfurl her flag over my place. But that was before...

Before I had built walls too high to climb and doors without keys as far as romance was concerned, that is. Solidly in place for the time being, at least, they were my heart's way of protecting me from another broken heart. It was too soon to think of another in the way I had once thought of Rebecca. I simply refused to risk another case of the self-inflicted heart break. I was absolutely certain that intimacy now, without love, would only momentarily diminish my feeling of emptiness. There, I said it. In spite of everything, I sheltered an underlying feeling of personal emptiness. I could use a friend. I could even be comfortable with Michele Lowry as a friend so long as it stayed that way. My current mind set was that being with any one now romantically was out of the question, but having a good friend, even one as pretty and sexy as Michele was not. Not knowing of anyone who could settle for that, I guessed the answer for me was to immerse myself in my work

I smiled to myself, as I walked along the yard's fence line perimeter to count the number of steel posts I would need to get to the corner. Twelve posts later, my brain had shifted to the task of replacing several corner posts. The auger I used was one of those that screwed itself into the ground with a lot of help from the operator. Twice I encountered rocks I could not pry loose with a crow bar, and twice I was forced to start over again at another spot.

My hands were blistered, my shoulders felt like a horse had kicked them, and I wanted to sit down and cry. But I didn't. What I did, instead, was fall back on a technique I remembered from my fencing experience of 30 years earlier. It was simple enough. Fill the hole with water. Move on to the next hole. Do the same. Do it again and again, then return to the first hole. By then the water had soaked in, making digging the next several inches much easier. Now instead of clay as hard almost as concrete, the bottom of the hole had been turned into something just short of mud. It was messy but it worked. When I finished it was dark. I was exhausted and hungry. But I had accomplished what I had set out to do this day, and the satisfaction and pride I took from that was worth the sore shoulder muscles, the aching back, and even more blisters.

The headlights on my truck pointed me down the road toward Jenny and Claire's Rafter M ranch, well after dark. By dumb luck, more than anything else, I avoided hitting a whitetail doe and her fawn. The porch light was on when I pulled to a stop in front of the house, and before I reached the door, it opened to reveal Jennifer standing there with her outstretch arm holding a cold, frothy glass of beer. I loved that woman!

"We knew you wouldn't be here early tonight," Jenny quipped. "Come wash up. Supper's on. Warmed-up supper, I should say."

When I finished shoveling the beef stew and buttered bread into my mouth on its way to a churning stomach, I learned that my friend, Jim Madsen, had called to tell me the job was mine and that I should report when I could. That was good news.

A second message was from my attorney in Baltimore informing me that the hearing had been moved up two weeks, and that I should arrive the night before for a briefing. It was too late to call him now, so I waited until morning. I saw no reason for the two of us to meet unless he knew something I didn't, and I conveyed that message to him.

I also called my friend and former colleague with the Port Authority to let him know that I had landed a job. He told me that when he learned I was moving to Montana he had wagered with a mutual friend that I would be back in Baltimore within a month. It pleasured me immensely to be able to stuff that mistaken notion back down his craw. I even gave him my office and cell phone numbers as documentation that I had established a genuine connection in Big Sky Country. I thought it only fair to remind him that out here near the end of the world, as he called it, reception was chancy. It's the clean, fresh air, I said. We both laughed at that and promised to stay in touch. I told him if he were smart he'd stay as far from my place as he could, for should he venture out my way intentionally or by accident, he'd find out what real work was like.

So did I. For the remainder of the week, I slaved away at the fence, completing it just in time to see Claire and Jennifer drive through my gate. On their heels, I am sure by design, Michele Lowry, skidded her truck to a stop behind them, and jumped out to join us with a six pack in each hand.

She tossed one of them to me, as she said hello to my other guests. They...the beers, that is, were cold and a trifle foamy. I, for one, gulped mine down as a preventative for sunstroke. We sat in the shade of the old cabin, ate the lunch Jennifer brought, and looked out over the valley below. Four sets of eyes fixed on the distant Madison Range told me that we were all thanking the powers that be for allowing us these kinds of small pleasures. Omniscience I did not possess, but the premise for my assertion was based on the mountains. How could one look out toward the Madisons and not be thankful?

Chapter 3

The first leg of my flight to Baltimore was non-stop from Bozeman to Minneapolis, where I had less than an hour layover. Time-wise, it was a short flight and I slept most of the way. I managed to grab a quick cup of coffee at one of the kiosks and went directly to my gate on the green concourse. Airborne, my window seat afforded me a full view of the landscape below, but its monotony swept me up against troubling thoughts about events of tomorrow.

Up to now, I had succeeded in stuffing the reality of what tomorrow might hold back into one of the dark recesses of my brain. Who would ever have guessed that my marriage would come to this? But in a few hours, it would, and my family would be dealing with a new reality, the prospects of which had alone already sent shock waves through our extended families and even friends we had made over the years.

It struck me that this whole process was undoubtedly less traumatic for Rebecca and me than it was for the children. We would move on and, in some fashion or other, begin rebuilding a life without each other. I had already begun. Rebecca had as well. But the children, Michael and Morgan, were like flotsam tugged this way and that by the troubled waters of matrimony. As parents we would do everything, short of reconciliation, to soften their anger and sadness but, in the end, they would deal with the dismembering of family or it would destroy them.

During the past week, as the days grew fewer before I would make this flight, my thoughts had run to the children time and again. Could we somehow shield them from the truth? No, I was sure we not only couldn't but that doing so was unwise. What we could do, though, was to try to soften many of the undesirable impacts, by agreeing to employ damage control measures wherever we could. I felt Rebecca would be receptive to anything that might allay some of the hurt.

With that in mind, I called her at work on my cell phone and suggested that the two of us meet for dinner to discuss steps we might take to subtract "nasty" from the proceedings. I was not looking for a way to absolve myself in my children's minds. I was only hoping we could jettison personal rancor and suppress any anger, bitterness and resentment that might be ignited as we bothered the details of our divorce.

She answered after the second ring, and remained silent for a few seconds when she heard my voice. "It's me, Becky," I said, and I was wondering...."

"Jim," she said, "I didn't expect to hear from you until tomorrow."

I told her it was good to hear her voice again, asked her how the kids were doing, and suggested we meet for dinner at a location of her choice. "We need to talk about tomorrow," I said. "Maybe we can make it easier on everyone, including the two of us, if we can enter that court room tomorrow with a plan we both agree to."

"A good idea," she said. "A really good idea. I was thinking along those same lines too, but didn't know where to contact you. Should the children be involved?"

My thought was that they should not. I told her as much, and she agreed. We set a time and place. I took a short nap, then showered and called a cab. We met at a small out-of-the-way restaurant we had visited several times before. She was there waiting for me when I got there. She stood up, said hello and planted a fleeting kiss on my cheek. We exchanged perfunctory questions about how we were doing, and then we ordered. The meal was excellent, the wine was our favorite, and two hours later, we had our plan.

"How are the kids doing?" I asked.

"As well as might be expected," she replied, "though Morgan is having the toughest time of it. I think Michael not only saw this coming but thinks its best for both of us. He is a wonderful young man, Jim. He is thinking of his mother and dad, not himself. And he is working hard to help Morgan not only understand but accept. They will come around."

I asked her to tell them both that I said hello and that I missed them but suggested, that for now, the less they saw of me the better.

Neither of our attorneys earned their fees the next day, since neither of them was given the opportunity to argue for or against anything. The division of assets and responsibilities we presented were incorporated into the preliminary decree without dissent. We were formally granted joint custody of the children, but we agreed that the best place for them now was with their mother. One day, perhaps, they would consider letting me come for a visit or, better yet, would think of coming to Montana to see me.

"Are my folks okay?" Rebecca asked as we prepared to go our separate ways on the courthouse steps.

"Yes, they are, I think. We had a nice talk, your mom and dad and I, at their place in Moccasin. They are sad but I truly believe, that once they began to understand the whys, they'll think it is for the best."

I threw in a bit about my having purchased a small place in the shadow of the Tobacco Root Mountains west of Norris. She said she was glad, and wished me luck. I did the same, and we walked down the steps together. She walked to the parking ramp for her car, and I hailed a cab to the airport. I couldn't wait to get back to Montana.

I won't say that I didn't spend some time staring off into the distance on my flight home, but when I wasn't staring I was either calling the Macintoshes or I was doodling or leaving notes to myself on my sheet of graph paper. I knew it was not simply a matter of getting back to Montana. It was a matter of returning to my place, to my new home.

The plane landed in Belgrade within one minute of the scheduled time posted on the concourse flight information board. I called Jim Madsen from the airport to tell him that I would be in on the following Monday morning, then I headed straight down 91 to Four Corners. A cup of good coffee there, and I pointed my truck's nose at Norris and proceeded to break the speed limit by at least 20 miles per hour, that is, until a Highway Patrol vehicle appeared in my rear view just shy of Norris Hot Springs. Another milestone! My first traffic citation in Montana. And the Patrolman's first opportunity to direct me to get a Montana driver's license within 30 days.

Benny Tovar was working in the Quonset when I pulled up before the house. I quickly walked over to him and asked him if he had time to haul one of the loaders over to my place before he called it a day. He said he had nothing but time. Claire and Jennifer were meeting friends in Ennis and weren't expected back until later

I rummaged through the fridge looking for sandwich meat. Slapped three slices of bologna between two slices of whole wheat and drained the coffee pot into my thermos. Before I left, I laid a note on the kitchen table telling them I was camping out at the place the next couple of nights and that I had robbed the fridge of sandwich meat and cheese. My larder also included what was left in one of the half gallon plastic milk jugs, a pound can of coffee, the hard stuff, a small bag full of celery, carrot slices, half an onion, a small cast iron frying pan, a pot without a cover, and a couple of knives and forks. I would need them for the stew I planned to whomp up tomorrow using the pound of cheap steak I bought in Norris. Benny was waiting for me when I dragged my loot through the door, most of it in an oversized cooler, the bottom half of which held all the ice cubes I could find.

"She's full of diesel," Benny said. "You ever run one of these things?"

"Been a while," I admitted, "but I'll figure it out."

Satisfied that I would, he followed me out on to the road. I wanted to get out in front to avoid eating his dust.

The second item on my clipboard priority list was to clean the rubble from both the inside and outside of the cabin. I tossed everything I could lift into the bucket and hauled it to a spot far enough from the building to allow for burning later. Everything was attached to something else, so I put my wrecking bar to good use, prying things apart for ease in carrying. Some of the roof timbers and braces tested my strength to the limit, but even these found their way to my burn pile. My plan was to let them rest there until the ground was covered with snow and the chance of scorching the countryside had disappeared.

I can't find the words to tell you how good it felt to wrest load after load of debris from the cabin, but I knew I was only high-grading it. Now, I had to start cleaning it out. I mean really cleaning it out! That would have to wait until next week, for I had no solvents or brushes. The best I could do was to take an old broom I found in the shed and brush what was left of the floor and the seams between logs to determine the size and shape of the gaps.

The better part of the week, if I included the weekend, lay before me. When the sun had passed from its noontime, directly overhead position, to its slow descent to the west, I shut the loader down and took an hour to set up my camp for the night. The small plastic-like cloth I had swiped from the Quonset served as the moisture barrier under the 2-person tent I had purchased at a Bozeman farm supply store. One look at the clear blue sky, and I decided not to use the rain flap included in the package. It was a nice tent, but too small to stand in. Had it not been for the fact that the mosquitos took over the country after dark, I would have slept under the tarp and left the tent in its canvas bag.

Scraps of wood to use for building my fire were everywhere, so I hauled an old tire rim close to the tent and began piling up kindling and burning-size pieces of wood so I wouldn't have to do it later when I was tired. My plan was to work straight through until dark. I had cheese and sandwich meat for my supper, and I made half a pot of coffee, but otherwise my cooking would have to wait 'til tomorrow.

I played out well before dark, so I pulled the truck up close to the tent and began adding to my list of tasks to be completed at some point in time. One was to calculate what I would need in the way of planks to replace the floor. Another was to mentally stake out a route to bring the power into the property. Then there was the permit I would need from the Forest Service to harvest lodge pole pine trees for my corrals, one section of fence, and a small, three-sided shed. Somehow I would have to lay my hands on enough larger logs to repair the house, and build the planned addition. I hoped to secure building logs from standing dead pine only; trees that had been killed by the pine-bark beetle or had been destroyed by fire.

If running water was somewhere in my future, I would have to make arrangements for the well driller to come out and rework the well, which had not been used for years. So many things to do. Having help, at least on the weekends when I could be there, would make some of the tasks much easier. Benny or Claire might know of someone.

The small fire I started in my tire ring just before dark was little more than embers by the time I fell asleep. But it had burned long enough for me to fry a couple of scrambled eggs, with a little cheese mixed in, and a second pot of coffee. I stared at that fire for an hour thinking about what I had done that day, what lay ahead for me, and how lucky I was. I knew I did not want to report for work on Monday or ever, for that matter, but I knew I must.

The next day was more of the same hard, sweaty, wonderful work. The small shed that had once been used to house a team of horses fell victim to the front-end loader. Careful inspection showed that it would be easier to replace than repair. Needless to say, my burn pile grew larger by leaps and bounds. By supper time I was thinking about pulling stakes and heading back to the ranch, but I knew I should tough it out here until I ran out of food. I was tired of my own cooking, but I had that steak to cut up for stew and all the other makings, so stew it was going to be.

By Saturday noon, every muscle in my body was screaming for a reprieve. How long it had been since I last asked my body to perform physical labor from before dawn until after dark I could not remember. Maybe it was because it had never happened. In any case, my head quit and my body followed soon thereafter. It wasn't long and I was on my way to the Macintosh place and several cans of cold, cold brew.

That night I proclaimed, during supper, that Sunday was to be a day of rest for me. I offered to drive all them into Bozeman for breakfast at the Over Easy. Jennifer and Claire accepted. Benny and Odin chose fishing over a town-breakfast. Country folks that we were, we were up and on the road early. Did we stand in line? You bet. Montanans were early risers, I guess. I ordered about 3,000 calories of food, while Claire and Jennifer showed more restraint. We talked about my Baltimore trip some, but mostly about my place.

We were getting serious about leaving when I heard them call out Jim Madsen's name. Entering from the hall, he saw me immediately and headed for the empty table next to us. Introductions were made all around, and we settled into some nice Sunday morning conversation while they waited for their order. I asked him if my message about starting in the morning had filtered down to him, and he said that it had.

"I suppose I might just as well tell you now, Jim, that we are sending you to Denver on Tuesday to represent the firm at a Housing and Urban Development meeting. We have just entered into an agreement with HUD to do some appraisal work for them on properties that have come back to them, and you know your way around HUD better than the rest of us. Their properties often come back to them needing repair and general refurbishment, so we feel we need to get a better handle on their guidelines and criteria. We want our bids to be competitive."

What could I say other than that I would be pleased to make the trip on their behalf. I hadn't thought the job would involve such travel, but occasionally a trip out of state could be rejuvenating. Some of my best ideas came to me at 37,000 feet but, like a lot of my dreams, their beauty and worth evaporated soon after we touched down at the airport.

"Your tickets will be ready on Monday. You'll be back in Bozeman late Tuesday night. We can talk more tomorrow. Right now, I better get to eating. Anne says I am wasting away to nothing." We all laughed at that, including himself.

The Over Easy was like Grand Central Station, with people coming and going as rapidly as orders could be cooked, fried or roasted, brought to a table, and eaten. With so many waiting in the halls, the inclination was to eat rapidly and move on out. One of those waiting proved to be Michele Lowry. My heart skipped a beat when I saw the tall man standing with her near the entry. I couldn't believe it, but I think I was just a bit jealous.

"There's Michele," Jennifer cried out when she saw her standing in the doorway. "She's with Martin."

Martin? I hadn't heard his name mentioned that I could remember. My question was quickly answered when the two of them walked toward us. Michele said hello. The tall man waved a jumbo sized hand to acknowledge us, as Jennifer pulled away from the table to stand and hug the huge hombre. "Marty," she said, "this is our friend, Jim Pengilly. He bought the old Tovar place from us and, this morning, he's springing for breakfast. Jim, this is Marty Larson, Michele's brother."

I stood up and shook his hand, thankful that he was only a brother. Hey, wait a minute. What was going on here? I had no business caring one way or the other? Hell, I had no idea what I was thinking. I tried to keep myself out of the conversation, since I shared none of the experiences and knowledge the rest did. But Michele was having no part of that. Answering her questions practically forced me to tell Marty my life story, or at least the part that could bear some public scrutiny.

They got the short version too. It hit me that Michele knew little more about me than Marty, so it was clear she was fishing for a clearer picture of just who her neighbor was. She might have been wondering, as I had myself, how this stranger could so quickly become so close to the Macintoshes. I don't know. In any case, Marty seemed a nice fellow. He was an attorney, but he was also a big-time rancher, and I was a guy who owned a run-down 160 acres; neither disposed nor well–equipped to discuss the pros and cons of ranching, the law, or anything else, for that matter. On the way back to the ranch, I laid out my plan to add on to the cabin.

"It sounds great," Jennifer commented. "I can't wait to see it when you are done."

"Well, I did a little better than I had anticipated in my settlement with Rebecca," I said, "so I can afford to hire some of the work done. I'll do everything I can by myself. I want it to reflect me and not someone else.

"But this surprise trip to Denver," I continued, "is going to put off a start."

"Sounds like you're planning on staying for a while, Jim," Claire said.

"It does, doesn't it," I replied, smiling at both of them.

My familiarity with Bozeman meant I could drive directly to my new base of employment without ever having seen it before. The street was one I had traveled countless times in walking years earlier from my small apartment to the campus.

Jim's partners, Myles Hoetzer and Abel Kryzmarzyk, were there to welcome me. Myles was from Indiana and had graduated from Purdue. Abel had grown up in Des Moines, but had graduated from Montana State. They didn't have to be there, but their presence gave me a good feeling and helped me see that working for a small firm could be the basis for some new friendships.

We talked a bit about my Port Authority position in Baltimore and what my job with them would entail, but after I mentioned that I had bought some land west of Norris and was rebuilding an old log cabin, we talked of little else. I think they envied me, in spite of all my personal problems, which I am sure were made known as part of Jim's briefing. I knew it was absolutely what Jim owed to his partners, notwithstanding our long history as friends.

Jim acted as my personal tour guide, and we worked our way

between cubicles and desks to reach the space reserved for me, introducing me to other staff as we passed by. My office was adequate, but nothing compared to what I was accustomed to, of course. But that was just fine. I wanted to be out on the job, in the fresh air, as much as possible, and so long as I had enough room to spread out a set of blueprints, I would be happy.

The receptionist, a lovely young girl by the name of Lori, helped me fill out a mixture of forms for payroll, health insurance, and income tax withholding before I left the building for a tour of some of the firm's ongoing street projects.

"Oh, Mr. Pengilly," she hollered, as I was about to open the door of my vehicle, "I nearly forgot to give you your plane ticket. There is a confirmation number for your lodging in there as well."

I took the ticket from her, thanked her, and asked her to call me Jim. "Yes, Sir-I mean yes, I'll do that, Jim." I winked at her when I left. She blushed. We were going to get along just fine.

My flight to Denver departed on schedule early Tuesday afternoon. A short layover in Salt Lake, while some passengers departed and others came aboard, afforded me an opportunity to leave the plane, stretch my legs, and purchase a cup of Folger's hard stuff The flight was uneventful between Salt Lake and Denver except for the buffeting winds along the front range which, at times, had the 727 bucking like an angry bronco. I'm sure there was never any danger of the plane breaking apart and flying away in a thousand different directions, but it certainly felt like it could. I was glad when I felt the tires pound the runway in Denver.

Denver's state-of-the-art airport and terminal, located several miles east of downtown, had me admiring the engineering skills that went into its construction. Despite problems with baggage handling and other glitches, it was almost a work of art. My motel was miles away in the heart of downtown, but I had no trouble locating the motel limo.

It was early, so the first thing I did was retrieve the agenda for the following day's meeting from my brief case. It was pretty straightforward, taking little of my time. The pad of graph paper and a sheaf of notes I had already written to myself were soon spread out on the surface of the small motel desk, and in no time, I had laid out a preliminary sketch of a floor plan that included two bedrooms, a large bathroom, and a third, smaller room to serve as my office and library. It would have several closets and enough windows to let in the sun's light and warming rays.

I had almost nodded off when the phone rang. I picked it up and said hello. I knew the voice immediately. It was Jordan Reveri. We had been lovers for several years, and she was a big part of why I was now, or soon would be, officially single again. She was calling me from the Denver airport. She was in town and had called the moment her flight from D.C. landed. She asked if we might get together for an hour or so tonight. Apparently she had called my office in Bozeman and was given my cell phone number.

My first inclination was to tell her I was tied up and couldn't get away, but it dawned on me that since my meeting wasn't until early tomorrow afternoon, seeing her tonight might be the best way to place a stamp of finality on our sometimes wonderful, often stormy affair. So I said I would. It was only then that she told me she would be checking in to the same motel. We agreed to eat in the motel dining room, and I arrived there only a few minutes before her.

She was dressed fashionably in a skirt and blouse discreetly proclaiming her femininity. Blue and white had always seemed to highlight her greenish-blue eyes and dark blonde hair. An aura of self-confidence and class surrounded her like a halo, and for a time I shamefully wallowed in the envy of several men and women seated nearby. She was stunning, and she exuded the promise of ecstasy in a way that few women could...or would dare. She had one principal nerve in her body, one card to play, and she used it to her advantage. My mind jumped back to an earlier, happier time.

It was August, and outside the air was heavy with humidity and the threat of severe thunder storms. The sun's rays invaded the conference room, sending razor thin shafts of light against the wall and making it difficult for many of us not to lose ourselves in our private thoughts. A dozen or more upper level management individuals, including myself, were seated around a long, oval-shaped table waiting for the man who would walk us through the several phases involved in designing and constructing the gigantic water conveyance system, the National Water and Power Alliance.

NAWAPA, as it was called, had never reached beyond the concept phase, but from the designer we hoped to learn how to manage our own large projects. We would learn more about management techniques, critical path analyses, logistical tools, even dealing with the public. My project happened to be the simultaneous upgrading of several components of the facilities owned by the Port of Baltimore. It was a minuscule undertaking, by comparison, but the largest single, most costly port project ever attempted in the Baltimore-Chesapeake Bay area. It was a phased project that jumped from the completion of one to the beginning of another, with little breathing space in between. It was my job to oversee it all.

The speaker's presentation was polished, detailed, and provocative, conveying enough food for thought to last a lifetime. I knew without being told that I was the beneficiary of a brilliant man's largesse and mental gymnastics. I was excited about what lay ahead, but I was also frightened. Was I up to it? Did I have the skills, and could I forge techniques that would keep me on top of the project's multitude of phases and facets, all of which must move ahead on individual timetables yet in sync with dozens of other endeavors. My position with the Port of Baltimore did not involve design, per se, but I was responsible for tending to the Authority's business in connection with everything else. Even the engineers who monitored compliance with specifications were assigned to me.

I would remember that session in Atlanta for a good long time, but not because of what I learned about management and problem solving. What I would remember longer was the stunning woman who sat across the table from me now. Her entrance had the effect of stopping casual conversations, raising heads, and engendering fantasies about what it would be like to know, I mean, *know*, such a woman. During the question and answer phase, she demonstrated that she was much more than just beautiful. Her inquiries were incisive, and she raised questions herself that helped to educate all of us.

That exquisite woman was sitting across from me now sipping on what had been our favorite wine, and she had grown more beautiful over time. We small-talked our way through dinner, but the time came when we both knew we had to confront the real reason we were here. And, as I had anticipated, she broached the subject.

"I'm really disappointed in you, Jim," she began as she reached out to touch my hand. "We need to talk...to talk about us."

"Oh, I don't know, Jordan," I ventured. "What would be the point?"

"The point is," she stammered, obviously distraught with my attitude, "the point is that we strayed away from each other for a while. We both know we shouldn't have, but I think you still have strong feelings for me. Must you be so distant? For God's sake, Jim, we were lovers. I remember when we couldn't get enough of each other. We can't just walk away from that. You owe me an explanation. We owe something to each other. What happened? Why didn't you answer my e-mails when I asked you to meet me?"

"I remember the e-mails, Jordan," I said, trying hard to get my brain out in front of my mouth. "I remember them, of course. I never answered because...well, because, frankly, I thought your questions were best left unanswered."

"What kind of answer is that? It's no answer at all," she snapped.

"I saw your questions best left unanswered, because I didn't have any answers," I said, "but if you must have answers now, I'll try to give you some. I have mixed feelings. When I see you across the table from me, my heart tells me to try hard for a reconciliation. My head tells me run away as fast as I can. I thought meeting you again would be a mistake, at least for me, until I was sure."

"Don't say that, Jim," she interrupted.

"You asked, Jordan," I said. "My answer might be different if I were sure one way or the other. In time I suppose I might even change my mind, but if you insist on an answer now, I'm afraid it is that I don't believe our being together again would ever work. Not only that, but I think this is the last time we should ever see each other. Think about it. Wouldn't you at least agree that it probably wouldn't work?"

"No, I wouldn't," she snapped. "Can't you understand that I am trying to tell you I want us to go back to what we had. I made a mistake when I let you get away from me. A big mistake. I know that now, but I want to be with you. I'll move to Montana if you want."

Her answer conveyed to me the certainty that none of my words had connected with her intellect in any way. It was as if I weren't there, that I hadn't spoken.

"What makes you think we could make it work this time?" I asked. "Aren't you forgetting why we drifted apart and eventually went our own ways?"

"No, I remember," she said, "but that doesn't matter any more."

"I think it does, Jordan," I countered. "We parted for a lot of reasons. One of them was my age. I am old enough to have children not much younger than you. You once said that made no difference, but it did, and I think you know it did. It was probably the main reason you walked away from what we had. If it couldn't work for you then, why would it work now? And, in case you've forgotten, we were both married at the time...unhappily, as I recall, but married just the same. And I know neither of us wanted to destroy that. In my case, there were children involved."

"Don't think I didn't think about the consequences," Jordan said, "but that was then. Everything is changed. The past doesn't count. Can't we wipe that slate clean? Ralph and I are separated. We haven't lived together as man and wife for almost two years now. Your marriage is in shambles. You are living in Montana because the life you knew back east is over. You share the same itinerary as your wife as far as your kids go, but that's all. Otherwise, you have nothing. I think of you all the time, Jim. I can't get you out of my mind. You're always there. I need you, don't you see?"

I told her once again that I thought it was too late.

"You're making this awfully hard for me, Jim." she said in a voice that hinted at her growing impatience and frustration with my resistance and with herself for not being able to convince me that we could rebuild a relationship. I believe she had come convinced that she could win me back.

"Everything has changed,' she said yet again. "I have changed."

I looked into her eyes, and I could see she was near tears. They told me she truly hoped for a rekindling of what had been, but it couldn't work. I knew it. She couldn't come to grips with the fact that too many harsh words, too many slights, and too many lies stood between us and any hope of resurrecting what had once been the perfect love affair. Rebuilding the foundation of that love seemed utterly impossible to me now. Where once it sustained us, it was now little more than a pile of rubble at our feet. Where once it was love, it was now nothing more than a collection painful memories.

"Jordan," I said, "I'll grant you that things have changed, but the change has not been your's alone. I have changed too. Once I cared deeply for you, but for reasons only you know for sure, you left me. Oh you were there physically right up to the end, but you were gone just the same. I may have been as well.   I don't mean to be cruel, Jordan, but that's the way it was.

"You walked out on me," I went on.   "I called. You seldom returned my calls. It was as if you needed to convince yourself that you could have me back anytime you wished. And, I suppose, for a time that was true. But not any more. I felt then like I had made an effort, that I had stepped up to the plate and struck out on several occasions that I won't soon forget. If you don't remember, it is only because you were already gone. After awhile, my pride kicked in, I suppose, and I learned to tolerate life without you.

"I loved you, Jordan," I added. "Thought of you a million times after we parted, but time heals. And now, I am healed. I just couldn't chance having my heart broken again. I won't do it!"

"Please, Jim," she said, her eyes begging, "can't we at least try?"

"No," I said. "It's too late. I'm not being obstinate in order to punish you. We are both to blame, I'm sure. It's just that love has gone from my life, and I'm not sure I want it back."

"Can't we at least spend the night together?" she asked, in a low pleading voice.

"I'm sorry, Jordan. I'm so sorry. But no."

"Is there someone else?"

"No. No one."

She stood up then and looked down at me. The small tears trickling down her cheeks came close to washing away my resolve but, as they say, I maintained. It was time...time to end it. I sat there for a long time, lost in memories that flashed across my brain like wildly dancing Northern Lights. The carafe of Merlot was nearly empty when I stood up to leave. What little remained I poured into my glass and finished it in a symbolic toast to myself for having cast off another of my past indiscretions. I never saw her again, but I would be lying if I said I never again thought of her or remembered how it felt to hold her in my arms.

Back in Bozeman, I surrendered to my job during the day, but nights and weekends belonged to the cabin and everything remotely connected. Every morning, early, before either Claire or Jennifer were up, I aimed my truck at either Bozeman or Belgrade. Street projects in two new subdivisions occupied a good part of my mind until I drove away each night. If I happened to be in Bozeman at quitting time, my only stop on the way home was at one of the fast food joints on Main. In Belgrade the menu was usually a made-up roast beef on whole wheat from the Deli section in one of the convenience stores. From that point on until I dropped into my bed it was the *place*. Half the time, I never bothered to stop at the ranch on my way to Pengilly Acres.

Headway, I was making on crossing items off my clipboard priority list, but not enough and not fast enough. It was the middle of summer, with its long days but, when I looked at the calendar, it was apparent that I needed help. Earlier, I had come to the same conclusion and had mentioned it to Claire, but somehow I never got around to actually looking for anyone.

The cabin was shaping up nicely. A new floor made of tongue-and-grooved 10 inch planks was complete, the gaps between the logs had been re-chinked, and replacement windows were stacked on the new floor waiting to be installed. The power company had been called, and I was on their schedule for bringing electricity to the place. The forest service had approved my permit for corral poles and fence posts, and Claire had helped me make arrangements with a moonlighting logger to supply me with all the logs I would need for my addition. But being on someone's schedule could mean an interlude of weeks before I saw results in the form of a meter on a post or a pile of logs in the yard.

Other than the work I had done on the cabin, my two other major accomplishments were a completed fence around about 80 acres and the foundation forms for the new addition. A stop at the lumber yard in town on my way home one day netted me the 100 sacks of cement I would need for the foundation and a slab at the bottom of my front steps. My plan also called for a good-sized concrete slab on the northwest corner of the house, but that might have to wait 'til next year.

Progress on the foundation itself was slow because I had to mix my mortar batches with a small portable mixer Claire had stashed away in the Quonset. But on the plus side, and there always is one if you look for it, was the fact that between batches I had time to rest. Concrete work, whether it is placing a load of ready-mix or a wheelbarrow full, is hard, grueling work if you are out of shape. I might have made it far easier by calling one of the ready-mix outfits. But I wanted the foundation's face to be that of rocks placed one at a time. Besides, the foundation became a repository for all kinds of scrap iron lying around the place. Ready-mix meant just what it said. Concrete dropped into forms then on to another job. No, I had made up my mind to do it my way or not at all. I was placing rock against the outside wall to determine where best to use them when Michele drove into the yard. She was carrying two cans of beer which had become the trademark of her infrequent visits.

"Hey, Jim," she said in her deep voice, "things are looking good, huh?"

"Coming along slow and not so sure," I replied. "but I like what

I've done so far. It more or less matches the existing foundation. Problem is, I spend more time hunting down rocks than I do fitting them into the foundation wall. I see a few rock piles here and there, but they are on private property. Don't know who they belong to. So, I'm pretty much restricted to the Forest Service land. Don't even know if that's legal."

"I can help you with rocks," she said. "Jump in my truck and I'll have you a load in a couple of hours."

She delivered on her promise and then some. Two hours later a pile of stones of all sizes and shapes were piled next to my forms. They had come from a good sized rock pile located on her land up again the National Forest Service boundary. I told her I was grateful and offered to return the favor anytime she wanted.

"I've got an idea there too," she said. "I'm hauling a load of yearling steers into Three Forks early Saturday morning. I could use help pushing them into the trailer. If you feel like it, why don't you just ride up there with me and look the place over?"

"What time should I be at your place?" I asked.

"About sunup would be perfect."

My truck was parked in front of her place well before the sun peaked over the eastern horizon. Headlights shining against her barn told me I might even be a little early. I was happy to help, despite the early start. This is where I lived. I wanted to be a part of things. I vaguely remembered her saying something about riding along to Three Forks, but I wasn't sure. If she did ask again, my *yes* would be immediate.

The livestock auction phenomenon was not altogether foreign to me, but the years between the present and my last sale were more than 20. We pushed the steers off the trailer and down the ramp where yard workers sent them on their way to one of the pens. The café served huge, tasty omelets and mine wasn't on my plate long enough to get a good look at me. Hers either as far as that goes.

We carried our Styrofoam coffee cups up to the top row of seating and watched as farmers, ranchers and onlookers like myself filed in. If there were any in the amphitheater who weren't stuffing one side of their mouths with sunflower seeds while spitting them out the other, I did not see them. Back in Moccasin, we called them Russian Peanuts. The funny thing was most of them came from North Dakota. Figure that one out if you can. It was like sitting in a peanut bar. When we went back to get a fresh cup of caffeine, the tiny shells crackled and crunched under our feet like Rice Crispies. Michele introduced me to dozens of people. She seemed to know everyone.

"Buying or selling today, Michele?" asked an old man, his pot belly hanging over his belt buckle and his ears crushed down by a hat that would easily win a prize for sweat stains and manure.

"Need some cash. Does that answer your question?"

"Well, good luck," he said. "The market's off a little you know."

"The market's off?" I asked when he was out of earshot. "You know that, and you're selling?"

"My purse says *sell*, and my purse never lies."

"Damn," I blurted. "Maybe I ought to be buying."

"It's a good time. Are you set up for it?"

"Water in the creek and fence on 80 acres. I'm ready."

When we pulled away from the auction barn and slipped out on to the highway, the trailer was loaded with 13 black-baldy, bred heifers, and they were mine. My check book had skinnied up some, but they were mine. Michele was smiling at me like I was the only first-grader in Norris holding a bag of licorice and jelly beans. And, damn it, it felt just about that good. When we dropped the ramp on the trailer and let them trail out on their own at my place, I felt like I had taken another step toward legitimacy in the valley community. I had a brand inspector's clearance report, a bill of sale, a vet's certificate, and the optimism of a man who, in the spring, knew he would be the proud stepfather to13 babies.

Michele hung around for about half and hour while I gave her the grand tour.

"You've got some good looking heifers there, Jim" she said as she walked to her truck, only to spin about and walk back to me and plant a kiss on my cheek, a moderately wet one at that. "Thanks for every thing," she said. "I'll be back one of these days to collect my commission for all the good advice I've given you."

I knew she was teasing me and enjoying it. "I'm a little short on cash." I replied, "so don't be expecting much."

"I expect as much as you've got," she said, and turned the switch to start her truck's motor. Her truck's ignition switch wasn't the only thing turned on that afternoon. She had tripped one of my switches, and any notions I harbored about being as worthless as her steers, vanished like wispy-white, scrambling clouds, tumbling over each other trying to get out of the way of one of those Alberta Clippers.

Chapter 4

Not long after the 4th of July, the driller came to rework the well, which was another way of saying he would pull as much of the old casing as he could and then re-drill it. It was the only way he could know for certain what he had to deal with. The well hadn't been used in 15 or 20 years, and it may not have been much of a well to begin with. He needed to know: Had it caved in on itself? Did it need new casing? Were there lenses of sand and gravel that would be an escape route for his drilling fluid? Did he need to seal them off? I left it to him to answer those questions, but I told him I wanted a well that would pump no less that 20 gallons per minute, hopefully more, and I wanted a pit-less unit installed to guarantee that I would have water in my house and at the stock tanks during the coldest of winters.

Odin Norgaard's nephew, Olaf, the young man who was to harvest the timber the Forest Service had granted me earlier in the summer, drove into the yard a few days after the well driller had departed with his equipment and a few thousand of my hard earned dollars. Behind Olaf were two logging trucks: one piled high with logs for the walls and timbers for the ceiling joists. A hydraulic hoist operated by the driver of the larger truck placed the heavy, dead pine logs on the ground as softly as a masseur. When he finished with the large logs, he pulled up along side the other load and dropped it to the ground where I wanted them.

The jumbo job of hoisting those logs into place was now in the hands of contractors. I had finished the foundation, and the power company would begin stringing lines on Monday. For me there remained a hay feeder and a three-sided, open shed for the cows when they chose to hide from the winter wind. I was in the middle of installing a set of cupboards in the kitchen, but before I did much more, the electrician had to pay me a visit.

Most Sunday afternoons I spend with Claire and Jennifer. Jennifer's specialty, beef post roast, was the usual fare, and I shamefully admit that I usually ate more than my share. Now and then one or more of the couples they grew up with were invited as well. Pot luck on everything except the roast seems to be the rule.

Today, we are joined by the Morrisons for a second time. They live south about three miles. Bill and Gertrude, Gertie as she was called, had attended elementary and high school with the Macintoshes and they are dear friends now a half half century later.

Bill is in his late sixties and whatever hair he once had is disappearing rapidly. He isn't totally bald, but he will be once he loses those stubborn but straggly remnants of what had once given him a sense of pride. His body is slim and muscular, but stooped slightly, no doubt from a lifetime of hard work. He is average in height with a narrow waist and broad shoulders, but he weighs less than 160 pounds. His eyes are as blue as can be and his nose is straight but longer than average.

His better half is almost as tall...and ram-rod straight. Her hips, unlike most women her age, have gone the way of Bill's hair...to parts unknown, and she wears glasses thick enough to start a fire if she were to hold them to the sun. Her own hair is thin on top, but despite her

Olive Oil-like appearance, her large brown eyes speak of a loving, caring wife and friend to those lucky enough to know her.

The two of them are a made-for-each other couple, according to Jennifer. Gertie's ever-present smile testifies to her positive outlook on life, one that seems contagious when others need a pick-me-up for whatever reason. Her positive outlook on life matches Bill's from what I can see, which probably explains her conviction that she was never more than moments away from winning as long as she kept yanking down on the one-armed bandits. That is, at least, the story Bill tells me.

The two of them shared similar backgrounds. They are the progeny of early homesteading families turned ranchers. She is quick to say that without her, Bill would not survive long. She is active in the community and a pillar of strength for her husband who, despite his strength and resolve in virtually everything he does, apparently has frequent bouts with this or that illness. Some say his most serious illness is galloping hypochondria. They are quite a couple, and as we get better acquainted, I am learning to like them more and more.

While the women slaved away in the kitchen, Bill leaned over to me and said, "She's a wonderful woman, Jim, and she thinks I can't live without her, but I let her think so. It makes her feel needed, and I guess we all need that. I let her run with the bit in her mouth for the most part, but I get nervous when she comes within smelling distance of a one-armed-bandit or a blackjack table. She is addicted to taking chances whether it is her left arm cranking a slot machine or betting on the Denver Broncos. I let her run loose as long as the bottom line doesn't sag too much. When that happens, I stand her up and lead her to the buffet."

Here I am, almost a stranger, and this old-time Montana rancher is confiding in me like I'm a young priest just out of the seminary. Only in Montana! I enjoy these Sunday dinner occasions very much.

Where else could I learn so much about these early day pioneers? And what better way to work my way into the community? Already, the lady at the service station-convenience store in Norris calls me by my first name.

I have yet to meet the Lustres or the Weers, but I have no doubt but that I will. This Sunday's get together ended after we had polished off supper sandwiches and ham and bean soup. Bill's parting words to me, were to call him if he could be of any help. He could of course. All he had to do was write me a large check, and from what Jennifer had said, he could do so. But I envied him not one whit for I was convinced that the good feeling that comes from being satisfied with your work and with yourself is far more important than having a huge wad of money in your pocket.

The word was, according to Jennifer, that he was one of the wealthiest men in the area. Money was not a fetish with him, and he seldom mentioned it, but his eyes and his head were always looking for a way to earn more. The foundation of his wealth was the vast acres south and west of Norris, a majority interest in a hardware-lumber business in Three Forks, a ready-mix concrete company in Townsend, and several thousand board fee of merchantable pine timber on the east side of the Tobacco Root Mountains.

I hung around for one last cup of coffee after the Morrisons left. Benny joined us and proudly displayed a nice stringer of crappies caught that afternoon while fishing with Odin. When he was gone, I lingered long enough to tell the Macintoshes that I was feeling much better about myself all the time, given the progress I had been making on the house, but that my job was not at all fulfilling I was going to work and giving the firm a full day's work for a day's pay, but I longed to be elsewhere.

"And the elsewhere?" Jenny asked.

"You know where, Jenny," I said. "Out here working on my place and going back and forth with the two of you."

"Anything we can do?" Claire interjected.

"No. You've done so much already. I can never repay you. No. I have to deal with this myself."

"Well, we are here for you, Jim," Jennifer offered. "Let us know if we can help."

"I'll be fine. I guess I'm feeling a little sorry for myself. I'll get over it."

I knew what the problem was. I was lonesome. I was spending an awful lot of my time by myself. Nobody was waiting for me with supper or a hug or anything else when I came home each day. I hadn't seen my kids for months. Nobody really cared about me other than my parents, I suppose, and Jenny and Claire. It suddenly occurred to me that, in spite of what I had told myself, I wanted someone. But that kind of thinking could toss me right back into the maelstrom that could break a heart that was beginning to mend itself. Still, it would be nice.

Feeling down and lonely, I drove slowly home. It was my own fault. I had so much to feel good about, but maybe it was just the letdown in the wake of the divorce and, earlier, the breakup with Jordan. Three or four miles down the road my melancholy disappeared like a magician had waved his wand. It always happened that way. The closer I came to home, the better I felt. After all, I had electricity now. I had a stove, a fridge, a washer, and a dryer. I had modern, double-paned windows, a storm door, and a queen–size bed to sleep on. How in good conscience could I ask for more?

Once I got the addition finished off inside, I'd have a reason to be proud. I had come to feel I had met the test, but I knew I needed something more. Another challenge, I suppose. Something to distance myself from the *project,* a respite from the routine that was grinding me down. I began making plans for a trip up into the Tobacco Roots and Hollow Top Peak before I was half way home.

I had a week to think the climb through, and that was enough. My first thought was to drive up to Pony, the jumping off place for climbing Hollow Top Peak from the east side. From what I had been told, a "jeep" trail brought you part way to the peak. My truck was no Jeep but it had four wheel drive and oversized tires that gave me plenty of clearance. I should have no trouble. From the end of the jeep trail, I would be one my own, but a climb could be therapeutic as well as physically challenging for a novice like myself. I needed a diversion. I loved my place, but I needed to divorce myself from it and all the work it entailed for a day or two. Next Saturday was the day. I was in pretty good shape, and I reminded myself that I wasn't exactly climbing Everest. I could do it. Yes. I could do it! Watch out, Hollow Top! Here comes Pengilly!

It was still early when I got home. I walked around the yard sizing up the outdoor tasks I needed to attack during the coming week. It was the sound of an approaching vehicle that broke my concentration and brought me around to see Michele pull up along side my truck. She was lugging a 12-pack with one hand and a package of something else in her other.

"Your fridge working?" she asked. I told her it was. She handed me the beer and I followed her into the house. I extricated two cans from the carton and handed one of them to her.

"Want to go for a walk, Jim?"

"Sure," I said. "Sounds like a wild adventure."

"Could be," was her abbreviated answer.

She led me out through my gate where we turned up the road leading to the west and the high country. I asked her if our destination was known to her. She told me it was, of course. Half the time she was several feet ahead of me on the winding, two-track road leading up to the mountain. After about a mile, she made an abrupt left turn on to a steep, and barely discernible game trail leading to even higher ground. I watched as her head dropped out of sight momentarily only to reappear again. When I caught up, we were perched on a flat outcropping of fractured granite, with an incredible view of the sweep and breath of the valley. Below us, reaching slightly above the level of the outcropping floor itself was a thick stand of pine over which we could look and behind which we could hide, if we wished.

"What do you think, Jim?" Michele asked, her eyes never leaving the panorama below.

"It's incredible. You could build a house on this slab and no one would see it from the highway. Does anyone else know about it?"

"Sure, but not many, I don't think. Marty and I stumbled across it on one of our horseback rides when we were kids. I've never told anyone about it."

"The view from here is absolutely stunning," I said. "Thank you for bringing me here. I'll keep your secret."

"Well, I wanted to show you why you're here and why you'll never leave," she said.

I knew just what she meant. The country had reached out with another of its caressing tentacles to draw me closer. Shivers ran up and down my back when I thought about how fortunate I was to be here. We put our backs to the rock wall behind us and sat there for over an hour. The sun was shining and the air was fresh but cool. Neither of us said a word. Just looked and immersed ourselves in private thoughts. Half the time, my eyes were closed, but I could still see images I would never forget. On the way back to the road, Michele reached for my hand and led me down. I grabbed it and squeezed it hard to let her know I was thankful for such an unexpected adventure.

When we reached the road, she dropped my hand and moved ahead of me, but its warmth lingered for a long time. When I caught up to her, I put my arm around her waist, pulling her against my side, and thanked her again. "The view was beautiful, Michele, and...well, so are you."

"I'm ready for another of those brewskis," was all she said.

We walked in silence the mile back to my place. Could there be a more pleasant way to top off a lazy Sunday? I didn't think so.

My "lucky 13" were standing with their heads resting against the top wire of the fence, looking at us like a puppies waiting for table scraps. I had a couple of sacks of ground barley and rolled corn in the bin. Usually, when they came, I spread out a baker's dozen piles on the grass for them, hoping doing so would routinely bring them up towards the building and keep me from going out to look for them.

"They're waiting, Jim," Michele said. "Better do your duty."

She turned and walked toward the cabin without another word. I struck out for the grain bin on a mission designed to make my 13 expectant black-baldy heifers happy. When I got to the cabin, Michele was standing over my new stove surveying two large t-bone steaks, sizzling in a combination of butter and onions. Now I knew what was in the package. I did what any good host should do. I set the table and dropped a bottle of Merlot into a 5-gallon milk pail filled with ice cubes. I liked my wine chilled, but I did have a backup bottle under the sink if she didn't.

"Chilled or not?" I asked holding the bottle in the air.

"Chilled is fine," she answered. I filled two glasses with ice cubes, drowned them in red, and held my glass up to touch hers. The tinkle of glass against glass was just the touch we needed to make this more than supper, to make it a shared moment between two friends.

The steak was delicious, and so were the fried spuds. Now I knew what else was in that package. "Perkins could use a cook like you," I said, "and I'm not ashamed to say that their gain would be my loss."

"Flattery will get you everywhere," she said, "everywhere."

"I'm not interested in everywhere," I replied. "Here is where I want to be, where I belong. No place else. You made me see that again up there on the rock.

"This has been one wonderful day," I added, "and I owe all to you. Thanks."

"You sound like it's over," she replied.

"No, I didn't mean that," I said contemplatively. "It's just that everything has been so perfect. The view, the time we spent up there in that jumble of rock and pine, the steak, the spuds, the wine, everything. I've been feeling a little down lately, and you put an end to that. You went to a lot of trouble to cap off a day I won't soon forget."

"Pour me another glass of wine, Jim, and I'll tell you something."

"Chilled or not?" I asked again.

"Chilled would be fine," she replied again.

For a long while, she sipped her wine, nursing it like someone beginning to feel tipsy, but wanting to avoid the next step. When she did finally say something, it had nothing to do with anything that had transpired today. It had to do with us. With her. With me.

"My motive for being here today, Jim," she almost whispered, "is to collect my commission. You remember the commission, don't you?"

I had an uneasy feeling that I already knew where she was heading, and my uneasiness flowed from the caution switch in my brain which told me not to get involved.

"I remember," I said, "What are the damages?"

"You haven't got enough money to pay me. There isn't enough money to pay me," she said, "but what you can do is take me to your bedroom."

Like I said, I saw it coming, so I wasn't really shocked when she spoke the words. My answer hinged on my resolve to keep in place the pledge I had made to myself about female entanglements. I had earlier told myself that in spite of my feeling of loneliness, it was prudent and wise to keep women out of my life until I was sure I was ready. It has been weeks and months since I last thought of either Rebecca or Jordan in this way, so maybe I was ready. What could I do? Here was a beautiful, desirable woman, a woman who said she wanted me. I made a choice, and I never regretted it. I stood up, reached for her hand and led her toward my bed.

That night we slipped into a mutually satisfying physical...no, sexual-relationship. We were mature, experienced adults, minus the old days and their runaway hormones. We took turns carrying each other toward the blinding crescendo that could only flow from kindness and tenderness. We fit like a pair of expensive, silk gloves, and we both knew this was a new beginning. I had convinced myself that sex without love was hollow and empty. Our night together was the undoing of that theory. As if to somehow bear witness to ourselves that we saw what we had experienced as being filled with right and goodness, we partook a second time of that juicy sweetness.

She was gone when I rubbed my sleepy eyes open to see the sun's early morning rays filtering through the partially open window blinds next to my bed. Propped against a half filled bottle of wine was a note. I lifted myself out of bed and reached for it.

Jim, it said: *"Last night was wonderful. You were wonderful. It has never been better.*

You took care of one of my needs and I'm afraid you triggered a need for more. I loved it. But I don't love you. You need to understand that, and I want you to know why.

I loved my husband as much as a woman can love a man. He is gone, and with him went my broken heart. The healing process may have begun as we held each other last night. I don't know. Maybe it even started the first time I saw you. But I can't stand another broken heart. A heart can break only when one loves someone deeply. I can't let that happen to me again. I couldn't cope with it. I can't stand to miss someone so much again, and the only way to guard against it is to not let love creep into my heart once more. I just can't. Not now at least.

If the sun is shining in your window, you are late for work. Call and tell them you are running late. But go to work. You need to focus on something besides last night. About now you'll be wanting a cup of the hard stuff. I plugged the pot in before I left. If you don't call, I will. Michele

The coffee was just what I needed, but I ignored her advice about going to work. I reached Jim Madsen and told him I wouldn't be coming in today. He didn't ask for a reason. I didn't volunteer one. He just told me Bailey would take over for me. I spent the better part of the day walking around the place in a daze. If ever a man had his plate full, it was me. I was technically still a married man, I had just made a final break with an old lover, I was working on a job I didn't like, I was buying a piece of Montana real estate I wasn't sure I could afford and, now, I was caught up in a relationship with a wonderful woman who said she wanted me but couldn't love me.

Under other circumstances I would have cut and run from what promised to be a loveless affair. My liaison with Jordan had been a search for love, but it had ended in a bed of hard feelings and rancor. At the time, my marriage was imploding, and I longed for someone, anyone, with whom I could share my hopes and dreams and, I suppose, my body. I believed in love then, and I believed in it now, but I couldn't run away from the feeling that I was setting myself up to get hurt once again. Cut from the same cloth we were, Michele and me. Both of us were alone and lonely. Both of us were troubled by the prospect of stumbling into anything binding. We were perfect for each other! She wanted a man now and then to satisfy her womanhood. I wanted the physical comfort she could give me but no more. She yearned for a friend. I did as well. Someone to talk with, someone to share ideas and dreams, someone who could be counted on to tell it to you the way it was.

By noon I had done all of the rambling about I needed, yet I'll admit it had been an educational walk-about. I now had a better feel for the general lay of my land, and I found noxious weeds and wild flowers I had never seen before. Wild flowers, I loved. Noxious weeds I could do without. Next time I saw Michele, I would ask her how best to deal with them.

My walk-about finished, I focused on building partitions in the new addition. Actually, partitions didn't fit well with my hope of keeping things open from floor to ceiling. I wanted air circulation and a feeling of not being cordoned off into a compartment with a bed. The bathroom needed walls for privacy if nothing else, and I had already framed the closets I wanted.

I was tracking sawdust over the floor and into the kitchen and living room, so I stopped pounding nails and began pushing a broom. The bed was a mess so I pulled the sheets, pillow cases, and mattress cover and tossed them in the washer. It was the first time I had actually operated the washer and dryer, but they worked well, and when I finished making the bed, I tackled the dishes. That I could do. I dried them with towels Jennifer had given me and stacked them in the cupboard. Someday I would make some lucky woman one hell of a housekeeper. I remembered back to when I was a kid and had discovered that washing dishes was the surest way for a farm boy to get his hands really clean.

The place was looking pretty good when Jennifer and Claire drove into the yard. They were on their way to their upper pasture but wanted to see what had transpired here since their last visit. They complimented me on the progress I had made and asked if there was anything they could do to help. I told them I thought I could wrap up the loose ends myself.

I think their real reason for coming had more to do with my being scarce at their place than anything else. I felt a bit guilty about that, but time fell into the precious commodity category. I knew they would be starting on their second cutting of alfalfa soon, so I offered to help evenings and weekends. I had run a baler before. I was intrigued by a mechanism that could lift hay out of a windrow, push it into a chamber, cut the edges smooth, tie it tight with two lengths of twine, and then drop it on the ground. Every time one of those bales dropped to the ground, I remembered having had a good feeling.

Claire said they would call if they needed me.

"Help is hard to find," Claire said. "Given any more thought to coming to work for us?"

I repeated what I had said earlier. Didn't want to quit a job I had just started. Not just yet, anyway, but when winter came and I expected to be laid off, maybe.

"We'll talk then," he said. "Take care."

"Oh, by the way," I said, "I'm taking a little vacation this coming weekend. Need a break. Going to try and climb Hollow Top and maybe camp out a couple nights."

"Sounds wonderful," Jennifer said. "I agree you need a break. You've been going at it pretty steady. Is it dangerous, you know. The climb, I mean. Are you going by yourself?"

"Not if you guys want to come along" I said, ignoring the danger part of her question. I knew that danger was always present when climbing in rocks. If it weren't for a bit of danger, that I felt I could handle, where would the adventure be?

"My goodness, no," Jennifer snorted. "Besides, Claire would have to attach some wings to those crutches, and we couldn't do that on such short notice. No, you go and have a good time."

"Yep," I said. "I will. Haven't done much camping the past several years, but I love doing it. I think its partly the challenge of making the climb and partly the solitude."

"Well, have a good time," Claire offered. "We better get going, Mother. Stop in and see us on your way if you can."

"Probably on the way back," I said. "I might be hungry for some decent cooking by then." They left then, heading west, gradually dropping down over the top of one of he hills and disappearing from sight.

I used my cell phone to call Michele, but got her voice mail. "Just called to see how you were doing," I said. "Call me when you can." I needed her cell phone number. She was gone from her house so much of the time.

Fifteen minutes later she drove into the yard.

"You're home early," she said.

"Not really," I confessed. "I didn't go to work like you told me."

"Shame on you. Did you see my note."

"Yes."

"And?"

"The coffee was great. Thanks."

"I'm glad. The other part of my note? Are you mad at me?"

I told her I was not the least bit mad. "I appreciate your candor," I said. "I really do. The truth is, I'm about where you are when it comes to relationships."

"Do we need to talk?" she asked.

"I don't think so," I said. "Not now, anyway."

"I'm sorry."

"You needn't be," I said, and meant it, "but I will tell you I didn't want last night to be a beginning and an end."

"I never intended that it would be," she replied. "I still want to be with you when we can."

"Can you stay the night?" I asked.

"I need to run home for a couple of hours, but I'll be back. Why don't we go away some place?"

"We can. I had planned to head up Hollow Top way this weekend for a little camping and climbing, but I can change that. Where would you like to go?"

"Hollow Top sounds good to me. When do we leave?"

"How does late Friday afternoon sound?"

"Sounds great. I'll be ready. Right now though, I better run. I'll be back for supper. What are we having?"

"The best Shipwreck stew you ever tasted," I said.

"Sounds interesting," she said, and then she left.

I was talking to my cows when the hum of an approaching vehicle tickled my ear. Michele had somehow been able to short cut whatever she had to do back at her ranch, and she was already on her way back, or so I thought. Instead of Michele it was Claire and Jennifer coming down off the mountain who pulled up along side of my baker's dozen.

"Jim," Jenny said, without getting out of the truck, "Claire and I had an idea."

I was sure they had changed their mind and were accepting my obligatory invitation to accompany me, but again, I was wrong. "An idea?" I answered. "Tell me about this great idea, please."

"Well, we think you should see if you can talk Michele into going camping with you," she said. "She spends so much time alone. She might enjoy it. She can cook. Why don't you ask her?"

"Sure, I suppose I could," I replied, with some feigned hesitation, hoping the relief I felt wasn't reflected in my voice.

"If she says she'll go, we'll meet the two of you at the Bear Claw Bar and Grill for supper, say a little before five on Friday. We should try to beat the rush. Their steaks are superb. We'll give you a proper send off. Call us when you know. We have to get home. Benny and Odin like their supper at six. We'll bring them along if it works out with Michele."

Their departure was of the same whirlwind variety that brought them. I had been thinking about what they would think should they somehow learn Michele and I had spent the weekend hiking. No need to worry now.

Wouldn't you know, my vast culinary skills all but deserted me as I tried to recall the steps involved in creating a roaster full of shipwreck stew. I had a thawed beef steak, so, I cut it up into one inch squares and tossed them in a cast iron frying pan, sizzling with melted butter and a half a cup of water. I kept the heat low to avoid scorching. That much I remembered from watching my mother make it 20 years earlier. Added to my growing conglomeration of ingredients were two large, white, sliced onions, the very critters I was counting on to give my batch of togetherness a taste long remembered.

After that, I wasn't sure, but my recollection was that the term, shipwreck, carried with it permission to use just about anything in the fridge leftover from yesterday. My noon meal the day before had been tomato soup and crackers, so I tossed in what was left of the soup and added a dozen crumbled whole wheat crackers. I stirred what I had so far, as if I were frying potatoes in a wok. I added several chopped stalks of celery, two cups of cut-up carrots, a half can of beef broth and salt and pepper. The whole mess, I tossed into a heavy roaster and shoved it into the oven. When tenderness began to creep into my concoction, I added several potatoes and a bit more water.

Two hours later I scooped globs of my creation onto to our plates, and sat there waiting for the only real chef present at the time to voice her opinion. She said it was very good. I didn't hear any resounding, "it's great, Jim," or "I love it," or "can I have your recipe", but she didn't leave anything on her plate either.

Afterward, we sat out under the covered porch I had added to the original building and drank half a bottle of Australian Cabernet. I confessed to her that I was closer to being a wino than I was to being a connoisseur and that I couldn't tell one wine from another, but I liked the taste of them all. I also told her that Jennifer and Claire had stopped by on their way home to suggest that I should invite her to go camping, because they said you were lonely.

"Not any more, I'm not." she said wistfully. "Not any more."

"Me neither," I said. "We are lucky. We are so very lucky."

Later, after we had talked of many things, we carried our empty glasses back to the kitchen on our way to the bedroom. I shut out the kitchen lights and followed her into the bedroom. I think we were both still a little nervous, and it showed in our tentativeness. We kissed as we stood beside the bed, and we slowly undressed each other, never speaking a word, yet knowing that this is what we both wanted. She leaned back to flip the switch next to the door, arching her back and pressing herself against me as she did so. She came to me then with desire and passion. I met her with as much, and we were almost instantly joined with her straddling me and rocking against my hardness.

"Lie still," she said, "let me do this. You'll get your turn." I relaxed as much as I could while my hands held her hips as she rocked slowly against me, moaning softly with every stroke. Her breasts were firm and I reached out to them, my finger brushing against each nipple's hardness. When I could lay still no longer, I pulled her face towards me and moved my lips and tongue slowly in and out of her inviting, searching mouth.

"It's your turn," she whispered. Slowly she lifted her self off and pulled me with her. We joined instantly, and now it was my turn to probe the depths of her womanhood. I moved in an out slowly alternating between teasing and deep strokes. Neither of us were hurried, wanting to enjoy the moment as long as we could. We paced ourselves, searching for that instant when we were both ready. When it came, she whispered *now* and reached for my buttocks to hold me against her, fearful I would fall away in the slipperiness following orgasm. I drove against her and she was there to meet me. From both of us came the moans of the moment, and we clung to each other long after, moving slowly, not wanting it to end.

We slept in each others arms, and again I was going to be tardy at work. But I didn't care, and she held me in a way that told me she wasn't finished. My priorities had shifted sometime during the night. A metamorphosis you could call it. But unlike Gregor Samson, who couldn't get off his back, I could have rolled my legs to the side of the bed and got myself ready for the 40-mile ride. I just didn't want to. So I didn't.

Michele was waiting for me in the kitchen, and my senses caught the sound of sizzling bacon, crackling eggs and the faint odor of toasted bread as I pulled my jeans to my waist. She came to me with a spatula in one hand and a kiss on her lips. God, I thought, could it get any better?"

Later, after she was gone, I made a hurried call to Jennifer to let her know that Michele had agreed to the camping trip. "Wonderful," she said, "Just wonderful. See you on Friday, if not sooner."

And later still, a long time later, I was working on the Belgrade project, verbally kicking myself in the ass for coming at all. On my way home that night, I stopped at one of the local sporting goods outlets and picked up a few more items we could use on our camp out. I asked Jim for Friday day off, hinting that I had some *personal* matters to attend to. I hated doing it, this playing on his sensibilities about my divorce, but practicalities told me I didn't want to drive all the way to town for what would be a half day's work.

"Are you sure you are up to this?" I asked Michele as we loaded our camping gear in preparation for our trip to the Bear Claw tavern and then on to Pony."

"I'm sure," she said. "It should be fun."

An hour later, we were sitting at the bar nursing a draft beer and waiting for Jennifer and Claire to arrive. Already, the Bear Claw was beginning to fill. Benny and Odin were the first faces I recognized, which put Michele up on me by only about 100 to three. I say *about* 100 to three because there was a long-haired, scruffy looking guy at the end of the bar I may have seen before. Michele, well, she knew everyone, it seemed, but I consoled myself, knowing that this was a bar and grill frequented primarily by locals, so why wouldn't she?

I glanced over my shoulder again to see Benny and Odin running interference for Jenny and Claire. As usual, when the two hired men stepped away from the ranch they did so with their traditional out-on-the-town scrubbed look. Benny's hair was slicked back like an Aberdeen Angus. Odin would have done the same were he actually in possession of hair. From Benny's neck hung a gold colored pendant of some kind, weighing a couple of pounds, and he strutted in there like he owned the joint. Fashion gurus could be found just about anywhere, it seemed.

"Will you look at that," Michele said, nudging me with her elbow. "Claire has shed his crutches. Hooray for Claire!"

Hellos were said all around and I invited them to sit with us and have a drink while we waited for a table. Jenny slipped in next to me, and the men took up bar stools on Michael's left and right

"Jim," Jenny almost whispered, "I am so glad Michele agreed to go with you. I think it will be good for both of you to have some time away from the steady grind of working seven days a week. Michele hardly knows what end is up, she's so busy. We feel so sorry for her. We try to involve her in things to help get over losing her man. She's so lonely.

"Believe it or not," she continued, "when we were younger Claire and I climbed to Hollow Top Lake several times. Never tried the peak. In later years, we would go with our boy. It's not an easy hike. Pretty steep at times, and lots of rotten rocks. Michele misses her husband so. It will be good for her."

"I'm glad she agreed to come too, Jenny," I said, "I think she will enjoy it."

"Oh, Jim," she blurted. "I almost forgot to tell you. Your son called as we were leaving the house. He asked me to have you call. You must have given him your phone number while you were in Baltimore." I hadn't but I had given Rebecca my cell number and the Macintosh number.

"Is there a problem back there?" I asked quickly, for I could not believe Michael would be calling if there weren't."

"No. No problem. He specifically asked me to reassure you that everything is okay, but he wants you to call when it is convenient. It's convenient right now, Jim. Why don't you call?"

"I will. Did he leave a number?

"No, he just said call him at home."

When we heard "Macintosh" called, we moved from the long bar and walked single-file like a bunch of penguins into the dining room. I waited 'til we had ordered to excuse myself, with a simple, "I need to make a call". A couple of heads nodded but for the most part the conversations continued as if they either hadn't heard or considered my leaving of small consequence."

Outside, I retrieved my cell phone from the truck and dialed my old number in Baltimore. It rang three times before I heard Morgan's voice.

"Morgan," I said, "this is your dad. How are you?"

"I'm fine." Then silence.

"Did Mike tell you he had called me?"

"No, but he's right here."

"Morgan-Morgan," I said but there was no answer.

"Hi, Dad," came Mike's voice. "You've probably sensed that Morgan is still angry with you. How are you?" I told him I was fine and asked if there was something I should know about.

They were all looking at me, as I slipped back into my chair. It was clear Jennifer had shared her news about Mike calling with the others. That was fine with me. "It was my son, Mike," I said, "He wants to come out for a visit before school starts again. I told him to come, of course."

"Well, that's just wonderful, Jim," Jenny said. "I'm so glad."

"We are all happy for you, Jim," Michele said, as her hand crept up to my leg beneath the table, leaving reassuring pats.

We talked about Mike while we waited. I told them he was a handsome 17-year old, taller than his dad, and shaving every morning before he goes to school. Has his mother's hair, which he wears cropped close to his head. His eyes are about the same color as mine, but his face is broader and, well, he's just a nice looking boy. Not only that, I said, he's an athlete who does very well in school. He hopes to become either a physician or research chemist. We never had to worry about him and homework, I said proudly. He did it and went looking for more.

"He sounds like a very nice young man," Claire said. "I could use a big, strong, conscientious young man to help me with the work Benny and Odin labor so hard to avoid."

Everybody laughed, including the two hired-men. It was Benny who asked innocently, "What is this 'con-see-en-shus' word you said, boss?"

We were still laughing when the waitress brought our orders. Once again, I was reminded that being back in Montana was good. I sneaked a look at Michele, thought about Michael coming, and I knew all was well again with Jim Pengilly.

The sun still stood high over the western horizon when we reached Pony. It was an interesting old mining town nestled up against the Tobacco Root Mountains. My highway map listed it but showed no population, which probably came pretty close to being right. Steering with my left hand and holding Michele's with my right, I herded the truck past several derelict buildings on to a decidedly less-than-smooth, narrow road that climbed gradually for a mile or so before we came to a fork. We took the left fork another half mile, dropping down to the North Fork of Willow Creek. We found the bridge over the creek I had been told about. We could have parked there had we wished, but decided to drive on to the trail head.

It was about a half mile from the creek-side parking area, and there was plenty of room. We lifted our packs from the rear of the truck and crossed over to the north side of the creek, following a stream-side path until we came to yet another bridge. This one was even more primitive than the first, safe only, I think, for pedestrian travel. Anyway, from this point on we climbed steadily on a rough, 5-foot wide trail, said to be useable by jeeps or other narrow wheel vehicles, including motorcycles. We saw none, for which we were thankful. We stopped several times on the trail to rest and glance out over the valley below. It was warm, with a bright sun doing its best to sneak beneath our hat bills.

The trail was never far from Willow Creek. Even when we lost sight of it for a few minutes, we could still hear the rush and gurgle of water across its rocky bottom. We followed it until we reached the signpost for trail # 333. Here we climbed a steep ridge leading slightly south east, and then, after roughly a mile, we turned right for a half mile to Albro Lake, our campsite for the night. I was proud of Michele. She shouldered her pack without complaint, but by the time we reached the lake, I could see she was hurting. I helped her get out from under her pack and steered her to a table-size but smooth boulder she could either sit on or prop herself against. Her spirits perked up noticeably when I pulled two cans of beer from the six-pack cooler I had secretly stashed in the bottom of my pack.

"You think of everything, Jim," she said. "I had no idea our little adventure would be so strenuous, so early."

"I'm sorry," I offered. "Why don't you just sit back and take it easy. I'll pitch our tent and build a fire so we can have coffee."

"Sounds wonderful," she said, "Where do we take our showers?"

"In the lake, I'm afraid. "I hope you don't mind water that's a bit on the cold side."

"I mind it, but I mind being dirty and sweaty even more."

Campers had been here before. In fact someone, probably the Forest Service, had brought up the wheel rim from a large truck to be used for a fire ring. I had packed in four or five newspapers and a small packet of kindling wood to help me start ours. Firewood was plentiful. My two-cup aluminum coffee pot, which actually held closer to three cups, was light to pack in and it required the smallest of fires. When it was done perking, I carried a cup to Michele. She smiled and reached out to squeeze my hand.

Our tent was small but more than adequate for two people. Neither of us could stand up in it without stooping, but it had vents on both ends to let the fresh air flow through and screen-like hangers above and on the side for storing clothing and other light objects. The two twin-air mattress we had brought filled the interior and then some, pushing the wide, bottom section of the tent out. Thank God for small, portable air pumps and size D batteries. Atop the tent, I fixed the rain shield in place with built in tie-downs. It could rain if it must but I hoped not.

We had no beach as such and I doubted there were many to be found anywhere on the lake. From the shore, it was easy to see that the water was probably no more than four or five feet deep within 20 or 30 feet of the edge.

I was deep in thought thinking about Michael's coming, together with the immensity of the mountains surrounding us when I felt a hand on my shoulder. I turned around to see her naked except for panties and a bra.

"If you go in," she said, "I will. I want to be clean." I stripped down to my shorts, without being asked, and tentatively tickled the water with my toe, knowing that I was going in no matter what. I reached out and took her hand and, together, we slipped slowly into its frigid fingers. It was cold but in a minute or so only our heads showed above the water surface. In time, it felt less cold, and we cavorted about like two kids. We didn't stay long, though.

When Michele was ready to come out, I was waiting for her with our only towel, technically a towel substitute, in the form of the small flannel-like plaid blanket I had found compressed in one of my pack's side pockets. We were both back in our traveling clothes quickly. I reached out for her and she came to me. I held her at the waist and looked into her eyes. Then we kissed, but it was a kiss not intended to fan any smoldering fires, not just yet. "What's for supper," she asked. "More of that shipwreck stew, I suppose?"

I told her no. In the cooler, I had made-up hamburger patties, two day-old boiled potatoes, a small onion, and a can of no-stick cooking spray. That and four slightly squashed hamburger buns were to be our supper.

"I supply the basic ingredients and the fire," I said, "and tonight your are my special Chef Boyardee."

"Fair enough," she said. "Let me at it."

We leaned against a boulder with our feet toward the fire and ate as if we were dining in the Space Needle's upper level dining room. We drank another beer each. We were determined not to carry a single, full can of beer down the mountain side. We talked about a lot of things. Actually, it was me who did most of the talking. I told her I would like to spend all of my time on my place instead of driving to Bozeman every morning.

"Claire says he would hire me full time right now," I said, "but I'm really hesitant about quitting Jim and the others just yet. It's too soon. I haven't been there long enough and, besides, I don't want to leave them in a lurch."

"I admire you for that, Jim," she said as she held out her coffee cup. "But you have to look out for yourself too."

"Come winter slow down," I said, "I might just give Claire's offer some serious consideration.

"It's funny, Michele," I continued, "but the job in Bozeman was to be a place I could go to and forget. But, you know, I don't need it. All I need, for now, is my place...and you. The job has become an encumbrance. It robs me of time to do what I really want to do. I want to be up here in the valley, I want more cows, I want a couple of good horses, I want to begin building a world where friends are important, where I don't drive 80 miles every day, where I can have you guys over for the weekend, for Christmas, or the 4th of July, that sort of thing. I want to belong."

"You already do, Jim," she said. "I'm so glad you're here. I won't let you break my heart, but I'll let you do almost anything else, if you get my meaning."

I got her meaning but, for now, with my arm around her, her head resting on my shoulder, and our eyes focused on the fire, that was enough. I wanted to tell her I cared, and I did, but I thought back to her note, and decided that to do so was asking for trouble. She would give and give and give...everything except her heart. I could live with that.

We drank our last cup of coffee under a full moon. We were

ready for bed. The two sleeping bags we had packed in were zipped together to make one. We made love again, and lay there living off our own body heat until the altitude blanketed us with it's cold. Even then, we clung to each other like two pieces of wet wallpaper.

Two nights we spent up in the high country, the second night at Hollow Top Lake. Once again our camp was on the water. We made love again and then once more when we returned from our climb up Hollow Top. I was beginning to have serious reservations about my staying power. I think Michele went home just in time.

It was a month before I saw her again. I called many times, sometimes two or three times a day. I reached her voice mail time and again, but never her. I left messages: they went unanswered. I was worried about her. It was unlike her not to answer my calls. Obviously, I had done something to anger her. If she wouldn't confide in me, I was sure it was because she wished not to. My own response was to let matters ride and to wait.

Michael came on a Friday night, I met him at the airport in Belgrade, and we drove into Bozeman for supper. He filled me in on what was happening in Baltimore with his mother and sister. Rebecca was still seeing her doctor friend, and she had gone back to work full time. Morgan was caught on the horns of a dilemma where, on one hand, she had us reconciling, and on the other, she was facing the prospect that her mother might marry her steady companion. It was a heavy load for a 15 year old girl to bear.

I told Michael, bluntly, that there was absolutely no chance of a reconciliation but that he and his sister needed to come to grips with the possibility that their mother would remarry. If not her doctor friend, then someone else. It only makes sense, I said. She's young. Maybe she can still find happiness.

"I suppose I should tell you that the house is up for sale," he said. "That says a bunch, to me at least, about her plans for the immediate future. I want her to be happy, but who am I to tell her what to do?"

"We must, each of us, travel our own path in such matters, Mike," I said. "Your mother and I have made several tough decisions these past few months, and we must live with them no matter how painful they are at times."

"I understand, Dad," he said. "I do. But that doesn't make it easy."

"Of course not," I said, "but being difficult doesn't change the fact that you must plot your own course. Your mother and I are both doing just that. It can't be any other way. I love your mother, and I always will, but not in the way I did when we married. This hasn't been easy for me, and nothing is going to be easy for you. Just remember, I am here for you if you need me. I can't tell you how happy I am you decided to fly out here. How long can you stay?"

"For a while, I think," he said. "At least a couple of weeks, perhaps a bit more. I want to sample a few bites of the life you have here."

I told him I could not be happier and that I had a place for him as long as he wished. It was pitch dark under a cloudy sky when we reached home. I offered him my bed, but he refused and pulled out the folding bed from the sofa in what passed for my living room. Before I turned out the lights, I took the time to check my phone for messages. I was doing it to the point of distraction these days, hoping, I suppose, that one time it would be Michele. I had one. And it was from her. She said we needed to talk. Would I call her in the morning?

I did so as soon as I was out of bed. Would I meet her up at our special place in the rocks? Yes, I said. When? I'll be there in 20 minutes she replied. I hurriedly wrote Michael a note telling him that I had to run out and check on my cows. Should he wake up before I got back, would he please turn on the coffee pot.

She was there when I arrived. I pulled my truck up along side hers and walked up the trail to the rocks. She was perched on one of the boulders when I stepped on to the outcropping. I walked to her and put my arms around her. We held each other for a moment and then she stepped away.

"I don't blame you if you are disgusted with me, Jim," she said, "but I needed time to think. I should have called earlier."

"That would have been nice," I said, "but I'm not mad. Just confused. I was worried something bad had happened."

"Something bad *has* happened," she said. "I know I told you I couldn't let myself fall in love again, well, I've gone and done it. With you." She was sobbing softly now, but she kept her composure and held me off when I tried reaching for her.

"Is falling in love with me so bad?" I asked.

"It sounds crazy, I know," she said. "I should be happy, but I'm afraid."

"Afraid-afraid of what?"

"Afraid I'll have my heart broken again" she said.

"Don't be silly, Michele. Please," I begged. "You can trust me. I promise."

We sat there for quite some time as she tried to explain her paranoia. She said she did not want to push me away and that she couldn't stand to be away from me.

"I told myself when I was driving home from your place Monday morning," she said, "that loving you simply couldn't be. I told you that, but then I heard your voice on the phone and something moved inside of me, something I can't control. I want you, Jim. I do. But I need time to get my head screwed on straight. It's not fair to you for me to be the way I am right now. Will you give me that time?"

"I love you, too, Michele," I said, "and you take as much time as you want. How should we do this?"

"For starters," she said, "I'm going away for a while. I've hired someone to look out for my place and my cows. Earl Carmack. He's married, and he and his wife and their boy will live at my place. I am going to go to Disneyland with Marty and his family and then, maybe, on to Hawaii. I'll be gone for a while. I won't write. I won't call. But when I know, I'll let you know."

We left it at that. I watched her drive away, tears streaming down my cheeks. I didn't know it could hurt so bad, but I had made a promise. My fate...our fate was in her hands.

Chapter 5

My Montana background told me that the subtle changes in morning and night time temperatures during the past week were harbingers of yet greater changes to come. It was nature's way of prodding construction workers, loggers, farmers, ranchers and others to pour that concrete, fell those trees, fill those grain bins, and bring those cows down from the high country, while they still could.

I now consider myself an official cowboy, and my eastern born and raised heir to the throne claims the title as well. Standing in the corral next to the open shed are two registered quarter horse geldings, both of them bays with black points and, in the tack room, are bridles with braided reins, leather and rope halters, horseshoes, horseshoe nails, hoof picks, various liniments and salves, and two slightly used saddles. We have already surveyed the width and breath of my vast holdings twice, and we are planning a repeat trip today.

My job in Bozeman is no more. I couldn't wait 'til the snow banks piled up, and I told Jim as much. He was understanding and, I'm thinking, a little relieved. Contracts had fallen off significantly and, come winter, the firm shifted, out of necessity, away from construction into design. Our parting was warm and cordial. The three partners sprung for lunch, we shook hands, and I was on my way.

My new employer is my friend, Claire Macintosh. I think Claire and Jenny are both happy to have me. As to Benny Tovar and Odin Norgaard, I'm not sure. Odin hadn't completely abandoned his shack next to the river, as Benny had done, so at least he had an out if the workload grew beyond his wishes. Though Claire covered Odin's health insurance, he was technically only a seasonal employee, anyway. He spent most of his time at the ranch, but absolutely refused to work full-time beyond Christmas. Guess he could live with out Jenny's good cooking once in a while. But fishing, now, that was another matter. Benny. Poor Benny, he was stuck with me. But he wasn't going anyplace and neither was I. I had landed.

Benny confided in me one day that Odin would be working full time, even during the winter, if he could take off any time he wished for ice fishing on one of his favorite lakes. "He don't like feeding cattle when it gets real cold," he said, "but you just wait. Odin will be moving in once he is eating his own cooking day after day."

Odin faced a decision and so did I. Mine was spur of the moment. Mostly because Mike was still here. His stay had lasted far beyond what he had planned when he first came to the place. The good relationship we had enjoyed before his mother and I split, still demanded some conciliatory tinkering. I did my best, knowing that in nine days, I would haul him to the airport, put him on a plane headed east, and wonder when I would see him again. Being away from the place all day long at least seven of those nine days, certainly wasn't conducive to bringing our relationship back to an even keel. Still, I wanted to try, so I shamefully made arrangements with Claire not to report to work until after Mike had left for Baltimore. I was always asking folks to let me put off working. Not much in keeping with the Montana work ethic.

The place was all but finished except for laying the cedar shakes on the roof and cleaning up around the yard. Odin had stapled down the heavy tar paper to lay the shakes upon. We hauled them from the shed in the bucket on Claire's loader and placed them ever so gently up on the roof without so much as breaking a sweat. Neither of us had ever laid shakes before, but we both had a general idea of what was to be done. Truth be known, it hadn't hurt to take a peak at the shakes on Claire and Jenny's rambler home.

It took us the better part of two days to complete the job. When Mike pounded in the last ridge line shake, we stood back and admired our work. It was the first project we had ever undertaken as a team, and we both were aware of that. A high-five exchange while yet on the roof told me we had made some progress in working our way back to where I wanted us to be. If ever a celebration was called for it was now.

My phone was busy for two hours contacting the Macintoshes, their old friends and my new friends, the Lustres, Morrisons and Weers. I even called my former employers in Bozeman, and two of the partners said they would come. Jenny asked if she could bring a couple house guests I hadn't met, and I said of course.

"Did you know that Michele is back?" Jenny asked. I told her I didn't.

"Well, why don't you give her a call and see if she can come." I told her I would, gladly, but I wasn't sure I should. I didn't think she was waiting for a call from me, and I had said I would give her time.

It had been nearly three weeks since I last saw her, and she hadn't called to let me know she was back. Maybe she hadn't had enough time. Still, I wanted to see her. I wanted her to meet Mike before he left, so I dialed her number. For almost the first time ever, I found her at home.

"Hello," she said in her soft voice. "This is Michele."

"Hi, Michele, this is Jim." Silence on the other end of the line.

"I heard you were back from your trip," I continued. "Jennifer just told me. I'm having some friends over Sunday afternoon for a cookout, and I'd like for you to come. I want you to meet my son, Mike."

"Oh, I don't know, Jim," she said after a pause. "I don't think I'm ready to see you yet."

"Please come," I said. "There will be close to a dozen people here, so it isn't as if we'll be alone, and I do want you to meet Mike. Besides I'm doing this to show off my place to my friends, and we are still friends, aren't we? Please come."

"Well, I suppose," she said haltingly. "Can I bring anything?"

"Just bring yourself, Michele," I replied. "Just yourself."

"Okay, I'll come," she said, "and I'll bring something, a salad or some beer or something."

"We're sitting pretty good for beer," I said, "but shy on salads, so if you want..."

"I'll bring a couple of salads, okay?"

"I missed you," I said before she had a chance to hang up.

"I missed you too, Jim. Bye."

Luck was shining on us that day in the form of clear skies and a soft breeze. It was the middle of August, and the days were still warm. I sensed Mike's nervousness. Understandably so, since he had met none of my guests other than Claire and Jenny. They had stopped by the day we finished our roofing project. "Couldn't wait to see your young man," Jenny had said.

The first to arrive were the Weers, Jim and Maddy. They were friends of the Macintoshes from Manhattan. They had recently become absentee landowners in the Madison Valley when Jim's health problems forced them to rent their place to their youngest son and find a place to live that boasted a smooth road to Deaconess Hospital in Bozeman. Jim suffered from Parkinson's disease to a point where he was besieged at times with tremors in his extremities he could neither conceal nor control.

In his prime, he had been a vibrant, vigorous man, capable of impressive feats of strength. He stood a head taller than most at six-feet-six inches. His craggy features were accentuated by substantial weight loss since the onset of his disease. I had met him for the first time a scant three weeks earlier, and I found him to be friendly and outgoing.

Maddy was Jim's wife of almost 50 years. Her height fell short of matching Jim's by about 16 inches, and she weighed almost 75 pounds less. She was not what one would call pretty; she was what most would call plain. Her dishwater blonde hair was unusually sparse, especially at the front, and she was very self-conscious about it. Her pretty green eyes sparkled, though, when she spoke of her children and grandchildren. Her personality was bubbly, and she was well liked by everyone.

She was one of those individuals who had opinions on everything. She also had a temper Angered by remarks with which she took exception, she did not hesitate in reading loud and clear from the Book of Maddy. I had witnessed one of her outbursts the first time I was introduced to her. Her disagreement was with her husband, and it involved the pros and cons of crossbreeding Angus bulls and Hereford cows. I stayed as far away from that one as I could without actually leaving the room.

"Thanks for inviting us," Maddy said, as I handed her a bottle of her preferred brand of cola. I knew she preferred it to wine or beer. "That son of yours is way easier to look at than his Daddy," she said.

"And who isn't," I asked with what I thought was a snappy rejoinder.

"You've got this place looking first rate," Jimmy said, as he looked down on my barely six feet from his lofty height. How's the job going in Bozeman?"

"Not working there anymore," I said. "Couldn't handle all that money they were throwing at me."

"Democrats, I suppose," was his smiling response to my failed attempt at humor.

The shiny, dark blue, Lincoln Town Car that pulled up to the house was one I had never seen before. Out of it piled a sprightly Jennifer and a freshly scrubbed Claire, followed by two of the most stunning female members of the human species I had ever seen, except for Jordan, maybe.

Jennifer gave me her customary hug, and turned to introduce her house guests. I recognized the older of the two as their daughter. Her picture adorned any number of walls and table tops in their living room.

"This is our daughter, Megan, Jim," she said, "and our granddaughter, Taylor. They flew up from Denver for a long weekend before Taylor's school starts. And of course, the tall, handsome man standing behind them is Claire, you know, you're new boss."

It is nice to meet both of you," I said. "Thank you for coming."

"Claire," I said, "Good to see you. New car?"

"Nope. Been parked in the shed next to the plane. Mostly, Jenny and me we drive trucks."

"Well, I'm glad you could come."

About then, Mike came out of the house with the Weers. He had assumed the role of tour guide and had, no doubt, called special attention to the shake-covered roof. I introduced him to Megan and Taylor, and I could tell he was nervous by the way he shifted his feet. They were like twins, born twenty years apart. I couldn't get over the similarities and, I soon realized that the photos of Megan in her parent's house did not do her justice.

Her slender but full figure was the first thing I noticed about her, once I got past her eyes. They were as dark as her thick, brunette hair, but the iris in each was spattered with flecks of white like the white tips of minuscule waves rushing against a beach in the moonlight. You could not see them and forget them. She was as tall as her mother at about 5 feet 9 inches, and she carried herself gracefully but with a built-in but unintended suggestiveness.

Her mouth was wide and filled with large white teeth. To see her as simply pretty was to do her an injustice. She was so much more than that. She was absolutely stunning and, in this unsophisticated Montanan's eyes, she possessed the kind of beauty that sent timid, male members of the species, including me, hurriedly scrambling away, knowing they were in over their heads with such beauty and class.

Her beauty was intimidating, and it was easy to see why. It was one of those "How could someone so beautiful ever give me even a second look" sort of things. But overpowering everything else, including her eyes, was a smile that could melt the coldest heart. My inner self responded to her like any man would and should, but outwardly my emotions were checked by what had become a wariness I could not dispel. My heart had grown as cold as any wintery day, except when I thought of Michele.

Mike wasted no time latching on to Taylor though, I must say, I was surprised. He had always been too busy, too involved, to get into the "girl thing" seriously. Was he making an exception today, I wondered, or had he reached a new plateau? Taylor was the next thing to a carbon copy of her mother with the same hair, mouth and eyes, but she had the youthful slenderness of a 15-year old and a quickness in her step that her mother had probably known at the same age. I had been told that it was her father who had passed on the olive-colored hue of her skin. I would bet money she had never been sunburned in her life.

She would one day be as beautiful as her mother and, while

outwardly that probably seemed of little importance to her now, it was a dead certainty…well, at least in my mind, that one day men would make fools of themselves over her. I was chuckling inwardly when it occurred to me that should Megan and I ever marry, which was as unlikely as malted milks in hell and, if Michael and Taylor should one day marry, in Megan's eyes, Michael would be relegated to step-son-in-law status. I didn't want to think of how that improbability would change my relationship to my own son.

In quick succession the rest of our guests, including Benny and Odin, appeared. Michele was the last to arrive. She was carrying two large bowls, covered with some type of plastic wrap, which she handed to me. She smiled as she did so, but quickly looked beyond me. She had a fresh, clean look about her, and she was as pretty as ever. She needed no introduction except for Michael. Megan and her had known each other all of their lives, and they were soon involved in an animated discussion.

We found chairs for everyone under the trees and out of the sun. Mike came around with the coffee pot and took orders for lemonade, soft drinks, iced tea and, yes, beer. Let it never be said that we were lacking in graciousness. Moreover, both Mike and I overheard guests expressing their surprise at how much the place had changed. I accepted those comments as compliments. After all, a few short months ago, the building site was sagging with the ravages of time and providing little more than the opportunity for camera buffs to capture photos of what life had once been. It is probably correct to say that the historical significance of the place had been diminished or wiped out by my handiwork, but I was proud of the improvements, anyway. That's why they were here. I wanted to show off, maybe even brag a little!

I am forever surprised at how something triggers something else in my mind. Today, it was an actual, for certain, original idea. My life back east had imploded, exploded and flown away like Cottonwood seeds because, in all those years, I labored without any set of clear objectives. I never had a dream. That was it. I never had a dream. I had one now. It was my cabin on the shoulders of a line of mountains. And it had become a reality.

But that dream did not stand alone. There was Michele. She was a dream not fully realized, for I saw her standing next to me forever. She was here today. Maybe...

I suppose it was my lack of experience in the culinary arts that prompted the ladies to take over the cooking, or had Michele told them of my Shipwreck stew?   Mike brought out a large platter of hamburger patties, tenderloin steaks, brats, and dogs. Megan took orders, and Taylor brought dishes, chips, silverware, glasses and cups from the house. As if by magic, Michele's salads found their way to the table. I added a bottle of pink champagne nestled in a spanking new, galvanized, 5-gallon milk pail filled with ice, and a dozen dollar store, plastic wine glasses. At some point I intended to propose a toast to my new friends.

Through all of this I stole occasional glances of Michele. Occasional, only because I did not want it to seem too obvious that I was staring. She was huddling, for the most part with Jenny and Megan but, more than once, I caught her looking my way. After awhile, she stood up and came over to me as I was spreading a table cloth across my kitchen table.

"Can I help with that, Jim?" she asked. I told her, yes, I could use some help

"How was your trip?" I asked.

"It was one of those 'are we there yet trips?' with my brother's kids doing the asking...about every five minutes. But it was fine."

I asked her then if she could hang around for a while after the others left.

"I shouldn't," she said. "No, I better not."

"Then meet me up at our place in the morning. I'll bring a thermos of coffee."

She stood there looking in the distance and then back to me before she said, "Okay, I will, but I can't stay long."

"Early? When?" I asked.

"Yes, early would be better. How is 8 o'clock?"

"I'll be there.

"I waited 'til noon. She never showed.

Mike and I drove into Bozeman that afternoon. We looked for a gift for Morgan, something small enough to put in his suitcase, and finally found it in one of the specialty shops on main which stocked all sorts of *Made in Montana* items. I found a key chain, a jar of huckleberry jam, and a book by a local author called, *You Can't Love Too Much*. Mike found his mother a magnetic outline of Montana for her fridge.

Afterwards, we drove south and followed Hyalite Creek up to the reservoir. I told him Hyalite Creek had, maybe, a dozen or so waterfalls visible from the trail. "Let's hike up there," he said.

Before we were done, we had hiked the trail, stopped momentarily at each of the falls, rested on the shore of Hyalite Lake, and climbed Hyalite Peak, his first 10,000 plus foot mountain ever. We were exhausted and starving when we reached the trail head at the bottom. We ate sandwiches and pickles at a cramped little place on College Avenue, called, of all things, the Pickle Barrel, and then drove home. In the morning, I hauled him to the Bozeman Airport and waited until his plane lifted off. The last thing he said to me before we parted at the entrance to the secure area was, "Taylor wants me to write to her when I get home. I have her phone number. I love you."

It was a bitter sweet moment for me. I was about to return to my place in the foothills of the Tobacco Root Mountains, a place filled now with loneliness without Michele, but I was saying goodbye to a son whose love and respect I had regained. Mike had edged his way cautiously back into my life. Michele, on the other hand, was gone from my life. I knew it. Ironically, we had both found love again, but her irrational fear of losing that person, and the pain that went with it, was too much for her to bear. It was nuts. It was crazy. Yet I felt so sorry for her. I had been willing to try love again. She hadn't. Once again, I had lost at love. Never again, I swore. Never again.

On Monday morning I went to work for Claire and Jennifer. Benny and Odin were in the kitchen eating breakfast with the Macintoshes when I drove into the yard. Claire outlined what we were to concentrate on before the weather turned bad. A third cutting of alfalfa from one of the sprinkler systems was ready to harvest. He wanted to haul two trailer loads of long-yearling steers to the auction yards in Bozeman before the market sagged any more. Six-hundred and fifty round bales of alfalfa and brome grass were still on the ground waiting to be hauled home. Two of the feed lots boasted gigantic manure piles to be loaded on truck-size spreaders and placed on the contract barley acreage. The barley itself had been harvested and hauled up to a collection point on the Sun River west of Great Falls. But the barley straw left behind by the custom combines had to be baled with the John Deere 336 square baler and stacked near the buildings. Some of those small straw bales were to be hauled to my place, and a truck load of large hay bales would eventually sit on the west side of my shed.

Benny and Odin began cutting the alfalfa, using machines that cut, crimped and windrowed at the same time. Claire had contracted with a dairy close to Bozeman for 300 round bales of the stuff; and any left over came to the home place. I pulled the square baler down the road four miles and started on the straw, coming home each night with a double-axle, flatbed trailer loaded with just under 200 bales.

By the time I got to my place, it was well past dark, and I had time only to throw a bit of feed at my heifers, eat a couple of hot dogs, and go to bed.

I finished the barley straw in three days, and then pitched in to help haul the big round bales home. Working with concrete was a tough job, demanding strength and endurance, but one thing could be said about working for Claire: It was different, but you never had any trouble going to sleep at night.

Exhausted or not, when my eyes closed in the darkness of night, memories of Michele swept over me and, magically, we were in our tent up on Hollow Top, or bathing in Lake Albro's frigid waters, or sitting on the porch on a warm, summer afternoon, nursing a cool beer and holding hands. When the desire and passion subsided, we were still soul mates who somehow missed seeing that we had become such good friends. Both of us had overlooked our symbiotic friendship. Together we were more than the sum of each of us as individuals.

No one had heard from her, including Jenny, but I still went to bed every night wishing my fellow camper was with me. She had a lot of people scratching their heads, wondering what had come over her to prompt her sudden disappearance. I knew, of course. But I also knew that her leaving should never have been because of me. I would have been happy to have her as just a friend.

Her hired man knew more about her whereabouts than he let on. I was sure of it. But he was closed-mouth, and volunteered nothing. Raising the Rock of Gibraltar with a gigantic crowbar would be easier than prying something out of Earl Carmack. I know. I tried. He was one of those big, silent types to begin with, so the prospects of learning anything from him were slim. Still, reading between the lines led me to believe that wherever she was, she was spending money. Why else would she be selling stock?

When we herded our trucks and trailers up the winding road that led to the grazing permit acreage, Earl Carmack and his son, Jason, were there with us to bring down a couple of trailers full of steers to be sold at the sales barn in Bozeman. Michele's 50 head brought a tidy sum. Maybe she had payments to meet. Or maybe she was spending the fall and winter in the south of France. One could only speculate. If I knew her location, I would hurry to her.

But I didn't, so I couldn't. If anyone knew anything, it would be Jennifer and, if she did, she was admitting nothing. The steers were part of a large herd spread out over thousands of acres of rangeland. Working together, the five us slowly but surely moved the half wild critters toward the holding pens. Earl, his son Jason, and Benny rooted them out of the draws and pointed them toward the pens. Claire, who surprised us all when he climbed up on his sorrel mare, and myself hazed them into the pen. It took us the better part of two days to hunt down a hundred steers mixed in with a large herd of cows and calves and them haze them toward the holding pen. Our first night out, we camped next to the pens, happy to have found as many as we had. Half of them were in the holding pen before sundown. The others took longer to find but, by nightfall the second day, we had them sorted by brand and loaded in the four trailers. It was close to 11 o'clock when we pushed Claire's steers off the trailer and into one of the pens at the home ranch.

After two grueling days of physical labor, we all slept in the next morning. The sale didn't start until 11 o'clock, so there was no reason to hurry. While I sat and ate breakfast, the phone rang. The only calls I ever got were from either Jennifer or Claire or Michael so I was surprised to hear Rebecca's voice on the other end.

"Hi," I said, "This is Jim."

"Jim, this is Rebecca. I hope I didn't wake you up." My first thought was that she would not be calling to pass the time of day, so

I girded myself for bad news and waited.

"No," I said, "I just plunked down for a little breakfast. I'm actually running late this morning.

"Well, anyway," she said, "I'm calling to tell you that I sold the house. There are papers you need to sign, so I'm calling to see if you have a fax number."

"I don't have a fax machine out here," I said, "but you can send them to my old office in Bozeman. I'll call Madsen and have the girls look out for it." I gave her the number and then asked how we made out on the sale. We had agreed when I was in Baltimore for the hearing that should she decide to sell the place, we would share in the proceeds after the closing and realtor cost had been deducted.

"Your share is going to be just over $325,000, but I hope you know you're going to get hit pretty hard on capital gains."

"Wow, that's a lot of money," I said. "Didn't we pay less than 200K for it 20 years ago?"

"Yes, I think you are right, and we had it nearly paid for," she said. "Inflation actually worked to our advantage in this case. When you get the papers, sign them, have your signature notarized, and send them back to me by fax immediately."

She went on to tell me that I should also go to my bank and have papers executed which would authorize an electronic, direct deposit. I agreed to do it. I thought to ask her about the small lake cabin we had bought several year earlier over in Virginia. She said she was also looking for a buyer, but that it might be too late in the year for a quick sale. Of course, she said, we'll be lucky to get a hundred thousand out of it.

"And where are you going to be living, when the new owners take over?" I asked, half knowing what her answer would be.

"Well, Jim, that's the other reason I called," she said. "I'm getting married and, of course, I'll be with Arthur." Arthur was her doctor friend.

"I'm happy for you, Becky," I said. "How is Morgan taking it?"

"About as I expected," she said. "Not well, but I think in time she'll be okay. I have heard her and Mike talking about maybe spending their Christmas vacation with you in Montana. Would you be agreeable to that? Arthur has been talking about a Caribbean cruise over the Holidays."

"More than all right," I said. "You tell them they are both very welcome."

She said she would and then said goodbye. Suddenly my world was looking up again, not that things weren't going pretty darn good already. But my pocketbook was about to get fattened up a bunch, and my kids might be spending Christmas with me. If only Michele...

When I drove into the yard, I could see that Benny and Claire had backed one of the trailers up to a loading chute and were ready to start pushing half of the steers through the sliding end gate. An hour later we had loaded the second trailer and were having coffee and doughnuts in the house. I dropped my news about Morgan and Mike almost before we got seated.

"That's wonderful, Jim," Jenny said. "Michael was such a nice boy. I can't wait to meet Morgan."

"Well, it's not for sure," I said, "but my fingers are crossed."

It took us an hour to haul the steers into Bozeman. Benny drove one rig, me the other. Claire rode with me, and we jabbered about nothing much except that in the morning we needed to start cutting the corn.

"It froze some last night," he said, "and tonight they're saying temperatures are going to drop into the teens. That means the corn is done growing. We might as well bring it in."

I had no experience in silage corn, but I knew enough to know that, once cut, it had to be piled into what was called a ground silo, compacted, and covered with heavy duty poly to foster the fermentation process. Come winter the silo would be tapped every day and a feed wagon would drop it into feed bunks.

In Bozeman the steers were unloaded and hazed into pens. The seller's name appeared on a ticket clipped to the heavy plank doors so prospective buyers would know who owned the stock. We had some time before the sale, so we stopped in a small café, operated only on sale day, for coffee and a caramel roll. If there was anyone seated inside who did not know both Claire and Benny I would have been surprised. They had been coming there for years. Even the waitress, who was also the cook and owner, called them both by their first names.

"Eat up, boys," she said. "Shutting this place down in a couple of weeks."

"And then what are you going to do, Amy?" someone asked.

"Gonna run off somewhere and spend the money I've been making off you boys all these years," she responded. "Been over charging you all along, but you've been so busy mucking around in the manure, you never caught on...never got close to catching on."

I ate my caramel roll as the small talk roamed from booth to table and back again. It was like one big, happy family sitting at half a dozen different tables.

But there was money jingling in this cowboy's pocket or, at least, there soon would be, and I can't tell you how big I felt when I was the high bidder on two lots of young black Angus cows, whose calves had been taken from them only days earlier. I drove out of there tall and proud, as they say, with a bill of sale for 53 head.

"Good buy," Claire said as I was coming out the door of the yard's business office. "They're bred good, and you'll have some nice calves on the ground come spring. You're going to need a bull or two, you know, along about June first."

"I know," I lied, "but I was thinking you might part with a couple of your older bulls, cheap." The necessity for having bulls, now that I had cows, had completely slipped my mind. My transition from port engineer to cowman had a ways to go, I guess.

"I think we can work something out there," he said.

I was still small potatoes, really small potatoes, compared to the average rancher in the Madison Valley, but, well, I was just getting started with much to learn and I had no plans for getting much larger. My game plan didn't include any provisions for expanding my herd in an attempt to catch up to the others. My brain was focused most of the time, and that included this morning, on Michele. I hadn't been thinking about cows even as I sat in a sales yard. I had been thinking of Michele to the exclusion of just about everything else.

It seemed like there was no ideal moment, so, out of the blue sky, I asked Claire if they had heard from Michele. He hadn't he said, but admitted Jennifer and Michele had talked on the phone more than once. He thought she was someplace down in Colorado, but, reading between the lines of what Jenny had said, he didn't think Michele was ever coming back. I asked him what made him think that, and he said only that one of his old pals in Norris had heard that someone else had heard from someone else that she might be interested and willing to sell her place.

Well, there you are, I thought to myself. She had made up her mind. Damn. Damn. Damn.

We had the corn packed in the silo before we got our first dusting of snow. The cows were down from the high country, and we were running them on a bit of winter pasture but their noses were mostly in the bunks lining the south side of the feed lot. I fell into the routine of feeding my own stock and then driving down to Claire's to help Benny and Odin. Late fall was a slack time if you had done your late summer's work. Both Benny and Odin were now living on the place full time, so it was easy for one of them to check on the cattle, water tanks, feed bunks, and what have you, so I sometimes I spent the entire day at my place feeding my heifers and cows, and surfing, as the say, the internet.

The snow was fairly deep, but the road leading to my place had been graded and made relatively smooth. Earlier, when the breeze was from just the right direction, I had burned the heavy stand of grass from the ditches. Doing so was supposed to cut down on the formation of snow banks on the road itself, and it did. So I had no trouble going back and forth. Several times I had bundled up in sweat pants and shirt to jog up to the rock outcropping, to what had been our special place. I couldn't get that woman out of my system.

Only once or twice had I found it necessary to lock in the 4-wheel drive on the truck. Claire and Jenny were hanging close to home themselves but had plans to spend a month or so with friends in Prescott after Christmas. I was happy for them. Earl or Jason stopped by now and then to see how I was doing. I know they thought I was lonely there all by myself, and they were just trying to help.

Michael and Morgan would be arriving on the 23rd, and we would spend Christmas Eve at the cabin and Christmas day at the Macintoshes.

The check for my share of the house was in the bank. I had made my payment to Claire and Jenny early. My cows were doing fine. The two bays grazed the fenced yard like a couple of elk over in Gardiner at the edge of Yellowstone Park, and all was well in the shadow of the Tobacco Roots.

My evenings spent alone, and they were many, were a time for contemplation. More than once I caught myself staring off into nothingness, as if I were looking into the mesmerizing, dancing flames of a lonesome mountain camp fire. At such times, my mind was truly blank. It happened, usually, as I struggled to pull together in my head, how the past months had changed me.

And, change me they had. I looked different, in my out-west jeans and belt buckle uniform. I was thinner. I was far more relaxed. Nowhere in my work at Claire's was there stress of any consequence, other than that engendered by a need make haste in order to beat the rain or snow. In Baltimore, the stress had been everywhere, every day, all the time. My voice was softer now, and I spoke the language of rural Montana. No one would have guessed that I had not long ago been one of those wear-a-tie-everyday, so-called professionals who rubbed shoulders on a daily basis with corporate CEO's, high-level bureaucrats, and politicians.

My way of looking at things was dramatically altered as well. I had made a mid-life career change, a shift away from self-proclaimed importance and lofty aspirations to the life of a single father living apart from his children under the shoulder of a mountain range in a log cabin, part of which was nearly 100 years old. And I was missing virtually nothing of the past; it was, at times, as if I had no past because some facets of it were now but dim recollections and others were too painful to think about.

Michele's loss had been unexpected, decisive, and devastating. I couldn't help admiring her though. She was much stronger than I. I had come to accept my loss, but the vacuum her absence created would, I hoped, be filled by my children. They were the stuff of what I was and they helped define me as an individual.

My quest for understanding was interrupted time and again, but slowly it led me to understand that before one can find himself, one must be truly lost. One must become immersed in something, in anything that is a distraction from the source of pain. And I had been so immersed in rebuilding a forlorn set of 19th century buildings that I somehow became separated from myself and was able to step back and see Jim Pengilly with clarity for the first time in a long time.

Before me now was a future without romantic love, a future filled with my children, I hoped. It was what I longed for as I waited for their visit. They were coming soon, and I was prepared to take the first momentous steps back to them after years of neglect, but I was apprehensive about outcomes, particularly with Morgan.

I loved my new life. What is there about jumping out of bed early and riding out through the bitter, frosty cold of a December morning toward the high country that adds to a person's regard for himself? Part of it flows, I think, from every man's need to occasionally step back and gaze, both inwardly and outwardly, upon his existence in the most elemental ways. I believe there is in each of us a mysterious, indefinable, perhaps primal urge to occasionally reach back to an earlier time when we were, as a species, more self reliant, more involved in living, and somehow more alive.

Without knowing it at the outset, I now recognized that I had been doing exactly that. The means used and the paths followed to reach back to your beginnings, and perhaps your true values, can be so down to earth as a night time fire beside a small lake high on a mountain. I know it to be so, for it was while I stared into a fire at Albro Lake that I came to understand that without love, one has very little and can never, ever be truly complete.

But other settings can work as well. It can be nothing more than a lonely walk on a moonlight night or an overland hike during the light of day when you are hungry or thirsty and far from food and water. Or it can be a ride over snowy, frosty trails on the way to check your cattle. The ways and means are never ending, but there must be quiet and solitude. And, well, I was having my share of both at the moment, but I welcomed a change, and change was about to swoop down on me from far away Baltimore.

The plane carrying Morgan and Michael arrived on time. They were famished, so I drove in to Bozeman for supper at the Food and Ale restaurant on east main where I introduced them to the best burgers this side of Missoula's Big Sky Drive-In. Our ride to town was Morgan's first ever in a truck. I made up my mind right then and there that, before they left, she would be driving that truck down the road, with me riding shotgun.

Long ago in Whitefish, I had read a sign in the window of a local eatery pronouncing it to be a poor place to eat because it was always full and there was always a waiting line. You were supposed to infer from that message that the reason there was a waiting line was because the food was better than good and everybody wanted to eat there. That was the Food and Ale. I had never been there during meal times when it wasn't teaming with waiters and waitresses dashing about with large round trays held overhead, on their way to serve the customers in this large, former warehouse.

While we waited, my kids joined ranks to update me on what was happening back in Baltimore. Surprisingly, I thought, Morgan talked some about her mother and Arthur and about the new home they were living in on Chesapeake Bay. "We've got a boat and everything," she said, "and I've made friends with the two girls living next door.

"I like it out there," she added wistfully, "but I miss our old place too."

"I've made friends with the girls too," Mike said, looking at me and winking, "at least with their older sister." What was happening to this family of mine, I asked myself? My daughter, who months earlier had refused to speak to me on the phone, and at one point had even said she hated me, was now talking to me as if the past did not exist. And Michael, though he and I had spent time together in August and had come together to a degree that surprised me, was now telling me he hoped to get better acquainted with the girls next door.

When we had stuffed ourselves with tenderloin steak, burger platters and a huge, flower-like deep fried onion, we all sat back for a time and fell to people-watching. Morgan sat there in a semi trance watching the mixture of individuals come and go. She saw strapping young college men, ski bums, older couples dressed fit to kill, as they say, and any number of individuals attired in any number of outfits ranging from the semi-formal to the second hand store.

"There are some really cute boys here," she said. "I may have to extend my Christmas vacation."

It was time to leave. My daughter was talking about boys, and Mike was glancing furtively at the comely and slender waitress who brought our check.

"The food was great, Dad," Morgan said. "Can we come here again?"

How could I possibly say no to my recently estranged daughter who was now calling her father, Dad?

"We will," I said, "but lets give someone else a chance to sit down now."

We drove home through the west end of Bozeman and through Four Corners. It was dark, but I wanted them both to see the landscape bathed in the light of a Christmas moon and washed with a dusting of new fallen snow. I toyed with the notion of turning in at the Macintoshes, but it was late so I passed by and drove on home.

The house was a shocker to Morgan, mostly because of its modest size, I think, but I felt it was warm and cozy within. Outside I had draped strings of blue lights from the gables and eaves. I built a fire in the fireplace, hoping to add even greater ambience to the overall atmosphere. We popped Jolly Time in the microwave and sat on the sofa watching television.

"This is really nice, Dad," Morgan offered. "It's like looking at one of the pictures on a Christmas card." An hour later she was sound asleep, her head on my shoulder. I didn't want that to end just yet, so I wrapped my arm around her shoulder and held her close until she moved and came awake.

"It's time for bed, Honey," I said. "Let me show me to your room."

Her room this night was my room. I grabbed her flight bags and brought them along. What happened next was almost more than I could have wished for. She came to me, put her arms behind my back and hugged me.

"Thanks for inviting me, Dad," she said. "This is going to be the best Christmas. I'm sorry about what happened earlier."

I knew exactly what she was talking about, and we let it rest right there. The best Christmas gift I could ever receive was to know that my young daughter had turned the corner on her despair and seemed to be headed straight for her dad.

Chapter 6

When breakfast was over the next morning, we bundled up and walked out to survey the less than vast Pengilly domain. We stepped down from the porch and stepped away from the cabin to see it in the light of day. It was rustic, for sure, but there was about it a sense of being connected to the surrounding country. The snow, though not particularly deep, crunched and crackled beneath our feet as we crossed over to the corrals to see the horses and cattle. Horses, as is their wont, shied away from the presence of strangers, but were eventually enticed to come closer by the whole oats Michael and Morgan held in their cupped hands. While Mike pushed some hay to the front of the feeders being crowded by the cows, I stepped back and took a good look at my daughter. Her hands were caressing the soft muzzles of the two saddle horses now, and she seemed oblivious to my presence, lost in a private moment of discovery.

She had matured since I last saw her. As tall as her mother, or nearly so, and resembling her in so many ways, she was nonetheless very much her own person. She had my hair, which was never quite willing to yield to the command of a comb or brush, but it was becoming to her nonetheless. I could see some of both her mother and me in her with Rebecca's slender but shapely young body, and eyes that flashed like a Mexican hat dancer's. From her old man, she got a broad forehead, heavy, curled eyebrows and a perpetual look of seriousness. That was her old Dad, not the new one. With chores out of the way, we piled into the truck to hunt down just the right Christmas tree.

Without their knowing that the place I drove them too was all but a shrine to Michele, we crawled up into the rocks and looked down upon a country blanketed in white with smoke curling out of chimneys in every direction. We poured from the thermos the hot chocolate Michael had made, holding the warm cups against our gloved hands like mothers holding their first baby.

The tree we selected was a six-foot, white pine. Decorated with colored lights, tinsel, multi-colored ornaments, and strings of popcorn, it was soon standing straight and tall a safe distance from the fireplace. Around it we stacked the presents I had purchased in Bozeman earlier and some they had brought from Maryland. I wanted it to be a Christmas to remember, and it was shaping up that way. There can never be a prettier tree than one cut and decorated by your own hand.

Michael and I grabbed our heavy coats to rush out and finish our evening chores. It was shaping up to be a nice night with a bright moon and stars galore. Our supper was a roasted pheasant I had shot out of season, creamed corn, and mashed potatoes. No chef's delight, but tasty and nutritious and the only full meal I had ever cooked for my kids. Before we stood up to wash the dishes and do a quickie cleanup job in the kitchen, I poured them each a small glass of chilled Cabernet, with Morgan's being by far the smaller portion.

"Here we are this Christmas Eve," I said, our glasses touching, "together in a way we have never been before. You have given me the greatest, most treasured Christmas gift a father could ever receive. You have brought yourself to Montana to be with me, and I will never forget it. Thank you. Thank you."

Our glasses tinkled against each other again, and slowly we raised them to our lips.

"Tally ho, the fox," I added. "Tally ho, the fox" they echoed in unison, with absolutely no idea of what it might mean. But to me it meant a great deal. The fox was symbolic of the lives that lay before us and, unless I was badly mistaken, we would chase it with all the heart and spirit we could muster, together.

The fire was blazing, the tree was aglow with colored lights, and we were about to exchange gifts when the sound of an approaching vehicle stopped us in mid stride. My first thought was a lost traveler, my second Michele. But it was not to be. When I opened the door what I saw, instead, was another lady as dear to me. It was Jennifer's sparkling face that looked out at me from under her white, Santa Claus beard.

"Merry Christmas, ho! ho! ho!" she said in the worst Santa Claus imitation I had ever heard. "Merry Christmas to all!"

"Come in, Santa," I shouted, "and a Merry Christmas to you."

The man who followed her in, lost somewhere in red, white, green and blue Christmas packages was, of course, Claire. Following him were Megan and Taylor. I could not believe it, and I said so.

I hugged Megan and Taylor, then blurted, "What are you doing here? I thought you would be basking this night in Denver's spring-like air."

"We wanted to surprise Mom and Dad," Megan said. "Didn't Michael tell you?"

I looked at Michael searching for an explanation of some sort. How did he get involved in this?

"I knew if I said anything, Dad," he said, "It would spoil everything. "Taylor told me on the phone before we left Baltimore."

"Well," I said, "surprise or not, come in, come on in."

I thought back, asking myself if there had ever been a Christmas to compare to this one, but failed to pinpoint another where happiness was so pervasive. We opened gifts, popped popcorn, cracked nuts, played Monopoly, sang carols, and a few of us even bundled up and went for a walk.

The night air was cool, but being able to look out across the valley and see the twinkling lights of dozens and dozens of ranches and farmsteads was well worth it. Before I went back to the house, I grabbed a pitchfork and threw an extra ration of hay to the cows and the horses.

For a while, we adults played whist while the kids played board games spread out on the kitchen table. Setting a totally un-Christmas-like precedent, Jennifer and Megan made a huge bowl of goulash consisting of elbow macaroni, lots of hamburger, chopped onions, and two cans of tomato soup. Jennifer cried out as she placed two large bowls before us at the kitchen table, "It's not fancy, but there's lots of it." It was delicious and everyone of us had a second helping. I hated to see them go, to see it all end, but I knew it must. Our goodbyes and hugs signaled the end of one mighty fine Christmas Eve.

The very first thing on our, or should I say *my*, agenda was to plant Morgan behind the wheel for her first driving lesson in a ton truck. Michael opened the gate to the pasture, and we drove through. I stopped the truck and turned off the ignition switch, showing her how to start the engine. Then I dropped the gear shift into drive, and let the truck move forward slowly without any prompting from me on the accelerator pedal. Light pressure against the brake brought the truck to a smooth stop. I moved the seat forward slightly and stepped to the ground.

"Now," I said, "it's your turn."

"Oh, I don't know, Dad," she said "It's so big. What if I don't do it right?"

I reminded her we were close to a half mile from the nearest fence, so there was room for a mistake or two if she was absolutely determined to make one. She stepped in then, pulled the door shut and slowly turned the switch. She looked at me with a smile at the corners of her mouth and dropped the gear stick into drive. The truck moved forward like a turtle until her foot hit the foot pedal...too heavy. Immediately she lifted her foot just enough, and we were off, dodging rocks, rough spots, and an occasional clump of sage brush. Heading northeast as we were and staring intently at the ground in front of the truck, neither of us realized that Michael was riding at our side on one of the bays. Fifteen minutes later, Morgan was herself looking about to places other than the ground immediately in front of the bumper, and she was carrying on an animated conversation with me. When we stopped in front of the cabin, she had two questions: how did she do and when could she ride one of the horses? I told her she did great and that her day to shine on the back of a good horse wasn't far off. First though, there were chores to do.

It amazes me how we sometimes find wonder in the simple things. We live in an age of computers, I-pods, floppy disks, and DVDs but, for the moment, pitching hay to the cows, turning the switch that pumped water into the stock tank, and measuring and dumping portions of ground feed into a string of feeders made of discarded tires, was far more intriguing to my city-girl daughter than any of the others.

Inside, after changing out of our chore clothes, I encouraged, no, admonished both of them to call their mother.

"Let her know you are fine and wish her a merry Christmas."

As we drove out the gate and unto the road later for the short ride to the Macintosh ranch, I mentioned how lucky we were to have such a nice, sunny day for all the people who would be traveling much further than ourselves. I told them to listen for the sound of our tires as they touched the hard packed snow, and remember it because they would not likely hear those lyrics again unless they came back to Montana during the winter. The clouds overhead were white and fluffy, floating along almost imperceptibly, as if mother nature herself was in the Christmas spirit. Welcome, mother nature, I thought to my self. Come be a part of our celebration.

"Keep a warm heart, kids," I said, "for warm hearts count for something. They always do." The words had barely left my lips when Michael, hesitantly dropped his major bombshell.

"Before we reach the ranch," he said, "I need to tell you both that Taylor's mother and father have split. Megan may not have told her parents yet, so we shouldn't say anything. Taylor told me on the phone while we were still in Baltimore, but asked me not to tell anyone, including the two of you. But, I had to. I was afraid one of us might say something we shouldn't. I knew that if they knew we knew it would have changed our Christmas eve in a big way."

I suppose it was shock I felt at hearing this news, but dismay might better describe my reaction. The truth was, I didn't know Megan well enough to have feelings about her one way or the other. But Claire and Jennifer certainly did, and I was sure the next level beyond shock is what they were feeling, if they now knew. They were just now beginning to show signs of crawling out from under the trauma and grief of losing their son. They needed no more tragedy in their life, and that is exactly what this was, take it from me. All I could think of was that I was sorry. All I could say was poor Jennifer, poor Claire. If ever I needed to be there for someone, this was it.

It was a somber threesome that pulled up in front of their house. "Now, guys," I reminded them, "let's do our best to pretend we don't know anything."

Our reception was as warm as I had expected, and I was sure Megan had yet to tell her parents. I squired Morgan and Michael around the ranch while we waited for the enormous ham to get done. Mike had been here before, but even he was discovering things and asking questions as we roamed through the sheds, along the rows of round hay bales, and along the fence holding in over a thousand head of mixed stock.

Benny and Odin were there, of course, clean and spiffy as if they were leaving here on a date. I doubted that, but they turned on the charm to their upper limits, where Morgan was involved.

"Bet there's a bunch of boys back in Ball-tee-more," Benny said, "who can't wait for this young lady to come home." Morgan was embarrassed but took it in stride.

"It's too bad you're older than me, Benny," was her rejoinder, "or I'd be taking you back with me." Benny knew, immediately, he was in over his head with this young lady, and backed off before she had another go at him. Most of our afternoon was dedicated to playing cards, board games, listening to Jennifer play the piano, and, then, of course, to eating.

Megan and Taylor were leaving the following evening, and the kids and I volunteered to take them to the airport. I knew neither Claire nor Jennifer liked driving on snow packed roads. They said their goodbyes while we waited. The ride into Belgrade was a quiet one. Reading minds was not my forte, but I was guessing that, as far as Megan and Taylor were concerned, their silence was one of melancholy brought on by the simple act of leaving loved ones. It could have been that Megan had spoken with her parents, but I didn't think so.

Their plane was almost an hour late, so we sat around on the lower level killing time. The kids ran off to have their go at a couple of pinball machines. We watched, content to enjoy the bustle of other travelers moving about or checking their luggage.

"I have something to tell you, Jim," Megan began slowly. "My husband and I have recently separated. Part of why we made the trip up here was to tell Mom and Dad, but I couldn't. I lost my nerve. I'll call them from Denver so they know we made it home, but I think I'll write with the news that I know is going to be devastating for them."

"I'm sorry to hear this," I said. "I have a good idea of what you are going through yourself. I've been there, and done that, as they say."

"Well, I wanted you to know, Jim." she said. "You are far more to them than a hired hand and a neighbor. You are dearer than you might guess, and for that reason, I am hoping you will help them through this. I would spend more time here right now, but Taylor has to be back in school on Tuesday. I could use a shoulder to cry on myself once in a while, but I think I can handle this better than they can."

"I'll do what I can," I said. "Count on it."

"Thanks, I knew you would. I'll let you know after I tell them. Okay?"

I asked her if she had my number and she said no. I was handing her a slip of paper with the number when we caught sight of the kids walking toward us.

"How is Taylor taking it?" I asked

"Hard, but she is a perceptive young lady, and I think she saw it coming long ago. There were just too many nights when her dad didn't come home."

We needn't have, but on our way home, we stopped at the ranch to let Claire and Jennifer know the girls were no longer earth bound. Jennifer would not let us leave until we ate yet another ham sandwich and tasted her homemade peanut brittle."

"Have a good time over in Missoula," she hollered as we piled into the truck, "and watch out for avalanches."

She knew we were driving up to Deerlodge so the kids could see their grandparents and then on to Missoula and Lolo Pass for a day of cross country skiing above the clouds. We spent the next day tidying up the house after our wild Christmas Eve party and then, in the afternoon, Michael and I together taught Morgan to ride. We chose the mare I had purchased from on of my neighbors, instead of one of the geldings, because she was easier to mount and inclined to be the least skittish.

By noon Morgan was riding the mare around in the circular corral, and she had learned the rudiments of neck reining and leg pressure. These horses were trained to neck rein and to move away from leg pressure. Had you attempted to steer them like plow horses, which they definitely were not, they would have been totally confused. After lunch, Michael saddled up and, with a cotton halter rope, led Morgan and the mare around the yard just to give her a feel for being away from the corral. Ten minutes of that, and she was tagging along behind Michael. The were walking and trotting, but once they were in the open pasture, Michael had her floating along in a slow canter. She was ecstatic when they returned to the house.

"I love it, Dad," she shouted. "I love it."

I was grateful that there had been no mishaps. She was a Chesapeake Bay girl born and raised, but her Montana blood had found its home on a horse.

Our trip to Deer Lodge and Missoula was filled with eye-opening experiences for the kids. Neither of them had ever crossed over a mountain pass in a truck or any other type of vehicle, for that matter, so they were thrilled as we topped out at Homestake Pass and started the rapid descent into Butte. The curvy road added to the ride down. We had a schedule to meet so we didn't stop in Butte very long, but we did brush up against the Berkeley Pit, once the largest copper mine in the country, and managed to drive through the downtown area with all of its history.

Grandma and Grandpa were waiting when we pulled up in front of their house. They hardly knew their grandchildren, but you would never have know it by the way they hugged and kissed and went on about how glad they were to see them. We managed, all of us, to tip-toe around the fact that Rebecca and I were recently divorced, by talking about the place over in the Madison Valley, my cows, the Christmas Eve party, the Christmas Day menu, and the horses.

We ate at the 4 Bs that night, feasting on prime rib and some of my mother's very own banana cream pie. She cried when we left, and my dad turned his head to the side, I think, to hide a few of his own tears. I felt guilty only spending the day, but our schedule was necessarily tight because of Michael and Morgan's need to be home right after the first of January to resume school again. Still, I was glad we took the time to make the trip. My parents went so far as to pledge a trip to Norris in the spring.

Lolo Pass and 14 feet of snow beckons hundreds of people from both sides of the Montana-Idaho border on any given winter weekend. We were fortunate that the time we had chosen to test our abilities was mid-week. We weren't sure about ski rental opportunities at the pass, so we rented skis at Bob Wards in Missoula and drove up the Lolo highway in a mixture of climatic conditions. The Bitterroot Valley itself was shrouded in dense fog. Halfway up it was raining hard, and when we reached the warming house and purchased our pass from the State of Idaho, it was snowing so hard it was difficult to find our way to the trail head a few hundred feet away. But the trails were groomed perfectly, and the moderate traffic down the two double rows of tracks was enough to keep the trails smooth. My experience was very limited, though the quiet of cross-country had always appealed to me. Morgan and Mike were like blank slates. Neither of them had ever been on skis of any kind. We all made our fair share of mistakes, but we muddled our way down the trail as best we could.

The brochures in the warming hut said several of the trails led to camping spots used by the Lewis and Clark Expedition but, well, I guess when we looked at the distances, the shorter trails were more inviting. We soon discovered that cross country skiing was not terribly difficult but that strong arms and shoulders were as important as strong legs. For several hours we stretched out single file on the trails that led us between towering Engelmann Spruce covered with snow, forming grotesque figures looking very much like ghosts draped in their white sheets.

"I've never seen country that changes the way Montana does," Morgan observed. "We've been through deep river valleys, open plains, over mountain passes, and now we are driving through country unlike anything we've seen since we left home."

I liked the sound of that, if by "home" she meant my cabin near Norris.

"Montana is a big state, fourth largest if you count Alaska," I said, anxious to toot my home State's horn. It covers and area of almost 150 thousand square miles. Maryland, less than 10,000. Montana has about 800,000 people, Maryland close to five million. Think about that a minute. My arithmetic says you could stuff about 33 Maryland's into Montana and have some land left over. Maryland is blessed with an Atlantic Seaboard climate with lots of rain and humidity. We're so large, we have several different climates.

"Western Montana, because the Northern Rockies roughly form our western border, has a climate a little bit like Seattle. Not nearly as much rain of course, but more clouds and lots of wintertime snow up high. The country dries out as you move east. Some parts of extreme southeastern Montana gets less than 10 inches of rain per year.

"At any given time, the wind will be blowing someplace in Montana. Violent thunderstorms, occasionally even a rare tornado, can be found somewhere in Montana on a given summer day. The humidity in the summer hovers around 15 percent or slightly more. How does that compare to Baltimore? I know. You can wring water out of the air back there. Climate has everything to say about how people make their living. Iowa, with its rain and humidity, grows corn. We grow wheat, oats and barley, unless we irrigate, and then it's mostly alfalfa."

"Ask some people the time of day, and they'll tell you how to build a watch," Mike said, smiling.

"We can do without the geography lesson right now, Dad," Morgan echoed as she peered out the window to look at the distant blue silhouette of a small range of hills. "When do we get there?"

"Half an hour, maybe a little less," I said.

My estimate was not far off. I called the Hales on my cell phone when we were within a mile and announced our arrival. They were on the porch waiting when we pulled to a stop in their yard.

Bob and Carmen rushed off the porch and came quickly to the car. The kids threw the doors open and ran to them.

"Hi Grandma., Hi Grandpa," Morgan hollered. "Did you think we would never get here?"

Grandparents on their mother's side, the Hales had traveled to Baltimore numerous times over the years. They seldom stayed long. Bob couldn't stand sleeping in someone else's bed for more than three nights, he claimed. And Carmen was restless when Bob was restless. All the same, they always enjoyed their stay and, to the extent that Rebecca would permit it, indulged Michael and Morgan as much as possible. Bob acted as chef for the short duration we were in Moccasin country, bouncing back and forth between the warmth inside to the grill standing on the porch ankle deep in snow. The steaks and burgers were excellent, and the potatoes, fried in sauteed onions and butter were mouth watering.

Over the course of the evening, Carmen succeeded in coaxing both of the kids away from the living room conversations and one of the early bowl games, to measure how they were doing in the wake of the blowup of our marriage. She confided in me later that they both seemed to be doing well and were enjoying their trip to "end-of-the-world" country. She said they were not only enjoying Montana and all they had seen of it, but they were fascinated by its diversity and the character of its people. I was proud of them.

We lingered the next day until mid-afternoon, wanting to foster a continuing spirit of togetherness. But, when we could wait no longer, if we were to make it back to Norris before dark, I finally cried "all aboard", and we were on our way.

Time passes rapidly whenever you hope for a string of days where you can enjoy life and family. Their last day was spend a "our" place, riding the horses, behind-the-wheel practice, and packing. Morgan had always been a bit of a mystery to me, disinclined as she was, at least with me, to share her more private thoughts. Mike was more outgoing and sharing in that regard, and to my delight and embarrassment, Morgan was showing signs of cracking the door slightly. The subject of our little daughter to dad talk while Mike was feeding the cows was an extension of her remark earlier that she was sorry for having refused to talk to me and for telling me she hated me.

"Can I say something, Dad?" she began our conversation. "Mike and I are leaving in the morning, so I have to say something now or it won't get said."

"Fire away," I said, "just don't be too hard on old Dad here."

"Okay, I'll try not to be too hard on you," she continued. "I've already told you I was sorry for my behavior before, but I want to try to explain why I said what I said. I hear you say that you are busy here with your cows and over at Claire's, that your plate is almost too full. Well, that is what was happening to me when I first heard that you and Mom were divorcing. I was busy in school, having trouble with math, and not getting along with one of the fellows I liked, and then you guys spring this separation and divorce thing on me. Right then, my plate was overflowing, and it was more than I could handle.

"I struck out at you, she continued. "Why, exactly, I don't know. But it was probably because Mom and I, girls that we are, were naturally closer. When I heard what was happening, I fled to Mother, and I wanted to strike out at something, somebody, anybody. Can you understand that?"

"Yes," I conceded. "I do understand. I don't want you to agonize about any of this. I understand, it's all part of the past. We can move on can't we, as friends, at least?"

"We are more than friends, Dad," she said, "I am your daughter. I love you more than you might think, and I want to tell you that our trip out here has been...well, healing. I have enjoyed myself since day one, and you have been a wonderful host. But I want to be more than an occasional visitor. I want to spend time with you and Mike, I hope, right here on "our" place. I want an invitation to come whenever I can."

Those were words any father in my situation wants to hear. I was ecstatic, and I told her so. "You have that invitation, as of now, Morgan, and you have made me very happy. Summers and some of the holidays would be wonderful."

We had come a long way, the three of us, and I knew in my heart it was more than I deserved. I think it had added some clarity to how I saw myself because they had come to me. It had always been Jim, it had always been just Jim. Oh, I had paid token attention to the others and their needs, but it was fleeting and perfunctory. Somewhere along the way I lost my sense of what counted. Incredible as it sounds, my kids were bringing me back to my senses

"When school ends in May," Morgan added, "I'll be in a jet

streaking this way and, thank you for telling me you want to see more of me...and Mike."

I hugged her like I had never hugged her before, and we were both near tears when Mike came in from the corrals. "There's someone coming," he said. "I think it might be Claire and Jennifer." Minutes later they drove into the yard and walked to the door. No knocking. Just walking in, which is as it should be with friends.

"Party time," Jennifer announced. "And we brought it with us. Tonight you kids will want quiet time with your dad, but this afternoon, you'll have to contend with Claire and me. Benny and Odin said they will be over in an hour or so. Said they wanted to say goodbye to their best girl who, in case you haven't noticed, Morgan, would be you."

Morgan rushed to Jennifer, threw her arms around her waist, and kissed her on the cheek.

"Thank you for coming, Jennifer," she said. "We have an early flight in the morning, and I was afraid we might not get a chance to say goodbye."

"Not on your life, child," Jenny said. "We would have fired your dad if he had hustled you out of here without a goodbye. Besides, we have gifts for your mother, and we're going to take you on a little trip."

"Yes, a trip," she said. "Now if you have bathing suits, dig them out and let's go."

We had bathing suits, all brand new, purchased for our night at the motel in Missoula. I didn't ask questions about the trip. It was something they wanted to do, and we assumed it involved immersion in water. We climbed into their car, drove to Norris, hung a right and stopped at Norris Hot Springs. Into their bathing suits quickly, the kids were soon in the warm water. They had the pool to themselves, and before long I was in there with them.

Claire & Jennifer, stayed in their car for a time and then, they too, joined us. Claire had a time of it lowering himself into the water, but he made it. We soon learned the reason for their not climbing in to begin with. Jennifer had called Benny on her cell phone to put in her order. He came with chips, pretzels, snack crackers, beer and wine for the adults, and soft drinks for the kids. Benny and Odin were decked out in a flowered bathing suits that hung below their knees.

"Jump in, boys," Jennifer said. "If you want there's a small pool next to us where you can indulge in a little nude bathing if you wish."

"Good thing I didn't know that," Benny quipped, "or you guys would have had to catch up to me. I always try to do a little skinny dipping before Christmas." Of course, we laughed and blushed at the thought of the two of them stripping down to their birthday suits. Benny was a part of the Macintosh family and had been for 30 years, so he was a part of our family as well. Odin was edging up to it and, like Benny had predicted earlier, it was just a matter of time and he would settle in on the Macintosh ranch permanently. I think he figured he had already done that, but we all knew he still sneaked away once in a while for his fishing.

Back at my place, Jennifer started cooking...well, warming our celebration meal. The table was set with seven places with the Macintoshes seated at the ends, Benny, Odin and myself on one side and the kids on the other. The meal consisted of hot dishes, one with macaroni as the main ingredient and the other a stew, heavy on ground beef and potatoes. Together we toasted our week of Christmas good will and fellowship, but the hit of the day was the Norwegian lefse Jennifer brought to the table. Of course it was something new to the kids. At first they were tentative in their tasting adventure, but with gobs of butter spread across each slice together with sugar, white or brown, according to your tastes, they were soon hooked.

There were those who argued that anyone who did not love the stuff, invariably harbored a flawed character and, inevitably, a fatal physical deficiency.

After our company departed, Morgan and Michael packed their luggage except for last minute items to be packed in the morning, and we sat around the house jabbering, watching television, eating the lefse Jennifer had left for us, and dreading, I think, the moment when we would say goodbye at the airport.

It came too soon to suit any of us, I'm sure. Not many hours later, I watched as their plane left the airport heading west before it banked to the left and gradually turned toward the east. I was invited to be at the Macintosh ranch for New Year's Day, and I accepted, but it was not the same with the kids back east with their mother. We watched a few bowl games, ate too much, and I went home early feeling severely bloated.

Winter ran its course before we knew it, and spring rushed at us with gobs of work and what seemed like a million things to do. Odin told me, privately, that he was doing his best to hang tough as far as his full-time *seasonal* employment was concerned, and that he was working overtime to resist the temptation to pack it in and go fishing.

I was surprised to learn that Claire and Jennifer had acquired almost 2,000 acres of new range and farmland. They were talking about another hired man. The land, to my dismay, was Michele's. She had given them the right of first refusal, and they had bought it without so much as a word to Benny and Odin or myself. The acquisition meant that the two places were now connected with a strip of land three miles long and one mile deep. I think they waited to tell me because, by now, they had deduced that Michele and I were more than casual friends and that selling her land was a signal to everyone that she did not intend to return.

I have to admit it is no longer that difficult to accept the idea of her never returning, because I saw that as likely months earlier. No letters, not a word. I was pretty sure it was not a matter of her having found someone else. The unlikeliness of that happening was clear to me. She had run from love, not towards it.

Life's experiences have a way of piling up on each other, some good, some bad. My divorce was at the bottom of the pile of bad. Stumbling upon Jennifer and Claire was a definite candidate for the good pile. Having my kids with me for Christmas would certainly be something I would lump in with the good. Michele's decision not to return to Norris from wherever she was, had to be part of the pile of bads. Letting her go, when I should have fought to keep her with me, also qualified for the bad pile. My after-Christmas attitude was one of optimism, though, knowing that with the advent of summer, I might see my kids again.

It's funny. When I was younger and my kids were living in the same house, I often walked past them, so caught up in some facet of my work that I hardly noticed them or, worse, saw them as mild encumbrances. Now when I look back, I am filled with shame.

My calf crop was 100 percent, meaning my herd had doubled in one year That went into the good pile, of course. A couple of the young heifers, knocking on the door that lead to motherhood, gave me fits when their time came but I managed. I had already begun to think about another younger bull, or possibly two, and next year's calf crop. My almost-new refrigerator required a new compressor. That was bad. The bank paid me nearly $15,000 interest on my CDs. That was good. Uncle Sam and the IRS folks reached out and grabbed close to $9500 back. That was bad. Still, I was, as they say, learning to roll with the punches, some of which were self inflicted. In spite of the yo-yo character of my life, things were looking good.

But all of that changed during the last week of May. I was working on one of the large sprinkler system's drive mechanism when Benny drove up and told me Claire wanted to see me at the house. The moment I walked in the door, I knew something was wrong. Jennifer was sitting at the kitchen table, her head cradled in her arms, as tears rolled down her cheeks. Claire stood at her shoulder trying to console her.

"What's happening here?" I asked.

"It's Megan," Claire said, "She called a few minutes ago with some very, very bad news."

And...?" I asked.

"She found out yesterday that she has cancer," Jennifer said as she lifted her head to look up to me. "It's pancreatic cancer, she said, and it's one of the worst kinds. By the time you have symptoms, it is almost always too late. She may die. My God, hasn't she had enough to worry about, the poor thing. Taylor. Now this."

"She's pretty much by herself, I'm afraid," Claire offered. "Her husband is no longer with her, and that leaves only Taylor. Luckily, school is out for the year, so Taylor *can* be there."

"So what can I do? I asked. "I'll do anything. Anything."

Jennifer looked up then and stood to put her arms around me. Times like this are perspective creators for everyone close to those who suffer. My own problems instantly fell away as I stood there in the company of people with *real* problems. It was too early for consolation, but not for hope, and that is what I tried to give them.

"Let's not jump to conclusions," I told them. "We don't know enough yet to know if the outlook is as bleak as it seems. Let's find out more."

"They are coming in the morning," Jennifer said, brushing away lingering tears at the corner of her eyes. "Would you go with us to Bozeman to meet the plane?"

"Of course," I replied. "When is their plane due?"

"About 10:30."

"I'll be over early," was all I could say.

The commuter jet from Salt Lake edged up to the terminal in the middle of a rain shower. Discerning that one of the two women, who walked through the gates into the waiting area, was seriously ill was impossible. She looked as vibrant and alive as the last time I saw her. Taylor led the way and rushed to her grandmother as soon as she saw her. Megan embraced her dad, but there was no crying. She was remarkably collected for one facing a future filled with so much doubt. I silently admired her strength, all of the time knowing its source. We had all had time to collect ourselves since first hearing the news of her illness, so talk was on the mundane and food.

It was your's truly who inserted the subject of food into what were serious, strained, uncomfortable moments. I knew they would have their discussions once back at the ranch, but for now maybe some light hearted conversation between them might be the best medicine. I suggested we stop somewhere for lunch. That was my thinking, but it worked only up to a point. An innocent question asked by Jennifer opened the flood gates when she asked, "So Megan, how are you feeling?"

"I feel fine. I can't believe that I'm sick," she replied. "I had some pain in by lower abdomen about a week ago, but it left for a time only to return. Never as intense as it was in the beginning, but it was there."

She went on to explain that she thought the dull, but persistent pain was probably caused by either a bladder infection or, perhaps, a kidney stone. Not wanting to contend with the discomfort any longer, she had taken the day off and checked into the Walk-In Clinic at a local hospital. The doctor she was given agreed that her diagnosis about bladder infection was probably on target, but that they would want to do some blood work to make sure and before deciding on an antibiotic.

"To make a long story short," she said, "the doctor told me my white blood count was normal which meant I didn't have an infection. But, he was concerned about the severity of the pain, and that led him to think it could be a kidney stone. He advised a ct-scan. That's when they found the mass on my pancreas.

"I'm not absolutely sure where the pancreas is located," she continued, "but I didn't think it was anywhere close to where my pain was. Anyway, they did more tests. They say surgery is my only recourse, and it will have to be done soon. The big questions now are when and where."

The ride to the ranch was quiet. Taylor sat in front with me. I asked her in a whisper if she was okay. She said she was, but she was looking inward now, wrestling with what had happened and what might happen. I left her alone with her thoughts, for I knew that for now, she had to deal with her grief in her own way. I did lean toward her again, offering to help in any way I might. She nodded her head but looked straight ahead. Jennifer invited me in when we arrived at the ranch, but I declined. Now, it was family, personal time. They treated me like family and we had grown very close, but they had to grapple with their concerns and fears in their own ways, in private.

Saturday was one of the most pleasant days we had in an otherwise, cool and damp spring. Try as I might, I could not totally divorce myself from what was going on down at the ranch, so I drifted from one project to another out in the yard. None of them succeeded in shutting out the latest trauma in my life. Admittedly, my link was tenuous, became it flowed indirectly to me from those who were directly involved. Megan, Taylor, Jennifer, and Claire. I liked and admired Megan, but little of me was vested in her life other that what flowed to me from Jennifer and Claire. That was enough if it came to that, but I needed to distance myself from it if I could.

Always, in the past, immersion in a task or project was the answer, so I fell back on that today. Out in back of the corrugated-steel grain bin was a stack of left over logs that I had been thinking of using to build a small shed to store our tack. Small though the timbers were, moving them even a few feet was strenuous and tiring. Just what I needed.

Several months earlier, long before the snows came, I had sketched out a floor plan for the shed and had poured a 10-inch high concrete foundation and filled it with concrete 5 inches thick. If that seems like over-kill, let me explain. For as long as I can remember, I have had a personal aversion to a head-on encounter with a badger or with a back-end face-off with a skunk. The foundation encouraged them to take up residence elsewhere.

Megan showed up just as I stepped out on to the porch after wolfing down three hot dogs and a can of Budweiser. The meat slipped down my esophagus without my throat noticing, but I stretched out and savored the taste of a cold beer, a taste which is like none other in the world. Megan was dressed in the uniform of any Montana ranch girl wearing high heeled boots, jeans and a baseball cap. I was struck once again by how pretty she was and how "in control" she seemed in spite of everything. And those eyes. The were so unique, truly mesmerizing, and it was hard not to peek.

"Come in, Megan," I said. "You picked a nice day to hunt down some fresh air."

"Yes, it is a nice day," she said, "but I'm not here to talk about the weather."

"Of course," I said. "Should we go inside. The coffee pot is on and I've got cookies."

"No, lets just go for a walk," she said. "I think better when I'm moving."

Walk we did for better than an hour, with her doing the talking and me the listening. The subject came as no surprise. I listened attentively as she tried to depict her situation from a personal perspective. I sensed from her tentativeness that she was doing it as much, if not more, for herself than for me. The picture in her own mind was clouded and in a state of flux, no doubt. Talking about it was her way of defining and clarifying. I'd been down that road myself, so it was easy to see that she saw me as a sounding board of-the-moment. More than happy I was, to be that or whatever else she saw in me that promised illumination or relief.

She explained that she has been trying to discuss with her parents her future in terms of the scenarios facing her.

"They are so distressed," she said, "that each time we touch on something specific, Mom cries and Dad does his best to console her. They aren't much help, frankly. I know they are crushed by what has happened to me. I need to talk to someone not so personally involved and...well, that's you if your are willing to let me cry on your shoulder."

"Cry on my shoulder all you want, Megan" I said, "and I am a good listener."

"Well, for starters," she began, "I might be dying. You already know that. No, let me start again. It is more accurate to say that I am *probably* dying. If it is pancreatic as they expect, it has very likely already spread, and I will probably die within a few weeks or months. I haven't had any symptoms, and that tells me they may have found it early. It was an accident, you know. I thought I had a bladder infection. The people at the clinic thought maybe a kidney stone. We were both wrong. I did have some lower back pain, and apparently that is one of the indicators of bladder and kidney problems *and* pancreatic problems.

"I'm trying to be positive," she continued, "but I don't want to die. I think I can cope with death if it comes to that, but it certainly isn't part of the plan I had for the rest of my life."

She went on to say that the doctor she had dealt with in Denver was a gastro-enterologist, not an oncologist, but several staff oncologists had confirmed that the scans pointed to a pancreatic tumor. They told her they could operate on it there, but they also pointed out that Johns Hopkins, the University of Minnesota, or the Mayo Clinic all had more experience in such surgery. They do the kind of surgery she needed all the time. The doctor in Denver said that he would make all of the arrangements, but she must decide where she wanted it done.

"So what do I do?" she asked. "Where do I go?"

Megan was asking for my help. The decisions she must make could potentially spell the difference between living or dying or, at least, between living for a short or longer time. My preference would have been to not be involved, but I was because she had asked. My brain had been sifting through all of the potential outcomes and I didn't like any of them.

"Well, Megan," I said, "before I give you my opnion, let me just say that I am so sorry that this thing is happening to you. You deserve better. I won't tell you not to worry, that everything is going to be fine, because I just don't know. And, I won't tell you where to go. That is a decision only you can make. All three of the places you mention have fine surgeons, I'm sure. But you might want to consider Taylor and your parents. They will insist on being there, and travel is a consideration. Strikes me that the Mayo clinic in Rochester would be easier for them to get to and to move around in once they get there, if only because of its smaller size."

She said she had thought of the travel part of it and that she agreed with me. She could arrange for them to stay at a hotel near the clinic and the hospital so they could walk to either without worrying about transportation. Most hotels had limos that took you to and brought you back from the hospital or clinic. "So that's what I am going to do," she said.

"What about your husband?" I asked. "He's going to want to be there."

"Ex-husband, you mean, don't you? I don't know. He might if Taylor asked him."

"Then why don't you talk to Taylor and let her decide."

"Yes," she replied. "I'll do that. I hadn't thought of it to be honest with you."

"There's something else you haven't mentioned, Megan," I said, "and that's Taylor and her school."

"I've already taken care of her school. Only a few days remained. I spoke with her teachers and the Principal, explained my dilemma, and they all agreed to waive the final test requirements. As of right now, she is through with her Junior year. I worry more about next year, but I'll cross that bridge when I come to it, *if* I come to it.

"You know what?" she said, "I'll take that coffee now. I feel much better, You've helped me a bunch."

"I'll make a fresh pot," I said. "How about a hot dog? Are you hungry?"

She said she wasn't but that she would eat one anyway. "I feel like celebrating just a little," she said. "I've got answers I didn't have before I came over this morning."

I told her I was glad to have been of some help but that she had already made up her mind about most things before she got here. "You answered your own questions by yourself," I offered. "All I did was try to help you see your options more clearly."

We sat there in the kitchen, two strangers really, who had moved a few steps closer to being friends. She must have felt something of the same, because she confided in me that she was not as afraid of dying as she would have guessed. It was more a matter of not wanting to miss so many things. Taylor graduating from high school, going to college, marrying, having babies, and those sorts of things. Her Mom and Dad she would miss terribly. They were not getting any younger. She wanted to be around to help them when they needed help.

"Good hot dog," she added, as she bit into a jumbo dog. "Can I have another?"

We chuckled at that, especially after I told her I had accidently picked out a package of mixed turkey and pork dogs instead of beef. She ate it anyway, right here in the heart of beef country.

"Jim," she said as she stood by the car door, "I've one last favor to ask, and it is the biggest of all. You can say no if you wish, and I won't blame you."

"Ask away," I said.

"My Mom and Dad are going to need help getting through all of this and so will Taylor," she said. "I hate to ask, but could you....?"

She never finished whatever it was she had begun. Instead, she stood up and walked toward the door. I followed her, and before she opened the door, she reached up and brushed my cheek with her lips. Then she was gone. She had either changed her mind about asking me another question, or the answer had come to her without my help.

A phone call from her while I could still see the plume of dust made by her truck led to my being part of the entourage that traveled to Minnesota. I felt like an intruder until I saw the pleading look in Jennifer's eyes later that evening. I was there and I was glad to be.

Non-stop flights east out of Bozeman to almost anywhere are as infrequent as Thanksgivings without a turkey, but we found one that would take us to Minneapolis as long as we were willing to fly on Sunday. Megan's first appointment was scheduled for 11:00 am Tuesday, so we had plenty of time to get settled in Rochester. Highway 52 out of the Twin Cities was a nice four-lane drive, and we reached Rochester well before dark. Behind us lay mile upon mile of corn, beans and alfalfa, which were the cornerstone of the area's agricultural economy.

It was Taylor who wondered aloud why we never saw any cattle. Seldom did we see any grazing in the area's lush greenery. They were, for the most part, housed year-around in spacious, well ventilated and climatically controlled loafing sheds, some stretching for a city block in length. I had read where one dairy located south of Minneapolis, along the Minnesota river, milked 64 cows at a time all day long, every day. Montana had some distance to travel before they could match that, though the likelihood seemed remote since Montanans were more inclined to family-type farms and ranches, operations that could function with a family or two providing the manpower.

The multi-towers of the Mayo Clinic stood out against the horizon, inviting the ill and not so ill from around the world. We were a somber group, and growing more so as we approached the downtown area where the clinic and our hotel were located. Had we elected to do so, we might have moved between most of the clinic's buildings via the skyways and subways that connected them.

I could just about imagine the anxiety and fear Megan must be coping with, as we parked the rental car, but it was her character that kept her from letting us see that side of her. Going through her mind must have been fear, hope, depression, and anger, but she never let on. It was one of those things each of us must face on our own. Having family close by helps, but nobody can jump on that cancer horse but the one who has to make the ride, no matter how much they might want to shield a stricken loved one.

We had all of Monday to familiarize ourselves with the vast Mayo Clinic complex. Most of Megan's appointments were scheduled for the Gonda Building, 9th floor, so we found the elevators and made a practice trip.

On the day of her appointment, we went with her up to the 9th floor, a floor which seemed to be devoted exclusively to cancer treatment. When her name was called, Jennifer and her stood up and together they passed through the gaping, electronically controlled door, holding hands. Taylor sat between her Grandpa and me, with her arm around Claire. It seemed like they had barely gone in and they were back.

"They are studying Megan's scan, the one she brought from Bozeman," Jennifer said, "but they want a radiologist to come and analyze it as well, so they said we should just wait out here."

In less than half an hour the name, Megan Tivoli, was called once again, and for the second time, the two of them disappeared behind the door. Ten minutes later, they were back again, this time both of them near tears. It was not a good sign. Crying could only mean bad news.

Megan came directly to Taylor, brought her into her arms, and began brushing away *her* tears, for she too was now crying. I watched as people around us glanced our way, assuming we had just received the worst news possible, that nothing could be done, that it was too late. And, to a person, they were probably all thankful it was not them. Jennifer took control and led us away from the others to hear the bad news from someone who knew.

"You can stop crying, guys," Megan said. "I think I just received some good news. Tomorrow I have to have another ct scan, X-rays, blood work, and an endoscopy, but if the tests confirm what the doctor thinks, I may not have pancreatic cancer. That's why Mom and I were crying. We were relieved."

"So, Mom," Taylor asked, "are you saying you don't have cancer; is that what you're saying?"

"I wish it were so but, no," Megan replied. "I have a large tumor, and there is a chance, a very small chance, it is not malignant. The doctor says that with this type of cancer that is highly unlikely, for almost always they are malignant. Benign tumors can turn malignant, so one way or the other, it will have to be removed. If their hunch is right, I have a cancer called sarcoma which began on my stomach and has spread to the tail of my pancreas and my spleen."

"What did the doctor say about the tail of my pancreas, Mother?" Megan said as she glanced at her mother. "I'm not sure I understood all of that."

"He said the tumor seemed attached only to the *tail* of the pancreas, which is good news, because only a small fraction of enzymes ...or whatever... are produced there. So it can be removed and the pancreas can still do its job, whatever that is. Their concern is that it might have already spread. That's the reason for another ct-scan and X-rays tomorrow. They must also determine for certain what type of cancer it is in order to select the appropriate type of surgical treatment and chemotherapy. "

"Then there is reason to celebrate?" I inquired.

"If we don't wait too long," Megan said, smiling for the first time all day. "I can't eat anything after dinner, because of tomorrow's blood tests."

The tests confirmed that Megan had a sarcoma cancer, and immediate steps were taken to have it removed. The doctor said it was impossible to know just what they would encounter until they opened the abdominal cavity. One possibility was that if the tumor covered most of her stomach, it would have to be removed and another stomach manufactured using a part of her large intestines.

"Remember what I told you earlier, Megan," I asked

"What? I don't remember."

"I told you not to cash in your chips just yet, because they are working miracles in places like the Mayo Clinic. The Clinic makes no claims as to being the worker of miracles, but if they can make you a stomach if you need it, I call that a miracle."

"I'll take it, Jim," she said, "and anything else along the way that I might need."

Her surgery was scheduled for two days later, early in the morning, and she had to be there by 6:00 o'clock for preparatory work. Jennifer went with her to the prep room then joined us in the waiting area when they took Megan to the operating room. We spent four hours, four restless hours, pacing back and forth, speculating about what stage of surgery they had reached, and silently praying for good news. When the surgeon came to the waiting room, she told us that everything had gone well, and that because the tumor was attached to the stomach like a mushroom on a log, she did not have to replace it.

"She won't starve to death with what I saved of her stomarch, but she'll have to eat six meals per day instead of the customary three," she said. "Because of her stomach's reduced size, she'll need a vitamin B12 shot once a month for the rest of her life. Megan's sarcoma tumor is very rare, with fewer than 10,000 people being diagnosed with it each year. That seems like a large number, and it is, but compared to the thousands even millions of people worldwide with colon, lung, or breast cancer, it is rare. She's in the recovery room, and unless the pathology report indicates otherwise, we are quite confident we got it all."

Now, some of us were crying again, this time for joy, for certain. I said goodby to her once she was assigned a room. Circumstances afforded us a moment alone as the others ran to the hospital cafeteria. It was then she told me she had all but made up her mind to return to Montana not only to recuperate but to stay.

"I want to be here with my parents," she said. "They will go crazy not knowing how I am doing on a daily basis. They all say everything is going to be okay. What else can they say? I'd be doing the same if one of you were lying in this bed. But, I know that it might not be so. A positive attitude is what I have, but positive attitudes don't cure cancer. Doctors and research and medicine do. If the worst happens, I want to be with my parents. There is nothing left for me in Denver except bad memories."

"It's your decision, Megan," I said. "Just let your heart decide. I have to run, Megan. I've got a plane to catch." Work was piling up for me in Montana and, besides, her husband, or was it ex-husband, had arrived. I left thinking I had done right by her and by the family, but I also felt a bit extraneous.

Back in Montana I divided my time between the Macintosh ranch and my own place. Benny and Odin were struggling to bring in the first cutting of alfalfa. The big loader tractor, with me sitting in the padded seat, buzzed around the field chasing bales and then lifting them up on the flatbed trailer for a ride to the pole barn hay storage shed. When the field was cleared, we set the sprinkler system into motion and moved on to the next task.

A small bunch of late calving cows had to be moved to the grazing permit but, in the interests of time, we loaded them in trailers and hauled them up to the permit instead of driving them west between two rows of barbed wire fences. I felt good about the progress we were making, but there was no end to the tasks yet to be completed. Benny was assigned to feeding the hundred or so head of steers still in the feed lot pens and to the nasty job of cleaning out the accumulation of manure and bedding straw from the corrals and pens now empty of stock. Odin, the carpenter man, tackled repairs on the feed bunks and in the sheds themselves. I drove the self propelled Air Coupe sprayer south to the barley field and applied the herbicide needed to keep the valuable, malting contract free of weeds.

Every night when I got back to my place, there was at least one message from Claire or Jennifer. Megan was doing very well, and her spirits were good. Had it rained? Megan was up and around, walking the halls of St. Mary's Hospital like a crazy woman, rushing to build her strength. Had we moved those late calving cows up to the pasture? Taylor wants to know why Michael never calls. Megan is on a morphine pump to help with pain but is trying to use it as little as possible. Had we cut the alfalfa? Megan started taking chemotherapy pills today. How about the barley? She gets a little sick each day from the pills but it doesn't last long. Megan's ex-husband stayed only a day. There's some frozen lefse in the freezer for you guys. We will be coming home soon. Can you pick us up at the airport on Tuesday?

We had toiled long and hard during the week, so once we had the steers fed on Saturday morning we called it a day. Odin went fishing, I'm sure. Benny retired to the bunkhouse to watch television. My place was waiting for me, but before anyone of us left I went to the freezer, withdrew all of the lefse, frozen though it might be, and divided it equally between the three of us. If I didn't, it was just a matter of time before I would have to make a quick run to Deaconess to remove a large mass of you-know-what caught up somewhere in Benny's digestive tract.

I left mine to thaw on the kitchen table when I got home and ate it for a mid-afternoon lunch. I should have been working on the shed-building project I had just begun the day Megan came to me for advice. I should have but I didn't. Instead, I saddled up one of the horses and struck out for the rock outcropping formation southwest of my place. My mind set was one of euphoria, made so because it seemed Megan might have dodged the big C. I knew too that in the dark recesses of her mind every day of the rest of her life she would always harbor the thought that a slight turn in the road could bring it all back. I had been surfing the internet to better understand this sarcoma type of cancer, and discovered that 65 percent of the time it returned, sometimes more aggressive than before. I truly hoped she would fall in the 35 percent category, where it never came back.

Walking across the shelf of the expansive granite outcrop I had come to think of as Michele's and mine was always uplifting. Far below, the valley stretched for miles to the north and south, as if reaching for the ends of the planet. And this day, the mountain ranges were punching holes in the clouds that moved slowly over them, etching indelibly in my brain a sight I could never forget no matter how I might try. I came here now and again for the express purpose of connecting with Michele, but today was different. For now, I just wanted to prop my weary back against the rock and lose myself in my good fortune.

Life for me had been a series of upward surges followed by halting plunges where I felt shut off from everything. Yet, inexorably, I moved forward and, in small, hesitant, steps, upward. I am not a philosopher. Not long ago I could lose myself in numbers, graphs, flow charts and cost estimates. Details were the stuff of life for me. I was a detail man back then. But, more so than anyone else, I knew that had changed. I could still use a mean pencil and my brain was essentially intact, but I was much more inclined to sit back, wonder about things, and let life come to me. Today was one of those days. Things were definitely looking up for Jim Pengilly, small-scale Montana land baron.

On the spur of the moment, I dropped down off the granite shelf and rode back home to collect my camping gear. Before I forgot, I called Benny and told him I would not be in until late Monday evening. Then I hastily packed the sorrel mare with a tent, tarps, pots, pans, fishing rods, coolers, and my camera. I was going camping up on the grazing permit, and I was going to stay there until I had to come back down to meet the plane.

It was my first attempt, ever, to load the leather panniers I had purchased at a local auction sale, but I managed to distribute my supplies more or less evenly in terms of weight. The tent, I strapped between the two panniers along with a small sack of whole oats and two blocks of salt, one white, the other the darker trace minerals variety. The salt blocks legitimized, in my mind, my spur-of-the-moment trip by persuading me that this excursion was all part of my job. My prized, lever action Winchester .30-.30 rifle rested in my saddle boot. Watch out coyotes and gophers!

Up on the east slopes of the Tobacco Root Mountains, I found the panorama of valleys and mountains below even more exhilarating, mind boggling, really. I was surprised at the ruggedness here on the shoulder of the mountains. In the nooks and crannies of far off slopes, I could clearly make out pockets of dirty-white snow hiding from the sun. Everywhere there were good stands of grass, but they were often sandwiched in between crumbling walls of granite. Boulders the size of small houses rested against a far slope or stood in the middle of a canyon like sentinel rocks in the middle of a river.

It was under the northern brow on one of these gigantic, fallen boulders that I set up my camp. It was perfect. I could dip my pot into the small, clear stream that bounced off the west end of the boulder and sliced its way toward the east. The front end of my tent faced to the east, so I could watch the spectacle of flickering nighttime lights below, including those of Norris itself.

I had barely enough time to fashion a rain flap over my tent before darkness clamped down on me like a coffin cover and put an end to my roaming about. One never knew in this high country. I was prepared to sit right where I was for a while if I had to. This late-of-Baltimore pilgrim would attempt no descent on terrain dominated by rain-slick rocks.

It was a time to hunker down, twiddle my fingers, and read a good book. I knew it was crazy, but one of the good books I carried in my saddle bags was the dictionary. I had started reading it from page one when I was in college. Now 20 year later I was on page

694. One could make a strong argument, I suppose, that I am a slow reader. In any case, next to Lapland was a checkmark telling me where to begin next time. The second book was Jack London's, *Call of the Wild*. I had carried it for many years and could recite full pages if they brought back to me the unconditional love dog and master shared. Which reminds me: I need a dog.

I fell asleep thinking about Michele. My memories of her were still very much a part of me, but they had softened. I still thought about her every now and then but not every day. Here, now, cradled between two perpendicular walls of pine and rock, her memory came rushing back at me like a massive avalanche. Maybe it was being in the tent, where our bodies had come together in love, or it might simply have been the flicker and crackle of the fire that brought her racing back to me like a runaway 18-wheeler on I-90.

In the morning, while a shadowy darkness clung tenaciously to the deepest recesses of the canyon walls, I was frying bacon in a small cast iron skillet and making coffee with the crystal clear waters of the small stream that crowded up against the boulder and my tent. Michele was gone from my mind, Megan's plight was faceless, and my son and daughter were hidden from me by hundreds of miles. I was here to steep myself in the cleansing power of this jumble of rocks and grassy plateaus, to wash away the array of negatives I had bumped up against in recent years.

Michele was at times but a fuzzy memory, Megan's prospects were promising, Jennifer and Claire's life was returning to some semblance of calm, Michael and Morgan were back in my life, and I was enthusiastic about my own prospects. I felt as though today marked the onset of a life of promise and fulfillment. I wanted to discard the garbage, cleanse myself of any lingering remnants, and embark up my new life beginning now.

My first thought was to change my camp, then I changed my

mind, only to change it once again. My objective was two-fold. In the first place I *did* want to take a quick look at Claire's...and Michele's cows and make sure they were okay. The few I encountered were usually slurping in water from the creek, and few of them gave me anything more than a oblique and hasty glance.

Secondly, I wanted to explore new country. This was only my second trip into the Tobacco Root high country, so I would be feeling my way. It was not to be a mountain climbing expedition, though there were 42 peaks, 10,000 feet or higher, in the sweeping breath of the range that I hadn't climbed. Only Hollow Top, the highest, had seen my footprints. This was one of those trips to help me see things clearer and to give me the feeling of self-reliance that flows from being alone and of being in charge in quiet and lonely places. No Jennifer to cook my noontime meal. No one to make my bed. No one to greet me in the morning. No one to invade my private thoughts.

Quiet and solitude is precisely what I experienced during the rest of the day, other than for the scream of a bald eagle clutching a newly caught fish in it claws as it lifted itself back into the updrafts above a small lake just below timberline. At each turn, as I caught sight of a new picture-window scene, I absorbed a bit of the wonder mountain man, Jim Bridger, must have felt as he explored the northern Rockies more than a hundred years earlier. The quiet was deafening, as they say, but it had not always been so. Here and there beneath my horse's hooves were traces of old mining roads, and off in the distance I saw the scars of switchback trails used for both mining and lumbering. Between last night's camp and my new one, three thousand feet higher, I counted 25 white tail deer, dozens of ptarmigan, countless pika, and the fleeting shadow of what I believed was a mountain lion.

We climbed slowly but steadily through a wild land, with the only the sounds of saddle leather creaking and the snorting and grunting of the horses as they fought the steep slopes. We stopped for the day when both the horses and me were exhausted. The horses I picketed in a pocket of lush high–country grass, and the tent I pegged down beside a pond less than an acre in size. In bed early, I slept without interruption throughout the night, raising myself up on one elbow at 5:30 to look at my watch and to begin extricating myself from my sleeping bag.

The ride down was quicker, but far from easy. Mountain trails, especially a rocky Tobacco Root trail, could get mighty exciting on the way down, should one of the horses stumble or slip on a loose rock. Lunch lasted long enough for me to make a small pot of coffee, gnaw on some jerky, and make myself a peanut butter sandwich, using my finger as a knife. And they say Jim Bridger had it rough! Maybe.

Too late to head down to the Macintosh place after I rode into my yard, I unloaded my pack, rubbed down the horses, fed them a bait of oats, and walked to the house and collapsed on the sofa. I was still there in the morning when the sun's first rays crept into the cabin.

Chapter 7

The Bozeman airport was beginning to feel like a second home for me. Flight 1309 was on time, but we waited half an hour for the baggage. Megan looked a little peaked, which came as no surprise to anyone, but Jennifer and Taylor were laughing and acting like they were Christmas shopping at the Mall. The women hugged me, and Claire and I settled for a hearty handshake.

"Megan and Taylor are moving to Montana, Jim" Jennifer announced as we waited. "We are excited."

"I should hope so," I said, acting surprised and trying not to give away the fact that I had been alerted to a possible move while Megan was still in the hospital.

"Yes, It's true," Megan said. "They tell me I have a long period of recuperation in front of me, and Mom and Dad offered to put us up at their place until Taylor and I locate a place of our own. I have to have blood work every week to begin with. When they are sure the chemotherapy pills I am taking aren't damaging my kidneys and a few other organs, I'll go less frequently. Anyway, we are thinking maybe in Bozeman, close to Deaconess."

"That's wonderful, Megan," I said. "How are you feeling?"

"Except for the fact that I can't find a comfortable way to sleep yet, just fine," she answered.

"That will change, I'm sure," was my feeble answer. "How about eating. Does that give you any problems?"

"No, but for now, at least, smaller portions are the order of the day."

"Here comes the luggage, Mom," Taylor sang out, ending our conversation.

Back at the ranch, I helped carry the luggage into the house, and then took Claire on a tour of the place, showing him what we had accomplished while he was gone.

"You should have seen that girl, Jim," he said, without so much as a hint that he was remotely interested in what I had shown him. "She was walking in that hall in the hospital like she was training for the Boston Marathon. Instead of the flimsy little slippers they gave her, she insisted we get her a pair of "walking" shoes.

"She was an inspiration to a lot of other patients and the medical people as well," he continued. "I was so proud of her. I just hope..."

"She's a strong girl, Claire," I said, reassuringly as his voice trailed off. "If anyone can beat this thing, it will be her."

"You know what, I think so," he acknowledged. "Yes, she's one tough Montana cowgirl. We want her to live at Michele's place, at least to begin with. That way, we can keep an eye on her and Taylor. Buy them a couple of gentle horses, I think. We haven't said anything yet, but we will soon. Maybe yet today."

"She has the strongest support group on the planet with you and Jennifer and Taylor," I said. "That will help when she gets down which, I am sure, she will from time to time. I'm waiting in the wings to help where I can."

"You've been there for her and all along, Jim. We appreciate it."

"It's the least I could do for my best friends. Come on, let's get some lunch or we'll start to get mushy."

Before I left to go out to work, I told Jennifer I wouldn't be there for supper. Things to do at my place, I said. It was true. I could always find something to do, but today it was a matter of not wanting to impose on what should be private, family discourse. During the rest of the week, I made myself scarce, stopping in only for lunch. I was usually out in field at supper time doing something away from the buildings while the others ate, so I loaded myself into my truck and hightailed it for home without stopping.

I did stay for supper on Friday night, but spent the weekend trying to con myself into resuming work on the shed project. Why I was dragging my feet, I don't know. It was one of those wonderful early summer days, and I just wasn't in the mood, I guess. So without agonizing over the matter, I saddled up my gelding for a ride up into the rocks. I heard a vehicle coming my way before I saw it. Once again, I was being paid a special visit by Megan. I knew she had something on her mind, and I waited for her to drive into the yard.

"Looks like you're heading out," she said. "I came at a bad time, I guess."

"There are no bad times for visiting with a friend," I said. "Why don't you come on in. I've got coffee, soda, beer, wine, iced tea. What's your pleasure?"

"Iced tea, would be nice," she replied, "but you were getting ready to go weren't you. I can come back."

"Don't be silly," I said, "I was just going to ride up to the rocks and take a look at the world about me. I can do that another time."

"How far is it? Michele pointed it out to me once, but I have never actually been up there."

"It's less than a mile, but you can drive up to within a couple hundred feet."

"Will you show it to me?"

"Sure, when you are feeling stronger."

"I'm strong enough now. Take me there please."

I agreed to do it if she was sure she was up to it. She said she'd like to try. If she couldn't make it, she'd say so.

"Jump in the truck, then," I said. "I'll bring along a jug of iced tea and some coffee."

We drove up there, but I was apprehensive. I could about imagine how much she was still hurting. Somewhere I had read or heard that to get at the organs within, most of the muscles that stretch across the abdomen and hold them in place must be severed. Only time lets them re-attach.

"Don't worry, Jim," she said, as if she could read my mind. "I wear a girdle like contraption to help hold my belly in. Just stay near enough for me to grab on to you if I must."

Slowly we climbed up the steep trail to the rock outcropping. Once on top, we stopped to catch our breath. Nothing in the world compares to the wonderful feelings one experiences at times like this.

"It's awesome, Jim," she cried out. "Michele told me about this but would never divulge its location. Thank you. Thank you very much. I'll keep her secret which, when I think about it, must not be much of a secret if you know."

"She took me up here in a weak moment, I guess," was my response.

I lead her to one of the spots where you could shinny up on and use a rock wall for both seating and leaning. We drank the iced tea before the cubes melted, and it really hit the spot on a warm day.

"Jim," she asked, "can I bend your ear for a little while again?"

"You know you can, Megan," I answered. "Bend away."

"Well, for starters," she began, "I want to thank you for your help these past few weeks. Mom and Dad were basket cases for a while, a bit more than I could cope with alone."

"You're folks are stronger than you might guess," I said, "but there for a while, they were struggling to deal with knowing you were sick, in a serious way."

"I know you and I have talked about this before, about my moving back, I mean," she said, "and I remember you're telling me to go with my heart. That's what I have done, but I am having some second thoughts, mostly because of Taylor."

"She doesn't want to make the move?" I asked. "It wouldn't surprise me if she didn't. She's young. She has friends in Denver. There is always some apprehension when children change schools and have to find new friends."

She said my assessment was the same as hers, that change is always tough no matter how small it may seem. Should I be asking her to do this, she wondered. My marriage is over, and my ex-husband's behavior tells us that he wants nothing more to do with either of us.

"What if I told her she could live with her dad for her last year of school, if she wished, and then she found out her presence was an inconvenience to him? He is a very selfish man. She would be devastated, and so would I."

"Tough decision," I said without offering any advice. I found myself going back to my own recent divorce and how Morgan had at first refused to talk to me. As much as it hurt, I had accepted it. I decided to share with her how I had dealt with Morgan.

"For what it's worth," I began, "let me tell you what I did when I learned that Morgan was solidly in Rebecca's camp, with an outright aversion to being a part of my life. It's not quite the same because I would have welcomed her with open arms had she wanted that. But as much as it hurt to know she detested me, I told myself that it was far more important for her to think well of at least one of us than it was for me to force her to be a part of my life, even if only because a judge said so."

"So what are you saying?" Megan asked.

"I'm saying you should talk to her about it, and let her make her choice. If she elects to go with her father, which I don't think she will, let her go. She's a sharp girl, and my bet is that right now she isn't thinking of herself. She is thinking of her mother. She knows what you are up against, and she will choose to stand with you."

She agreed that my approach had merit but wondered if forcing her to make such a choice was asking too much from someone so young.

"I suppose one option would be for me to stay in Denver. She could split her time between the two of us if that's what she wants. She's only a child, you know."

"What she wants," I said, "it to have her mom and dad together again. You say that is not in the cards. She needs to know that, if she doesn't already. I think she is a sharp girl. Trust her to make the right choice.

"Shouldn't you be asking yourself what you want, Megan?" I continued. "This shouldn't be all about Taylor. It can't be. What about you?"

For a few minutes she sat there looking off into the distance, as if the answer she was looking for was out there someplace. Finally, she said, she wanted to come back to Montana. If she was going to die she wanted to be here. It's selfish to feel that way, she said, but that's how she felt.

"Then tell her," I said.

She said she was inclined to do so but had to think more about it. Then she raised yet another plea for help, when she asked me what I thought about her and Taylor moving into Michele's old place, should she definitely decide to say. She had mentioned earlier that she thought Bozeman was her best choice because of its hospital and clinics. I remembered her saying that, but I knew her mom and dad were counting on her being close, so I suggested that she take up residence in Michele's old house, live there most of the week and drive to Bozeman only when she must. In time she would likely only have to make the trip once a month or even less frequently.

"Knowing that, what would your choice be?"

"I think you just made the choice for me," she said. "Earlier, I asked myself that very question. I wanted to be where I could look out my window, see the Tobacco Roots off to the west, the Madison Range to the east. I only asked because I thought a second opinion was important, so I had to ask Dr. Pengilly."

My eyes followed her car as she drove slowly down the narrow road toward home. About half way there she stopped in the middle of the road and sat there for fully ten minutes. She was either deep in thought or she was crying, and there was not a damned thing I could do about it. After a few minutes, she began moving again. I watched until she turned left on Highway 287 and drove north.

She had come looking for answers. Had her trip been wasted? Had I been of any help? I don't know. When asked, I knew of no other way but to tell her what I honestly thought. Go with your heart I had said. It was a simplistic response to the complex and complicated set of issues she was facing And, indeed, that is what she was dealing with. Issues are not to be confused with problems. That much I had learned in one of my engineering classes.

Partly, I was told, it is a matter of semantics, but issues arise only when you began dealing with solutions *to* problems and when a variety of divergent opinions surface. That is where she was. She had defined her problems, but she hadn't solved any of them, because she was still sorting through lists of potential solutions. She might have narrowed her choices today but, at some point, she must decide. There were, for example, several courses of action she could pursue in dealing with Taylor. One was to let her return to Denver for her Senior year in highschool. Another was to force her to stay in Montana. Yet another was to give her a choice. Selecting the latter option, effectively put the burden on Taylor's shoulders which, in my view, was precisely where it belonged. Any choice Megan made for Taylor was potentially destructive to their relationship anyway, so why not let the youngster decide.

She had asked and I had given her my opinion, but at least in Taylor's case, I thought it was a moot point to begin with. Nothing, including her father and her friends, could prompt Taylor to do anything but stay with her mother no matter where that was. I was sure of it. Why didn't I tell her that? Or had I in a round about way? I think maybe I had.

There were matters which must be addressed in a context of practicality too, and my suggestion that she live at Michele's old place and drive into Bozeman when she must seemed to address that criterion.

She certainly had my sympathies. She was dealing with a form of cancer that might cut short her life in her prime. She was dealing with not one but two heart wrenching sets of problems Barely through a divorce, she was now staring directly into the face of cancer and uncertainty, or worse, an early death. What could I do to ease her burden, what could anyone do? We could tell her everything was going to be okay. But what did we know? She had said as much herself. Still we said it again because we wanted it to be true, hoped that it might help, and because we didn't know what else to say.

I had never had cancer, hoped I never would, but I also wasn't buying into the notion that a positive attitude could beat it. I think Megan knew that better than any of us, and she was bearing the burden of that reality, make no mistake about it. No, a positive attitude might help maintain a decent quality of life and help one contend, but that was all. Megan already knew that, better than all the rest of us. She had said, hadn't she, that what cures cancer is research on causes and prevention, pharmaceutical breakthroughs, sophisticated diagnostic tools, treatment trials, and competent, dedicated physicians. How do I know that? Too many obituaries, spoke of the gallant battle the deceased had waged against cancer but lost. In such cases, positive attitudes were not enough. Megan was dealing directly and responsibly with things like the strong person she was. Who could ask for more?

Charlie, my smooth riding gelding, had been waiting in the corral for over three hours. I didn't want to disappoint him so we went for a ride around the quarter section, with the little mare tagging along behind. Then I put a halter and lead rope on the mare and we rode the three miles to Michele's Ranch. I had been there several times to help her with this and that, so it was familiar to me, but there had been one big change I didn't know about. Back under the trees behind the ranch house sat a new double-wide mobile home. Earl and Jason were installing skirting around its bottom to keep rodents and cold winds out. Clearly, Jenny and Claire had already made their decision. Megan's approval, in their minds, was but a formality.

With the addition of Michele's land, they had expanded enough to warrant hiring another full time hired hand. Earl was steady and he knew cows and machinery. Jason was just a kid, but he had Montana cowman written all over him. He was involved in his High School rodeo team, riding saddle bronc, bareback, and team roping. His weekend heading partner at amateur rodeos in the valley was his dad, and they both swung a mean rope.

I knew the place was in good hands with the Carmacks. The place couldn't run by itself, and we were already stretched pretty thin. As ranch manager...that's what they were now calling me... I knew I would be bouncing back and forth between my place, the Macintosh Ranch and here. Michele's interests had been acquired through a turn-key transaction, which meant the land, cattle, machinery and everything else on the place now belonged to Claire and Jenny. They had parted with a wad of the green to acquire this place, which made my transaction with them slink off into a dark corner, like the embarrassed kid who had just farted in Sunday School.

They both stood up when they saw me and waited for me to ride up to them.

"Don't you guys ever take a day off?" I asked.

"Oh, yes, we do," Earl replied, "but Mom wants to get settled before Megan runs us out of the house."

"Megan was just over," I said. "She never mentioned anything about moving in here."

"I know, but they're counting on it, Claire and Jennifer, I mean," was his reply. "We don't mind this double wide at all. First new place we've ever lived in. Got three bedrooms, too."

"Well, I'm glad, boys," I said, "You do a good job for Jenny and Claire. Lucky they've got you."

"Appreciate that, Jim," he replied. "We do our best. Jason is a big help too."

Jason hadn't said a word up to that point. He was a quiet young man anyway, unless he was playing basketball or baseball, and even then he let his jump shot or his bat and arm do his talking.

"How you doing, Jason?" I asked.

"I'm doing good, Jim. And you?"

"Been having a stretch of good these past few weeks, and it's going to get better if my kids can make it out here for a while."

"Yes, sir," he said. "I'll bet."

"You ever meet them?"

"Nope."

"When they come I'll bring them over."

"Yes, sir."

"Morgan must be about you're age."

"Is Morgan the girl?"

"Yep. She's a nice girl. You'll like her."

"Yes sir."

Jason was a good kid, but he didn't waste much breath on long conversations. "Well, boys," I said, "I'll let you know when Morgan gets here. Bye."

I was smiling as I rode away, and I could think of no one I'd rather see take Morgan to a movie at the Mall in Bozeman than Jason. I had already made up my mind I was going to fix my daughter up with one of the valley's nicest young men.

In and out of the Macintosh house every day, I bumped into both Megan and Taylor several times. They seemed to be settling in nicely, and Megan was cheerful and talkative. I asked her if she had been to the doctor yet and she said she had. Everything was normal. So far so good. I prayed it would stay that way. She was out and about the ranch, often with Jenny and Taylor.

During lunch, Megan announced that she and Taylor were going to spend the afternoon in Virginia City. Taylor had never been to this old time gold rush city and one time Capitol of Montana. Many of the old buildings had been designated as National Historic Places, often with much of the period furniture still in place. Others, of equal historic significance, housed a host of specialty shops, and there were guided tours of the town highlighting events which occurred there more than a hundred years ago. They would enjoy it.

Jennifer had one of her lady friends coming so she begged off. Mrs. Weer, I think. I was working in the Quonset repairing a busted sickle when Jennifer showed herself in the yawning doorway.

"I'm in a hurry, Jim," she said, "but I wanted to ask you a favor."

"Sure," I said, "anything."

"Take Megan to town for a show and dinner, will you?" she said.

"I think it would be good for her. Would you mind?"

"No, I'd be happy to do it," I said. "What about Taylor?"

"No, it's Taylor's idea. She thinks her mother needs a diversion from the routine around here. Too much time to sit around and think."

"Okay, if she'll go. I'll ask her tonight."

She didn't buy my suggestion that I needed a night out and that I was hoping she would come along for company.

"They're paying you to do this aren't they, Jim?" she asked as she slipped into the shotgun seat of my truck. "This is my night out, not yours, right? I don't need a night out. I'm perfectly content to sit around, doing nothing."

"No, it's not what you think," I lied. "I thought we could both use a break. Ah, what the hell, I guess they thought you needed a little therapy compliments of Dr. Jim. It wasn't my idea, I'll admit, but I don't recall anyone having to twist my arm very hard before I became an accomplice."

"Oh, they mean well, I guess, so what the heck. Anyway I didn't get all gussied up to sit around home and watch television."

And all gussied up she was. She was wearing a beige skirt and a loose fitting blue and white blouse tucked in at the waistline. A row of tiny white buttons ran from her neckline to her waist, and they were made of the same pearly material as her ear rings. Her hair was combed back on the sides of her head and pinned there to keep it from tumbling over her shoulders. She had a scrubbed, outdoor-living, clean look about her, and I knew she would be by far the most beautiful woman in Bozeman this night. I would bet my place in the foothills that no one would come close in the eye department, and I would win.

I felt both conspicuous and out of place sitting across from her in my nearly new jeans and a long-sleeved, grey chambray shirt buttoned to within one button of the top. But I would tough it out. I was on a therapeutic mission, and I meant to do my duty.

We were leaving early because my plan included dinner, followed by a movie, followed by a stop at one of the local clubs for a couple of drinks. It wasn't until we reached Four Corners that I made up my mind as to where we would eat. When I reached the intersection that was the focal point of the town, I knew I was heading to Belgrade. I knew how to get there, I just couldn't recall the name of the establishment Ask me precisely where we were going, and I couldn't tell you. But I knew I would find it eventually, and I did. The Bar Three supper club, located on the west side of a large downtown brick building, had a rustic, western motif but the menu was varied and extensive.

It was already starting to get busy, but we didn't have to wait. The young waitress we followed to a corner table leaned over and whispered that the young man playing the guitar and singing country was her boyfriend. "He's really good," she said.

Megan turned a few heads as she walked ahead of me to our table. An older lady two tables away waved at her and asked her how she was doing. This was Montana. The word was out. Everyone knew everyone and everything.

The food was excellent and we small-talked our way through dinner, then sat and nursed our coffee for an hour or so.

I looked at her over my steamy cup of coffee and asked her straight out, "So, Megan, the truth. How are you feeling?"

"Good." was her reply. "Good. But of course I'm a bit worried, I suppose."

"Wouldn't be normal if you weren't," I said. "Maybe what you need to do is immerse yourself in something other than worry. That's what my place gave me. I needed something to lose myself in, and building it up to what it is now gave me that."

"Sounds like you think I should get a job," she offered almost absent mindedly."

"Wouldn't have to be a job. It could be almost anything. With your background in financial counseling, though, you could probably figure a way to work at home, using a computer. The commute would be a short one, from your kitchen to your bedroom office. You'd still be free to make your trips to town for blood work and ct-scans, but you could hang closer to your parents and enjoy a less hectic lifestyle."

"And...?"

"And it might help you back away from thinking about problems and issues all of the time," I concluded, "but it is only a reprieve, and eventually you will have to deal with them. If you don't, external forces will do it for you and, perhaps, not in a way you'd like."

"Makes sense," she replied. "Shouldn't we be going?"

She was right. I paid the check, dropped a ten dollar bill in to the singing cowhand's hat, and we left for Bozeman.

The movie was a tear jerker about an elderly couple struggling to cope with the loss of a daughter who had taken her own life. In its own way, it was instructive. Its flashbacks pulled at your heartstrings and you wanted to shout to them that it was okay or that, no, they were making a mistake. In the end, they were consoled by knowing they had done their best under circumstances largely beyond their control and that only faith in her own goodness and worthiness could have saved the daughter. Not exactly what I would have selected for our movie fare, but it was Megan's choice, and I think she enjoyed it. Tears spawned by the filmic experiences of people like yourself, probably reflect an actual emotional connection with what is occurring on the screen. It's a little like the "hook" journalists talk about. Movies made for entertainment alone are inherently failures unless you are a teen-ager, or in doing so, they touch your emotional self in some manner.

We bypassed the after-movie drinks and headed for home. When we got there we sat in the truck talking about nothing and everything, both of which had a way of dovetailing with the state of her health.

"You know, Jim, when I heard that doctor in Denver tell me I had pancreatic cancer," she said, "my world collapsed before me in a nano second and I was sure I was going to die."

"Sounds like some of what you were thinking turned out to be incorrect," I observed.

"I know, but do you mind if we talk about it anyway?" she asked. "I need to put into perspective what has happened to me, and telling someone else of my thoughts seems to help."

"No, you go right ahead, Megan," I said. "We've already agreed that our experiences of tonight falls under the heading of therapy, and if you want to tell me something, the night is not over."

"Okay, and thanks," she began slowly. "I've never said any of this to anyone, so you are the unlucky recipient. Let me begin again. When I first heard that I had one of the more aggressive and deadly forms of cancer, I was so stunned. I was speechless. I walked out of that doctor's office in shock. There I was, a girl in her early forties, being told that surgery *might* save my life, but that it was a big *might*. Rogue cells left behind could come back and attack my body even if the surgery seemed successful, they said."

"I can't begin to comprehend what you must have been thinking about then," I said.

"What was I thinking about then?" she mused aloud. "I was thinking I was as good as dead. That my time had come. But, you know, I couldn't fully grasp what was happening, and I think that is why I didn't bust into tears or scream in anger. They had never been very definitive about my chances. When I look back I think I know why. They didn't know. I had a chance, but I was still a walking, stare-straight-ahead Zombie when we went to Rochester. I told myself, no, this couldn't be happening. I knew I needed something to shield me from having to face a future forever changed, a future that meant I had to wrap myself around the concepts of living and dying. In fact, knowing what I knew about pancreatic cancer, I thought it was really a matter of preparing my self for death."

"You could have fooled me," I said, "when you say you had all but accepted the worst possible outcome. I never picked up on that. Not from you."

"But that *was* my frame of mind," she responded, "when I watched one of the nurses plaster my abdomen with some type of antiseptic solution, I was trying to be brave, but it wasn't easy. I had always thought that when my time came, I would make a kicking and screaming exit, but just then I was doing none of that. I was half convinced I wouldn't even survive the operation. And I don't remember agonizing over the denial...why me...anger...depression... acceptance gauntlet. Or is that where I am right now? It might be, and it might explain why I am so accepting of whatever lies in store for me. I feel like I should be angry with someone."

"Be angry at me, if it helps," I said. "That's what friends are for."

"I do remember saying to myself, damn the luck!" she continued, "but that was about it. Some might argue that I am in the denial phase right now but don't realize it or won't admit it. I don't think so. I had accepted whatever was to happen...good or bad...almost immediately after first being told that I had cancer and, in doing so, had erased the need to agonize over something I couldn't control. Whatever the outcome, I had already pretty much accepted the fact that dying is, in many respects, nothing more than the final step in the living process. I'm not one of those wonderful souls that makes more of it than that. But, there were things I wanted to do, and I needed to get after them if I could. I didn't have the time to start feeling sorry for myself. It just wasn't a good time for negative thinking. I carried that one more step and stopped thinking period."

"You know what?" I said, "I think you are forgetting something."

"And what is that...?"

"That the surgeon told you she believed she had removed all of the tumor, that you would be placed on a chemotherapy program for a year, and that your chances were much improved from what they seemed before the surgery."

"No," she said pensively, "I haven't forgotten what I was told. And, you know, I do believe I have a good chance of winning. I feel good. No, I feel great. The chemotherapy pills are not as toxic as I thought they might be. I still find it difficult to believe that I am actually sick."

"Maybe, you're not," I said. "You were once, but maybe not anymore. Why not just assume you are going to make it. If it doesn't turn out, deal with it then."

"Damn you, Jim," she said with the resurgence of a wide smile. "You are good."

I told her that with that profound statement, we should call it a night. She agreed and thanked me for a good time. She had the door half open when she leaned toward me and planted a sisterly kiss on my cheek. Then she was gone. I drove home satisfied that I had done my duty.

I saw her only once or twice during the ensuing week. Other matters begged my attention. My kids, as it turned out. They sent me a text message while I was in town with Megan, announcing that they were leaving Baltimore early the following morning. I met them at the airport and brought them home.

"You guys could have knocked me over with a feather," I said, "when I read your message. I hoped you wouldn't wait too long after school ended, and you haven't. What does your mother think of all this, and how long can you stay?"

"We're here aren't we?" was Morgan's flippant reply. "As far as the length of our stay? She left it up to us. Don't get your hopes up too high about getting rid of us soon, though, because just between you and me, we bought only one-way tickets. When you want us out of here, you'll have to spring for the tickets."

"Sorry, no *dinero*," I said, "You'll be here at least until my ship ties up to the dock. You might as well unpack your luggage.

Seriously," I added, "when did you decide now was the time to come?"

"We've been talking about it for a couple of weeks," Morgan said, "but Michael was busy applying for admittance this fall to a couple colleges. Said he couldn't go until the matter was settled. He got the answer he wanted, so here we are."

"And, pray tell me, Michael," I asked, "what have you decided?"

"I'm going to the University, Dad. I've known I wanted to since last year."

"He means the University of Montana, Dad," Morgan interjected. "The University of Montana!"

"I don't believe it," I said, "I don't..."

"It's true," Mike said. "They have a good pre-medicine curriculum and a reciprocity agreement with the University of Washington. Washington accepts a certain number of U of M pre-med students each year, and I plan on being one of them. The clincher was our trip up there at Christmas time. I was pretty sure way back then that I wanted to be a Grizzly!"

"That's is absolutely wonderful, Mike. Now if we could just lure your sister out here on a more permanent basis or, at least for longer stays, that would be a double wonderful."

"Whoa, Dad," Morgan cried, "I just finished my junior year of highschool. I have one to go."

"I know," I said, "but when the time comes, I hope you'll at least consider..."

"I'll have to check out the boys before I make my decision," she said teasingly. "Right now, the University of Maryland has the edge in the boy department."

I jokingly told her that, when the time came, I would be putting on the full court press to line her up with some big, tall cowboy. I failed to mention that I would be starting sooner than she might guess with my down-the-road buddy, Jason.

"Well, we'll see about changing that if we can," I said, "but right now I want you to get unpacked. Jenny and Claire are coming over for a cook out. I've got the makings. Oh, and Megan and Taylor will be here to. You remember Taylor, don't you Mike?"

"Vaguely," he replied with his worst attempt at holding a straight face.

"Anyway, they have decided that they are moving to Montana, but you probably knew that too. They'll be on Michele Lowry's old place, just down the road from here. Claire and Jennifer purchased the place a few months ago.

"There's a cowboy down there you'll want to meet, Morgan," I added.

"No thanks, Dad," she quipped, "We Baltimore woman are much too discriminating to bother with broken down saddle bums."

That girl, I thought. Her newly acquired confidence frightens me. Where is the nearest Nunnery?

The gang from over east came tooling down the road in two vehicles, loaded with sundry food stuff, folding tables, folding chairs, coolers, soda, beer and wine. The front seat of the second vehicle carried Benny and Odin. Benny had been a member in good standing of the Macintosh family for decades: Odin seemed to have found a home there as well, as long as occasional fishing on the Madison

River was part of the job description. They were both good workers and neither could have found homes in a better place.

Pitch dark it was when they pulled out of the yard and headed back to the ranch, minus Taylor. Morgan and her had conspired with myself and Megan to countenance a hastily organized sleep-over. The girls wanted to talk about our trip to Ennis in the morning to haul home a couple of new saddle horses. They didn't know that the new horses were for them. Neither of them had any idea just how much money I had on the range these days. Thanks, old-time cowhand!

In any case, I planned to let them choose, but only after they had ridden them around to demonstrate that they weren't too much horse for their meager riding skills. They were novices, but there would be no plough horses on the Pengilly ranch. Michael rode with us in the rear seat of the extended cab, stealing glances at Taylor, I'm sure.

The horses the girls would choose from, I had seen earlier. The two I had ridden when I visited the small rancher south east of Ennis would have been my choices, but I made up my mind to let the kids choose. My choices were well broke horses with good temperaments, but he had other well broke individuals he was willing to part with if he could get his price...or something close.

Morgan's eyes fell on a 15-hand registered 5-year old Paint mare with a show horse confirmation. Sorrel and white, it was a pretty thing. Girls seem partial to color, but in this case, there was more than color. I had asked that none of the horses be caught up and ready for us. The girls were going to have to catch their own horses when they got back home, and I wanted to see how easy or difficult that would be before I plunked down any money. Morgan rode her mare around the large corral, starting with a walk and ending with an easy canter. It was neither first nor second on my list, but it was sound of confirmation and easy to catch. If she wanted it and the price was reasonable, it was hers.

Like Morgan, Taylor had limited riding experience and was certainly no judge of horse flesh, but she knew what she liked and finally selected another mare, slightly smaller than Morgan's. But she did so only after trying two others. She made her decision, I'm sure, only when she sensed she could handle the horse and when she was comfortable with its gate. It wasn't as flashy as Morgan's *overo* paint, but it had a nice blaze on its face and two stockings on the rear. Both horses were sound in conformation, and both had good looking heads and small ears.

While the girls rode around the corral, I settled up with the owner and bought two more used 15-inch saddles and a couple of bridles and halters. What I liked about the two mares, as much as anything else, was the fact that they handled well with D-ring snaffle bits instead of the harsher curb bits. They loaded without any problems, and we were on our way home after a short detour to a local drive-in for burgers and fries. The girls were looking forward to spending a lot of time in the saddle, but they had no idea as we drove north toward Norris that they would soon be proud owners.

When we got home we threw the new horses in with my two bay geldings and my sorrel mare to let them get acquainted. Mike tied in with us, and we spent most of the afternoon riding around and over my 158.8 acres. The girls made supper...fried egg sandwiches and cokes...before we piled into the truck to haul Taylor home.

On the way I announced that the horses were a gift from me to them so long as they stayed at my place or over at Michele's, in Taylor's case. They thanked me with screams, a peck on the cheek, and a hug. I wasn't just softening Morgan up for Jason. I had plans for a trip into the back country when they were ready for a lot of ups and downs, overs and unders. I knew they would feel better about that if they were mounted on their own horses.

Juggling work and play wasn't easy. It never is when the work to be done is work that *has* to be done. It was a busy time at the Macintosh Ranch, with no end of tasks to look after. Weather was always a consideration and I, for one, was always looking over my shoulder for angry clouds lurking on the horizon.

Rain and haying are a bad mix, and at the moment, we were baling the first cutting of alfalfa, which took most of my time and all of Benny and Odin's. Rain, rain, stay away! The hundreds of round bales kicking out the back end of the baler had to be hauled to make way for the next crop. Claire's open-sided but roofed pole barn provided the cover needed to maintain its high quality. The sprinkler system had to be serviced and made ready. That job fell to me when I could find a couple hours of slack time in the bale hauling. A couple hundred head of crossbred steers housed in the feedlot had to be tended to every day. Manure built up in the other pens, waiting to be removed.

The Carmacks were running Megan's place like they would their own, which was just what we needed. I was spread pretty thin what with having to manage things on Jenny and Claire's place as well as my own. Luckily, Megan was there to help occupy the girls, and Taylor had her driver's license so the two teens could make a run to town on their own if they got really bored.

No one expected me to be a one man entertainment committee, least of all the kids. They were really young adults, and they could take care of themselves. Michael needed nothing to fill his idle hours, because he had none.

When Claire learned he was going to be at the University in the fall, he had hired him immediately. So far, he was doing odd jobs, of which there were many, but as he learned to operate the tractors, he found himself dozing out the feed lot manure, loading bales, or grading the road between the ranch and my own place. He was one of those young men who saw in each task he was asked to complete an opportunity to learn. Out in the sun all day long, usually stripped to the waist, he was as tan as any kid spending the summer as a life guard at the pool.

We did manage a short canoe trip on the Upper Yellowstone one Saturday afternoon. We rented canoes in Livingston and hauled them upstream to an access area near Emigrant and floated and paddled about fifteen miles to another public access point where we spent the night. We had some current to help us along but, thankfully, no white water to test our limited skills.

It fell to Michael and I to steer the two canoes between river stretches boasting a profusion of rocks in the channel. The girls took their turn but were totally inept. It was a perfect stretch for novices. And we all marveled at the number of drift boats and rafts close against the banks, with fishermen's fly rod lines cutting the air like whips. None of that intrigued the kids, but I can't say that for tubing. Dozens of young people floated on the water, laughing and hollering back and forth. Most of them were drinking beer and being somebody. It looked like fun. I envied them.

On a warm and cloudless Saturday afternoon near the end of June, I sat alone on the porch with a wistful eye on the Madison Mountain Range to the east. Megan and Jennifer had taken the kids into Bozeman to bum around and to cruise the many shops on Main. Michael had gone as well at the insistence of Taylor. So, I was on my own, wondering if I should just sit there and relax or get up and busy myself with something. Riding out to check my cows and calves won out. Life had been good to me lately, and semi-lazy weekends were a part of that. Life was good. Things were definitely looking up.

I could not have been more mistaken. What started out as another great day in what had been as a string of great days brought me news that sent me spiraling downward to the depths of despair, sorrow unlike anything I had ever experienced. It started with a soft knock on my door as I sat at the kitchen table nursing a second cup of coffee before I stepped out to saddle my horse. Filling the doorway when I opened it was Michele's brother, Martin.

I hadn't seen him since that Sunday morning several months earlier when he had come into the Over Easy Café in Bozeman while we were having breakfast. He lived up near Coeur d' Alene, Idaho, where he was both a rancher and a partner in a large law firm. That was all I knew about him. Had I met him on the street I might not have recognized him. He was well known to Claire and Jenny, but an unknown quantity to me. I wondered why he would be at my doorstep, and I quickly found out why. I naturally assumed it had something to do with Michele. And, indeed, it did.

"Please, sit down, Marty," I said, "A cup of coffee?"

"Thank you, but no," he replied. "I've been over at the Macintosh place for the past couple of hours talking to Claire. He plied me with enough coffee for two men my size.

"But a glass of cold water would be nice," he added.

I dropped some ice cubes in a large glass, filled it at the kitchen sink and handed it to him.

"I'm afraid I am the bearer of bad news, Jim, very bad news," he began. "I'll dispense with the preliminaries and tell you that my sister, Michele, was killed in a car accident three days ago near Durango, Colorado. Her brakes failed going down a steep grade, and she smashed into the mountain side."

"Oh, God, no!" I cried. "Not Michele!" I was transfixed, petrified as if turned to stone. I could say no more. I was instantaneously in shock. Tears ran down my face. I stood up, trying to collect myself, but I couldn't, and I began sobbing uncontrollably. I could barely stand. I felt a steadying and consoling hand on my shoulder, and I looked up to see Marty Larson, bear of a man that he was, crying like a baby too. I don't know how long we clung to each other, but it was obvious he hadn't fully come to grips with her loss himself.

"Let's sit down, Jim," he said after a while. "There's more."

"More?" I said, "How could there be? I was trying to gather myself, but I could not shut off the flow of tears from my eyes. My world had just ended. The love of my life was gone.

"My wife and I have been worried for some time about Michele's health," Marty said haltingly, "her emotional health, more specifically. I have traveled to Colorado several times these past few months to see if I could get to the bottom of her sorrow. That's what is was. I know that now.

"Anyway," he continued, "she finally confided in me about two months ago that she had fallen in love with you some time ago but had left you for fear her heart would be broken a second time. She never really go over the loss of her husband, you know."

"I know and, yes, it's true," I stammered. "We did...we both fell in love. I knew that the loss of her husband had left deep wounds in her heart, and she missed him 'til I think she began to think she couldn't stand it any more. And I believe she came to believe she would lose me too. I don't know why, but she was never able to cast out that doubt and fear. I tried to persuade her otherwise, but she was having none of it."

"She told me as much, Jim," Marty concurred.

"I loved her more than I have ever loved anyone in my life, Marty," I sobbed. "She said she needed time to deal with her fears, and I said I would give her that time. The last words I said to her were that I loved her. Hers were the same. I was a fool. I should never have let her go. I should have kidnaped her or something. I should have held her against her will. I'll never forgive myself for letting her go."

"She was coming back to you, Jim," Marty said, "if it's any consolation. When I visited her about a month ago, she told me so. She has been working at the local hospital and had given them her notice when the accident happened. She needn't have worked. She did so only to fill her mind with something besides the memory of her husband and her love for you. She was a wealthy woman, Jim. She owned our mom and dad's place, and her husband had several hundred thousand dollars of insurance. You may not have known that."

Speech deserted me again. What could I say?

"I have something I need to give you," he said, handing me a large manila envelope. "It's from her, and I know, among other things, that there is a letter for you enclosed."

I opened the package slowly, and withdrew its contents. It contained several sheets but the first was a hand written letter to me, dated less than a month ago.

Dear Jim, it began, *You said you would give me time to make a decision.*

I should have known that only a man who loved me dearly would do that. I am writing to tell you that I have made up my mind. It never was a matter of loving you or not loving you. You know that. It was always a matter of whether I was strong enough to take a chance on having my heart broken again. I know now that I was wrong and silly not to take that chance. So, if you will have me, I am yours. As soon as I can get packed and attend to a couple of other things, I'll be on my way back to you. I'm sure you already know I sold the rest of my land to Jennifer and Claire. So I have no place to go but to you.

Oh, if you look at the attached papers you will see that I have signed a quick claim deed giving you the land we came to think of as our special place. It's all perfectly legal. Marty did it for me. I hope you will take me there often. Love you, Michele

I sat there for minutes saying nothing. What was there to say? Fate had dealt our love a crushing blow. What should have been, what almost was, could never be. She had left me the task of dealing with the loss of a loved one, the very thing we both feared.

"I loved her, Marty," I said. "Goddamn, I loved her." Tears were falling again, and I couldn't stop them. "I'll always love her, and I'll never forget her.

"Can we bury her up among the rocks and trees?" I blurted.

"She would love that, Jim," Marty replied.

"She wanted to come home. This is home," I said "That way, we can always be together."

Three days later, on by far the worst day of my life, her friends laid her to rest up in the rocks among the pine trees, with the vast valley spreading out below her. Two hundred people attended, driving 4-wheel drive pickup trucks, Lincoln Town Cars, Cadillac's, Chevy Cavalier's, jeeps and, yes, even motorcycles. She was loved by many from all walks of life. The lone black limousine had brought the State's Lieutenant Governor and the President of Montana State University. Marty gave the eulogy and every person there, regardless of their station in life, wept for her memory.

For many I was a stranger, a newcomer to the foothills, and only a neighbor. But I was also the only one present dying inside and not convinced I could go on. I silently pledged to myself and to all of them that I would love her forever and would never forget the joy she had brought to my life. In the car we were quiet, each of us looking inward at our thoughts We leaned on each other for support and comfort. Tears trickled down Claire's cheeks, while Jenny, Megan and I cried unabashedly. I failed miserably in showing my strength. My kids followed behind in wonder.

No one knew, except for Marty and his wife, that Michele and I had been in love. I think Jennifer guessed, but she had never said anything to me. In fact, I would not have been at all surprised to learn that she hoped, in time, we might marry.

My children were confused by my outpouring of grief, for this person they had never seen, but they too remained silent. One day I would tell them.

Chapter 8

The assertion that when it rains it pours is a platitude common-ly used to portray times in our life when stuff piles up before us faster than we can deal with it. I use a platitude now and then. Who doesn't? Most of the time they are given more credibility than they deserve but, now and again, they are absolutely true. We bur-ied Michele on a Tuesday and two days later, Megan learned that her Thursday ct-scan contained the shadow of a large mass pressing against her left lung. Her Bozeman doctor notified the Mayo Clinic immediately, and her doctor there called her an hour later advising her to return to the Clinic for tests. He said that he didn't wish to alarm her, but a biopsy was needed as soon as she could get there. It may be nothing, he observed, but we are concerned. That mass just shouldn't be there.

Claire's phone call that evening brought me the news. The kids and I immediately dropped everything, jumped into the truck, and drove over to the ranch. They were all doing their best to hold up under Megan's devastating news, but the red eyes told me otherwise.

"You didn't have to come over, Jim," Megan said. "I told Dad not to bother you."

"I'm glad he did. *We* are glad he did," I said, nodding my head in the direction of Michael and Morgan. "What exactly did you hear from Mayo?"

"The doctor in Bozeman found a mass up against my left lung," she replied. "He said not to be alarmed, but what else am I supposed to be? The surgeon in Rochester said it might be a collection of fat-like substances that formed within the abdominal cavity, following surgery, but that a biopsy would be needed to confirm what it is. The surgeon admitted she was concerned but only mildly so."

"I don't get it," I said.

"Well, you're talking to the wrong person if you're looking for a clear explanation," she said. "I only know what they told me. They think it might be this fatty material that came together inside my abdomen following surgery as a result of weight loss. But it could be more of...well, you know what."

"Have you been feeling okay?"

"I've been feeling just fine. Better every day for that matter."

"Well, let's hope that is all it is," I said. "What happens now?"

"Back to Rochester, I guess. Mom and Taylor will fly down with me."

"Do you want me to come along?"

"Thanks, but no," she said, "I know my way around down there now far better than I want to, and Mom and Taylor will be there, just in case."

"I'd certainly be willing to accompany you," I said. "Benny and Odin and Mike can handle things around here. How about Claire, wouldn't he feel better if he were there?"

"I think *I* would feel better if you were all there, but I want to do this myself."

"Well, if you're sure..."

"I'm sure. I'm sure."

The kids and I settled for that, but I reminded her before we left that we were a phone call away should she need us. She would only be gone for three days if the biopsy came out negative for cancer, she said. The doctor in Bozeman had told her that if the results were negative, they would continue to watch it on future scans, hoping it would disappear or grow smaller over time.

Three days later, Claire and I were at the airport to pick them up. The test results confirmed the surgeon's surmise and, for that, we were all truly thankful. Her oncologist did tell her that her red blood cells were elongated, which probably meant that her down-sized stomach was of insufficient size to absorb the Vitamin B12 her body needed and, that beginning immediately, he would increase the dosage of the shot she was getting once a month.

I liked what I saw. The good news had erased the worry lines from her brow and softened the thread like vessels of redness in her eyes. That old sparkle was back there where it belonged, highlighting the tiny, incomparable white flecks in each iris. I was beginning to see some evidence, through her transformation, that there was a connection between the mind and the physical self.

The 4th of July fell on a Friday, and I decided the firecrackers, rockets, and sparklers should be augmented with a special celebration for Megan. Oh, to be honest, it wasn't my brainchild alone. Morgan, Jennifer and Taylor were the perpetrators or, should I say, the actual brain trust when it came to details. It would be held at my place, at my request, because it was the only way we could pull it off without Megan knowing ahead of time. If my plans came to fruition, there would be a surprise for Michael and Morgan as well, because I had surreptitiously made phone calls to the Pengillys and Hales, inviting them to come...and to stay awhile if they could. Other guests included the Carmacks.

I had never met Earl's wife, Ellen, but she answered the phone when I called. I introduced myself and explained that we were planning some Independence Day festivities at my place and that we hoped the Carmacks could be there. She accepted immediately and asked what she could bring. I said I wouldn't have any idea what that might be, but if she wanted she could call Jenny. I had the steaks, brats, dogs, hamburger patties, and beer in my fridge along with a couple dozen cobs of sweet corn.

"Just bring yourselves, Ellen," I said, "and be sure Jason comes along. There's three kids over here who would like to meet him."

I had barely hung up the phone before it began ringing again. It was Megan. She said she was coming over. Come on over I said. Half an hour later she drove into the yard in one of her Dad's trucks.

"Hi, stranger," I said. "Things are going well with you?"

"They are," she replied, "and for that I am thankful."

I told her to come and sit with me on the porch, thinking she had something specific she wanted to talk to me about.

"Alcohol?" I asked. "Can you drink any?" She said she could drink it, but only infrequently and in small amounts.

"I'm going to have a beer," I said. "You? I've got wine as well."

"A beer sounds good. As long as it is very cold, almost freezing."

I skipped into the house long enough to grab two frosty ones, flipped the tab on hers and handed it to her. She said nothing in the world was as good as the first sip of cold beer on a hot day. I agreed completely, having reached the same conclusion long ago. She also said out front that she wasn't there for her usual counseling. I told her it was a good thing. My session rates had skyrocketed because of demands for my services. I guess the word had got out, I said, tongue-in-cheek, how good I am. We chuckled at that, but neither of us said anything more 'til we'd finished our beers. We sat there lost in our own thoughts, as we panned the valley and the Madison range.

"Want another?" I asked.

"Nope," she replied. "I came over to go for a horseback ride with you. I feel strong enough, and I wanted to check out the mare you bought for Taylor. You didn't have to do that, you know."

"I know," I said, "but I wanted to. She's a good kid. Morgan and her have become best friends and, besides, I figured any self respecting Montana cowgirl needed her own horse."

"I hope she thanked you," she said.

"She did, profusely," I answered, "and I'll thank you if you'll get yourself out of that easy chair and come with me to saddle the horses. Anyplace special you'd like to go."

"Back up into Michele's rocky outlook for starters. Then I'd like to just ride up into the mountains."

"Let me pack some lunch and make a pot of coffee," I said.

"No, I'll do that, Jim, while you're saddling those horses. Okay?"

It *was* okay and I trotted off toward the horses. I tied a small tarp behind my saddle and slickers behind both. The tarp was for sitting; the slickers for rain. I never went into the mountains without a bit of preparation. Resting at the bottom of my saddlebag was a jar of peanut butter. It was a quick source of energy, and a person could live off it a long time if necessary. I didn't come by that gem of information through experience. But I had met a man who worked at the Smithsonian Institution in Washington who swore by it. He was a man who had logged thousands of miles hiking on dozens and dozens of trails throughout the world. "As good as trail mix," he told me. It seemed to me that when he wasn't eating peanut butter, he must have been writing, for he had authored 12 books about his adventures.

Both my gelding and Taylor's mare were experienced trail horses. That much we knew from the riding we had done around our place which, of course, lacked the dramatic topographic features of the Roots. Still, there were enough ups and downs to give all of us a good workout. I led them to the water tank, but they snubbed the offer. Then I draped their reins over the hitch rail I had put up in front of the cabin, and walked up the single step to the porch. Megan met me at the door and told me I had a phone call.

"It's a woman," she said. "Asked for Morgan. Probably Rebecca."

The voice *was* that of Rebecca. She called frequently asking for Morgan or Michael, if the former was not about. If I happened to pick up the receiver, we usually had our obligatory *how-are-you* exchange but seldom more than that.

"I was calling for Morgan, Jim," she said. "I take it she isn't there."

"No, the voice your heard was Jenny and Claire's daughter, Megan. I think I mentioned her last time we talked. She's recovering from some pretty major surgery. We were just ready to go for a ride up into some pretty rocks near here."

"Well, that's nice," was her terse reply.

"Morgan isn't here just now," I said. "Truth is I'm not sure where she is. Probably another shopping run to Bozeman. I'll have her call when she returns."

"No, that's not really necessary," she said wistfuly, "Nothing special to talk about. I was just lonesome for her."

"Then I'll be sure and tell her you called. She has her lonesome times too. Daughters and Moms need to talk every once in a while."

"Thanks, Jim, I'd appreciate it. Bye."

Megan was waiting for me on the porch. "Are you ready to hit the trail," I asked, trying to sound as much as I could like Ward Bond. She nodded her head, and we mounted up, riding toward a sun that was just beginning its gradual decent. The day was perfect for something like this. I was glad she had asked.

It took us only about fifteen minutes to reach the side trail leading to the rock formation. We ground tied our horses at the bottom and worked our way slowly toward the top. I offered my hand to her to help her keep her balance on the rocky ground, and I stopped a couple of times to ask her how she was doing. We spent only about 15 minutes up in the rocks, part of the time staring down at Michele's native head stone. Upon it were etched in lower case the words, "*a love lost*". They were my words, with her family's approval, but they meant far more to me than anyone would have guessed, or so I thought.

"You loved her, didn't you, Jim?" were the words Megan uttered even as I stood there trying to paint a picture in my mind of her lovely face. I was taken aback to say the least. Never had I given Megan or any of the others even the slightest hint about my feelings.

I looked straight into her eyes as we stood shoulder to shoulder next to her grave, and said, "Yes, I did. How did you know?"

"Your eyes," she replied. "I never guessed until this moment."

"It wasn't meant to be, I guess. I thought it was, but..."

"I'm sorry Being unlucky in love, as the both of us have been, doesn't mean there isn't someone out there we were born to be with. I have to believe that."

"Hope your right," I said. "Come on, we better get high-tailing it up the hill or we'll have to find our way back by the light of the moon."

"A silvery moon?" she asked. "You know what that could mean, don't you?

"Nope. Tell me."

"It could mean that it's shining for you and me alone."

"Not likely," I said, wishing immediately I hadn't.

"Okay," she replied. "Bad idea huh?"

"Not bad, just improbable."

"Why do you say that, Jim?"

"You can do better. You deserve better."

Was she teasing or was she fishing? I wondered. Those were the questions I continued to ponder as we rode up the road toward the mountains. If it were the former, I could tease back with the best of them. If she was fishing, her creel was still empty. I wasn't biting, but I *was* sorry about my knee-jerk response.

"A silvery moon wouldn't be that bad," I said, hoping to take the edge off my earlier response. I guess any moon is a good moon when you're riding towards the mountains in Montana."

"Let's bring the kids up here soon," she said, ignoring my feeble attempt to soften my hasty words. "Before school starts and they all head out in different directions."

"Good idea. Can't wait long. Morgan is probably heading back to Baltimore in the next couple of weeks. I think her mother was calling today to find out when."

I opened the barbed-wire gate next to the cattle crossing, and she led our horses out on to the grazing permit and the real beginning of the mountains. It was exactly where I had begun my solo trip up here earlier. But, the sun told me we shouldn't penetrate the wild canyons very far before we turned back and headed home. Even in the moonlight, silvery or otherwise, the back trail was treacherous in the darkness.

The Tobacco Root Mountains must be very old, I'm thinking, for they were falling apart like the bodies of used up humans and all sorts of animals. In the distance, we could see massive collections of crumbled rock clinging to the sides of slopes or resting on the bottoms of canyon floors. Granite debris, some as small as coarse gravel and others the size of a pickup truck, littered the base of the slopes and even crossed the valley floor to come to rest part way up the other side. From Claire and Jenny's place, the Tobacco Roots were an awesome sight but gave not the slightest hint of their almost four dozen mountain peaks that reached nearly two miles above sea level.

That was the view from afar. Close up it was even more spectacular with deep canyons and broad vistas at every turn in the trail. I had traveled well beyond the point where we turned to start back down. Our back trail was littered with boulders and shelves of rocks perched trail side and, in some ways, it was more exciting than the trail that led up into the clouds. Heading up we faced a seemingly never ending high country that looked impenetrable from where we stood. Below was the Madison River Valley and the Madison Range beyond. Beyond that the Spanish Peaks, the Gallatins, and the Bridger Range north of Bozeman. Taken together, it was sufficient to catch the breath of even a world traveler.

On the way down, we stopped more times than I can remember. Several were to make sure Megan was okay and others simply to take in the country below and beyond. I think I recognized well before she did that we had reached too deeply into the Roots and that we had a very difficult ride ahead of us to reach the foothills and home. It was almost dark when we pulled up to the catch pens and the small lake located on the east edge of the grazing permit.

"Let's stop here for a minute, Megan," I said. "We'll water the horses and then make for my place."

"Must we? Couldn't we just stay here by this lake?" she asked.

"We're not really set up for staying the night," I said

"Couldn't we throw something together in the way of a lean-to?"

"We could, but we're only about five miles from my place. We could make it easily, though it would be a dark ride."

"Then let's stay." she said, "There's all kinds of kindling along the lake, and we could make a shelter from branches off those pines."

"Or, we could call Benny and have him bring up a trailer to haul us home," I offered as an alternative. I wasn't altogether opposed to staying. It was a nice warm night. No sign of rain. We wouldn't freeze.

But I was worried about her. Was roughing it in her best interests? Did she have medicine she should be taking?

"Give me your cell, Jim," she said, "I'll call." I handed it to her thinking she would heed my suggestion that Benny bring up a trailer.

"Mom," she said, "this is Megan. Jim and I rode up into the mountains this afternoon, and it's too dark to try to make it home tonight. We're going to stay. We are camping near the catch pens, and we have sandwiches and a jar of peanut butter to eat. We've got a big tarp and our slickers. We'll be just fine. Don't worry. This is my idea. I need a night out under the stars. Okay?"

When she handed my phone back to me, she looked straight into my eyes, pleading for my approval. What could I say? It was a done deal. We turned the horses into the pens and began setting up camp. The spot we found a few feet above the lake was level, and I found traces of earlier camps and campfires. I built a lean-to and covered it with the boughs of pine cut from the bottom of nearby trees. Using boughs from the same tree, I covered the ground under the lean-to until we had a veritable mattress shielding us from the irritating slivers of rock beneath. The tarp was large enough to easily cover us during the night when it cooled down as I knew it would. Our fire was just to the front of the lean-to, its heat bouncing back from the cut bank we were perched upon.

We had several sandwiches to eat but no coffee. Still we hung close to the fire and talked. Not about her medical problems as I suspected we would, and not about our being out here under a silvery moon, as I hoped we wouldn't. Mostly we talked about the Madison Valley, the mountains and how privileged we were to be here. And, then there were the horses. We both had an affinity for being mounted on a good horse. Riding through the pine clad foot hills, and feeling the incredible delight of the outdoors that seeps into your heart and spirit, was an added perk.

I had only known her for a few months, but I sensed we were kindred spirits almost immediately, at least as far as Montana was concerned. It was in both of us to siphon off as much of what the country offered as we could. Montana reared, we had both left and returned before we really began to appreciate what we had come back to. In my case, I had returned to Montana but back to a place I had never been.

I watched as she lost herself in our campfire, sounding, I'm fairly sure, the depths of her being and wondering about what the future held for her. In her position, I would have been likewise engaged. She said very little. I was sure she was trying to wrap herself around her future to better know how to deal with whatever joy and sorrow it might portend. She made me want to take her into my arms and hug her hard, but I deliberately avoided doing so. She made me think of a young girl who had encountered a slight of some sort by one of her friends, and was needing someone to hug her and tell her how great she was. Still, I did not want to insert myself into her thoughts, in any way, but I'm sure she knew she was here with a friend who shared her love for the beauty of a night such as this.

I believed, absolutely, that on this night, the eastern slope of the Roots was hosting a sure enough Montana girl and a sure enough Montana guy. And I think it was that thought that brought me around to seeing us as *compadres* who would always know where to go when we were feeling down. I had come to understand that I had become her principal confidant regarding her health and her concerns about the future.

To another, she might seem wrapped up in her health, to the exclusion of everything else, but I knew better. She was simply one of those people who, when forced by circumstances to sound the depth of her beliefs and values, had the courage to do so. I wonder. Is it something we all must in some fashion do when our mortality hangs in the balance? I don't know. What I do know is that she could count on me to help her search for the essence of what she was.

She said she was beginning to feel cold...and tired. Together they were reason enough to crawl beneath the tarp to seek both sleep and warmth.

By morning, I was thankful for the lean-to and the tarp, for high altitudes bring cool evenings even in July. All-in-all we slept on a comfortable bed of pine boughs through the night long after the warmth given off by the embers of our fire had turned to ashes.

When I came awake, I found her back pressed against my chest and I carefully moved away from her. When she stirred, I was already pouring water over the coals of last night's fire to make sure they would not flare up later and send sparks out unto the grass. As is frequently the case, when sleeping on the forest floor, we were both up early and were saddling up when we heard the roar of a truck rushing up the road towards us. Behind the wheel sat a sleepy, smiling Benny Tovar.

"Morning people," he said, as he threw open the truck door and stepped down. "Jenny said you'd be wanting coffee about now. Everything go okay?"

"It was a perfect night, Benny," Megan said, "but I'm glad you came. I've a bunch of things I want to do today."

While we nursed our coffee, Benny backed up to the corral gate and opened the trailer door. Accustomed to being hauled, both horses walked in and stood looking at us through the side-wall slats, as if to say they were anxious to be back in their corral among friends.

We crowded into the front seat, and in 10 minutes we were driving through my gate. Benny left almost immediately with the truck and trailer. Megan opened the door of her truck and slid in under the steering wheel.

"Anytime you want to do this again, Jim," she said, "I'm game, silvery moon or not. I'll be over early on the 4th. These celebrations need a woman's touch." And then she was gone. I watched as her left arm, balancing on the truck's window opening, waved goodbye. We would do it again faster than either of would have guessed, for Morgan announced to Michael and I, while we were doing our supper dishes that night, her plans to leave less than a week after the 4th.

Her declaration advanced our trip with the kids up to the canyons of the Tobacco Roots, and it also prompted me to think about the life our children had inherited in the wake of their mother and father's divorce. The divorce itself had been without rancor, almost friendly, so the scars left by parents determined to blame each other or to pit the children against one spouse or the other were absent. But all that aside, they were now "shuttle" children, never quite knowing where they would be sleeping from month to month, and fearful of alienating one parent or another by seeming to prefer one over the other. Divorces were never children-friendly. Regardless of age and maturity, they needed stability in their lives at a time when parents were least able to provide it.

The court said we had joint custody, but I knew from the outset that sharing equally made no sense. It didn't begin to address the problems the children had to face. In Michael's case, custody had become a moot issue. He was going to do what he was doing, custody notwithstanding. He was working away from home, had been admitted to the University, and knew what he wanted from life. Custody simply did not pertain to him anymore, even though he was yet under the age specified by the court. But Morgan was a different case all together. She had a year left in highschool, she was still mama's little girl, and she was uncertain about college and the future. I felt sorry for her but didn't have a clue as how I might ease her pain.

Ten minutes after Megan and Taylor arrived to help us set things up for our 4ᵗʰ of July bash, my Mom and Dad drove into the yard. Morgan and Mike were genuinely surprised and delighted to see them. Both hurried to greet them and help with their luggage. Grandparents, especially grandmas, are always stabilizers in the lives of their grandchildren, and I never learned why. Even Mike was closer to my mother than to my dad. Someone please explain that to me. Double surprise was the order of the day when half an hour later Grandma and Grandpa Hale lumbered to a stop in their Durango. Morgan and Mike were both flabbergasted and, once again, delighted to see both sets of grandparents. Good kids that they were, they made everyone feel welcome. I introduced Taylor and Megan all around. I had told my mother about Megan's bout with cancer, and had asked her not to bring up the subject unless Megan herself mentioned it.

I found myself scrambling to find chairs for everyone while Megan and Taylor went back into the house to gather dishes from my neither fancy nor coordinated collection. The Carmacks were next and, as host exemplar, I rushed to introduce them. I knew they were nervous since they were, of all the people there so far, known only to me and Megan and Taylor. Earl wore the cowman's uniform, jeans, large silver belt buckle, clean felt hat and a long sleeved shirt buttoned to the top. Ellen was a pretty woman, tall and slender.

Standing next to her, shuffling his feet ever so slightly, stood my pal, Jason. He was as tall as his father which made him taller than either myself or Mike, and he was a handsome young man. I had never seen him without his hat until today. His hair was dark and curly. His eyes were dark as six feet down, and his shoulders were broader than mine. Always when I had seen him before, he was wearing a beat up straw hat or a baseball cap. The long-sleeve shirt, and a gray bandana around his neck were a part of a typical young Montana cowman's uniform. I watched as Morgan hesitated in mid-step when she came out from the cabin and caught sight of him. My plan to show her that Montana's young men could stand toe to toe with any of those Chesapeake Bay dudes was off to a good start.

Claire, Jennifer, Benny and Odin came an hour later, their crew cab truck's box overflowing with plastic chairs and two folding tables. Benny and Odin hauled out two huge coolers filled with plastic soda bottles and several six-packs of beer. It was their contribution, and the smiles upon their faces, as they sat the coolers down, attested to their pride in having come up with the idea...with the idea seeded, of course, by Jenny.

The kids saddled up and went for a ride up into the rocks and then over and around the foothills. As far as I knew, no one yet had any idea that I now owned the 80 acres holding the huge outcropping of granite.

I noticed that Jason was the quieter one of the four youngsters, but Morgan was doing her best to draw him into the group. Way to go, Morgan! When they returned a couple hours later, Mike and Jason fired up the grills without any urging from me, which I took as a signal that they'd had enough chips and soda pop, and were now ready for meat.

My own tarnished reputation as a cook brought Megan and Jenny to the grill to work their culinary magic. I knew Jennifer had blended onion soup and yeast into the burgers. It was her specialty. Claimed the yeast, if given time to work, kept them open enough to internally store the meat's juices instead of letting them seep out on to the briquettes. I couldn't argue with her. They were delicious, and I noticed she got no complaints from the kids, whose tastes ran toward fast-food fare.

I also saw that Jason and Mike were both nursing a can of the frothy stuff. I didn't say anything. What the heck, they were hard working young men, talking about cows and grass, oblivious, or seemingly so, to the two pretty young ladies who were stealing glances when they could. Both had their heads screwed on right, and I had no doubt that one day soon they would be very successful in whatever field they chose Mike was headed toward a career in medicine or chemical engineering, and I had only recently learned that Jason had a full-ride scholarship at Montana State waiting for him when he graduated from highschool in Ennis at mid-year. Why was I not surprised to learn that he would pursue a degree in range management. What else for a young man who was so much a part of the Montana landscape? Ironically, his scholarship was for his skills as a baseball player, but I knew him well enough to know that most of his attention would be focused on range management.

The food was delicious and if there was one among us who did not over indulge I didn't know who it was. Not me, for sure. We sat for a long time, each of us feasting on the scenery in every direction. Not long after darkness closed in, the grandparents inquired as to sleeping accommodations. Finding a place for them to bed down was easy. The Hales slept in my bedroom and the Pengillys in the smaller room Morgan had been using. She slept on the sofa, and I spread my air mattress out on the porch. Michael had gone home with Jason. There was some chemistry there, and I think it had to do in part with their shared seriousness and in part because they were contemporaries possessed of uncommon maturity and optimism about their futures. Watch out world. Those two are marching in your direction!

When everyone was gone, and while the stars twinkled above us, Morgan and I finished washing the dishes and talked about our family brouhaha. We agreed it had been a huge success.

"You know, Dad," she said as she stacked the washed coffee cups on the top cupboard shelf, "I don't really want to go, but I think I better."

"Your Mom's lonesome, right?" I observed.

"She is, and I'm lonesome for her."

I wanted to tell her that I missed her mother too, but it was not so. Oh, I thought of her every once in a while, reminiscing introspectively about the good times. Other times I wondered about her life today. Was she happy? From what I could gather from the kids, she was. I hoped so. Did she have regrets? Of course. As did I.

"Of course, you are, honey," I said, "and well you should be. No matter what happens, no matter the future course of your own life, you will always love her. And you will find love for yourself. Be careful not to mistake a moment's pleasure or companionship for love. Save your love for one you know to be worthy. Do not squander it. It is too precious. You are talking to someone who knows."

"I know," she said. "I won't. Is that what you and Mom did... squander your love?"

"No, in the beginning and, for a long time, we loved each other deeply," I said, "but we let time and love of self erode it and, before we knew it, it was gone. I will always love your Mom, but not in the same way I once did. Looking back, it seems we rushed into marriage, without really being ready. One could argue, I suppose, that our getting married at all was a mistake. How could that be when from that marriage came two wonderful children? No it wasn't a mistake. It was simply a case of two people becoming too wrapped up in themselves. Don't let that happen to you, Morgan."

"I'm going to try not to," she said, "and I need to tell you again that the anger I once felt for you is not there anymore. I blamed you alone when the truth is, I now see that you were *both* guilty of taking the other for granted, and now you are living with the consequences."

Her words moved me in a way I could not have foreseen. Here she was, a teenager, reading to her father from the Book of Morgan. There was in her a serious, contemplative maturity I had never seen before. I was as proud as any father could be.

"I love you, Morgan," I said. "I always will. You are precious."

"I love you too, Dad," she said as she slipped into my arms. "Don't ever take *me* for granted."

"Count on me not doing that, honey."

The folks left Monday morning with promises to visit again soon. Jason brought Michael home shortly thereafter but too late to say goodbye to them. He spoke for a moment with Morgan and then he was gone. I told the kids I had to run into Bozeman for a couple of hours and invited them to come with. Mike took me up on my offer, but Morgan hung back, saying she had to start getting ready. I said that was fine. Clean up the house a little if you get the notion, I said, and throw a bale of brome grass into the horses. She waved at us from the front door as we drove away.

"She has a date with Jason tonight, in case you're interested," Mike said. "It's a double. Taylor and I will be chaperoning."

"Jason's a nice kid," I said, "But does it take the entire day to get ready?" Mike smiled at me knowingly, but said nothing. When we reached Four Corners, he asked what I needed in town."

"Nothing," I said, "but you do."

"Nope. Not me. I don't need anything, period," he responded.

"Yes, you do."

"What?"

I told him he needed wheels. No self respecting working man should have to borrow his Dad's car to go out on a date.

"Besides," I said, "come fall and Missoula, you'll need some means of getting around....and to come home on long weekends. Now, what should we be looking for? A Mustang? How about one of those Sunbirds?"

"Neither," he replied. "I know exactly what I want. A used, red three-quarter ton crew cab, GMC Sierra Grande pickup...with a topper. Ressler's has one. I saw it last week. But I can't afford it. I want to use some of my summer wages for school."

"Here's the deal, Mike. You cut your deal with Ressler's. You sign the note. I'll co-sign. While you're in school, I'll make your payments. When you're working for Claire, they're your responsibility How does that sound?"

"Sounds great, but you don't..."

"But I do," I said. "Just make sure there's some rubber left on those tires."

We were home not long after noon, but I soon learned that prying any work out of Mike was out of the question for the rest of the day. He spent his afternoon washing his most precious possession, while Morgan I watched from the porch.

"When is it my turn, Dad?" Morgan inquired.

"Maybe next summer," I said, "if you decide to come see your old dad again."

"Count on it, old dad," she said as a huge smile crossed her face, "and, incidentally, in case you're interested, Montana boys may have moved up a notch as far as Maryland boys are concerned. Jason is taking me to the movie tonight. I want a red Mustang, new." I told her we would see, knowing she would probably get her way, and that ended that conversation.

Jason pulled into the yard plenty early, I thought, but arrangements had been made and I played no role in that. Taylor was with him. I had almost forgotten that they lived on the same ranch. I sat back and watched the moment unfold. Mike and Jason were pilot and co-pilot, occupying the front seats. Morgan and Taylor climbed in the back and they backed away from the house, only to stop before Mike swung the front end toward the gate. Out came Morgan, half walking, half running. She never said a word. She stood up on her tip toes and planted a kiss on my cheek, then she turned and walked back to the truck. She looked just like her mother. I stood there watching until they drove out of sight. This was a milestone for both of us. Morgan, on her first official date, as far as I knew, and her dad wondering what lay ahead for her and himself.

The cows were bedded down within sight of the house. I leaned over and carefully pushed myself between the two top strands of barbed wire and walked the short distance to them. The two old bulls Claire had loaned me were off somewhere else, having completed their mission, I hoped. Only two of the cows were grazing. The others were down on their bellies, chewing their cud. Most of the calves were lying down as well, stretched out full length on their sides like sun bathers. I watched two of them cavorting about, playing some sort of game with each other, then I turned and walked back to the house.

The phone was ringing when I came through the front door, and I was not able to reach it before the caller gave up and hung up. It was Megan. I called her back immediately. She was inquiring about our trip with the kids we had discussed briefly before the 4th.

"We'll have to do it in the next day or so," I said, "or we won't be doing it. The forecast is for rain Friday and Saturday, possibly Sunday."

"Why not tomorrow," she said. "We could haul the horses up in Dad's gooseneck and be back in one of the canyons before dark."

"Then, I better get busy pulling things together," I said.

"Good, I'll look after the food. I'll tell Taylor we're going when she comes home from the movie. What about Jason?"

"If Mike doesn't take him home first, I'll see if he can make it," I said. "Otherwise I'll call him. We're going to need a couple more horses. Can Benny load up a couple of your Dad's geldings and bring them when he comes with the trailer? And saddles and all that stuff, too?"

"He will," she said. "Are you concerned at all with the short notices we're giving the kids?"

"They'll cope. Morgan knows she is leaving soon, so she won't drag her feet."

"Good. I didn't think it would be a problem. Kids are resilient. Besides, they are going to have to deal with a lot of short notices in their lives. Let's call it part of their education. I'll be over early. It will take some time to get packed."

Early the next morning, Jason pulled into the yard with a 2-horse trailer. The first horse to back out was a good looking quarter horse, black in color with a blaze and one white sock. On each side of his withers, was a smooth-edged spot of pure white, a tell tale sign that this was a roping horse. Sometime in the past, he had suffered saddle burns that rubbed away the hair. When it came back, it came back pure white.

A breast collar which helped hold the saddle in place was the only other adornment aside from a set of saddle bags and a yellow rain slicker. The other mount was a stout 14-hand bay gelding with a pack saddle already cinched down on its back. Our four horses were added to the three Benny brought in the gooseneck, and the two Jason had come with stayed with his trailer. Three rigs left the yard. Michael and Taylor led the way in Mike's buffed, slightly used pickup, pulling a two-horse trailer containing Taylor's mount. Jason and Morgan ate Mike's dust in Jason's rig, another heavy duty ranch truck. Benny, Megan and I brought up the rear.

In less than a half hour, we were at the corrals, unloading our gear and pushing all ten of the horses into the largest catch pen. Benny lingered only long enough to hand me a half dozen horse shoes, some nails, a nipper and rasp. We all stopped to watch him back the trailer up and get his front end pointed at the gate. With not so much as a waving hand, he was gone and headed down the road, kicking up a cloud of dust like a drag racer. Mike and Jason parked their trucks inside the fence near the corrals.

The first task facing us was to spread out all of our gear to assess just what we had and didn't have. I had brought what I had as had the others, and we soon learned we had more of about everything than we needed. Jason was the only experienced packer, so he took charge. The rest of us stood back and watched or handed him items as he asked for them. I had used panniers on my one trip up, but there was nothing very professional about how I had packed. Jason meticulously assessed what we had not only in terms of utility but also in terms of weight.

We brought the four pack horses out of the corral, and he began dropping smaller, difficult-to-tie-down items in the panniers according to weight. Atop this he placed tarps, some tents and one of the large coolers. Then he moved over to the next pack horse and began strapping on a larger rolled-up tarp, two small tents, sleeping bags, air mattresses, back packs, and sundry other camping items such as lanterns, cooking utensils, coffee pots, and a gleaming Port-A-Pot. Before he finished, all four of the pack animals had something strapped to or hanging from their saddles. Over the tops of each pack, he spread a lightweight tarp that was soon cinched down with ropes running in every which direction until he had fashioned a diamond hitch. All of the packhorses carried modest loads; none of them carried more than was reasonable.

Jason was finished in no time and I, for one, marveled at his dexterity and skills. Some one had taught him well, and I expected it was none other than the senior Carmack. As we were preparing to mount up, he ran to his truck and brought back several coils of rope and a few of the stiff lariats. He reminded us that there would be no pens or corrals where we were going. Each of us wound up with one or more of the coils strapped to the swell of our saddle. We carried with us several one-leg hobbles, but where we were going it was going to be rocky with scanty grass. So a rope corral made sense.

We gave the horses a chance at water, and then we were off, with Jason in the lead. I rode drag with the four packhorses immediately ahead of me. Their lead ropes were tied to the pack saddles of the horse ahead of them, and they followed along nicely. They were not about to be left behind. This was the trail Megan and I had taken, and I recognized several landmarks as we pushed ahead, but we were soon on a part of the trail we had never reached. The climb was steep, and at times we were riding on the side of the mountain, using switchback trails winding slowly upward. We stopped when Jason stopped. He seemed to sense when horses and riders needed a respite.

At noon, we pulled up to stare into a small, dark side canyon which my eyes told me ended abruptly at a vertical rock wall several hundred feet high. The canyon walls were steep, but the sun must have found its way into the canyon for at least short spells each day. How else could anyone explain that a hundred yards into the side canyon's darkness, we found a stretch of level ground with enough soil to support a nice growth of lush, green grass?

It reminded me of what I had always called "slough" grass, but it was different in that its blades were narrower and sharper, with shafts of green with small heads, containing tiny round seeds about the size of Pigeon Grass seeds. Whatever it was, the horses chomped on it greedily. We all dismounted and walked to the head of the canyon out of which trickled a small but steady stream of water. At its bottom, an ankle-deep, small pool collected in a small depression only to trickle out and disappear almost immediately back into the ground through a series of cracks.

Megan had walked out to the lip of the opening for a look-see. She beckoned to us to join her, and what we saw was startling. Looking down our back trail was like looking down into the mouth of a funnel. It had not seemed so steep as we crawled upward, but looking at it now, we suddenly realized what we had accomplished. As the crow flies, we had probably covered no more than a couple of miles. According to the Forest Service map I carried in my saddle bag, the canyon we were in was several miles long, growing narrower and probably more difficult with each step.

"Are we in over our heads, Jason?" I asked, thinking that we should seek friendlier trail where we need not be unduly concerned for our safety.

"No, not as long as we go at it slow and easy," he replied, "but if anyone is apprehensive, we can turn back. I know of other easier trails. In some places we can even follow old mining or logging roads."

"What does everyone think?" I asked. "Should we keep going?"

It was Megan who spoke out, I thought somewhat hesitantly, to say that she thought we should keep going. Her words were echoed by both Taylor and Morgan. They were clearly excited about this first in a lifetime taste of the wilderness, and both were anxious to press on. Michael nodded his head in agreement. Determined not have any accidents on my watch, I asked a second time if everyone was sure. Same response. So, it was a go.

We each ate a sandwich and had something to drink, and we were soon on our way. I positioned myself at the narrow opening that led to the trail. First in line, Jason stopped when he came to me and said in a low voice, "It'll be fine, Jim." In exactly the same order we used before our stop, we began climbing again. I warned each of them as they passed to be extra careful about loose rocks. To a person they nodded and fell in line.

Two hours later we reached another wide shelf of flat ground where we stopped again to stretch our legs. It was set back from a huge chunk of smooth granite that hung out over the canyon wall at least a hundred feet, like a launching pad or a stubby diving board.

The main canyon wall sloped away from the overhanging section of boulder and eventually reached back into the timber. The small creek at the bottom of the canyon was no longer visible, and we were now riding in a mixed stand of Lodgepole Pine and Engelmann Spruce on our left, and a mixture of pine, twisted brush, and boulders on our right. This time we stripped the horses of their saddles and rubbed them down with burlap bags.

Opportunities to view the grand sweep of country below and beyond are infrequent when your eyes are glued on the trail ahead. So these stops were important. I made sure there were many, for I wanted everyone to inhale the sweet odor of the spruce and pines trees, catch the shadow of an eagle or a hawk's wings against the rocks, and soak up the fresh air and it's subtle high country fragrances. Megan and I edged our way to the lip of the granite slab to take in the view. The kids, more energized and curious, crept back out on our back trail to survey the Madison River Valley and the far away peaks of the Bridger and Gallatin Ranges. I thought our view was the better, but I also wanted to catch a few moments alone with her. I was concerned that the physical demands of our climb were tiring to her. She said she was holding up just fine.

The section of trail we had just covered wasn't nearly as steep as before but, if anything, it was narrower. The lower part hugged a smooth vertical wall of granite. Immediately below, grass and soil were scarce commodities. To the north of the creek, though, lay vast tracts of rolling hills covered with grass and interspersed with more pine trees. This was the main part of the Macintosh grazing permit. Now and again I was able to watch small groups of stock move across an open spot or dip their heads into a pool of blue water. In the heat of the day many would find respite under the trees.

"There is an open area among the rocks just above timberline," Jason said, "and in a couple hours and we can be there."

"And the trail between here and there?" I asked.

"Pretty good," he said, "we'll be mostly in the trees and, once we get there, we'll be within easy climbing distance to the top. Up there you can see forever."

I passed Jason's words on to the others, which seemed to infuse all of them with a renewed energy, and we were soon following him through the trees. The trip up was without incident, and we found a great place to pitch our tents. Jason and Morgan strung his ropes between stunted pine trees, scrubby, nondescript brush, and even rocks. Morgan poured ten small piles of whole oats on the rock surface, and the horses attacked the piles like soldiers coming out of a prison camp.

I was in charge of stretching our tarps out upon the rocky ground and matching them with tent sizes. All of the tents were free-standing, though here and there we found enough soil in cracks between rocks to drive in a few pegs. We were shielded from a west wind by a rock overhang that allowed us to place our tents and fire part way under it. It wouldn't keep us dry in a rain storm, but there was something comforting about its bearing, and though there were few trees, we were able to gather up a good sum of kindling and larger branches for our fire.

The front of each tent faced a rock ring built to hold a fire. Not our rock ring. Others had reached here before us. We were not, by any means, the first to use this spot for a camp. Charred chunks of wood still remained within the scattered ring of rocks, and remnants of rope clung to tree branches here and there, and, well, yes, there was garbage too.

The two coolers were placed away from the fire but near the tents. Megan had us eating like kings in no time. Even before the hot dogs, beef patties and brats started to brown, my eight-cup aluminum coffee pot was perking merrily away atop my small, back packer's stove. The first cup was mine. After that I didn't keep track.

The weather was perfect. Short sleeves appropriate. In the distance, a handful of fluffy white clouds skittered across the sky over the Madison Range, a light breeze tickled our ears, and no one could guess how many stars twinkled in the heavens above.

We were but a half dozen, but as we sat around the fire, several conversations were working simultaneously. Jason and Morgan were roasting marshmallows at the end of long sticks. They were talking and laughing...about who knows what. Occasionally Mike and Taylor became part of the dialogue. Megan and I said very little, mostly looking into the fire or piling on more branches. I could about guess her thoughts. Her recent health scare had been frightening, I'm sure, but it had been a false alarm, and since then she had seemed quite relaxed. I hoped she had really turned a corner and that her future was one largely without fear and anxiety.

We were the last to leave the fire. I poured each of us another cup of coffee. After a while, I stood up and walked over to the edge of the huge outcropping we were perched upon. I wanted to watch the parade of headlights that made their way north and south on the highway, the twinkling of stars that provided a heavenly blanket of light, and the distant, vertical shafts of light that brightened the sky over Bozeman. She joined me shortly, and we stood there for a long time gazing with wonder at landscapes near and afar, now shrouded in darkness.

"Some day, huh, Jim!" she offered, as her arm slipped around my waist. "I'm so glad we came. The kids are loving it. And me too."

"It's been great," I said, meaning it, "but in a few days, I'm going to be missing my girl. In less than two months Mike will be off at school." I don't know why my arm brushed her back and suddenly went to her shoulder. I felt her edge ever so slightly against my side, and we stood there silently for several moments.

"You've got friends, Jim," she said, "we won't let you get too lonely." And then she walked away. I told myself that our touching was nothing more than a bit of togetherness between two good friends. And then I walked toward my own tent.

I was up and out of the tent just as the sun edged a tip of its brightness over the Madison Mountains. My thought was to have the coffee perking long before anyone else was awake. As it turned out, I was only the second out and about. Megan already had a flame eating away at the underside of my coffee pot, and she was quietly rummaging through one of the coolers, looking for breakfast.

She looked up at me and smiled, but said nothing. She had this way about her that set me to thinking, well, you know what. Maybe it was part of a strategy of suggestion. Or was the stepping back only an expression of her own locked door? Was I reading way more into our subtle brushes with intimacy than was there? I hoped I was. I had loved at least twice, maybe three times, and lost each time. I was like Michele in that I too was afraid. Afraid, yes. And not willing to give in to it again. I remembered Michele's letter and her confession that she had been foolish for not taking a chance on me, but it wasn't enough. I had built a wall between myself and a new love, a door that was stuck, and I had made up my mind to keep it that way.

Taylor was the first to join us, but in no time at all we were all gathered around the fire. The sound and smell of bacon sizzling in a huge cast iron frying pan had something to do with it, no doubt. We ate a breakfast only possible on a mountain side. Whatever it was that made it so, Denny's and Perkins needed to send someone out for the recipe. After that we simply sat and talked about our experience so far and wondered what the new day held for us. We ate off paper plates, which had already been burned along with table scraps, but the frying pans had to be washed. I jumped up to do it but got shot out of the saddle by Taylor and Morgan.

"We'll do that, Dad," Morgan said, "then we are all going to climb up and look over the other side."

"It's a heck of a view," Jason offered. "You and Megan ought to give it a try too. You could handle it."

I didn't know about Megan, but all of a sudden I was feeling a little like one of those senior citizens. Megan caught the unintended inference as well, and we looked at each other mentally weighing the challenge.

"What do you think, Jimbo?" she said. "Suppose us two old timers could ever do it?" Jason's face was flushed. His *faux pas* had, of course, been unintentional.

"We can give it the old college try," I replied. "We can lean on each other."

In no time at all we were all clambering up the talus slope, searching for foot holds on rocks as large as my truck or as small as a golf ball with a cutting edge. I found it exhilarating, but my neck began to hurt from looking up constantly to see how far I had to go. I stopped to see Megan off to my right, slightly ahead of me. I was about the say something when I heard the shriek of a female voice from above. Then we heard it again. I was Taylor's, I was sure. Then it was Mike's screaming out to everyone and anyone.

""It's Taylor, "he hollered, "she's fallen down in the rocks She needs help!"

I looked to Megan. Her eyes were filled with panic and fear, as she tried to move faster across the rocks. I was closer. I'm closer, I told her. Let me look. Everything's going to be okay, I shouted, though I knew it wasn't.

When I reached Taylor, the first thing I saw was blood streaming down the side of her face. Her eyes were closed, and she was moaning softly and crying for help, her voice barely audible. Then I saw her leg. It was twisted in a way that could only mean it was broken. By then Mike and Jason were at my side, with and Morgan and Megan only steps behind.

"Now," I said in a loud, commanding voice. "Everyone keep your cool. Taylor has been hurt, but let's not panic. It may not be as bad as it looks." My words were the wrong ones, for before she had ever seen her daughter, Megan was screaming. I moved quickly to her side and grabbed her. She was sobbing and crying, "Oh God. Not Taylor!!"

I shouted at Morgan to grab Megan and hold her, then I moved down to Taylor's side to learn as much about her injuries as I could with a visual inspection. To my amazement, she looked up at me, albeit with eyes clouded and red. My worse fear, even more so than the leg, was a skull fracture. A fall of only a few feet was enough. Megan edged up against me then and got her first close-up look at her daughter. She was whimpering softly, but she was amazingly collected given what she had just seen.

"We have to bring her out of there, Jim." she said. "How can she even breathe, stuck down there the way she is? *Is* she still breathing?"

"She is and I have noticed some movement, but she has a broken leg for sure." I replied. "Now if everyone will step back, we'll try to lift her out of there and get her someplace where we can lay her down flat. She's probably in shock or soon will be. We need to get her out and see what we can do with the leg."

Mike and Jason were standing next to me and together we lifted her slowly from between the two rocks that held her captive. Her left leg was puffy and red, and it was askew from a point midway between her knee and ankle. We took a chance, and I knew it was a big one, that she hadn't suffered any spinal injuries. I had caught movement in both legs and arms, so once we pulled her up on the large rock up slope from where she had fallen, we laid her down flat and held her in place.

"Get one of those tarps from over by the rope corral," I hollered to anyone, "and someone find a couple of poles about eight feet long. We're going to have to fashion a stretcher for her. We need to immobilize her as much as possible so we can try to push that leg bone into place...and we're going to have to carry her out of here."

"What can I do, Jim," Megan asked over my shoulder.

"Jump on your cell phone," I said. "Call 9-1-1 and tell them we've had an accident our here. Tell them where we are located and tell them we are uncertain as to the nature of Taylor's injuries. We know she has a broken leg, and she may have internal injuries, and a concussion or skull fracture, but we're just guessing. I think 9-1-1 will contact the Sheriff's office, and someone there will decide if sending a chopper is warranted. Tell him that if it is a matter of money, I will reimburse Montana Rescue for all expenses."

Megan moved away from the group and the noise we were making.

"I hope they can pluck her off the mountain side," I said to the rest of them, " but I don't think so, at least not from here. I think the overhang will stop them but, if they can, so much the better. If they can't, we need to be ready to haul her down that trail by ourselves.

"Tell them if they have a basket they can lower, bring it," I continued. "It could be tricky, but maybe...just maybe they can reach her from above."

Taylor was awake and looking up at us in bewilderment. She asked what had happened and we told her. She couldn't remember it. I felt her head carefully to see if I could find something suggesting a fracture. It wasn't there, and I was beginning to believe, at the worst, she might have a concussion. It was also possible, I ventured, that she had internal injuries, but even that seemed unlikely. Her color was good and as time passed, her range of motion was increasing.

I saw the signs as encouraging, and I told myself that if we must, we could bring her down the mountain. I knew that her leg must be hurting a bunch but that it was going to hurt even more. She needed help as soon as possible, and I saw that as the strongest argument for using a chopper if possible.

We ate up better than a half hour fashioning a stretcher and sliding her on to it. She was stirring more, and she opened and closed her eyes several times.

"Let's start her down, boys," I said. "We have to get her out of this jumble of rock. You two take the front, I'll follow behind. Take it easy and don't either of you take one step backwards until you can see where your foot is going to land."

Slowly, slowly we began to pick our way downward through the rubble. I had never worked so hard in my life. My shirt was soaking wet, and my muscles were crying for rest, but we didn't stop, we couldn't stop. There was no place to set her down without risking further injury. When we reached the campsite, Megan and Morgan were waiting in each other's arms.

"I got 9-1-1," Megan said. "Bad news. The Montana Rescue team is occupied trying to reach a young hiker who has fallen from the trail to a ledge below the trail up north of Helena. The Gallatin Valley Search and Rescue group is down in Yellowstone on the Bechler River treating someone who went over one of the falls, and Deaconess doesn't have a helicopter. An ambulance is on the way though. So, it looks like we have to get her down to the catch pens by ourselves. How is she?"

"She's okay, I think," I said, not really knowing.

We had covered Taylor with two blankets and another light tarp. We were kneeled at her side when we heard a ruckus coming from the horse corral. None of us knew what had caused it but whatever it was, the horses needed some comforting. Taylor's eyes came open, and she looked up at her mother.

"What's that awful noise?" she asked. "I slipped. I'm sorry. Am I hurt bad?"

"The noise is nothing but the horses jumping around, anxious, probably, to get out of their little pen," her mother said. "You're going to be just fine, Taylor. Your leg is broken, but we think that is all. How do you feel?"

"Like Mike ran over me with his new truck," she said, with the slightest hint of a smile at the corner of her mouth. "But wow! My leg is really starting to hurt."

About all we could do to help with the pain was to give her aspirin, and then I would try to place the leg in some sort of splint. How to do it came to me suddenly once I had it straightened. I took one of the self-inflating sleeping pads, tied it loosely around her leg and then triggered the inflation action. It worked. Her leg was fairly straight and moving it was next to impossible. It gave us time. Just what we needed. At that point, we figured nothing was to be gained by waiting. One way or the other we had to start down.

"Here's what we are going to do," I said. "Mike and I are going to start down immediately. We'll do our best until the rest of you can catch up. I want Jason to look after the horses and get them ready to start down. Once he gets back to Mike and I, two of us will carry, and the other will spell when one of us needs rest. That way, there will be fewer stops.

"Megan," I continued, "you and Morgan fall in behind us, but before you do, help Jason with the horses. Give the horses each a hand full of oats, then saddle them. While you're doing that Jason is going to get our things packed. When he's done with the packs, he's going to hurry and catch up to us. When you're ready, you girls can bring the horses on down.   Don't ride. Lead a couple of them. The others will follow. Watch your step. Don't rush to catch up with us.

That's when accidents happen, and one is more than enough."

Gravity, our enemy on the way up, befriended us now. The trail was not as steep as it had been on some of the lower segments, but without gravity, we would have had to stop to rest more frequently. I didn't know if I could make it. My you-know-what was dragging. Jason and Mike were struggling as well. Working in our favor was the fact that the sun was yet below the south canyon wall, and we could feel a cool breeze wafting at us from below. We had traversed less than a mile, when Megan and Morgan caught up.

"How is she doing?"

"She's quiet, Megan," I said, "that's about all I know for sure. She's going to be okay, I think."

Where she could, Megan held onto her daughter's hand. Several times, Taylor squeezed back, which I saw as a very good sign. The boys and I changed places frequently, and we made steady progress downward. Once, I thought we were going to drop the stretcher when Jason slipped on a small rock, but he recovered in time. Mike was the physically strongest of the three of us, with Jason a near second. At least that is how it seemed now. That left me as the weak link.

But together we covered more than two miles before we had to stop for another breather. When we lifted the stretcher again, we were quickly back on a much steeper stretch of trail. There was no way to make our descent other than to stop and rest when we felt we must. Megan and Morgan followed a hundred feet behind us, and the horses moved down like they were tied together.

Our next stop was less than another mile down the side of the canyon wall. Here we took time to drink from the trickle of water flowing out of the cracks in the rocks and watered the horses from the puddles below. All the while we slipped and slid down the next segment, Taylor talked to us about everything under the sun. Her conversation was totally coherent, and I knew she was trying to help divert us from thinking about our fatigue, which was edging perilously toward exhaustion.

Our next stop lasted longer, for we were near our physical limits. We could see the catch pen still far below us, and our spirits were lifted considerably just knowing that we would soon reach the bottom. Megan called Deaconess to tell them we were probably about half an hour from the pick-up point. She explained again what had happened and gave them detailed directions for reaching the corrals. We were still half an hour from the corrals, but as we lowered Taylor down the last reach of the trail, we saw the flashing red lights of the ambulance coming at us from the highway.

The emergency medical people checked her vitals and hooked up an IV before they transferred her to their stretcher and loaded her in the rear of the ambulance. One of them announced that two persons could ride in the ambulance back to Bozeman, but they had to be relatives. Megan quickly said she was the mother and, to everyone's amazement, Morgan laid claim to being a sister.

We watched as the ambulance sped away toward Bozeman. Then we hurriedly tossed our gear into the boxes of our vehicles, and left for my place. Michael and I struck out down the road ahead of the others, relieved to know that Taylor was receiving professional medical attention. Jason followed close behind us with his truck and trailer. My phone rang as we were pulling into my yard. Megan's voice was on the other end.

"Fast trip, Jim. We're already at the hospital. On the way, the paramedics told us it is unlikely that she has a skull fracture, and she may not have a concussion. The doctors are setting her leg now. They say it will need a pin. She'll be on crutches for a while, but she's going to be just fine. I feel like I've been holding my breath for an hour, but I'm finally breathing again."

"That's the best news we could have gotten," I said. "I'll tell the boys. They'll be so happy." When I shouted out Megan's good new, they clapped and screamed like their favorite football team had had just scored a touchdown.

"She wants you all to come and see her when you can," Megan added.

"With any luck, we'll be there in an hour or so," I said, "but we'll be there."

"I owe you a bunch, Jim," she said before her phone clicked dead. "You were wonderful up there."

Benny was waiting for us with a tandem-axle trailer when we got to my place.

"Megan called," he said, "and told me to meet you here. Do you know yet how Taylor is doing?"

I told him Megan had called a few minutes earlier and that Taylor was going to be okay. He nodded, saying nothing, but it was easy to see he was relieved. We quickly had Claire's horses loaded in the trailer.

"Leave mine and Jason's here," Benny, " I said. "We're going to go straight to town to see Taylor."

An hour later, we pulled into the Deaconess parking lot on the east side of Bozeman, and we were soon in Taylor's room. She wasn't there yet, but was expected down from the recovery room momentarily. If ever there was a more motley, dirty, bedraggled looking reception committee, I hadn't heard about it. We actually made the next day's *Chronicle*, and that night, a small segment showed up on the local TV channel's 6 o'clock news. Taylor stole the show completely when she announced that the subject of her first theme at school this year was going to be, "The Tobacco Roots: Coming *Down* From *Above* on Your Back *Over* a Rocky Trail *Under* Emergency Conditions". She had made it. She was a Montanan.

Morgan left two days later, torn between lingering with her new found friends and being with her mother. Her mother, of course, won out but, I wondered, would it always be that way? She had taken to Montana's wide spaces and, I think, our way of living.

She already had what many would call the good life, living in a spacious home on Chesapeake Bay. But Montana was tugging away at her in subtle ways. I doubted even she could put her finger on what was happening to her. But I thought it probably had more to do, I think, with the life *style* one could embrace out here than it did with money, position, leisure time and all the factors that allowed one to enjoy a quality life back east. She was accustomed to affluence, but she was savvy enough to recognize that money, alone, counted for little. I finally embraced the idea that a quality life can be found almost anywhere.

Her life spent in Baltimore, had never given her a sense of what else lay beyond the verdant hills, waterways, and greenery of Maryland. Montana had done that. She was no silly girl, enamored of Jason to a point where she was willing to give up everything else for him. But she was a girl, I was convinced, who would make up her own mind about important matters and, when she did, I doubted there was much that would deter her from attaining her goals. Jason might be there when her time came to have a serious relationship. And, he might not. If I read the cards right, one thing seemed quite certain. If *she* decided her life partner *was* to be Jason, Jason it would be.

Heartening as it might be to know that Morgan had a kind of maturity already that would lead her down a life path that would be both rewarding and fulfilling, I knew there were no guarantees, whatsoever. All I knew was that her few weeks in Montana had been a windfall for me. I was a father who wanted her close, but I was also one who recognized that it might be a good long time before I saw her again. The latter fear dimmed slightly when she whispered to me, as I followed her to the entry of the boarding gate on her way back to her mother, "Those Baltimore boys better shape up if they expect to win me away from Jason."

She turned and waved one last goodbye to her friends. Taylor was there in a wheel chair, but nothing on the mountain had changed those eyes of hers or her exuberance for life. Jason stood off to the side, donned in blue jeans, running shoes, and a white T-shirt. Maybe he wanted her to remember him that way. Mike had said his goodbyes back at the place, and Megan stood to the side hating, I'm sure, to see Taylor's best friend leave. I gave Morgan one final "I love you hug," and then she was gone.

We straggled from the terminal all feeling a little sad. But, as they say, life goes on. Mike wouldn't be leaving for Missoula until the last week of August, and I had plans of my own. A couple of plans, actually. The first was to drag Patrick Macintosh's Cessna out of its shed and begin restoring it to working order.

The second was to take Megan, Taylor and Mike down to Yellowstone Park for a long weekend. Neither Mike nor Taylor had ever been there. There was much to see and do. I figured they would enjoy it. We could get a couple of rooms in the lodge, and dispense with camping for this trip. We could take turns pushing Taylor and her wheelchair over the boardwalks. I had mentioned the idea earlier and they had all agreed it was something they wanted to do. Taylor's approval was contingent on my guarantee that she wouldn't be going for any ambulance rides.

Chapter 9

It was never part of my plan that Megan and I would spend so much time together alone in Yellowstone. I thought of myself as group tour guide of sorts but never envisioned Michael and Taylor breaking away and embarking upon their own solo adventures after we completed the agenda I had laid out for us each morning. Their docket commenced immediately following lunch in the Lodge. It included more strolls on the very boardwalks we had tramped over earlier in the day, stops at the ice-cream parlor, drifting through the numerous gift shops, and resting on the outside benches or the leather covered sofas in the Lodge itself. Twice, they left Megan and me seated across from each other in the dining room, not knowing quite what to do.

The first time it happened, we walked some more ourselves out on the boardwalks. Traffic had abated. It was peaceful and quiet. When we found a bench to sit upon, we broke off our walk to engage in a bit of people watching. I think we both enjoyed just sitting there watching as dozens and dozens of couples, groups of cavorting youngsters, and solitary individuals passed by. They were a mixture of shapes and sizes, complexions, and languages, suggesting that at least some of them had come long distances to see what we took for granted.

One of the couples we spotted while they were yet a city block distant was our very own Michael and Taylor. Mike was still pushing Taylor in her wheelchair even though he had already logged several miles at chief pilot, and he couldn't help but be tired. They were engaged in an animated discussion about something, and when they came upon one of the benches, he pushed her up to it and sat down next to her. From where we sat, it was clear they were holding hands, and we watched as they kissed.

"Let's get out of here, Jim," Megan suggested, "and let them have their private moments."

I agreed, and we turned away from them and took the first path we found leading back through the trees to the Lodge. When we reached a puddle of water in the middle of the trail, Megan grabbed for my hand to help steady herself as she reached across the wetness with an extended leg. When I followed in her footsteps, she held my hand until we found a wooden bench under the verandah of one of the gift shops. She waited there while I went inside for ice-cream cones and coffee. The ice-cream occupied our hands and our minds exclusively for a few minutes in an unsuccessful attempt to avoid dripping all over ourselves. I looked toward her once, and watched as a rivulet of cream slipped down her chin. I was about to say something when I felt something trickling down my own chin. Needless to say, I held my tongue. In time, we finished them and started on the coffee.

It was one of those wonderful late summer afternoons, with a light breeze wafting through the trees to cool what had been an unusually warm day for this time of year. We were both tired, and it felt good just to sit. It didn't hurt that across from me was one of the most attractive woman I had ever known, and that we were friends.

"This is just wonderful, Jim," Megan ventured, brushing her hair back against her ear. "I don't know how may times I have been here, and I'd be surprised if I haven't sat on this very bench before but, somehow, this is different. I think maybe it is because this is the first time I've been able to relax so much in a long time."

"I'm glad to hear that," I said. "It's a good sign."

"It is, yes, it is, I think," she said slowly. "I may have turned a corner, an important corner, in terms of my health. The last scan and blood test showed no signs of the beginnings of a new tumor. And the longer I go without having one start up again, the less likely it is that it will happen. I have gradually come to believe that I have a future, a *this world* future filled with expectations. I owe a lot to you for that, you know. You've always been there for me, someone to lean on, someone to help me feel not so alone. You have helped me so much, by being a friend and by being there when I needed to bounce my ideas and concerns off someone. Today is another good example."

"No," I retorted. "I deserve no credit whatsoever. I haven't done anything that any real friend wouldn't do in a minute. Your words are exactly the words we have all been longing to hear, and they had to come from you. It is not enough for your friends, including yours truly, to assert time and again, as we have, that you will win your battle with cancer. How could we know? We couldn't. We hoped you would, that you would grow certain about your future, but we really didn't know. We were never sure you would win until *you* said you would win. And now you have. You need to tell your folks. They will be relieved to hear those words."

"You make it seem as though you were all holding your breath waiting for me to proclaim that I felt I was winning the battle."

"Truth is, in a sense we were," I admitted. "We knew when you were resting easy, we could rest easy. As crazy as it sounds, you have been our pillar of strength instead of the other way around. It goes back, I believe, to the view held by many that it is probably easier to die than it is to have to deal with knowing someone you love is going to pass on."

"Now, is that another of your professional opinions, Dr. Pengilly?"

"Dr. Pengilly is a fraud," I said. "He knows nothing. He talks too much. Doesn't listen enough. Pay him no mind."

"Well, if that's the case," Megan said, "will you listen to me some more?"

"Only if we break long enough for me to grab a couple more cups of coffee...or would you want something stronger? A beer? Some wine?"

"Just coffee," she replied. "Make it decaf."

When I returned with two steaming cups, I sat back and listened as she revealed details of the circumstances leading to her divorce. She had never related any of the details to me. I was amazed to hear her tell me things that reminded me in so many ways of my leaving Rebecca and our divorce. Her husband was one of those highly successful individuals who, like me, had become so immersed in his career that he had all but abdicated his family responsibility. Sound familiar? For a year or more before Megan learned of it, he had been romantically involved with a colleague. Her first knowledge of his infidelity came when he told her he wanted out of their marriage. Rebecca didn't know about my own affair with Jordan, and I didn't learn of hers with her doctor friend, until after I had moved out. I was surprised when I learned of it, but I think I understood. She was lonely and, like me, she needed to feel wanted.

Like Rebecca, Megan had a career of her own, a career that brought income into the household but never grew more important than being a mother to Taylor. And so it was for Rebecca. Morgan and Michael were always her first priority. Rebecca and Megan were clearly victims. Mario Tivoli and Jim Pengilly were the perpetrators.

Unlike Megan, however, Rebecca ultimately wanted out herself.

She had grown disenchanted with what we had, knew it was beyond saving, and recognized that dissolution of the marriage was the only course if either of us was ever to be happy again.

Megan confided in me that she did not want her marriage to end, and that she had pleaded with her husband to make a stab at reconciliation.

"It was hopeless," she said, as she looked off toward the distant mountain peaks, "and one day I finally confronted the certainty that he was already gone both physically and emotionally. I knew it was over. He didn't contest, and he gave me full custody of Taylor."

I could tell she was near tears, but I said nothing, thinking that maybe those tears needed to be shed as part of the healing process. The poor gal was healing on so many fronts.

"Now, if that isn't enough, Jim...Dr. Pengilly," she added, "listen to this. In spite of everything, I am having a very difficult time falling out of love with the man. He treated me like dirt toward the end, but I forgave him. You can laugh if you want, but it is true."

"I'm not laughing, Megan," I said. "The truth is that how you feel may not be that unusual. You just need some time. That's what you need. Memories get in the way of forgetting because they clog the road you must travel to reach beyond feelings. I'll always love Rebecca, I suppose, but not in the same way I loved Michele. And, don't be surprised if you don't harbor feelings for your ex-husband for a long time. Still, memories ebb over time. The trick is to figure out how to change from one kind of love to another."

"I suppose you're right," she replied, "but how do you get on the right track and how does one accelerate the process of change. I'm miserable, and I'm lonely. For the first time in a long while, I am lonesome."

"We've experienced some of the same things," I said, "so we are birds-of-a-feather in a sense. The big difference between us is your cancer; something I have never had to face. Another is the fact that I wasn't in love with Rebecca when we got divorced. And, she was no longer in love with me. So the formula that worked for me might not be exactly the one for you."

"But surely,"she replied, "you've learned what works and what doesn't work."

"Yes, I suppose I have. For me, it was immersing myself in building up my place. As long as I live, I will be grateful to your folks for giving me the chance. My job in Bozeman and, frankly, working for your Dad, were less important than the *place* but only because I simply could not get myself *in* to them the way I could with my *own* place. I felt like a pioneer, a homesteader, a person taking the first steps in building an empire, albeit a small one. A project of some sort produces results quicker than a job, per se, because each success, no matter how small, works to restore personal esteem. And, it is esteem that is severely injured when divorce enters into the picture. Self reliance builds confidence, and confidence nourishes esteem."

"But I don't have a project," Megan replied reflectively. "What could I do?"

"You have Michele's place don't you? You're a Montana gal. You've been ankle deep in the cattle business all your life. Take over Michele's place, personally and completely. Make decisions. Build it up to suit Megan. Build it up for you and Taylor. Develop a plan. What about a new home? What about shelter belts, more fencing, outbuildings, an arena for Taylor to run her barrels? How about a new breeding program? The list is endless if you have the will to try."

"My goodness," she replied, "don't do it all for me, please! I better get a pencil. I can see I need to get to thinking about such matters. I haven't done that. Not at all. "

"I haven't done it all, and I won't," I replied. "There's more. If you're not ready to tackle a major project, how about a job in one of the banks in Ennis or with one of the financial services firms? A job need not be an end in itself, but it could serve as transition from your life today to what you see for yourself in the long-term.

"You have you're MBA," I added. "You probably know more than all of those country bankers in Ennis. You've got built-in hired hands in Earl and Jason. They can do the heavy work. You be the brain, but you can get your hands dirty too if you want. And put Taylor to work. Once you have a project in mind, let her be a part of it. She could join the 4-H. Feed out a steer, plant a garden, raise some chickens, whatever. Nurture her. And keep her busier than she could ever have imagined. In the end she'll love you for it. One day, she'll be running the place."

"Any more, Pengilly?"

"Yes. Just one more thing," I replied. "Put some of what I have just mentioned together with a lot of your own ideas, and your love for Mario will fly away like cotton seeds in a summer wind. Your lonesome feelings will evaporate, and if they don't, do what Sigmund Freud recommended for erasing depression and killing loneliness: go across the street and help a neighbor."

"A neighbor? Are you forgetting we would be neighbors, Jim?"

"Not at all," I said. "Come over to the Pengilly spread and bring along your hired men as far as that goes. I'm expanding too. I have made a down payment on 1280 acres that lie between me and your grazing permit."

"Really?" she said, clearly startled by my unplanned announcement. "That's wonderful. I hope it means we'll be neighbors for a good long time. I'm going to be leaning on you a bunch, Jim. Do you mind?"

"How could I mind, if it makes you well again?" I replied. "You and me, we are friends. We've become pals. We lean on each other. You and Taylor, you both belong here, you know. I need someone to lean on as badly as you do."

"One more question, okay?" Megan asked. "And on this one I'll get right to the point. I can see you have built a barrier against taking another chance on love. How high is it, and how long is it going to be there?"

That woman, she was forever throwing one of her breaking-ball curves in my direction. I chewed on it like a mother cow chews her cud and finally came up with a resounding "I don't know," to which I added, "Ask me again when you're dead sure you have fallen out of love with your husband."

"Until then, we are friends?"

"Yes, of course, forever friends."

Our conversation had already ended when Michael wheeled Taylor up to our bench, and the two of them suggested we go into the Lodge for coffee. I was filled to the brim with liquid. I'd venture to say Megan was as well. We accepted their invitation, nonetheless, because neither one of us could say no to our children. But, I for one, was going to be imbibing something much stronger, something that came in smaller doses. Had I just made a left-handed kind of commitment to, Megan, I wondered? Had she slipped in a left hook I hadn't seen coming, or was it my resolve that was failing me?

I stared at the ceiling in our room for a long time that night, trying to understand what had prompted me to say what I had said and wondering about Megan's interpretation. Maybe my answer slipped past her like water rushing to the side of a rock, or was that wishful thinking on my part?

Our second day in the park was a repeat of the first in that we covered miles of ground to see what Yellowstone had to offer. And once again, following dinner, the kids left us alone. But that is where the similarity ended. Megan and I were far more subdued and, I suppose, more contemplative than we had been yesterday. Our conversations were largely small talk interrupted, thankfully, by a four hour *Everybody Loves Raymond* marathon on the local TV.

On our way home the next day we drove to Yellowstone Lake, which we were told was the largest freshwater lake in the country located above 7,000 feet in elevation. The park ranger spoke of the Yellowstone Caldera, which imparted a feeling of uneasiness in his audience. It had been about 600,000 years since the last major eruption, he said, but I couldn't help feeling we were dead in the middle of a potentially catastrophic event for someone, someday.

The trip would have fallen short of it's potential had we not taken the time to view Yellowstone Falls and the Norris Geyser Basin. On our way to Livingston via Gardiner, we stopped one final time to embrace the grotesque beauty of Mammoth Hot Springs. Elk grazing on the green, watered yards in Gardiner were like dessert, following a sumptuous meal in an classy restaurant.

During the following week, I was engrossed in my work at the Macintosh Ranch. I saw Megan and Taylor several times, but our talk was limited to the little that occurred during lunch. Most of the time, we were too tired to talk. I harvested Claire's contract barley, dumping hopper after hopper of the plump, malting grain into the box of one of his trucks. When I filled the box on one truck, Benny hauled it away and left me with another empty box to fill. I had removed the straw spreader from the combine, which left fluffy windrows of yellow straw and, as soon as I finished harvesting, I brought out the square baler and made 3500 small bales for bedding. Michael and I hauled 500 bales to my place to bed down the horses and the cows on stormy, cold nights.

Over the weekend, Benny and Odin helped me remove the wings from Patrick's Cessna 172. Parked in one of the ranch's sheds for years, it was a painful and constant reminder to Claire and Jenny of their loss. I had casually mentioned to Jennifer one day that I thought

I could put the plane back in running order and that it could be sold, if they wished to do that. She said, without a moment's hesitation, that I should do as I had suggested. It was time, she said, to reach beyond their loss of Patrick.

"Take it out of here, Jim," she said. "If you can sell it, do so. If you want to fly it, do that. The plane is yours to do with as you wish. If you need papers, we'll sign them."

"No, that won't be necessary, Jenny," I said. "I was just thinking..."

"I know what you're probably thinking, Jim," she cut me off, "but we have a daughter and a granddaughter who need us now. Patrick would want us to smother them with all the love they deserve, and we will never be able to do that with the plane sitting out there in the shed to remind us of our loss."

"Maybe if I succeed in getting it flying again," I said, "and you see it up in the clouds, you'll feel like Pat is still here."

"Maybe," she said. "In fact, yes, I kind of like that idea. Claire would too."

Benny and Odin helped me remove the wings from the still shiny, blue and white plane, and we hauled them and the fuselage over to my place in two loads. I had a shed now, large enough to house the plane so long as the wings were removed, and I could work on it in my spare time, even when it rained. The motor was frozen, and I had to remove it and haul it to the airport in Belgrade where I found a retired mechanic who agreed to overhaul it. His job was to disassemble each and every part, down to the last bolt, test gauges, and pumps, and put it back together with new parts where necessary.

I spent my time removing and replacing the tires, both of which were flat and badly weathered. The wheels themselves, I also removed, replacing the sealed bearings rather than taking a chance on their failure. The cables and linkages that give a pilot the ability to move the rudder, ailerons, and elevators and thus steer the plane and cause it to climb or descend were sound as near as I could tell, but I meticulously examined every single inch and replaced any I felt showed the slightest wear. The wing flaps were electrically driven, so it was essential that a dependable power source be maintained.

When I could find the time, I was in Belgrade logging a few hours of flight time to help me brush up on my own flying skills in hopes of earning my Montana license. I had soloed back in Great Falls many, many years earlier but had logged less than two hundred hours of actual flying time and my license had long ago expired. I was with an instructor now, but I flew the plane by myself the first time out. Several times, I took off and landed without his assistance. I knew I could fly, but I had the written exam to pass too, and that meant a couple of hours hunched over the manuals most evenings. The internet was a great help here, particularly when I needed more definitive information on some subjects that I was unable to find in the manuals.

Megan and Taylor stopped by occasionally on their way to the Macintosh ranch, but our visits were short. Megan had taken over active management of Michele's place soon after our return from Yellowstone Park, and her visits were largely to let me know how much progress they were making. We never talked about barriers and time lines. It was as if our conversations had never happened. We did talk about me flying her down to Rochester for her next appointment. She seemed unconcerned about flying in her brother's plane, and I agreed to take her there. We went so far as to agree that we would leave a couple of days early in case of weather grounded us along the way.

Taylor was still keeping her horse at my place, fearful that Morgan's paint would get too lonely without the company of her mare. She dropped by at least every other day to go riding with Michael. One

Saturday afternoon she came with her mother, and we all saddled up and rode up to Michele's grave in the rocks and then on up to the catch pens just inside the grazing permit. Megan had brought hand cut flowers from Jenny's flower garden, and we placed them upon Michele's grave during a moment of silence. In the back of my mind, I knew those flowers were for me as much as they were for Michele. We stayed only a few hours on the grazing permit, enjoying the land's rugged beauty and checking on cattle where we found them. I knew Morgan would love being here with us, but it was not to be for the time being, at least. On the way back Megan and I followed the kids along the road leading to my place.

"Any movement on that barrier, Jim?" she asked out of the blue. I shook my head

"Any movement on you know what?" I countered. She shook her head, and that ended it for now. But we were both smiling, and I took that to mean that we were enjoying a bit of banter between friends. I also took it to mean that both of us were edging toward the very type of relationship I had been mentally guarding against. "I've another question I need to ask, Jim," she said, "if you don't mind."

"Sure," I said, but my first thought was that it was going to be another of her hard ones, the ones that made me squirm. It wasn't. She only wanted to know the time. Now she was playing with me for sure and, damned, if I wasn't enjoying it a little. Along the way, we had slipped in to being good friends, maybe best friends. I liked that too.

"Why don't you and Mike come over for supper tomorrow night at Michele's—at our place?" she asked, as she climbed into her car. "Taylor's doing the cooking. She's going to grill some strip sirloins. About 7:00?"

Michael answered for us. We would be there. I made a mental note to check my stock of red wine, hoping Mike would rise to the occasion and make the toast, his first ever to my knowledge. I had my *"Here's to the bottom, to hell with the top..."* thing ready just in case.

We both quit early the next day so we could scrub up and rustle enough clean duds to make us look half way presentable. Taylor was at the grill when we arrived, with a spatula in one hand and a long fork in the other. And she was standing. Her crutches were no where in sight, but I did see a diamond willow cane propped against the grill should she need it. She welcomed us and told us supper would be ready before long.

"Mom's in the house," she said. "We didn't have room on the grill for the corn so she's blanching the cobs on the stove."

"I'll go see if I can help," I said. "Maybe I can carry something for her."

Megan was standing in front of the stove watching the steam rise up from the boiling corn. "Hi, Jim," she said, turning to look at me. "Thanks for coming. I could hear you guys talking to Taylor. Knew you were here. Taylor looks good, doesn't she? This is the first time she has taken responsibility for an entire meal, so she's a bit nervous. Be kind, will you?"

"She'll do fine," I replied, and I placed a bottle of Shirazz next to her on the counter. "And how are you doing?"

She turned to look at me then, and I immediately noticed she was looking a little peaked.

"Are you okay, Megan?" I asked, suddenly quite concerned. I shared with her the fear that the slightest backache, the smallest abdominal cramps, or a bit of nausea were a signal that her cancer had returned.

"I've been feeling a little lethargic since yesterday," she said. "I guess it's time for my vitamin shot."

"Dr. Pengilly suggests we uncork that expensive Yellowtail Schirazz I brought for us." I said. "Maybe a glass of the red stuff will perk you up until you can get to town for your shot."

"Pour mine over some ice, will you, Jim," she replied. "I'm starting to prefer it that way. Another bad habit I've picked up from you, I guess. And make it a big one."

"Something wrong, Megan?" I asked. "You don't seem yourself."

"Oh, it's nothing, really," she replied. "Probably one of those days I out to be off helping a neighbor."

Hoping to cheer her up, I flippantly asked if Dr. Pengilly needed to work some of his psychotherapeutic voodoo on her today.

"Maybe later." she replied. There was a miniscule sliver of a smile at the corners of her mouth, which hinted that our conversation was at least slightly uplifting.

"Dr. Pengilly may have to work some of his magic on me," she said, "unless Taylor's cooking brings me back to life."

"Then let's join Mike and Taylor," I suggested, "and see if eating does the job or if Dr. Pengilly needs to get involved."

Mike stuck his head in through the door about then to announce that the steaks were ready, unless we wanted them super, well-done. I lifted the kettle with the corn in it and drained the water off in the sink. Megan handed Mike the wine, two bottles of Coke, and two more glasses. She balanced a bowl of apple salad and a small relish tray on one arm and then somehow managed to wrap her other hand around bottles off steak sauce, catsup, and two raw onions.

The feast was on, and it was delicious. The steak was done just right, with a hint of pink in the middle, and the russet potatoes wrapped in foil with butter and onions were out of this world. Taylor was radiant, basking in the honest compliments we tossed her way. When we finished eating, we all sat back and relaxed. For a time we said nothing, just sat there nursing our Shirazz.

Our conversation was relaxed and casual, but it covered a wide array of subjects: their plan to add a Quonset-type loafing shed to an already extensive complex of buildings; Taylor's decision to attend highschool in Ennis; the fact that her cast was coming off in less than a week; the news that Claire and Jenny were flying to the Bahamas to vacation with the Morrisons and the Weers for a couple weeks; and the job interview Megan had with one of the Ennis banks the following Friday.

I volunteered Mike and I to clear away the table and wash the dishes, but Taylor was having none of that. Dishes were hers to do, she said, but she would allow Mike to help if he insisted. No one heard any arguments from me, so once again, in a left-handed sort of way, Megan and I had been abandoned by our children. I suggested we go for a walk, and she thought it was a good idea.

"Come on," I said, as I reached out for her hand. She gave it to me, and as we walked toward the north side of her property she slipped her arm about my waist and I brought mine to her shoulder. "Are you feeling better, Megan?" I asked, looking down into those eyes with their specks of white that made me think of falling stars.

"I got an e-mail from Mario today," she replied. "He offered to purchase my half of our house, and he wants Taylor to fly to Denver next week for a couple of weeks before school starts. I have full custody, but I think I should let her go if she wants."

"Does Taylor know about the invitation?"

"No I was going to tell her, but I wanted to see what you thought first."

"It's your choice to make," I said, "or is it? Maybe Taylor should spend some time with her Dad. He's had time to think about what he's given up. He's probably feeling pretty small about now for the way he treated you and her."

"I doubt that," Megan replied, "but what if he persuades her to stay and finish school there? I don't know what I would do if that happened?"

"Don't worry, Megan," I assured her, "Taylor will never agree to that. She belongs with her Mom. Kids are like chickens: when it comes time to roost they do it pretty close to home. And this is her home now, don't you see that?"

"I'm the next thing to a basket case right now, Jim," she admitted. "I was feeling so good about things and now all of a sudden I'm slipping backwards."

"Let her go," I said. "If you don't, you're going to forever worry about losing her. And you'll be worrying about nothing. She has made up her mind to go to school in Ennis. Mario is not going to change that. Just let her go, and I'll bet she will be back here quicker than you think. And when that happens, the entire matter of where she wants to be will be resolved once and for all. You should give her a chance to learn what I, for one, already know."

"Do you really think so?"

I told her I did, and I also suggested she might want to go off someplace by herself. Maybe you need some alone time, I said. Maybe you ought to take off a couple of weeks yourself. Go someplace where you can divorce yourself from the things that you find stressful. Occupy your mind with things that leave little space for what troubles you.

"Have you ever been to Vancouver Island?"

"No, Seattle's the closest," she replied. "What would I do on Vancouver Island that I can't do right here?"

"You could rent a car and drive north out of Victoria and cross over to the west side of the island. Half way there you could stop briefly in the port of Alberni and have a Big Mac. The scenery is spectacular wherever you go. Over on the west side you could stay in Ucluelet or Tofino. They are both on the Pacific, and the beaches between the two of them are expansive and ruggedly beautiful but, I warn you, the water is cold. Stick your big toe in the water and I can guarantee you that how you feel about Mario will fly away like a feather in the wind."

"Come on, Jim, it isn't that easy, I don't think."

"Maybe not," I said, "but I can almost guarantee that Mario won't occupy center stage in your thoughts. Give it a try. Both Ucluelet and Tofino are situated on inlets protected somewhat from the ocean, and they are both very picturesque. Back in Victoria, you can walk the streets and check out dozens and dozens of small specialty shops or stroll along the inner harbor and watch the ships work their way around the San Juan Islands. Natives operate stalls along the inner harbor hawking their beautiful handicraft, and you can grab a cup of delicious coffee or stroll down one of the side streets and go to an English Tea."

"I don't like tea. I have never liked tea. I don't intend to ever like tea," she replied, teasingly.

"Okay, forget the tea," I said. "I have saved my best idea 'til last. Find a good, secure public campground and go camping, all by your lonesome. Rent one of those small campers. Stare into your campfire. That will wash your brain more effectively than any psychiatrist could ever hope to do. For as long as you stare into it, Mario and even Taylor will be off somewhere beyond your awareness. Are you forgetting our impromptu night up on the grazing permit? Did that short stretch of therapy do no good whatsoever?"

"And what about Jim Pengilly?" she asked, ignoring my questions to raise one of there own. "Where will he be?"

"He'll be back in Montana slaving away where he belongs. Don't waste anytime thinking about Dr. Pengilly. He'll be occupied trying to win his pilot's license.

"Good luck on that license." she said, "I don't like flying unless the man at the controls has one."

"Good thinking, girl. Maybe we ought to head back. They should be done with the dishes by now."

They were, and after a round of *thanks for coming* and *thanks for inviting us*, Mike and I left for home. It had been a most enjoyable evening, though I'm not sure I'd made any progress in terms of boosting Megan's spirits.

The Macintosh Ranch was a beehive of activity going into August. As usual, it was the harvesting of feed of one kind or another that burned up most of our time. The silage corn was looking very good, but we were still running the sprinkler system around about once every ten days and would do so until it froze.

Spread out over the Macintosh Ranch's vast acres were thousands of bales of alfalfa and mixed hay. It was strung out from the main ranch up to Megan's, a distance of several miles. We had two gooseneck trailers hauling all day long. Each of the trailers carried exactly 178 small bales or 35 round bales. Stacks, a city block long, had already been built on the north and west sides of Claire's extensive feed lots, and several smaller stacks would be built inside a nearby, fenced hay yard.

My original quarter section was devoted totally to pasture to be used for summer and early spring grazing. The grass on the two sections I had just purchased had been grazed heavily; it needed what remained of this fall and the coming spring to recover, so 200 of the large round bales and 500 square straw bales had to be hauled either from the main ranch or from Megan's. The weren't a gift. I paid cash in Megan's case or their value was deducted from my salary. I insisted that they received fair value from me for whatever feed I purchased.

Come spring, the hundred cows I would purchase yet this year would calf out on the additional two sections of grass I had just purchased, but I would have to winter them at home. If my hay supplies were inadequate for the new cows, I'd be buying more from Claire or Megan. Their irrigation systems all but guaranteed a surplus each year. Next summer, unless something changed his mind, Claire said I could run up to a hundred head on the grazing permit.

I was satisfied with our progress in picking up the bales and moving them to where we felt we would need them. Benny and Odin would finish hauling them, and I would be spending a few days up on the grazing permit to check range conditions and to try to get a better head count. I expected to put in long days in the saddle, and I was toying with the idea of moving Claire's 24-foot camper up there instead of roughing it in a tent. Nights were cooling down pretty good, and I am one of the faint hearted when it comes to cool. Besides with each passing day and the weather likely to come with it, the opportunities for roughing it would grow fewer.

Until then, I would be studying for my private flying license. I was ready for them, and was present and accounted for when the written exams were administered on Tuesday and Wednesday of the first week in August. I passed them without too much difficulty and then went to the clinic at Deaconess for my physical. Dr. Michael Herron, a specialist in internal medicine, conducted the physical exam, which I passed with flying colors except for one small speed bump. I was red-green color blind, which I already knew and which meant I had to secure a waiver to get my license. The waiver simply prohibited me from night-flying. Runway lights were the culprit. In any case, I soloed and spent a total of seven hours in the air over the weekend. Most of the time I was looking down upon the Roots. Someone tell me if there is a better way of familiarizing myself with the landscape. From that, I was able to get a good overall count but, I wanted an on-the-ground check to spot health or injury problems up close.

The hours I had logged back in Maryland allowed me to grandfather in the right to fly with passengers immediately, but I waited to actually do so until I was comfortable in the cockpit myself. My Montana hours were logged either early in the morning or in the evenings before sunset in order to avoid the thermal updrafts on the mountain front.

I used my pasture for takeoffs and landings, with my imaginary runway on a north-south tangent when the wind was blowing from the north or south. When it changed direction and came at me from the east, I took off always into the wind. A strong wind rushing down the mountains from the west meant I didn't fly that day. A Cessna 172 simply lacked the power to lift me over the Tobacco Root range without circling about long enough to gain the necessary altitude.

It took only a matter of minutes, but there was no other way. Even the 727s and 707s that took off from the Bozeman airport often made a wide loop to gain altitude before they tackled the Bridgers or the Gallatins. From what I had been able to gather, the friend who was flying when Patrick Macintosh was killed near Rawlins, had overestimated his plane's capabilities and underestimated the height of the mountain he had crashed into. Eyewitnesses attested to the fact that the pilot had attempted to turn away but had made his move after it was too late.

I loved the 172. It was the first and only plane I had ever flown, other than a couple hours in a Piper Super Cub, and I thought it was a thing of beauty. Later models were far more sophisticated in terms of radio and navigational features, but it was a highly dependable pleasure craft from the day it was first manufactured. Rated to fly at a speed of 130 miles per hour, it had been flown as fast as 160 miles per hour but, of course, that was probably a test flight under unique atmospheric conditions. Empty, it weighed something over 1200 pounds, with a wing span of about 36 feet. Four passengers, including the pilot, could comfortably occupy its wrap-around cabin, and it could handle a payload of something over 2000 pounds. Its climb rate was over 700 feet per minute and it could be flown at an altitude of almost 16,000 feet. Its range of over 700 miles, meant it could be flown from Bozeman to Fargo, Cheyenne, or Rapid City without refueling. Never one to take chances in the air with respect to weather and fuel, I always kept a sharp eye out for the aircraft weather reports, and I never let my fuel gage drop anywhere near empty.

Michael was the first to ask me for a ride. We took off heading into a wind from the north-north-west, and flew along the front of the mountains long enough to gain the necessary altitude before we banked to the left near Three Forks and flew back over the Tobacco Roots. Looking down upon the rugged range below brought back some bitter-sweet memories.

We flew directly over Pony toward Hollow Top Mountain and looked down upon Albro and Hollow Top Lake where Michele and I had camped. The Tobacco Root Range is only about 40 miles in length. Some accounts say it contains 43 peaks over 10,0000 feet. I knew only a few of them, but was able to point out to Michael, Hollow Top, Potosi, Jefferson, Branham, Thompson and Cloud Rest.

We flew south in almost a straight line from the northern end of the range, searching for the specific canyon we had followed and where Taylor had broken her leg. When flying over mountainous terrain, I routinely try to fly well above the ridges rather than in the valleys and canyons. That way, if I have trouble, I can look to both sides of a ridge for possible landing or crash sites and choose the one that looks the most inviting. Down in a valley, and unable to gain in altitude, for one reason or another, there was but one option, the valley itself.

At 120 miles and hour, it took us just a bit over half an hour to cover its distance from north to south. At it's southern end, we could look down upon the Gravelly Range and Ennis and Virginia City. In the distance, toward the Idaho State line, we caught glimpses of Old Baldy, Cascade Mountain and Black Butte. Their elevations fell short of many of the Tobacco Root peaks, but they were impressive nonetheless. The sight of the lofty peaks in every direction made me want to climb each and every one of them. From the southwest end of the Gravelly range, we circled back and dropped down into the pasture next to the house without incident. The Cessna's performance was perfect. If it were sold, it would be to me.

Two days later, Megan and Taylor showed up for a ride over essentially the same route. This time we took off heading into a slight east wind and followed the Madison River north until we were more or less straight east of Three Forks before we cut back over the Tobacco Roots. Later, as we were about to touch down on Pengilly National Airport, I invited them to stay for supper but they declined because they were helping Claire and Jennifer pack for their departure the next day.

Mike and I drove over to the Macintosh Ranch after supper to say goodbye to Claire and Jenny. They were leaving early in the morning so we did not stay long. My discussion with Claire regarding the tasks he wanted us to focus on while they were gone occupied most of my time.

I had only one small chance to talk to Megan and to ask her when Taylor was leaving for Denver. Her reservations were for Wednesday night, two days hence. Did she want me to help get her to the airport? No, that wasn't necessary. When we had a minute alone in the kitchen, pouring cups of coffee for ourselves and Claire, I inquired as to her Vancouver Island reservations. "Not yet," was her economical answer.

Thursday afternoon was my target date for heading up to the grazing permit. I had long since changed my mind about using the Macintosh camper. Roughing it was what I wanted, so on my way home on the eve of the Macintosh's departure, I drove over to Megan's and borrowed a pack saddle from Jason. He said Morgan had called, was enjoying her time with her mother, but was anxious to come back to Montana.

"Did she happen to say when?" I asked.

"Maybe at Christmas," he replied, "though it sounded like she had yet to secure her Mother's approval. I sure hope she can come."

"That make two of us, Jason," I replied solemnly.

Later than night, I asked Mike to keep an eye out on Megan while I was gone. You're in charge here, Mike, I told him. Check the cows a couple of times every day and make sure the horses are fed.

Before I retired for the night, I painstakingly developed a list of everything I needed to take along. And, I was constantly reminding myself that my trip was part of my job and not an extended camping trip where I could strike out wherever I wished with no particular objective in mind. It took me most of the next morning to round up everything I wanted to take along. Most of the rest of the day was needed to get it packed on the two pack horses.

It was a proud man who rode out on to the grazing permit early that evening, and before dark I had the three horses in the catch pen and my tent staked down near the small nearby lake. I built a fire, perked a pot of coffee and leaned back against a tree to look into the flames. What I had told Megan about the magical powers of campfires proved true once again. I lost my self in that fire and, I mean lost myself, thinking about nothing, not wanting to think about anything. When I had finished my second cup of coffee, I walked over to the pens and threw a bale of mixed hay to the horses, checked the water trough, and rolled into my bed. It wasn't yet 10 o'clock, but I was tired, and I had a long day ahead of me.

For a time, I watched my fire flickering in the darkness, but I was soon sleeping soundly. The next thing I remember is sitting up and trying to rub sleep from my eyes. The sun was already signaling, with a faint, pale light over the Madison Mountains, that I was only moments away from actually seeing it begin its long climb. I jumped out of my tent, anxious to be on the trail with my tally book and my stockman's basic first aid kit. I was hoping that my practice sessions in the undersized roping arena I had built at one end of the smaller catch pen would pay off if I found it necessary to send my loop out to bust an injured or sickly calf. Older stock, if they showed signs of needing closer inspection or immediate attention, would be drifted back toward the catch pen and the squeeze chute situated in one corner.

Breakfast consisted of three fried eggs, two sausage patties, and three slices of toast made with my backpacking toaster. I washed my utensils, plate and cast iron frying pan in the creek, stuffed a couple of sandwiches, a jar of peanut butter, and a bag of day-old biscuits in my one saddle bag and, in my off side bag, I made room for my 2-cup coffee pot, a cup, and a plastic bag filled with coffee. It took but minutes to toss another half bale of hay in to the two pack horses, and I was on my way. The first cow-calf pairs I spotted were across from my tent on the other side of the lake. My binoculars told me they were in good health. A half wild mother cow wheeled to face me when I slipped in behind them from the east. The calves were putting on size and weight in the lush patches of grass found all over the permit, but their tails shot into the air, like their mother's, and the whole bunch ran off to the north. I watched them until they dropped below a knoll and disappeared from sight.

The trail I followed was actually the remnant of an old mining road. Ruts cut in it decades earlier were still clearly discernible, as it followed the path of least resistance up the mountain side. It was marked, in places, with severe erosion and, in a few spots, runoff from earlier downpours had cut through the side of the road, cutting small gullies into the side hill. But nature was working its healing powers even there, with brush clinging to its sides and small patches of grass hugging its bottom.

South of the road, the mountain sloped away gradually toward the creek under a canopy of pine trees growing even in the cracks of huge rocks. It was a ruggedly beautiful slope, and I would have bet that it was home to mule deer, elk and even and occasional moose. The trail I rode hugged the north slope, and I found myself constantly dodging huge rocks and large trees. It lifted gradually toward the north, its slope covered with a good stand of short grass. The higher I reached the more rugged it became. Here and there I spotted rocks whose face was wet from water seeping out of overhanging fractures. In places, pools of water collected beneath until their depth overtopped the bowl they were found in and spilled over the side unto the road and down the slope.

A few hundred feet increase in elevation brought me through a stretch of smooth, gray rocks jutting out from the trail's north side and interrupting my view of the largely grassed area to the north. They reached no more than thirty feet into the sky, but they sat immediately adjacent to the trail, and I had a hard time finding my way past. The deer tracks I followed took me through narrow passages between a jumble of rocks that had obviously fallen from above, until I came out into an open area bereft of trees and covered with a fine stand of mountain short grass sprayed with light blue and yellow wild flowers. In the middle of that big open were two hundred or more cow-calf pairs. This time, my binoculars did not reveal the presence or absence of injured or unhealthy critters, but the brands I could make out confirmed that these were Claire and Megan's cattle.

My position was downwind from them, and I was able to close on them for a better look before they saw me. Off to the right and slightly down slope, I spotted what appeared to be a yearling steer or a young heifer bogged down on one end of a good sized pothole.

When I rode over to see what I had, several of the mother cows looked my way, but there was no panic in them and, before long, they dropped their heads down to resume grazing. It was late enough in the day that many of the calves had spread themselves out on the ground for their forenoon naps in a bright sun.

What I found in the boggy spot was a young cow or first-calf heifer mired in scum and decayed plant growth. I dabbed a rope around her neck on my first toss, wrapped it hard-and-fast to my saddle, and slowly pulled her out. She had been there a while, and she was understandably gaunt and hungry. When she tried to return to her watery prison for a drink, I hazed her away. She looked at me like the dumb animal she was and then lifted her tail in the air and trotted away in the direction of another pool. Her black udder was swaying from side to side and it was swollen and dripping milk with every step she took. She moved on as if she had a destination in mind, which confirmed for me that she had been in the mud for a while and that she had a calf someplace.

I followed her long enough to see her stop in some rocks and paw at what was probably her sleeping calf. She never moved nearer than a few feet, and I knew something was wrong. She was snorting and pawing at the ground, but she did not approach near enough to touch her nose to her calf, if that's what it was. I rode up behind her, and she trotted quickly off to the side and then stopped to look back at me. What I found were the remains of what was probably a three hundred pound calf, whose body had been almost completely consumed by a rogue pack of wild dogs or a mountain lion.

As I carefully read the sign I found, it became clear to me that this was the work of a cougar, that the kill had been made elsewhere, and that the carcass had been dragged up into the rocks. Amateur though I was, I was soon convinced that it was the work of an adult-sized cougar. I found deer tracks all over the place, but they were ancient.

No, the fresher tracks were, without question, those of a cougar.

I found what seemed to be two sets of tracks which were, in fact, the front and rear tracks of the same cougar. The front tracks were larger than the rear, but both had pads roughly shaped like a pyramid with its top snipped off. The paws on the front feet were round. On the rear feet, they were smaller and oblong shaped. I saw nothing that even faintly hinted at claws, and that's what confirmed my belief that the calf had been the victim of a cougar. They had claws, rather long claws at that but, from what I had heard, they were retractable.

What could I do? Probably not much. I had a .30-30 lever action Winchester back in camp, but my chances of ever getting near enough to a cougar to get off a shot were slimmer than slim. Still, when I rode out in the morning, the rifle would be in my saddle boot.

Off to the north I rode, looking for more cattle. I spotted several small bunches here and there but never any heavy concentration of critters. Still I made my count and logged the number and locations in my tally book. Once again, I was riding across a wind swept slope covered with a good stand of grass, interspersed here and there with stunted pine trees that looked like they were lonesome and lost. My expedition turned up nothing, so I turned back and began feeling my way back down the mountain and to my camp. It was mid-afternoon when I turned about because I was taking no chances on being caught up here in the dark. I was unprepared for it, carrying only what was left of my second sandwich and a small jar of peanut butter.

When I dropped down out of my saddle at the catch pen, I was amazed at how stiff and sore I had become. The explanation was simple: this day's ride saw me in the saddle longer than I could remember at anytime in the past. I mean *anytime*, ever! I had earned everyone of those aches and pains, and I'll tell you right now, I was proud of them. I'd dabbed my rope over that cow's head on the first try, I'd counted over three hundred cow-calf pairs, I was about to set myself down to a fresh cup of coffee and three or four eggs fried in bacon fat, and I was going to sleep like a dog all night long. Then, in the morning, I was going after that cat!

Finished with my supper, I sat back and looked up at the clouds, whistling and holding a hot cup of coffee in my hand. And it was the hard stuff, too. It was still early, barely dark, but I wasn't going to worry about getting to sleep. I was practically there already, and my head had yet to touch the pillow. I sat there thinking that what I had done this day was a far cry from plunking myself down behind a desk and looking out across Chesapeake Bay.

Hidden somewhere deep within me were the remains of a civil engineer once capable of managing hundreds of lesser engineers; an engineer who would never again see the light of day. I was happy with myself, doing what I was doing, and I was a little bit proud. My fascination for numbers was still intact, and I had that analytical mind, but my heart was on the mountain side, and I knew I would never again be complete away from here.

I was a total failure in love. I had walked away from a good woman who was the mother of my children. I had lost the love of my life by letting her get away from me, but I had built something that would last, a spot for myself in the foothills of the Tobacco Root Mountains, and someday, a long way down the road, I hoped, they would plant me up here where the sun shined on me each morning and the moon and stars twinkled throughout each night.

That was the essence of my thoughts and my mind set as I leaned against my saddle and looked into my fire. The slate was clean. Not a tangible thought crossed my mind, and I felt cleansed by the day's events. I watched as flashes of lightning illuminated the lower slopes of the Madison Range. The absence of thunder told me it was too far away to pose any threat to me. Then suddenly, to my dismay, I watched as a pair of headlights pulled up in front of the gate.

I should have known my transition from eastern engineer to Montana cowboy was incomplete. A cowboy, even a kid-cowboy, would have known the difference between lightning and bouncing headlights. I made out my truck and immediately became concerned that Mike had come as the bearer of bad news. And it was Mike who pulled through the gate, parked up against the catch pens, and dimmed the lights.

"Hey, Dad," he said as he walked from behind the truck, which I now noticed was pulling a trailer, "Thought you might be in bed, but I came anyway."

"Nope, been thinking about it though," I offered, as I stood up. "What brings you up here? Something wrong?"

"No, everything's fine," he said, as he turned to look back at the truck. I watched as a figure moved out from the shadows leading a saddled horse.

There was no mistaking that individual's identity. It was Megan. Now what the hell was she doing here, I wondered? She was wearing a long-sleeved western style plaid shirt under a down vest, and her faded jeans were tucked into a set of rough-out boots that reached almost to her knees. The hat she wore, pulled down to her ears, was the very hat Claire had loaned me once and said he wanted returned.

"Hey, cowboy," she said, "can you tell me if I'm anywhere close to Vancouver Island?"

"Who wants to know?" I asked.

"You're neighbor, who just happens to hold a one-third interest in this grazing permit, and I'm here looking for trespassers. Call it a vacation if you want, but here I am. You got any proof *you* belong here?"

"Yep, as a matter of fact, I do." I said. "My boss has a *two-thirds* interest in the grazing permit, so if you have it in your head to be here, you'll take your orders from me. Okay?"

"You work for my dad?" she said, shrugging her shoulder as if suggest she did not know.

"I do." I said. "Yes, I do. And I work real hard."

"Well, then, that's different. Where's the bunkhouse?"

"If you didn't bring it with, you better turn around and go home. I'm not giving up my air mattress for anyone. "Now tell me, Megan," I added, "what in the hell are you doing here?"

"Jim, when I heard you were up here in these mountains playing cowboy, I told myself I wasn't going to let you enjoy all of this without me. You said I should take a trip. Here I am. You've got a camp fire. I'll stare into it."

"What about Taylor?" I asked. "Does she know you're here? She'll be worried."

"Left this morning for Denver," she replied. "A friend of mine said she needed to see her father."

I turned away from her then, because I knew she was baiting me with every word she spoke. She was throwing back in my face every suggestion I had offered back in Yellowstone. Her being here wasn't particularly troubling to me. I could handle her and her whimsical notions, but I wasn't at all sure about how it was all coming down with Mike.

I pulled him aside when Megan walked to the truck and began unloading her gear. I asked him, in the next thing to a whisper, how he got involved, and he said Megan had called and asked him to come over with my truck. Said she wanted me to drop her off at the grazing permit. I drove over, and she was waiting for me with her horse saddled and ready to load.

"What was I supposed to do?" he said. "Besides, Dad, you're best friends. What could it hurt?"

"My reputation with my son, for one thing," I replied.

"Dad, your reputation is on solid ground with me," he said, "so don't worry. "Anyone can see the two of your are in love, even if you don't know it. You belong together..."

"Belong together?" I interrupted. "We're both failures when it comes to love. Is this one of those cases where two negatives make a positive?"

"Could be, Dad. All I know is I'm leaving Megan here, and I'm going home to get some sleep. Call me on your cell if you need anything. Bye."

He turned then and walked away from me, his hand raised in a reverse *so long*. Megan stopped him when they met, and they spoke in low voices. She handed him an object I could not make out, pecked at his cheek, and then walked over to open the gate for him. When he had passed through, she closed it and walked toward me, her arms filled with her own camping equipment.

"Well, Jim,"she said. "Here I am. "Are you angry?"

"Nope. Come on, I'll help you get set up. Where's your tent?"

She said her tent was in the box of my truck, which meant that my tent was her tent. Unless I forced her to sleep out on the ground. No, she wouldn't have to sleep on the ground, I told her, and I admitted that I liked having her here.

"But aren't we rushing things a bit," I ventured. "I though we had an understanding."

"We did," she admitted, "but things have changed."

"And what is that?" I asked.

"If you'll build up that fire and make some more coffee, I'll tell you."

When the pot had perked long enough, I filled our cups, suddenly no longer sleepy, then I sat back and waited.

"It's true, I think, that we had an understanding," she offered, "but I've changed my mind."

"Changed your mind? In what way?"

With our backs propped against the huge log someone had dragged in from somewhere, we looked at each other, as if we were sizing up something we might want to purchase at the super market. She was a complete mystery me at times. I never knew where she was coming from. She always managed to catch me off guard. I liked her, liked having her around. She was my friend and she was a tease, no doubt about it. And God, she was pretty. Being with her was like being caught up in a dream, one of those good dreams, one that you remembered. Still, the ball was in her court, as far as I was concerned, and she knew it. I waited and, finally, she spoke.

"Bear with me on this, Jim," she said, "I'm still sifting through my thoughts, and what I have to say is important for both of us. I want to find the right words. When you left my place the other night, I was thinking how I didn't want you to go, ever, and how much I loved the feel of your arm around me. Maybe that was just a woman thing; you know, feeling secure with no sense of vulnerability. But I think it was more. It was a man-woman thing and, for me, the pheromones were buzzing about like fireflies. I have liked you since day one, Jim and, you know that, but for me this was something different. It was a new feeling I had about you. Mario was no longer lurking in the shadows. Had he been I would have known. No, he is gone. I don't love him anymore. That's the change I am talking about.

"So you want to know why I'm here, right?" she continued.

"Tell me."

"I will, Jim, in a minute," she replied, "but first let me explain how it came about that I suddenly pulled out all of the stops. After you left the other night, I went to the house to tidy things up a bit. The radio was tuned to one of the country music stations. One of those songs was playing softly, and I'll always remember the lyrics. Not the exact words, of course, but the notion that one can never know what the future holds until one tries it on, and that it is better to be sorry for something you did than something you didn't do.

"So, I'm here with my heart, and all of me, looking for a man who's not afraid to take another chance on love. I'm done tossing time away. I may have something inside me ready to flare up and eat me up; I may die before I should. Whatever time I have left, I refuse to squander. I'm not taking any chances. I'm going for what I want now. I'm not waiting.

"I'm here to tear down that wall of yours. Falling in love with you has not been easy, and God knows we have both bungled love in the past. Falling in love happens, but it can be difficult for a whole bunch of reasons: staying in love is even more tricky. I want the two of us to try again, together, to make it work.

"Someone once told me," she added, "maybe it was even you, that the woman always picks the man. Well, buck up cowboy, I've picked you!"

Chapter 10

We fell asleep in each other's arms right there by the fire. My air mattress spent the night alone, but I didn't mind. The cool air drifting down off the mountain during the night had me rekindling the fire while it was still pitch dark, but I tunneled my way back under our tarp and brought Megan against me. We were snuggling together like newlyweds and, in a way, I suppose that's what we were. No papers, no preacher, no rice flying through the air, no yelling or cheering crowd, and no tin cans tied to the bumper of an auto. But we had taken an important first step in that direction. I couldn't believe it had happened so fast. I couldn't comprehend how I had caved in as I had. Could it be that I was actually in love again?

I was up before her and had the fire blazing again when I saw her looking at me from under her coarse canvas blanket. We smiled at each other, but neither spoke. She could feel the cold air, and she could see that the coffee had yet to perk, so she settled back under the tarp and waited.

"It's ready," I said, thinking she had gone back to sleep.

"Can you bring me a cup, Jim?" she asked.

I told her I'd be happy to do so, but when I handed it to her I asked if waiting on her was to be part of some twisted *breaking in* process.

"No breaking in process, Jim," she said. Why don't you grab your cup and come back under the covers. We can watch the sunrise together."

"For a while," I said.

It was a fine morning at that. We nursed our coffee and relaxed as the sun slowly poked its head above the Madison Range.

"About last night, Jim?" she asked.

"What about last night?" I responded.

"Well, we didn't...you know...we didn't..."

"Nope, we didn't. To tell the truth, I fell asleep. Let's agree to go slow. We'll both know when it's time."

When we finished eating and had washed our dishes in the plastic tub Megan had thought to include in her stock of supplies and gear, I drifted over to the catch pen and caught up our horses.

"Are we going to camp up in the high country tonight, Jim?" Megan asked.

"Not unless you want to," I said. "This is a good jumping off spot for the entire permit and it's the first place people would look if they needed to talk to either of us. I recommend we stay her at least for tonight. I love being near the water, over-grown puddle that it is."

Her response was a simple *okay*. She said she liked it here too where we were out in the open and able to see for miles beyond.

"Among other things," I said, changing the subject abruptly, "we're going hunting today."

"Hunting?"

Yes, I told her, and then I described my find up on the north slope. Before I dumped upon her my vast knowledge about mountain lions, I admitted that what little I did know came to me in the form of printed words rather than actual experience. Mountain Lions aren't often seen up here, I ventured, but that doesn't mean they aren't around. They are very elusive and difficult to see. They are stalkers and are seldom seen until it is too late. They are also a species in jeopardy. Their habitat is shrinking but, in spite of that, they possess an uncanny will to survive. So, even if they feel threatened, they only rarely attack humans. For their meals, they prefer venison or elk, but if they are hungry they will eat porcupines, racoons, beavers, rabbits, dogs, cats and even insects. When they are starving, they will take on almost anything, including a full grown horse and, almost without exception, they kill what they stalk.

"They can weigh more than a good sized man," I continued, "and their athletic abilities are nothing short of fantastic. They can attain speeds in excess of 40 miles per hour and they have been known to leap 15 feet vertically. That cougar up in the rocks killed a calf at least twice its own size and dragged it several hundred yards. It's probably back in the rocks right now, slowly digesting the 300 pounds of calf it has eaten over a matter of a few days."

"How do you know all this?"

"Like I said, books, hunting and fishing magazines, that sort of thing, but I actually saw one up close once in the San Diego Zoo. A mature, male cougar is a thing of beauty. The one I saw was tawny colored with jagged patches of lighter hair on its underbody and about its face. He was close to eight feet long from the end of his nose to the tip of his black-tipped tail. He probably outweighed me, and he purred like a common house cat. From what I've heard they don't growl like a lion or tiger, but snarl like a barnyard cat. Their claws, which come into play when they pounce on their prey, are retractable."

"Are you sure we want to go hunting?" Megan asked.

"Well, I'm not crazy about killing a mountain lion as far as that goes," I replied. "They are a thing of beauty as far as I'm concerned but I don't like to see them eating up profits either. You do the screaming.

I'll do the shooting, and let's both hope I can shoot straight, if it comes to that."

The pack horses were nibbling on the half bale of hay I had thrown over the fence to them when we left. They would be fine and, the truth was, we really didn't need them. Whatever I thought we might need was in our saddle bags or tied behind our saddles. We were wearing jackets and scarves over our hats when we rode out of camp. It was cool like an late summer morning ought to be up so high. Later, after the sun's rays had moderated early temperatures, we would tie the jackets behind our saddles and the scarves around our necks. Our saddle bags were stuffed with sandwiches, strips of bacon, beef jerky and, yes, peanut butter. In mine, we packed the 3-cup coffee pot, one plastic bag filled with coarse ground coffee, another with shavings from a dead branch. I prided myself in being able to get a small fire going and a coffee pot perking within minutes of our arrival at a stopping place.

After we mounted, I pulled up along side of her, put my arm around her and pulled her against me. I didn't tell her I loved her. I just wasn't ready for that yet, but our kiss was a wet one, the promise of more was there, and neither of us wanted to stop. But we did, of course, and soon we were headed back through the same country I had traveled the day before. I wanted to show Megan the calf's carcass to give her a better feel for what had happened.

Cougars usually pounce on their prey from behind, so I asked Megan to take the lead when we came to the short stretch of jumbled rock. That way I'd be where I could see the cat, if it was there, and warn her. I was counting on our horses alerting us to the cat's presence. I had passed through the day before without sighting anything or detecting movement of any kind. Today, my Winchester was out of its boot, just in case, and it was cocked. But our passage was uneventful. As we moved along, I kept a sharp eye out for fresh tracks of any kind, but saw nothing.

By now, I guessed, the cat was likely resting somewhere with a full belly, and he could be miles away. Once through the rocks we hung a hard right and began riding up slope toward the outcropping where I had found the calf. Megan looked at the remains of the mostly black calf with revulsion, and we did not stay long. I didn't tell her that the carcass had been moved slightly since yesterday and that there were fresh tracks leading away from the rocks in the direction we were heading.

"Tobacco Roots, it's a strange name isn't it, Jim?" Megan observed out of the blue as if to direct their thoughts away from the pile of vissera and hair on the ground. "I know how they came to be known as such. Do you?"

"Nope. I've wondered," I said, "but never thought to learn why."

"Dad told my brother Patrick and me that they are named after the root of a Mullein plant that was dried by the Indians and miners, then ground up and mixed with Kinnikinic as a substitute for tobacco. He knew a lot more about it than I remember."

"Interesting," I said. "Figured it must have some connection to smoking."

"What about the plane?" she asked. "Wouldn't it be quicker to get a count from above?"

"Good idea," I replied. "We'll give it a try later this fall. I'll do the flying. You can do the counting. We could take pictures and then count them when we got home."

By the time we stopped at noon, we had reached beyond where I had reached the day before, and our rough count tended to compare closely with my cow-calf estimates of yesterday. The country we were riding into now stretched out in front of us on an easy slope with a thin stand of mixed pine and spruce, but our path was blocked by the rising vertical canyon wall we had kept in sight all morning.

This was one of those narrow canyons that led to the high mountain plateaus above and, hopefully, to a large herd of our cattle. Our count so far was roughly 400 head, and somewhere within the permit there ought to be another 700 cow-calf pairs and around 200 head of yearling steers. Over 350 of those cows-calf pairs belonged now to Megan. The cows were commercial grade. Only the bulls were registered stock. Megan had become an important producer in her own right, and coupled with her Dad's black-baldy herd, they were one of the larger producers in the valley.

Our noon stop was bean time for Megan and me, but it was also a respite for the horses. We unsaddled them, rubbed their backs down, threw hobbles on both of them, and turned them loose to graze. Under a lonesome old pine tree, I built a fire. While it heated our coffee, we sat back against the trunk and ate. I handed my binoculars to Megan and we took turns glassing the area far to the east and south. One could not really appreciate the size of things until he could look down from above.

Size has a way of translating and transforming individuals into microscopic specks, piddling presences, in the grand scheme of things but, at the same time, it empowers those who occupy the high ground. We didn't speak of it, but I believe we both felt extremely fortunate to be up here, close to the clouds.

"Jim, can I tell you something?" Megan asked, as if she had read my mind. "I don't want to leave here, ever. I have never been happier than I am this minute."

"I feel the same," I said, "but the folks down below would have search parties out looking for us after a while. Maybe we could find some middle ground."

"Such as just down the road from my place?"

"It's a thought," I said, "but speaking practically, I think we won't be able to stay. We have to climb up that canyon over there and see if we have any cows on the plateau. And we have to make it up and back before dark. Unless you want to live on peanut butter 'til morning."

"No thanks. Let's go."

The horses hadn't drifted far, and I had them caught up, saddled, and ready to go before Megan killed our fire and packed up what was left of our lunch. The trail up the canyon was steep, but it was the remnant of an old mining road so, at times, we were able to ride abreast. Below us to our left, we spotted a small bunch of maybe 40-50 cows bedded down on a grassy bench overlooking the creek. A closer inspection with my binoculars located no sick or injured individuals, so, as they say, we pressed onward and upward. The sun had moved some distance to the west by the time we topped out on a surprisingly level tract of grass that sloped very gently toward the south. Here we found most of the rest of the herd, including a handful of bulls we had left to catch any cows or heifers that hadn't settled yet.

We turned back almost immediately, satisfied that the herd was in good shape and had adequate grass. We did not expect to encounter diseased critters. This was clean range, never over grazed, with lots of water. Accidents were another thing. Calves cavorting about had been known to get too close to a precipitous edge. And, of course, predators could not be discounted. To my knowledge there were no Grizzly bears in the Roots, but black bears were fairly numerous. Then there was always the chance of running into a pack of feral dogs.

Half way to our camp, Megan spotted what appeared to be another calf down off to the north. We rode toward the mass of flesh and hair stretched out on the ground. When we came within a hundred yards, we both caught a flash of movement and watched in amazement as a large cat leaped across the carcass and bounded into the trees. The cougar had been feeding as we approached. He was almost instantly too far away for me to get off a shot, but I knew he would be back for more of the young doe he had brought down.

Finding another victim was an unsettling experience for Megan. I could see it in her eyes, so we left almost immediately. Our cougar friend or one of his friends was on the prowl again, and it was only the presence of that young doe that had spared another of our calves. I knew what I had to do. In the morning I would ride back, find a down-wind, concealed location, near enough to the remains of the doe to reach with my .30-.30. The cat would be back sometime the next day, and I would be waiting for him.

Megan was especially quiet during the remainder of our trip back to camp. My sense was that what had been a period of euphoria for her when we stopped for lunch, had suddenly changed dramatically. She had experienced the mountain at its best, and she had learned of the cougar's standing in the overall food chain. I wish I could have protected her from that, but I couldn't.

Thankfully, the more distance we put between ourselves and that bundle of hide, flesh and viscera up on the mountain, the more relaxed she became. By the time we reached our camp, she was talking again and acting like her old self. While I made supper, she disappeared below the bench where the tent was located, and I could hear her splashing about in the water. Later, I would do the same thing. Surprisingly the water was quite warm. It had been a long day, and we both felt the need, I guess, to wash away our memories of seeing the cougar bound away from his kill. We sat for hours beside the fire, staring into it as if it held some magical power to heal and, maybe it did, because all the while, she tucked herself up under my outstretched arm and reached around me to hold me tightly. She was sleeping when I nudged her awake.

"We can't stay out here again tonight, Megan," I said softly. "It's going to get too cold. Did you bring along anything warmer than what you're wearing?"

She never said a word, just stood up and walked to the tent. A few moments later she emerged wearing a set of blue sweats proudly proclaiming her allegiance to the *Montana State Bobcats*. Her rough-out boots had been replaced with a pair of blue and white running shoes emblazoned with a leaning "N".

"This is warmer and more comfortable," she said. "Now can we stay out a little longer? I want to talk."

"Sure, do you want a jacket? I've got a couple in my duffel."

"Later, maybe. I'm counting on some body heat, you know."

"Well, then, if that's the case," I said, invitingly, "come down here."

She snuggled up against me again, and I waited for her to speak. She told me that up on the mountain earlier, when she saw the gutted doe, she saw herself in the same light and she felt, momentarily, that it was a sign, a bad sign. The surgeons at St. Mary's Hospital in Rochester had opened her abdomen and removed part of her stomach, the tail of her pancreas, and all of her spleen. She went on to say that, since then, she had never felt complete; that they had taken a part of her and diminished her in some way.

"It's a childish way of looking at it, I know," she said, "but that is how I have felt these past few months. I'll forever have that foot long scar running from my sternum to below my belly button and, I suppose, it will burn and smart forever to keep me from ever forgetting the trauma of that experience. And, if that weren't enough, divorcing Mario, left me feeling smaller than I had ever felt."

"Time. Megan," I said, "Time will take care of all that."

"I don't need that time, Jim," she said, "Not anymore. That's what I wanted to tell you. My feeling of being reduced by the surgery vanished like a wounded pheasant running in the grass. It's gone. Guilt about my divorce too. It took a couple of hours, but it was dying up there on the mountain and, by the time we got here to camp, it was dead."

"That's wonderful," I said, "just wonderful. I'm so happy for you. But I don't under...

"Understand? It's easy, Jim," she exclaimed. "I realized that I *was* no longer incomplete. It was you, don't you see. You made me complete. Where were you 20 years ago when I could have loved you?"

"I wasn't at Stanford," was my lame answer.

"Well, I'm not at Stanford any more either," she said, "and I'm tired of waiting. You love me, I know. Now show me how much."

Nowhere under the sun or moon can there be a more fulfilling way of topping off even a great day than to hold the woman you love in your arms. Nowhere in the galaxy is there a greater feeling than that of holding the soft, yet firm, body of an impassioned woman who loves you and needs you to be complete. We were both nervous and tentative at the outset, but as we responded to each other's warmth and caresses, we moved against each other, meeting the other at just the right moment.

When I sensed I was getting ahead of her, my movement slowed and she dropped back effortlessly to give me the time I needed. At times she moved against me; at times it was me who led. We were pacing ourselves, and the amazing thing is, we did it without saying a word.

It was a sensing thing. And it was our senses that told us we were exactly where we needed to be as we raced together toward the final ecstasy. Done, we clung to each other for minutes, still caressing, still enjoying, and then we found the comfort of our mattress. Spent, yet still breathing heavily, we fell apart and lay side by side until we fell asleep. Before I slept, I found my self thinking about the man who had walked away from Megan. He was an utter fool, an idiot. He had to be. Thank you, Mario! Thank you!

My dream, the first I'd had in a long time, was crazy and totally unrelated to our passion. It involved the efforts of a host of branch line railroads to keep from being swallowed up by the main liners. Explain that, somebody.

We made love again toward morning, and this time it was slow and easy, but the result was the same. Megan confided in me while we were making breakfast that she had dreamed we were being driven against the rocks in the middle of a stream by a rushing current until we were washed ashore near, of all places, a beach near the bridge that crosses the Columbia River east of Ellensberg. My reaction was a simple *wow!* Her dream was at least as wacky as mine.

"What's on the schedule for today, Jim?" she asked.

"We have two schedules for today;" I responded, hesitantly. "One is mine, the other is yours." I could see my answer had confused her, so I explained.

"I'm going after the cat, Megan; you're gonna have to be staying in camp."

"No. I don't think so," she snapped. "Where you go, I go. Okay?"

"It could get a bit hairy up there," I said, backing off just a little. "It might be better if you stayed here. I won't be gone all day, I hope."

"Hairy is where I want to be, Jimbo. Hairy is where I'm going to be! You're looking at a gal who's made up her mind not to miss out on even the skinniest, smallest slice of life."

There are many good things to say about a strong woman. I just couldn't think of what that might be at the moment and, somehow, I knew there wasn't a list long enough to dissuade this particular woman any more from anything she made up her mind to do. So I acquiesced. No I folded. Acquiescence connotes a gentlemanly acceptance. I folded simply because on this one I was outmatched. My ego, though slightly deflated, was still largely intact because, secretly, I was proud of her. Still I didn't want anything bad to happen to her either.

"It could get a little boring," I said, throwing out what was my last ditch shot at keeping her in camp.

"Boring's okay," she replied, "but you and me, we've come far enough already to tell me we will never be bored as long as we are together and love each other."

"You win, Megan," I said. "What have I got myself into?"

"You've got yourself into a situation," she said, "where there's a cougar that needs killing and a woman who can't get enough of you."

"Saddle your horse," I said. What else *could* I say?

What had begun as a mild, sun-drenched morning changed slowly, almost imperceptibly to one of low hanging clouds and the promise of rain. With undersides dark and foreboding, they had drifted in from the east, rubbing gently up against the front of the mountains. The odds that the weather would make an end run around the mountains, and drift off to the north or south, were poor. And unless I missed my guess, chances for more sunshine were equally remote.

So we packed one of the horses with our tent, our sleeping bags, the mattresses, and as much of our other gear as we could. That included enough food to last until morning should the clouds suddenly collapse and let loose the moisture they couldn't possibly hold if they continued pushing against the mountain. The other pack horse I left behind with enough hay to last until morning, and keep him from wondering where his partner had gone.

I kept my eye on the horizon to see if the flow of clouds was changing. I had a cougar to think about. A diet of slippery rocks on a steep trail, I could do without.

Megan was quiet as she slipped into her saddle and waited for me to mount up. My pocket was filled with .30-.30 cartridges, so I took the time to drop most of them into one of my saddle bags before I mounted and moved up along side of her. I knew she wasn't really mad; she was only trying to make a point.

"I'm sorry," I said, as I slipped my right arm around her shoulder and pulled her against me. "I should have known you wouldn't want to stay down here."

"I'm not angry, Jim. Just disappointed. I want to be with you, that's all."

"I understand," I said, "and I want to be with you. So from now on we tramp the globe together."

It took us the better part of two hours to draw near to the doe carcass. For the last quarter mile, we advanced on foot, leading the three horses. When we came to within a hundred yards, I slipped my binoculars out of their case again and glassed the area near the remains. We took turns inspecting the surrounding area for more than an hour before we began to move closer. In my mind, I was sure the cougar would return. It was a matter of patience. There was that possibility, of course, that he had caught our scent long ago and was somewhere up in the rocks watching us.

We were too distant for me to have any chance of bringing the big cat down, so we moved slowly to the northwest, always with the wind in our face. We walked again, leading the horses, until we found a sizeable depression that would give us the cover we needed. The backdrop for our camp was a mixed grove of spruce and pine trees. We were obviously in a transition zone as far as the trees were concerned. Higher up it would be mostly Engelmann Spruce.

We were still staking down our tent when the drizzle began. We tried to make as little noise as we could, but doing so was all but impossible. We had three horses snorting and stomping about when the urge hit them, and even the sound of our voices could probably be heard some distance away. If it were actually raining, and raining hard, I observed, noise would be less of a problem.

We were now no more than 50 yards from the doe's remains. We took turns with the glasses throughout the morning and, when our eyes weren't glued on what remained of the doe, we were glassing the surrounding mountains watching for other wildlife. The images that floated across the binocular's circular view included surprisingly vivid snapshots of trails, individual rocks, birds and trees, in spite of the prevailing overcast conditions.

By noon, it was raining in earnest, and the wind had shifted to the southwest, which meant that it would be raining harder in the next hour or so. Our tent was up and we had built a hatful of fire under the lower branches of a large spruce tree. When the heavy rains began, I rushed under the spruce with a tarp that I was able to stretch over the lower branches, hoping to keep the rain from snuffing out our fire. It kept the rain from our fire, but it also prevented the smoke from rising up through the branches as I had hoped. Which was more important I wondered? Hiding the smoke or eating and drinking our coffee?" Suffice it to say, our addiction to coffee trumped smoke, and I never removed the tarp.

Hard rain sent us scurrying to the tent. We might have stayed relatively dry with our hats and our yellow slickers, but I thought the yellow stood out too much against a background of black, green and brown. With the shift in wind, it was likely that our scent had revealed our location to the cougar already and if it had, I was pretty sure we had made the trip for nothing. The other thing that concerned me was how little of the doe's carcass actually remained. The cat had devoured it almost completely, and he might have abandoned it for yet another kill somewhere on the plateau, or might even be actively hunting again. I admitted to Megan that I was speculating. I really didn't know.

Still, it was too late to head down. We were stuck there for the remainder of the day and perhaps for the night. The horses were tied to nearby trees, their heads hanging low and their bodies drenched with cold rain. They were accustomed to standing in the rain. They slept standing up, usually hip shot, and they accepted nature's laws. If you thought about it at all, what else could they do. We sought the comfort of our rain-proof tent. From time to time, probably out of boredom, with no real expectation of catching sight of the cougar, one of us donned one of the slickers, and went out to train the binoculars on the nearby rocks. We split that particular chore evenly between us, because my new found love would have it no other way.

Throughout the morning and early afternoon, we hunkered down either in or near our tent. Twice I left to rekindle our fire and replenish our supply of coffee and to steal another glance at the rocks. Dry wood was growing scarce, but I was able to cut away several of the dead branches always to be found near the bottom of most coniferous trees.

We cat-napped the afternoon away, threw together some supper, and retreated again to the tent. The rain had slackened somewhat, but the ground about us was saturated. Even the horses looked dejectedly at me until I dropped a bait of whole oats before each of them. I marveled as I watched their upper lip work to extract a single kernel of oats from the soaked ground.

Neither Megan nor I was particularly tired, given the amount of time we had napped during the day. We were stuck in that tent until morning, make no mistake about it. It was too dark to read, so we talked. No, it is more accurate to say that Megan talked. I was amazed at some of the weighty concepts she had floating around in her brain. She began by telling me about a person in Greek mythology named, Sisyphus. Archimedes I'd heard of. And Pythagoras, Aristotle, and Euclid were names I recalled. But no Sisyphus. In any case, Sisyphus, being punished for some deed Megan could not recall, was sentenced to push a large rounded stone up a very steep slope for as long as it took him to get it to the top.

"It kept slipping back on him and he kept pushing it up the incline," Megan explained. "We're supposed to believe he is still pushing it, I think."

"And your point?" I asked.

"My point is this," she replied. "Trying to reach the top of the hill is mostly what we humans do every day, all the time. We don't always know what's up there, but we keep trying. Because it is in our nature to do so. Somewhere within us is chemistry that behaves like a minuscule computer chip and makes us do it. We can't help ourselves.

"Think about it for a minute, Jim." she continued. "What would the world be like if we didn't keep pushing? For a long time now, I've been struggling to push a ball up that hill. I feel like a female Sisyphus. First, it was winning a job in a Denver bank, traditionally the domain of men. I kept piling up good work and after a while someone noticed. They couldn't ignore my performance. I got the job. I pushed the ball over the top. Then, it was my divorce. I pushed the ball that was Mario time and time again, hoping to reach the top so he could see what he was tossing away. It kept slipping back on me, and one day he walked out. I not only didn't succeed in pushing the ball up the hill, the ball ran away from me. Defeated again the way Sisyphus must have felt every time he tried and failed.

"Then along came the big *C*," she continued. "Since the day they told me I had cancer, I have been pushing that ball, trying to get over the hump as far as my health is concerned, but it kept rolling back on me. I was over the top, I felt, when they told me I was cancer free. Next thing I knew there was another ball waiting for me when they found that lump next to my left lung."

"But that turned out to be a glob of fat or something, didn't it?" I ventured.

"Yes, but I took a step backward and lined that ball up with the hill, until the radiology report confirmed that it wasn't a tumor. Then came the nausea. I'm still pushing against that ball, and I will continue to do so until my year is up."

"But didn't you sort of reach the top once more the last time they told you were cancer free?"

"Yes. But then there were the screwed up red blood cells. Another hill. Another ball. Vitamin B12 took care of that, but my point is that every time I felt like I was over the hump something came along to push me back. And that's the way it is going to be from here on. That's the way it always is, always."

"Are you pushing that ball now?" I asked, thinking her answer would be negative, but it wasn't.

"Yes, as a matter of fact, I am," she said thoughtfully, "and the hump I'm trying to get over is you, Jim Pengilly, the now famous Dr. Pengilly. You see, you're not to the top of that hill yet. You're not a sure thing for me. I need to help you push."

"And that's what you want?" I responded.

"Yes," she said. "I want one thing in this world I can count on. I deserve that for a change."

"And, you don't think you can count on me?" I asked.

"Not completely, no, I don't. When you've struggled to push that ball up the hill as many times as I have, you come to believe nothing is ever sure."

"Can I tell you one thing and then ask you a question?"

"Yes."

"You can count on me. I'm going no place. If you have to push another ball up another hill, I'll be there with you. Now, my question: Can we change the subject?"

Looking a little bit hurt at my impertinence, she said she would be happy to do so and, without missing a breath, launched into a discourse on the merits of crossing Hereford and Angus-Holstein heifers with Angus bulls. There are several dairies in the vicinity, she noted, who routinely breed their milk cows with Angus bulls. They breed them so because, cows have to have time away from the milking parlor and their stanchions. You can't milk them day after day forever. No matter how efficiently you recover the milk, over time they give you less and less.

"That's because the dairy people have always known what we beef folks have only recently begun to take seriously," she continued, "and that is that they need rest. Now, why Angus bulls instead of Hereford, Shorthorn, Ayshire or whatever? Because Angus bulls throw smaller calves, only once in a blue moon do they have horns, they have black udders, and they make more milk than any of the straight beef breeds. Bring those attributes together with the large frame and milking capability of the Holstein and you not only have bigger cows and far better milkers, you have bigger, stretchier calves that will fit a niche in the market for lean beef."

"I follow you," I said. "I've actually wondered about it myself, but is this a short course on crossbreeding, or are you headed someplace else with this?"

"I am for a fact," she replied. So let me ask you what you are using on your black-baldy cows?"

"Polled Herefords," I replied.

"Why is there something wrong with that?"

"It's not the best choice, Jim," she replied cautiously. "By breeding them back Hereford, you are cutting away some of the perks you got the first cross gave you. Mainly white udders again. And I think you'll rob your calves of the ability to eventually give more milk."

"I'm not sure, Megan," I told her. "I'm going to have to push that ball up the hill for a while to become a believer. I'm not sure."

"There you go," she said, smiling. "All of a sudden, you're pushing your own ball up the hill. But don't get to feeling too bad. I'm in the same boat; pushing my own theories up the hill. I'm not where I want to be yet, so why don't we join forces and do it together."

"Do what together?"

"Push the ball. Lets partner up and buy every damn crossbred heifer calf with a dairy background we can find. They'll probably look like black-baldies but they'll have dairy and milk in their background. We'll breed them with registered Angus bulls when they're ready, and we'll start building a herd of cows that gives more milk to their calves, and makes more money for us!"

"You know what I think, Megan?" I asked. "I think we should do it and, secondly, I think you should forget the bank job in Ennis. Put your imagination and your business acumen together with your brain, and you won't need to cross the street and help your neighbor."

"No," was her weighed reply. "I've been thinking about that, and I'm going to go for the interview. Working in a bank or one of the investment firms validates all of my time in school. Besides, it is work that I find challenging.

"You're the boss," I said. "I'll be in to see you for an incredibly low interest loan."

"I love you," she said. "Let's go to bed."

We went to bed friends rather than lovers and, in my mind, it was important that we did. If we were to make it up that love hill together, the glue that made us one had to be more than sex. Surely it was friendship that brought us to love. There had been no love at first sight, no shooting stars, no flipped switches, no electricity, just a slowly emerging friendship. And it would be that friendship that would get us over the speed bumps in our relationship.

Who could predict the future with certainty? No mortal had that power. But we commoners could at least say with confidence that whatever our future held it would not be without trial and travail. In Baltimore, directly opposite my desk, I kept a framed assertion along those lines in a picture frame. It read: *"the road to success is always under construction"*. They weren't my words. I don't know who gave voice to them in the beginning, but whoever it was, we owed that person something for his insightful reminder.

Love must entail more than sex, much more. At times, the parties involved must be *just* friends. And that was how our night played out. We held each other, and we kissed, and we touched, but there came a time when we simply slipped away and fell asleep.

In the morning, we spent a couple of leisurely hours eating and getting packed. We waited 'til the sun worked its drying magic on the land before we took to the trail. We had given up all hope now of killing the mountain lion. The rains had washed away his tracks and scent. The wind had switched from the west to the southeast, a harbinger, if it persisted, of more wet weather ahead. It was time to leave, time to go home.

We did linger long enough to inspect the doe's remains one last time, but found nothing to suggest the cougar had been there. No tracks, nothing to show it had fed again. It was already early afternoon before we started down, and we worked our way back to the trail gingerly. The going was slow, because some sections of rock were still slippery, exactly as we had guessed they might be. When we approached the jumble of rocks that could be negotiated only single file, we slowed again.

I sent Megan ahead with the pack horse. Something told me to hang back. If there was a cat up in those rocks, my best chance of killing him was to hang back and keep out of sight. I took stock quickly of where a cat might lay in wait. Two places stood out as likely launching pads. From one of them, a scraggly bit of brush, growing inexplicably in a crack in the rocks, spread out over the trail. The other protruding ledge seem more likely.

My instincts told me to pull my rifle from its boot, though it seemed unlikely I would need it. Megan was ahead of me at least 50 feet when I caught a flash of movement overhead. It was the cat! I could see it clearly. Actually, what I could see was a wagging tail. It was poised to leap down upon Megan or the pack horse. There was no time to warn her. When the cat raised up, ready to spring, I simply pulled the rifle against my shoulder and fired. Seconds later it fell to the rocks below only a few feet behind the pack horse Megan was leading.

Frightened by the thud of the cat striking the ground and by the scent, both horses instinctively jumped away from the sound, nearly unseating her. They buckjumped down the trail 50 yards before she was able to regain control. I watched as she turned to looked back at me, fear and uncertainty etched in her face. I stood over the downed cougar, my rifle pointed at its head. I jerked back on the trigger and sent another bullet into him. I might take a chances in poker, but not in this.

I turned again to see that Megan had dismounted and was cautiously approaching.

"My god," she cried. "I can't believe it. I watched the rocks above me before I squeezed through the slot, and I saw nothing. He was waiting there someplace, ready to pounce on me wasn't he?"

"Might have been the packhorse he was after," I said, "but he might have had you in his sights too. Are you all right?"

"Yes." She said, as she came running into my arms.

She suddenly began sobbing, and I could feel her body trembling. I did the only thing I could, and that was to hold her tight and stroke the back of her head until she relaxed again.

When the moment passed, she looked up at me and asked, "What happens now, Jim?"

"We're taking that cat's hide home with us," I blurted. "We've done our job up here, and we've earned the right to tack his hide against the wall at your place or mine."

I told her that before we did anything, we should get back to camp. I knew I had a skinning knife somewhere in my duffel. I had a hunting knife in my saddle bag, but I knew it was not particularly sharp. It would get the job done, as far as that goes, but I didn't think it was wise for Megan to watch that process.

"But let's try," she said. "It would save us another trip up here, right?"

"It would, yes," I replied, "but are you sure you want to be a part of this. It could get kinda messy."

"I want to be here, Jim," she asserted. "That's not *your* cat. That's *our* cat. We're a team."

"Okay," I said and, in a matter of seconds, I began dressing out the cat. I started at the sternum and opened the body up with an upturned knife blade that split the hide back to the groin. Then I sliced back over the rib cage and stopped when I reached the underside of the cat's jaw.

The viscera were lying on the ground shortly, and I dragged his innards away several feet where I measured its length with the soles of my boots. He measured over seven feet from the tip of his tail to his nose. He was in prime condition, with layers of tallow hugging his body here and there...and he had killed his last calf or doe.

The hide peeled slowly away from his body as I held it taut. Long strokes, not intended to bite deeply, saw the hide separate from his body. I looked up several times to assess how Megan was handling this rather grisly task, and each time I did, she smiled. Then and there I accepted the fact that she was one tough lady, strong in ways that both surprised me and made me proud.

"Can I try?" she asked. "I've helped Dad butcher a steer lots of times."

"Sure, if you've got the stomach for it," I said.

I held out the blood smeared handle of the knife to her, and she reached for it without hesitation. She had been watching closely, and she moved quickly to her knees and grabbed the hide, held it taught, and began skinning.I helped her roll the body over so she could come across the back, and then rolled it back so she could finish the other side. She stood up when she finished and handed the knife to me.

"The rest is your's, Jim," she said. "Did I do okay?"

I complimented her on the job, and she deserved it. She had done as much as me, but it was the head that stopped her. My own thoughts were confused, but tacked on the front door of the barn, it would look better with the head intact. I did what anyone who didn't know should do, I said no, the head would stay. We would wait and see what others who knew more than us had to say. The head stayed wrapped tightly in its skin after I severed the neck and separated the remainder of the hide from its body. It was surprisingly heavy, and I knew immediately I did not have the stamina to pull it the two miles to our camp down by the catch pen. Something told me that neither of our saddle horses nor the pack animal would tolerate the hide on its back. I tried to drag it up close enough to lift it up and hang it over the saddle, but both horses backed away, wild-eyed and snorting. Then I brought the packhorse up, and it too pulled away.

We had two options: leave it here or use our lariats. Combined they were about 70 feet long. I tied them together and draped one end over the cat's head and cinched it down tight. The other, I tied hard and fast to my saddle horn. Megan led the way down with the packhorse following behind on a lead rope. My gelding danced about a bit at first, but he slowly came to accept the rope against his body and the weight of the hide dragging behind.

When we reached camp, Megan used her cell to call the Macintosh ranch. No one answered so she left a message, then called Michael and Benny in turn. Michael didn't answer, but she got Benny on the first try. Everyone employed by the Macintosh Ranch had a cell phone provided by Claire. Everyone, that is, except Odin Norgaard. Odin refused to carry one of those "silly contraptions".

She quickly related to Benny what she wanted him to do, and in less than an hour he pulled up in front of the catch pens pulling one of Claire's triple-axle stock trailers. Michael was riding shotgun. They insisted on hearing the story about the cat before they lifted a finger to load our horses and our gear. Megan was the narrator, and she did a good job.

Loaded, we jumped into the rear seats of the crew-cab truck for the ride to my place. There we unloaded our gear and turned the horses into the corral. The truck box was full of our gear, pack saddles, and the hide. I had covered it with a tarpaulin thinking the scent would be blunted if it were covered. Once the horses were in the corral, I pulled it out of the truck and went for a ladder.

Benny supplied the technical advice as far as the cougar's head. Hang it with the head down, he said. Nature has a way of cleaning out that head, he added. We all knew what he meant. Stretch it out with its head down and its's tail nailed at the top, he said, for bragging rights, of course

I wanted to display it so that it would be seen immediately by anyone driving into the yard. It was my talisman, I mean, *our* good luck symbol, I hoped. I climbed the ladder, dragging the hide by the tail with me, and nailed the tail to one of the studs on the east side of the sliding door. The hide nearly reached the ground, even after I stretched it out and drove a couple more nails though it with the raw side out. In the morning, I would see what I could do to scrape away some of the meat and tallow and stretch it out even more. Eventually, when it had dried, I would turn the hide out. From the ladder, I could see my cows lined up against the top wire on the fence looking as if they were watching television.

When we finished the hide, Megan sent Benny home, telling him that I would drive her over to her place later. Mike rode back to the ranch with him to finish out the day and pick up his truck. Megan and I both took hot showers and then sat on the porch nursing a cup of fresh coffee and surveying our hide. Did it feel good just to sit there looking out over the foothills, feeling clean? I should say so! It was a relaxing time after all of the trauma on the mountain, but it was also a time for introspection.

Where do we go from here? That was the question we were both asking ourselves. We had walked away from the seclusion and refuge of the mountains into a world where friendly curiosity and benign scrutiny came into play. We saw ourselves as married in every way except formally and legally, but neither of us had even hinted that marriage was a likelihood in the near term. Maybe we were both afraid. Being in love involves expenditures; it involves putting something at risk. It wasn't that we weren't sure of our love. It was more a matter of still not being reasonably certain we could make it work. We were, after all, experienced in dysfunctional relationships that had trampled on our self esteem. The process of rebuilding was underway, but our hold on our new love was tenuous because we had both been wounded in some way by our pasts.

We agreed that in the short term our children were our first consideration. Michael was perceptive enough to know we had gone beyond the hand-holding phase. We didn't know if he knew we had become lovers, but we guessed he probably did. Taylor was another story, as was Morgan. They were both mature for their age and perceptive enough to recognize that we were special friends and that our friendship might blossom into something more. And, at least Taylor, seemed not to mind. Still we didn't want to conduct ourselves in ways that embarrassed them, and that meant we must avoid the "shacking-up" label. So discretion was essential and, in its footsteps, followed a certain amount of exciting intrigue.

Mike was leaving in a less than three weeks, but Taylor would soon be back from Denver, and Megan was cognizant of her sensibilities. Morgan was insulated to a degree by being away in Baltimore, but she and Taylor had become close friends, and the mails, especially those of the electronic variety, were certain to keep her fully posted. And then there were Claire and Jennifer. They left no doubt that they wanted us to be together, but their idea of togetherness involved a license and ceremony. We knew we could avoid a lot of trouble if we got married, but it was too soon. So in the meantime we would have to be satisfied with finding time together when we could.

Mike nibbled on table scraps when he returned with his truck. The supper dishes were stacked in the dishwasher, and the three of us retired to the chairs facing the fireplace. We talked about our trip and about our plan to invest in cross-bred dairy calves. We would purchase yearlings heifers where we could and three day-old heifer calves as we found them. Mike found the idea of building a breeding program using crossbred dairy heifers intriguing and asked if he could invest a few dollars of his own money in our new venture. Because he had only limited dollars, he wanted to limit his involvement to the calves that were only a few days old. They were selling for about $100 a head, so his initial investment was limited to five calves, and that consumed nearly one fourth of his total net worth. He agreed that because he was a small percentage owner who would soon be leaving for the University, he would care for the calves for the rest of the summer, leaving us free to spend our extra time actually hunting down more calves.

When he went to bed, Megan and I talked for only a few more minutes. I told her I could not believe the metamorphosis Mike had undergone in less than a year. Twelve months earlier, he was living in

Baltimore, uncertain as to what he wanted to do with his life. Today he was living in Montana, working on a large cattle ranch, earning wages, and investing in livestock himself. I was very proud of him, but I couldn't help feeling sorry for his mother.

Megan stayed the night, but she slept alone in my room. I slept in Morgan's room, and Mike sacked out on the sofa. We were up early, and the three of us had breakfast together. Mike left first and we left shortly thereafter. Megan was without wheels, so I drove her over to her place.

"My interview is tomorrow," she said, "and if I get the job, I'll probably start on Monday. Maybe this weekend we can all go scouting for calves. There's a small stock rack over at Dad's. We should use that in your truck instead of lugging on one of those big, clumsy trailers."

"Consider it done, boss," I said. "Mike and I will have it ready to go when you're ready. Okay?"

"Okay. I'll call tonight," she said. "Love you."

The following two weeks could not possibly have been more crowded with activity. Claire and Jennifer returned from their vacation, tanned and anxious to tell us about the highlights of their trip. Taylor flew in from Denver, pumped up about starting school on the one hand, and dreading it on the other. She had zero friends to lean on during the first days, but she shrugged it off, and persuaded Megan and Jennifer to underwrite a shopping trip to Bozeman.

Megan won the job in Ennis, and a nice concession in the process. The powers that be had tentatively consented to her working only four days a week, Monday through Thursday, and she would not begin until the day after Labor Day. The biggest surprise of all was a phone call from Morgan at the Bozeman Airport telling me that Jason had met her plane and that they would be at my place in less than an hour.

A welcoming committee which included everyone she knew, including Benny Tovar and Odin Norgaard, was waiting in the yard when they drove in. Jason was beaming, and I wanted to cry when I saw her. She was wearing a flowered cotton dress that hugged her slender body and she was gorgeous. She was carrying herself like the woman I hoped she would be in a few years. She had always been precocious, and that included an accelerated physical maturity, I guess. We lined up like the families of the bride and groom do at a wedding, and kissed, and hugged and squeezed her like a long, lost friend. When she came to me, her eyes were filled with tears, and so were mine.

"Sorry about the short notice, Dad," she said. "I wanted it to be a surprise."

"I'm so happy to see you, Morgan," I said, "I can't believe you're here."

"I can't either," she replied. "It took some arm twisting, but I persuaded Mom to let me come for a few days before school begins. I wanted to see Montana again."

Inside I was crying. My daughter had come home.

Early Saturday morning, Megan and I left for Billings and the Yellowstone Livestock Auction Yards. It was their regular horse and dairy cattle sale. We thought the kids might enjoy the trip and the experience, but they had other plans. Billings was a three hour drive from the Megan's place, so with a stop in Columbus for coffee, we were still in Billings for a late breakfast at the auction yard itself. The dairy sale lasted until 1 o'clock, then they switched to horses. The baby calves were sold in a separate barn beginning at Noon. The 10 crossbred heifers we purchased were black whitefaces, but we bought three straight Holstein heifers and two Holstein bull calves as well. The latter we would castrate and see what we could do about putting some meat on them. On average they weighed in a just over 100 pounds, and two of them were already nibbling on grain. We could have stayed overnight and loaded the cattle in the morning, but we didn't. It was one of those opportunities for us to be alone without raising eyebrows, but we wanted to get some milk replacer into our calves as soon as possible.

So we loaded 15 baby calves in the back of my truck and struck out for Norris. We housed them in one of my sheds temporarily, and began bottle feeding them immediately. The bawling and bellowing was continuous, but we were in the cattle business together and that's what counted. Claire and Jennifer drove over after Megan called them. Claire was a beef man but he too was interested in our little experiment and believed Megan might be on target in terms of filling a specific marketing niche. The kids came as well toward evening. They had run down to West Yellowstone to see the Grizzly bears.

Michael asked which of the calves were his. We gave him his pick and he took half of the black white-faced heifers. Observant for someone his age, his summer working for Claire had imparted more than just a little knowledge about cattle prices and breeds. He was no longer a pilgrim when it came to knowing his way around cattle, and I was proud of him. I think Jason had become his tutor. Morgan wondered how it was that Mike now owned some calves and she didn't. Mike explained that he had bought and paid for them with his own money.

"I've got some of my own money," Morgan interjected. "How many are Mike's?"

"Mike owns five of them," I replied. "

"All right," she said, "I want five of them too, all heifers. I'll pay you before we go to bed tonight."

"But...," I started to say

"But what about me?" Taylor interjected before I could finish.. "If I'm going to a Montana cowgirl, I need cows...or calves would be okay,"

"How about the money to pay for them?" Megan asked.

"I've got money. Dad gave me money before I left," she replied.

"But we don't have any of the crossbred heifer calves left," Megan said.

"I can wait 'til you find them. Do you want cash or a check?"

Megan looked at me, and I shrugged to let her know if was okay with me.

"A check would be fine, I guess."

"Good, because I don't have any cash."

I don't know who began laughing first. It might have been me, but it was hard to tell because we were all soon laughing at the same time. Here we were, after a ride of well over 300 miles to get started in building our crossbred herd, without a single crossbred heifer to our name. We had been wiped out before we got started. We were sitting there instead with five calves, only three of which would ever produce milk.

Megan was shaking her head, the kids were laughing, and Claire and Jenny were grinning from ear to ear. If there was anything on this earth that could have made them feel better than knowing those three young people had bought into the Montana cattle business, I didn't' know what it was. Jason was standing back from the others, and I was feeling kind of sorry for him. I need not have.

When the kids left to drive to Ennis, Megan confided that young Jason owned forty cows, and had 39 calves on the ground. Poor Jason. Here I was feeling sorry for him, only to learn that when he folded in his 20 yearling steers, he was a bigger operator than your's truly. Well, he might out rank me in the cattle business, but that was *my* mountain lion pelt nailed to my barn. So there.

Between Megan and me, we had a sizeable chunk of cash at our fingertips. Mine was largely tied up in certificates of deposit at banks in Bozeman, Belgrade and Ennis. Megan's was more liquid than mine, if only because she had more recently come into possession of her share of the sale price on the Tivoli house in Denver. The fact that I pinched my pennies harder than her might also have been a factor. I liked to go to the bank and look at my money once in a while, but I had an inbred aversion to spending it. Megan, on the other hand, was a disciple of the school that held that to make money you must spend money. In any case, I knew I would soon have to spend some of mine if I wanted to be a bonafide Montana stockman. Having a banker in our yet to be formalized family didn't hurt, and it took Megan a single phone call to arrange for a loan that would let me bridge the gap between maturity dates on my certificates and my immediate needs.

We had pulled out all stops when it came to curbing the magnitude of our cross breeding project. The more we looked, the more excited we became. Our little babies, with their backbones showing, were a pitiful sight compared to a nice Angus or Herford calf of the same age, but they would fill out and they would be milkers.

Claire and Jennifer's operation still far surpassed our resources in land and feed base, though between us we were masters of over four thousand acres of range, not counting the grazing permit, and three quarter sections of irrigation under pivot systems. My portion was a long way from being paid for, but it was mine to use as I wished until I defaulted on my loan. Our objective from the beginning had been to find maybe a hundred or so cross bred calves, and it was clear that we could easily manage that and several multiples if we wished.

But, finances were one thing. Time was another. It was out of our control, and the best we could do is work hard and then work some more. I was still holding down a nearly full time job with the Macintoshes, but they indulged me at every turn because they wanted us to succeed and because they cared.

But as they say, every coin has two sides. One side of ours gave us some flexibility in altering our daily routines to make it possible to travel in every direction looking for calves and either hauling them home or making arrangements for their delivery. These trips produced results most of the time, but when the small dairy operations had already marketed their calves, we consoled ourselves by spending nights here and there together. Megan argued that everyone, including our children, knew we were a couple in every way, that they would have to be blind not to see it. But we always tried to be discrete in terms of when and where we hazarded being seen. I suppose we did so more for Claire and Jennifer than anything.

One of our nights out found us in Chico Hot Springs over in the Paradise Valley. We had both been there several times but never together. Our departure from my place, where I now kept the Cessna full-time, was later than planned, and it saw us landing just before dark on the half-mile long, north-south service road leading to the Springs. We enjoyed a fine meal, took advantage of the hot springs, and spent a wonderful night together.

At breakfast, we met a local dairy operator who gladly sold us 20 crossbred heifer calves for a reasonable price and agreed to hold them until we could bring a trailer over to pick them up. It was while we waited for the bill, that my former employer, Jim Madsen, walked in with his wife and two kids. He spotted me first and waved. I knew we were going to have a visitor, one who would want to know who the beautiful woman was who sat at my table.

When he walked up to us, he was smiling, and before I had a chance to say anything he introduced his wife and children. The children were a boy and girl in their teens, and the mother was someone I had bumped into as I was leaving the office one day.

"Jim and Anne," I began, suddenly knowing I was not going to portray Megan as anything other than what she was, "I'd like both of you to meet Megan Macintosh. I work for her father over by Norris.

Megan and I are business partners and, when we can find the time, we are going to be married."

Megan glanced at me and, as I watched, a smile covered her face, and those eyes, those eyes, that twinkled like a million stars, were like a lighted chandelier in an otherwise darkened room. It was the first time I had openly acknowledged to any one else that we were more than friends and business associates. We were that and so much more and, while we both contended we needed more time to be sure, we were in fact sure. Most of the hesitation had been mine, but it was gone. Suddenly I wanted everyone to know it. She was bright, beautiful and a challenge, but I loved her. Yes, I loved this woman even after I had persuaded myself that love would never find a home with me.

"Why don't you sit down and join us?" I said. "We just cut a deal to buy some calves from a local dairyman, and are in no hurry to leave."

"Are you sure?" Anne asked. "We don't want to intrude."

I assured them they were not intruding and stood up to pull two extra chairs up to the table, and went so far as to help Anne and her daughter into theirs.

"The kids are anxious to get to the pool," Jim said, "but we said a light breakfast first."

We drank our coffee and traded small talk while they ate and then sent their kids to their room for their bathing suits.

"We both have teen age kids," I said. "Megan has a daughter named Taylor, and mine are a boy and girl. Michael works for Megan's father as a ranch hand and is headed for the U of M in a few weeks. My daughter, Morgan, recently visited us for a few days, but she's back in Baltimore now to finish her senior year in high school."

"They takin' to Montana?" Anne asked in a timid voice. "Some do, some don't."

"It's growing on all three of them," Megan offered. "Michael more so than the girls, but they are liking it better all the time."

"Jim," Madsen said, changing the subject abruptly, "been wondering what you've been up to. Busy at the office. Could use some more of that Baltimore expertise."

"Wouldn't have the time even if I were so inclined," I observed, honestly. "No, I've got my place over in the foothills of the Roots, and that's where my future is. Megan is my neighbor, and one of these days we'll be together in one place or the other. Mine I hope. We met there. It's small, but the atmosphere is what we both want."

"Probably be at Jim's place," Megan volunteered. "We've got a mountain lion pelt hanging on one end of one of the sheds. It's a fixture. We got him together. I was the bait. Jim did the shooting."

"There's a story I'd like to hear sometime," Madsen said, "but seriously, there's a spot for you with us, even if only part time. Two new housing projects. Both south of town. Damn place is growing like mad. But I guess you know that. Keeping traffic flowing on our small town streets is the city's biggest problem."

"Found my niche south and west of Norris," I said. "Sorry. But you and Anne and the kids should drop out sometime. We'll give you a tour and the kids can saddle up and check out my cows."

We said our goodbyes shortly, and in a matter of minutes I was taxiing the Cessna down the service road and headed for home.

"I've two things to say, cowboy," Megan said once we were airborne. "First off, did you mean it about...well, you know, getting married?"

I told her right there that I meant it and that there was no reason why we ought to hide how we felt about each other, including from her parents and our kids.

"Well," she said, "if that's the case, is it against FAA rules for a passenger to kiss a pilot during flight?"

∽ 291 ∽

"I'm the captain of this ship, lady," I replied, "so it's my call. But I will not permit it until I hear what else you said you wanted to tell me."

She said it had occurred to her while we were eating breakfast, that time was precious to us and that we didn't have enough of it to build our crossbred herd, before winter, in little bits and pieces, a snitch here, a snitch there. We need to head up to the Helena valley, she felt, and cut a deal with one of the big dairies. We are dealing in a dozen here a dozen there. Not enough. A hundred head in a bunch is more like it."

"I agree, I said, "and the sooner the better. Now, you may kiss the captain."

The Cessna fought a strong head wind all the way home, but we crossed the Gallatin and Madison Mountains by mid-morning, and both of us were hard at work well before lunch. We talked more about marriage, and agreed that it was too early to spring our decision on the family and that, in our own way, we would begin to feel our way around with our children.

"We can't let the kids change our minds, Jim," Megan said, imploringly, "can we?"

"Of course not, honey," I responded, "but on the other hand, I don't want them hearing about it from someone else. Let's make it as easy on them as possible. Think about it. Taylor still very much misses her dad, as she should, and even you have said she probably hasn't fully given up on the notion that a reconciliation between you and her father is possible. You know better, and you have said so, but let's give her a little time. I'm sure there are times when she pines for him to the point of tears, but that will change. She will come to understand that she can never be happy unless you find happiness."

"And you think I will find it with you?" Megan asked, teasingly.

"Yes. You like me. She likes me. And, after all, she's riding a horse

I gave her. Every once in a while I provide her with the chance to get cozy with Michael by taking you someplace to look for cows. How could she not like me?"

"Be serious, Jim," Megan offered.

"But, I am. I think she likes me. She likes my kids, and every day she spends here in Montana she sees how it is with the two of us and she grows more comfortable with seeing us as a couple."

"Yes. Suppose you are right, and I think Michael is already in our court. Morgan might be a hold out."

"Once maybe, but not any more, I don't think," I said, meaning it. "The girl has undergone at least a partial metamorphosis since the first time she visited me. She thinks she might be in love with Jason if I am reading the signs correctly. She'll come around to thinking you and I belong together too."

"For an engineer, you do a lot of making your way though life with your heart, Jim," Megan responded. "I'm oh so thankful for that. With a little time, we'll work our way through all of this …won't we?"

"Almost a done deal the way I see it, Megan. "I've got a son and daughter and you have a daughter who are minority partners in our cross-bred cattle venture. They have a vested interest in seeing us together. Most kids want dogs. Ours want calves, and they're sharp enough to know who's going to take care of them when they can't."

Which brought us back to talking cows. Megan volunteered to make a few phone calls and, thanks to mobile phones, she managed to arrange a meeting with the Hegary brothers, owners of the Helena Valley's largest dairy. The meeting date was set for the following Saturday, so we had some time to begin thinking through our business goals and objectives. I had eavesdropped on their conversation enough to know that the brother she had reached thought he saw a way to work something out that was mutually beneficial.

The day after Labor Day was Megan's first day on the job in Ennis, and when I saw her that evening the smile on her face told me it had gone well. Mike and I were having supper when I heard a truck pull up in front of the door, and I somehow knew intuitively that it was her. With her came Taylor, not long home from visiting her father in Denver. She grew to look more like her beautiful mother each day, and though I would need a tape measure to prove it, I thought she was now a hair or two taller than her tall mother.

"Celebration in order here, Jim," Megan said. "You are now, this instant, looking at someone no longer qualified for unemployment benefits, if I ever was."

"Wonderful! I hollered. Did they make you president?"

"No but they treated me very nicely. They were very friendly. I had worried that some might resent my being there, taking a job away from some local aspirant, but I guess my living south of Norris was enough for them. That, I think, and the fact that the head teller and me were in the same graduating class in high school."

"Are you suggesting you had a degree of academic nepotism working for you?"

"No. Not at all, but I knew I had one good friend there before I ever got started. She gave me a tour of the bank, but the president and two other administrative sorts briefed me on the job. I am now on the payroll, a member of the bank's investment panel, and I'm drawing decent wages for the four days I work each week."

"Four days? Great," I said. "You mentioned earlier that you had at least a tentative commitment to an abbreviated work week, but I thought that might change. When the other employees heard about it. You *did* have inside influence, right?"

"Not really," she answered. "I asked for it. Said I needed an extra day off 'til I got settled on my place, and that one day I could probably go full time.   Didn't tell them I needed the time to bottle feed a bunch of three day-old calves."

"Well, that's wonderful," I said. "You'll knock them dead before you're there a week."

Before we knew it, Taylor and Michael had slipped away from the kitchen table and were watching television and, I think, holding hands. Megan and I sat there, looking starry-eyed at each other, and we did a bit of across-the-table hand holding ourselves. God it felt great to see her sitting there, knowing we were in love and wanting each other in every way.

I stood up and walked to the fridge and brought back two bottles of beer.

"Not much of a celebration without some of the foamy stuff," I observed, as we touched our bottles against each other. "I'm so proud of you," I added. "Just don't get so wrapped up in your job that you forget to drop in to see me now and then. I might cry."

"You'll be crying, all right,"she said, "when you write a check for your share of the calves we'll be buying come Saturday, but never fear: you now have a friend in high places in the banking business."

"And, can I ask you if your financial wizardry includes fool-proof skills in embezzlement, should it become necessary?"

"We'll get by," she said in a normal tone of voice then whispered, "have you said anything to Michael about...well, you know what?"

"Nope. How about Taylor? Did it ever occur to you that we are concerned about nothing? Let's call them back to the table and tell both of them right now."

"You're probably right that we should do it soon, but let's wait until we come back from Helena. We'll have time to talk about it coming and going."

And that is exactly what we didn't do. Instead we spent most of our time working Megan's hand-held calculator, trying to figure out what we should and could offer for a calf no more than three days separated from its mother's womb, how much feed we'd need for each calf, how much feed we had, and whether or not we should limit ourselves to heifer calves. Megan remembered seeing small bunches of straight Holstein steers grazing in farmstead trees and small pastures as we drove from the Minneapolis-St. Paul Airport to Rochester.

"They looked damned good to me, Jim," she said. "Lots of stretch with a susrprising amount of meat covering those big bones. I think they are like everything else. Give them groceries and they'll turn it into beef."

"What about cross-bred steer calves?" I asked.

"Let's think about that, Jim. We can decide after we see what the Hegarys have."

Helena is located roughly 80 miles north of my place in an almost straight line. So we had barely begun our discussions when we pulled away from the north end of the Tobacco Root Mountain range, and that put us nearly half way to our destination. West of our path were ranges of mountains laid out like pieces of flawed corduroy and, with the sun spraying their eastern slopes with soft light, they were a thing of beauty. More than once we stopped speaking to each other in mid-sentence as the grandeur caught us in its clutches. To the east stretched miles and miles of rolling hills and plains. Devoid of trees except for small clutches here and there and adjacent to even the smaller waterways, they had their own beguiling beauty. Together the two landscape types spread their aura over viewers like gravy atop mashed potatoes. It made one forget everything else.

The Hegarys had a small private runway, and we touched down there, by-passing the municipal airport. We were turning off the runway and had just begun to taxi down a narrow, graded road leading to a large set of building when we saw a pickup truck moving toward us. When it came to within a football field's distance from us, the driver turned abruptly and slowly moved back toward the buildings.

I watched as an arm flew up from an open window, beckoning us to follow.

The driver was leaning against his truck, one leg crooked and resting on a tubular running board, when we got there. Wearing blue coveralls and rubber boots that came to his knees, he looked like a sure enough dairy man.

"Got me a clogged up manure pump," he said in a deep voice, as if to explain his sodden attire

"Damn thing's got a mind of its own but, what the heck, if you're who I think you are, you are interested in cattle and not what they spew out their back sides. I'm Flynn Hegary. My brother, Daniel, is busy in the parlor."

"Glad to meet you, Flynn," I said, "this is Megan Macintosh, my business partner, and soon to be my wife. You already know we are interested in buying a few yearling Hereford or Angus-Holstein cross bred heifers and some calves if you've got them."

"Hell, we got 'em running out our you-know-what," Flynn replied, as he threw a plug of Copenhagen in the left side of his mouth. "Danny and me have talked and we've got an idea on how we can do some business that is mutually beneficial. But first let me give you a quick tour of our operation here and, in the process, show you what we've got in the way of young stock."

We walked from where the truck and Cessna had been parked, and he led us into a cavernous loafing shed which fed cows into a circular milking parlor around the clock.

"We milk 32 cows at a times around the clock. By the time we finish with the last of our 1500 head, the first batch of 32 is waiting to get milked for a second time."

"Are all of your milk cows Holsteins?" Megan asked. "That's all I see from here."

"Well, we milk a mixed bunch of Jerseys and Guernseys, but we do it in another parlor. We increase our butterfat by mixing."

"Amazing place, Flynn," I said. "Didn't realize you were so big."

"Big makes us competitive, but it gives us a handful of headaches too. But I'm wasting your time here. You want to talk yearling and 3-day old heifers out of our Holsteins crossed with either Angus or Hereford bulls.

"But before we get to that, tell me a little about yourselves and your operation down in the Roots." Megan took the lead and I was proud of her. She left no doubts in Flynn's mind about two important things: she was a forward thinker and she knew cows. She explained the size of our combined outfits, our current feed base, range conditions, and reasons for wanting to begin a program designed to build a herd of dark-uddered, hornless, stretchy cows that gave considerably more milk than the good cows we now owned... and made us more money.

"We believe there is niche to be filled out there, and it involves lean meat grown under clean range conditions and a feeding program where nutrition is a primary consideration," I said, "and we want to build a program that makes it possible for our kids to stay in Montana."

"Good," Flynn said. "Damn, I thought we *might* be able to do business and, now, after talking to the two of you and sizing you up, I *know* we can."

Chapter 11

And business we did. On a scale neither of us had given a moment's thought to, and we were still wondering if we hadn't gone a little crazy when we slipped down along the eastern slopes of the Roots. If it turned out that we had leaped off the edge into deeper water than we could handle, the results could be devastating. But we had an out. There were contingencies. We hadn't signed anything, and even our tentative verbal agreement was based in large measure on whether or not Claire Macintosh was willing to throw in with us in terms of feed and range. The Hegary brothers both knew that.

My first thought was that in our excitement Flynn Hegary had reeled us in like a catfish, you know, big mouth, no brains. My second thought and Megan's as well, she admitted, was that no...Flynn was an astute business man in spite of his manure-pump-attire, who had seen in us two savvy individuals who were already working on the cutting edge of what would one day become a much more common practice.

Hybrid vigor was the key and, in the beef business, any cross gave you some of that. Straight Herefords, Shorthorns, Charlais, Angus, and what have you, were rapidly becoming a thing of the past, at least as far as cows go. At the same time, the demand for straight-bred bulls remained strong. More and more stockmen would eventually come to recognize the benefits of crossbreeding, and more and more stockmen would milk hybrid vigor for all it was worth. Flynn Hegary had told us as much before we left for home, and he admitted if he were in the beef business he would be doing the same. If he were in the beef business, he said, he wouldn't have any choice, but he'd be crossbreeding milk and beef not beef and beef. Did that make us feel smart? It sure did!

We walked away no, flew from Helena, not knowing for certain if we were up to the deal Flynn had offered, but our belief that we were on the right track was stronger than it had ever been. I dreaded to think of what lay ahead of us in the way of work, but telling me it couldn't be done was the next thing to a guarantee that I was going to try. And I don't think Megan was far behind me in that regard. When were ever going to find time to tie the knot?

"Tell me I'm dreaming, Jim," Megan said in a trembling voice, "did we just come close to cutting the best deal imaginable or committing the worst possible, amateurish blunder?"

"You know what, Love," I said, my own voice trembling like an earthquake with a 4.0 reading on the Richter scale, "I think we might pull it off and reap excellent returns on our money and labor, or...we might fall flat on our face if we've been outsmarted by the brainy business acumen of the Hegary brothers. But they are, I believe, as honest as we are. They see a way for them to cut their labor costs dramatically, and they like the idea of those replacement heifers growing up on good, clean grass."

"I hope you're right, Jim. I want to give our idea a chance. I want it to work."

"We agree about that," I said, "and I'll bet money that the Hegarys want this to work as much as we do."

I told Megan that I thought it hinged pretty much on what Claire and Jennifer thought and that if they thought we should back off, we'd be gone like a puff of smoke. Were that to happen, I reminded her, we could always fall back to the modest hopes and expectations we started with.

"But if he said we should take it on," I said, "I say we go for it. I don't think we'll ever again stumble into such an opportunity. You were way out ahead of me in your thinking about crossbreeding, and I think Flynn's assertion that, were he in the beef business he would be doing what we are doing, confirms that you were right. I believed him then, and I believe him now. But I have to admit that my heart is beating right now like a good-sized trip hammer. One way or another, sink or swim with the brothers or on our own, it's going to be one hell of an adventure."

We couldn't wait until morning to hear Claire and Jennifer's assessment of the deal we had been offered and tentatively accepted, so the prop on the Cessna had barely stopped before we were in my truck racing for their place. When we got there, Jenny was scooping huge portions of vanilla ice cream on slices of the apple pie she had baked the day before, and Claire, Benny, Odin and Michael were waiting with forks poised to attack.

"Two more customers, Mom," Megan shouted as we came in. "We're hungry!"

"Well then, Dear," Jennifer exclaimed, "you'll have to bring out the second pie from the counter over there."

The pie and several cups of coffee vanished in a matter of minutes, and when the others had leaned back against their chairs and loosened their belts a notch or two, it was Megan who charged ahead and related our experiences up in the Helena Valley.

They all knew that is where we had been, and they were anxious to hear what we had found out. She began by reminding all of them that she and I were already in the early stages of building a herd of cattle with the strong milking capacity, absent in most straight beef breeds. A lot of people talk about it and see merit in crossbreeding, she said, but not many are doing much about it. Change can be tough to implement, especially when what you've been doing has been working for you.

"But, like I said, we decided to give it a serious try. What we hoped to get with our trip up to Helena was a hundred or two of their crossbred calves. We have been searching for yearlings and three-day old heifer calves out of either a Hereford or Angus cross on Holstein cows. The Hegary brothers have got 'em coming out their ears. Our plan is to breed most of those cross bred heifers to Angus bulls. We believe that cross will produce calves that will look like any other Angus, but when those babies become mothers, they will produce three or four times more milk than any of the straight breeds. You all know how important it is for calves to have access to as much in the way of groceries as they can. Those cross bred cows would do that. We were also looking for some yearling Hereford-Holstein cross heifers. At least a few so we can make comparisons.

"We found out several other things," she went on, "including the fact that the Hegary brothers alone can supply us with all we'll ever need in the way of calves. We also learned that they have calves out of both Angus and Herefords crosses. The Hereford crosses are out of polled bulls, which means a lot of their calves won't have horns. We know them as black baldies, and we've all got a bunch of them on our three places. Calves out of Angus bulls can be anything as far as color, but they tend to be mostly black."

"Sounds like a big operation," Claire interjected.

"If you can believe it," she continued, "they milk around 1500, yes, 1500 cows every day, which means they milk 32 cows in a circular milking parlor, around the clock, seven days a week. The cows are housed in long, ventilated, loafing sheds. They only very rarely ever see grass. Block-long feeders are filled automatically with silage and other types of feed. Flynn Hegary, the younger of the two Hegary brothers, told us that, with urban sprawl and all, their land is far too valuable to be used as pasture. So they raise corn and alfalfa under sprinkler irrigations systems and purchase barley and other grains wherever they can find it.

"That's kind of where we came in," Megan added. "Jim, why don't you go ahead and tell them about the deal they offered us?"

"Sure," I said. "Hang on to your seats, boys and girls. This is it. We can buy as many baby crossbred calves as we can handle at $100 per head. They would be from a few days to as much as a month old, and the older ones would have been started on a mixture of rolled corn, barley and whole oats. If we want, they will sell us straight Holstein heifers that they won't be using for replacement milkers at the same price. Then, and here is where it gets interesting, we can buy four-month old Holstein heifers that have been vaccinated and are eating grain. They are destined to replace older or non-producing cows on the milking line. They will deliver whatever we buy in semi-load lots, and they will enter into a formal agreement to buy all of them back for $1100 each when they are with calf. When the time comes to breed them, they will send a man down to do the artificial inseminating.

"We haven't said yes or no, but we did give them our we-think-so," I continued. "Depends on what you all think, particularly you, Claire and Jennifer, because we would have to use some of your buildings and purchase most of the surplus hay and corn you are now selling every year. We know that between us we can handle the cost of the calves, and we feel we can manage the overall crossbreeding program if we can hire a full time hand and some seasonal help. Like I said, if the two of you don't like the deal or you think we are biting off too much, we will simply fall back to our earlier, far more modest plans."

We knew that the questions Megan and I raised weren't the kind that could be answered over a piece of pie and a cup of coffee. A "let's see-how-it-works-out-on paper" from Claire and Jennifer was not only the first step but the most important step in deciding.

For most of two days, we all but forgot the work we knew needed doing around our three places and, sat instead, at the kitchen table at my place, burning up a bunch of lead. In the end, it came down to an observation by Claire, the essence of which was: he thought it could be done, but suggested we bite off something less than the whole hog until we had earned our sea legs.

"The Hegarys are wanting to turn over an important part of their operation to the two of you," he said, "and unless you can largely meet their goals and objectives, they might go elsewhere. I don't think we want to do that, because I think we have a unique opportunity here. The trick is going to be to persuade them that it is in their best interests to see you start slow until everybody is satisfied it's going to work."

By now, Megan and I had determined how much we could responsibly handle financially, what we needed in the way of new pens, sheds and grain storage, and how much help we would need in addition to what Claire and Jennifer thought they could fold into the deal in terms of Benny and Odin. Jennifer did not back away from expressing the need for a bit of caution, pointing out that the Macintosh outfit, which was itself of considerable magnitude, would all go to Megan one day, thus obviating the need for her to take unnecessary chances.

"But that's just an old woman's view, guys," Jennifer said, as she made the rounds again with the coffee pot, "and what you are thinking to do reminds me of when Claire and I were taking our own chances in trying to scratch out a living right where we are all sitting. We did it. We did it together and, for me, I wouldn't trade that experience for anything. We succeeded. We didn't fail. But had we, we would have done it together and, when everything is said and done, that's all that's counts.

"When it comes to business decisions, Claire is my go-to guy," she said. "He has already hinted that it might be a once-in-a-lifetime opportunity for all of us, and I hope he's right."

Two days later I flew up to the Helena Valley and brought brothers, Flynn and Daniel, back to the Tobacco Root Mountains. We toured all three outfits, pointing out existing facilities, planned additions, and our overall layouts. In the end, it was Claire and Jennifer who sealed the deal with the Hegarys. It was hard to spend anytime with those two and not come away with feelings of confidence and competence. We agreed to a phased approach with the Hegarys, but promised to do our best to meet their needs as well as our own in a reasonable amount of time.

The first load of replacement heifers was scheduled for mid-September. They would go directly to my place, and I would be ready.

We flew at our work, all of us, and I hardly saw Megan. We communicated by phone or by hurried trips from one place to another during the day. And occasionally we managed to talk for a while late at night. Michael's classes didn't begin until the last week in August, but he had to spend two days in Missoula before that, as part of the orientation process for new students.

When he returned, he immediately pitched in and worked from before sunup until after dark, but I knew he still had some things to do to get ready before heading to Missoula for school. Take a few days off, I told him. Take Taylor to a movie in Bozeman. He did and they had a good time, he said, but he was back on the job early the next morning. Make a run to Yellowstone, I told him or climb a mountain. He didn't do either. What a kid!

He had to finish the baling, he said. Could any father be more proud? He had proved a big help to all of us since he moved from Baltimore, and I think he knew that when he left he was leaving a big hole, especially since we now had a bunch of calves coming our way. At some point we would have to take off enough time to find a hand to replace him, and it wound up being Jennifer who volunteered to look for someone.

The young lady who had a habit of showing up at my front door unexpectedly did it again. My phone jingled early on Friday, and a voice I recognized instantly as that of my sometimes exasperating daughter, Morgan. Pick me up at the airport at one she said. Delta flight 235. She had five days off and her mother's permission to see Michael off to the University.

"Can't stay long, Dad," she said, "but for some silly reason, I missed my horse, my calves and, well...you too...a little."

"You missed me a bunch, girl, and you know it," I said. "I'll be there." I was happy she came, because I knew it would likely be months before I saw here again. The kid had a way of growing on a person.

On the way back to the ranch...and that's what I was calling it now instead of simply *my place*, she was on the phone with Jason. Now and then she would hold her hand against the phone and announce to me that she was getting a C minus in Geometry or that her mother had sold the small lake home we owned up north.

She arrived on Friday but had to return to Baltimore the day after Labor Day. Her stay was short, but I didn't care. Something was better than nothing. The better part of Saturday and until noon on Sunday, she was on her horse, mostly in the company of Jason. Michael was leaving on Wednesday. Their time together would be brief, but long enough for them to say their goodbyes and, in Morgan's case, to cry a little.

Sunday evening saw all of us sitting around a table at my place. The dishes had been stacked, and the adults sat at the table drinking their after dinner coffee. Michael, Taylor and Morgan were there, sipping on their soft drinks and wondering, like the others, why I had earlier announced there were "family matters" to be discussed.

"Maybe Odin and me should go in the other room," Benny Tovar suggested. "We are not family."

"You two stay right where you are," I said. "You have been a part of the Macintosh family longer than most of us, certainly, longer than me and my kids. You stay right here."

When I had everyone's attention I began, measuring my words carefully because I wasn't real sure where I was going with them. Not one of them, I'm guessing now, had the slightest notion as to what it was all about. Michael was probably an exception, because he always knew more about everything than he let on."

"This is about cows, isn't it?" Morgan sighed

"Nope. Not about cows, Morgan," I said. "The long and short of it, folks, is that I wanted all of you to know that Megan and I have decided to get married as soon as we can find the time." There it was: impromptu, spur of the moment, unrehearsed, no forewarning, no precautionary briefing of children, nothing.

"We are in love. Yes we are in love," I added, "and if that surprises any of you...well, welcome to the club. We have both been unlucky in love, as they say, but we have come to believe that life without love is nothing, and neither of is willing to settle for that.

"I know this may be hard for our children to accept and, if it is, we are sorry for that. We love each other, and our love certainly does not diminish our love for all of you. Congratulate us if you can, bear with us if you can't, and try to accept that fact that two people who have seen little in the way of happiness lately, except for this family and Megan's good health, have found happiness. We are as anxious about all this as you might be, but we are determined to take a chance again and make it work.

"Megan? Do you want to say something?"

"I can't think of anything," she said, "that would paint a clearer picture of where we are coming from and where we intend to go. That's it. We love each other."

For what seemed a long time but was, in reality, a matter of seconds, silence was pervasive in the room. Then suddenly Morgan stood up. She's going to storm out of here. I knew it. In a second she'll be crying and full of rage. I knew she cared deeply for Megan, but hearing that her father had found another love besides her mother might be a pill she simply could not swallow. Time and time again I had thought of speaking to her about Megan and me, but just never did. I didn't not say anything because I was afraid, but rather because I knew nothing I could say would be convincing. She had to convince herself, and I was about to find out if she had made any progress in that department.

Still my mind was dancing a jig trying to get out in front of her reaction, trying to anticipate her reaction, but it was all for naught, because she was suddenly standing, clapping slowly and wearing a smile. The rest fell in behind her like packhorses on a narrow trail, and soon they rushed up to us with hugs, kisses and well wishes. When the group had emptied their store of hugs, kisses, kind words, handshakes and kidding, Jennifer announced that she had announcement. Ice cream, milk shakes, root beer floats, and coffee were next on the agenda. Then it was back to Morgan. I glanced down at Megan, as she pulled herself closer, and I could see both relief and concern in her eyes.

"See, I told you," I whispered, as my arm flew around her waist. "Nothing to it! I knew it would be easy." She smiled again and shook her head ever so slightly, as much as to say, "Is it always going to be like this?"

I looked out upon that small group of relatives, soon-to-be-relatives, and friends, and I knew I was just where I wanted to be and that I was the luckiest guy alive and residing in paradise. My daughter, I was proud her. She had matured so much it was hard to believe. But she wasn't done yet. I glanced out of the corner of my eye, as I talked with Jennifer, to see her stand again and tap her fork on her water glass. She had more to say. Oh God! What now?

"As the youngest of the group, I believe I have certain prerogatives, one of which is to speak my piece. Two things I have to say, if no one objects. First off, one day last summer Taylor bet me that these two would announce their engagement before Christmas and would be married before my birthday next June. She said she knew it the first time she saw her mom when she came back from the Mayo Clinic the last time. There was something in her eyes, she said, and that something was my dad. They were always looking at each other, a peek here, a glance there.

"Well," I told her, "that would be all right with me. It is obvious they are hooked on each other, but I thought she was reading into it more than was there. I said Megan would never settle, needn't settle for my dad. Sorry, Dad. But Taylor argued that the two of them were looking at each other like two starry-eyed love birds. I said it was impossible. No, I said it was double-impossible, that she was nuts. Michael said he would not speculate. I said let's make a bet, let's have a contest to see who is right and who is wrong.

"Michael refused to become a party to our bet. He said we were both nuts. So in the end, Taylor said that if her mom and my dad *did not* signal their intentions to marry by Christmas, she would give me one of her heifers and admit to everyone that I was right. So, Taylor, the contest is over and you are the winner. I will have Jason personally deliver your new calf to your place no later than tomorrow so long as he can work it in before we leave for the early movie in

Bozeman tomorrow night. If he's too busy...well, tough."

By now everyone was smiling and laughing again, but Morgan was not finished. "The other thing I wish say is on a more serious note. My dad once told me that if I mixed one dose of antidisestablishmentarianism with two does of califragilisticexpedaliotious I would produce, a triple dose of nothing. I know that hidden in there someplace was something he wanted me to know. I never found out what it was, but I have to admit that when I first thought of him and Megan as a couple, I felt like I had, on my own, done some mixing of many things in my life that produced a lot of personal uncertainty and confusion.

"I mean, after all" she added without missing a beat, "wasn't there a chance that my dad and mom might one day reconcile? No one ever told me it was impossible, at least not directly, but over time I began to see for myself that my dad was happier than I could ever remember him being. And my mom seemed so too."

Personally, I had not the faintest idea where Morgan was headed with her impromptu speech, but I was absolutely certain that those pesky things near the corner of my eyes were tears.

"Then to complicate things," she continued, looking directly at me, "I found myself once again loving the man I had once disliked intensely. He never deserved being disliked by me, but it took a while for me to learn that my mom and dad were *both* victims and that, had they stayed together, they would still be unhappy. My dad has taught me so much about love these past few months, and so has Megan. I wish them the very best. I hope they will be very happy, but I don't want to see any courthouse wedding. I want a fancy one where I have at least a chance to catch that bridal bouquet. Once again, Megan and Dad, you need to know that I could not be happier. End of speech."

Now I was brushing jumbo tears from my cheeks, and there was ever more clapping and more coffee. What could have been a disaster for Megan and me gave us, instead, a new perspective into the insightful maturity of our children...and greater appreciation for our small group of supportive friends.

Taylor got her calf. Morgan saw the movie. The rest of us looked the other way and worked our tails off on Labor Day. Michael was there all day in spite of the fact that he had to leave early in the morning. Monday night, Megan and I treated the entire bunch to dinner at the Food and Ale, and I made sure Morgan was squeezed in between Megan and me. Mike sat directly across from us at the large round table we managed to capture. I watched as he conversed with those around him, but noticed that when he was not so engaged, he was staring off into the distance, momentarily divorced from the small talk. I knew he was feeling bad about leaving, knowing how much work remained and how much he was going to miss Taylor and the rest of us.

We had done everything we could to ready ourselves for the influx of several hundred black and white critters, and up in the Roots were over 1200 head of cow-calf pairs and a couple hundred or more head of yearling steers that would have to be rousted out of the canyons and draws before winter hit. I didn't even want to think about how much we were obligated to do in the next couple of months but somehow we would manage...we must.

And we did, but not until we said goodbye to Morgan. Both of us had watery eyes when she turned away and walked to her gate, but we were a father and daughter team now, and that was enough for me. Come back, I said, as often as you can.

Jennifer found us two hired hands to finish the haying and then to help build the pens we would use to keep our calves separated. And we finished just in time, for a bit after noon on the 15th three long, tractor-trailer rigs pulled into my yard and unloaded 125 Holstein heifer calves.

We were ready for them, but they could have come at a better time, since we were up to our necks in work without them. The two hired hands were hard workers, and we could not have asked more of them. Together with two of Taylor's classmates from Ennis, we stayed out in front, but just barely. One of the girls drove a truck pulling a large flat-bed trailer while Odin and me threw bales up to Benny for stacking. The other one actually ran a front-end loader and cleaned out a couple of pens Claire had not used recently. It didn't take long before we began seeing neighbors who wondered what we were up to with so much black and white.

By the end of September, we had a total of 300 heifer calves destined to one day replace...well, possibly even their mothers on the milking line. We also had better than 400 crossbred heifer calves that would someday be part of the Macintosh-Pengilly herd. They were out of registered, polled Herefords. Their bodies were largely black and their faces white. Better than half of them had white on their bellies, but most would never require dehorning. Then, we also had a hundred yearling cross bred steers, and better than a hundred straight Holstein steers. We had taken a gigantic step into the cross breeding business and, so far, that step was proving to be in the right direction.

Megan and I got away only one time during September, and that was to fly her to Rochester for her semi-annual check-up. She passed with flying colors, and we were soon on our way back to Montana. We returned to the frenzied activity devoted to making and storing feed, and that continued until Thanksgiving. We took a few days off then, for the workload, even with hired help, was beginning to wear us down. My folks and Rebecca's folks came down for Thanksgiving dinner at Claire and Jennifer's, but they left the following morning, anxious to be back home and sleep in their own beds.

The rest of us loaded up a trailer load of saddle horses and headed for the grazing permit. It was intended to be a leisure trip, and it was. Claire and Jennifer both spent considerable time in the saddle as we scoured this canyon, that draw, this coulee, that water hole, checking the cattle. We all enjoyed the time away from work, but none of us escaped without a sore backside by day's end.

The first hard frost, which signaled that the corn would grow no more, hit us the first week in December. When it arrived, we attacked the irrigated corn like so many wild hogs eating their first square meal in days. Half of it we cut for grain and hauled it to the large grain bins to store. Even the stocks and leaves that fell to the ground in windrows behind the combine were baled and stacked next to the pens. The rest was silage corn. I lost track of the number of truck and wagon loads of silage we packed into the concrete ground silos, covering them with heavy plastic to foster the fermentation process.

It took a good bit of fancy footwork...no, a lot of fancy footwork to bring 1200 cows down from the grazing permit. But Claire knew what he was doing. He called the shots with regard to the permit cattle and when they must be brought to the ranch. He did not want to fight winter to get at them, so he was careful in assessing conditions and weather forecasts. He had done it dozens of times over the years and, when he felt the moment was right, we buck-jumped our way on to the permit.

Our first full day on the job was December 6th, and I can tell you that bringing half wild cows and even wilder calves out of the Tobacco Roots is no small task. Laced as they are with canyons and rugged draws choked with brush and trees, locating the cattle is a challenge in itself. We all spent hours each day in the saddle, and those were hours not fitting into the pleasure ride category. Tiring and...yes, dangerous those hours were. When darkness settled over us, we cared for our horses, ate and slept, figuratively standing up, while we waited to load out one load after another of stock destined for Claire's pens.

It might have taken much longer to locate the pockets of stock spread out over thousands of acres of broken country and high plateaus, were it not for the Cessna. Each morning before the updrafts began climbing the eastern slopes, Megan and I cranked up the 172, headed north or south, and climbed until we reached an altitude that allowed us to get on top of the mountains. With binoculars and a spotting scope we located, in minutes, large and small bunches of stock that would have taken hours to find on a horse. With our cell phones we sent the information to Jennifer, who was tending to what amounted to a command post in their new 5th-wheel trailer. She, in turn, sent riders on their way.

Our catch pens were too small to hold the entire 1200 head, but we managed to haul several hundred head to the ranch in stock trailers and a rented semi-tractor-trailer rig. The remaining 700 head, we drove to the ranch down the narrow, fenced alley that was a road. Keep in mind that nearly 700 calves, most of them weighing in over 400 pounds, followed as many mother cows. It was a sight to see and one I'll remember for a long time. The cows and calves passed within a hundred feet of my log house, but we didn't stop there. Later, Megan's cows and calves would be cut out from her father's, and trucked over to her place. And much later, several hundred of the calves would be sold either at the auction yards or by private treaty. When we were satisfied that they were all fed and watered and secure in their pens, every last one of us got the first good night's sleep in days.

In the days that followed, we all slipped back into our routines. Megan presented herself to the bank in Ennis, but she quickly found the job not to her liking. Oh, as far as that goes, I think she enjoyed the work. It was more a matter of not wanting to be away from the cows...and me, I hoped. Taylor reluctantly returned to her studies at Ennis High School. Michael called often, promising to be home for Thanksgiving. Morgan wrote me a nice, long e-mail with her congratulations on my choosing of Megan to be her future step-mother. Even her mother was happy for me, she said. Could she come for Christmas? I think you know what my answer was but, in my own defense, I did tell her that her mother would feel bad if she spent the holidays with me so soon.

And Christmas was just around the corner. We had no plans other than to be together. I couldn't get in the mood, probably because our daytime temperatures were above average. Mountain tops were covered with the white stuff, and most of the upper reaches were inaccessible until next June, but only splotches here and there were to be found in the valley. Good for feeding cows, but did little to foster a Christmas spirit.

For all of us, work days were piling up and falling away like dominos without our ever seeming to make any real headway. My days began in darkness with the black and white critters that always seemed hungry and bawling. Still it was rewarding to see how they were growing. Then it was over to the Macintosh place or Megan's to help out. Gradually, the pace tailed off as we hauled home or stacked in-place the last of the feed, and the slowdown came just in time. The last two weeks before Christmas were near normal in almost every way.

I say almost normal if only because between us all, we had most of our chores finished by early afternoon. Of course we always checked on the stock to make sure the feed bunks were full and the water tanks were open before we called it a day. We hadn't been standing still, by any means, as far as the crossbred segment of our operation. Spread between our three outfits were 300 four month old straight Holstein heifers, 500 cross bred heifers, more than half of which were black baldies. Besides that there were now 150 straight Holstein steers between four and eight months in age, 124 mixed cross bred steers, and 50 yearling Holstein steers.

Our two hired hands had been let go. We saw them now and again on weekends or at one of the basketball games in Ennis, but they never came out looking for work. Claire was back in the saddle again with only the slightest hint of a limp when he walked about *looking over* the stock on all three places.

Our first measurable snowfall came on the 18th of December. Four-wheel drive vehicles came in handy, I'd have to say, but the temperature was moderate for this time of year. I made up my mind to host the Macintosh clan at my place both on the day of Christmas eve and Christmas day. None of us lived very far from the each other, so I didn't have to worry about extra beds. Megan and her mother would cook the major dishes and haul them over at the appropriate time. I pledged to do everything else, including washing and drying dishes and a bit of sweeping and scrubbing.

For reasons I am just beginning to fully understand, the favorite meeting place for all of us gradually became my place rather than at the main ranch or over at Megan's. Mine was smaller but more cozy, and there was just something enticing about logs crackling in the fireplace of a log cabin that had many years earlier belonged to Benny Tovar. But it wasn't that alone. It was, I believe, because it had a longer history and because it was....well, more Montana.

Taylor was the one who suggested that the three of us ought to fly over to Missoula a day or two before Michael's classes were finished, and bring him back to the ranch. The woman never got any argument from me. I was anxious to see Michael again, and it seemed like a couple of days away from work, school, and the ranch might provide just the therapy we could all use after a hectic summer and an even more hectic autumn. When Benny and Odin volunteered to look after our cattle during our short absence, it was only a matter of two days before we literally hit the big skies.

The sun was low on the horizon and on our back when we lifted off from our landing strip that wasn't a landing strip. Sunny from the start, our departure was early enough to avoid bothersome turbulence and the wicked updrafts that plagued the fronts of most of Montana's mountain ranges. Our flight path roughly followed Interstate 90, and our ride was smooth all the way. Landing at the Missoula airport was delayed several minutes as we waited for two Northwest flights to touch down on the concrete. We taxied to one the private aviation hangers, stopped next to a chain link fence, and looked up to see Michael standing by his truck, waiting. So much for surprises. I made a mental note never to trust Taylor again to guard such important secrets.

She looked over to me with a noticeable smirk on her face as much as to say, "Ha! Gotcha!" And her mother was smiling as well, so I amended my pledge to myself not to trust *either* of them again with surprises. By now, Michael's head was pressed against the high chain link fence, and his fingers were intertwined with Taylor's. Megan and I might have been in another world, far divorced for their world of puppy love, young love or whatever it was.

"Meet you at the entrance," Michael said. "I have to hurry or I'll be late for my next class." And we did hurry and he did make it to his class in time. We rented two adjacent rooms and from both we could watch and hear the singing, gurgling, rushing Clark Fork River as it picked its way between and over boulders of varying sizes. Mike helped us carry our luggage in, then I drove him over to the University. He would call us as soon as his class was out and he had finished his shower.

Our plan for the day was no plan at all. The girls wanted to spend time at the mall and Mike and I wanted to make the 24-mile quick trip to Livingston where he had located a so-called "balanced-ride" saddle. He explained that he believed that most saddles put you back too far on a horse's back, which exaggerated the trot and made the horse work harder. I bought into the idea, I guess, because I was always unconsciously pushing against the swells instead of lazily slipping back to the cantle. The one he purchased showed some wear, but it was solidly constructed, and such saddles were no longer being made.

We met the girls at the mall for lunch then followed them around, spending most of our time sitting on one of the not-so-comfortable benches. Mike had purchased tickets for all of us to the Grizzly-Weber State basketball game, which was part of the annual holiday tournament held in Missoula. The Grizzlies kicked their you-know-what. But one of the things I'll always remember about that game was the speech the student body president made before the outset, admonishing Grizzly fans to be good sports. When he finished, the response was a uproar of boos followed by laughs. Another incident was not something everyone in the field house was privy too. Only those of us who happened to have nearby seats heard a young man, who came to the game wearing a western hat, shout out to one of the referees, "Hey ref., open your eyes, you're missing a great game".

Beef growers that we were, we left the game when the Grizzlies had a commanding lead and beat a path to one of the steak houses to take advantage of their "all you can eat" prime rib dinner. We sat around a bit, drinking coffee and listening to Mike relate his experiences so far at the U. Good school, he said. Pre-med program strong and challenging. No medical school as such, but a reciprocity agreement between Montana and Washington made it possible for four students from the U. to transfer to the University of Washington's medical school each year, provided they qualified. He was determined to be one of the four and, knowing him, I would have bet that he would.

Missoula's weather in late December can range from balmy to

frigid. We caught it somewhere in between, which meant light jackets during the day and heavier jackets after the sun dropped below the mountain peaks. Taylor and Michael dragged out their heavier jackets and went for a walk on the asphalt paths adjacent to the Clark Fork. Megan and I walked down the hallway to the lounge for a night-cap. The kids were just walking into the lobby when we came out of the lounge, and we walked to our rooms together.

I gave Megan a peck on the cheek before Mike and I walked down the hall a few steps to our own room. It had been a long day, and I was tired.

"You know, Dad," Mike said, "I can't hardly wait until tomorrow. I want to try out that new saddle. I don't care how cold it gets."

"Well," I said, "you should do that. Tomorrow at this time, we'll be back at the place and, if you're satisfied with the saddle, you can lay back and take it easy."

"Thanks for coming after me," he said, and then he was sleeping.

Chapter 12

Habitually early risers, Megan and I finished breakfast and were drinking our second or third cup of coffee, waiting for the kids to show up. Between sips, we discussed when we should have our wedding. My inclination was not to wait, to tie the knot right after Christmas. Megan leaned toward something well after the first of the year, maybe about Easter or even after the kids are finished with their school in the spring.

"You chickening out?" I asked with a healthy smile on my face.

"No. Not at all," she answered, "but to me, it is really important that all three of the kids to be there, and how can we decide when we really have no idea when Morgan will come again? Talk to her next time she calls, and if the subject happens to come up, ask her if she has any plans for another visit."

I said I would, and I admitted that her point was a good one. Having the kids there when we tied the knot was essential. After all, our getting married was a kind of symbolic pronouncement to them that there was no going back for any of us, including them.

"Based on her speech during our family meeting a while back," I said, "I think she's all right with the idea that we are going to be married, but she's young and she's very sensitive to such things. Her perfect world has crumbled down around her over the last year or so, and she is struggling to reshape her life with the pieces she's plucked from the pile. You know as well as I that no one can ever know what is in the mind of a person her age. Heavens, she hardly knows herself.

"Still, I'm going to take her at her words," I continued. "She said when she was here last time that she was ok with our getting married, and I think she meant at...at least at the time. The question is: does she still feel that way? The only certainty as far as I can see is that she would be terribly hurt if we ran off and got married by some Justice of the Peace.

"And I wouldn't blame her," I added, "and I want to say for that record, that if you toss that bridal bouquet anywhere near her, I'll sue for an immediate annulment."

Taylor's appearance at the restaurant entrance ended our discussion. She was alone. Michael was still sorting through his stuff, she said. He's worried their won't be room on the plane for the saddle and the other stuff he brought. He says we can sit on the saddle blankets, but thinks it will take some doing to get our luggage *and* his saddle in the space we have.

"We'll figure it out, I said. There's always a way."

Moments later, he plopped down into the chair next to me, thumbed his way through the menu, and poured himself a glass of orange juice from the carafe we had ordered.

"Trying to get organized," he said, as he handed the menu to the waitress who had come up to our table. "Had to make sure I brought the right text books home and then, of course, there's the saddle."

"Don't worry about the saddle, Mike," I said. "We'll find a way. Actually, our load is more a matter of bulk than weight. We didn't bring much in the way of luggage...not for a short trip like this. What we have is in small stuff bags which are much lighter than most suitcases. I've got some camping gear stowed back there, but it's light as well and, besides, we are way underweight. Your saddle and blankets are bulky but not terribly heavy. If it comes to it, you can hold that saddle on your lap. If we can't make it work, there's always UPS.

"I want to remind all of you," I said, "that it gets cold up above this time of year, and the heater in that aluminum can is no longer 100 percent efficient. You can sit on the blankets, and I think you'll want to wear your heavy jackets. You'll be thankful you brought them along before we get home."

"Good," Mike said. "I'm relieved to hear you think we'll have room."

When he finished eating, we got up without a word, as if we had all received a silent command to do so by some higher authority. An hour later, we were at the airport, quietly piling into our fully serviced plane. Mike made a hurried call to one of his room mates to tell him he could come out and get the truck anytime it was convenient. Keys were in a small black container held against the box's sidewall with a magnet.

By the time he hung up, Megan was walking out of the small terminal with two cups of complimentary coffee. We were set. I had earlier filed and now meticulously followed a flight plan which took us north out of Missoula into a light head wind for about 20 miles until we gained enough elevation to top out two thousand feet above the spine of the Bitterroot Mountains. Once there I dropped down a few hundred feet so we could fly under a line of clouds that weren't low enough to so much as brush the mountain peaks as they moved east. They looked like harmless little things that would dissipate once they crossed over the mountains, and I thought there would be very little, associated turbulence. They might drop a few snowflakes as squall lines often do, but I didn't think much of it.

South of us, dense fog gripped the lower valleys, wiping out our view of roads and small streams, but at our cruising altitude, it was mostly sunny. In a few minutes, we would hang a left and let the tailwind push us beyond the clouds and accelerate our short trip home. My thought was that we would skirt the Tobacco Roots on the west side, turn east when we could see Ennis, and fly over the Madisons, then head northwest to the ranch.

I caught a fleeting glimpse of Lolo Creek through a gap in the clouds and, for a few moments, watched cars climb the winding road leading to Lolo Pass. A year earlier, the kids and I had dabbled in cross country skiing there on our way to Moccasin to visit Rebecca's mother and father. I had hiked up in the Bitterroots a few times, looking for high country inspiration, I suppose, while I was still in high school. I loved the country out along the Continental Divide, and I was thinking that down the road, Megan and I would come out and climb both of the Trapper Peaks not far from Darby. Had an old friend living just outside that small town. He owned a tavern there, and I was pretty sure we could touch him for a cool one.

Immersed in such relaxing thoughts, I happened to glance at the oil pressure gauge and was startled by what I saw. My brain instantly told me we could be in serious trouble. If it was only a matter of a gauge that was malfunctioning to lock the needle in place, we would be okay. But if it was resting at the bottom because we had lost our oil pressure, well...that was quite another problem. My instincts told me it was the latter, that either the pump had failed or a line had ruptured, and if I was right, we were caught up in a life and death situation.

Moments later the engine stuttered several times, momentarily recovered, coughed a second time, then stopped dead, locking the propeller in a horizontal position. The oil pump had failed or the line had ruptured. I was sure of it now. The predictable consequence of either was a locked engine. It had failed, for whatever reason, and nothing I tried could bring it back to life We were going to crash. Megan glanced at me, her face cloaked with fear, but she said nothing.

We were barely 20 minutes from lift off, and we were in desperate trouble. We were fifteen hundred feet above the spine of the mountains, and I had still had the option of peeling off to either side. Only a few miles southeast of Lolo Pass, we were looking down at thick stands of Englemann Spruce, interspersed with snow fields, the larger of which I judged to be as much as a mile long.

"Hang on, guys," I said in the calmest voice I could muster. "We have lost our oil pressure, the engine is locked, and I have to set us down in one of those large snow fields below. Don't panic, please. We are not going to crash if I can help it, but our landing is going to be a hard one. Tighten your seat belts and stay calm."

Maintaining our air speed was critical, for if it dropped too low we would simply stall and fall out of the sky into the snow or trees like a belly-flopping pancake. The 1500 feet of altitude we had above the spine of the mountains was a blessing. Our air speed was dropping, which meant that we were closing the distance between ourselves and a set down. I doubt if any of the others had noticed, but the altimeter needle told me what was happening.   I knew I could maintain our speed for a few minutes, so long as I kept the nose down by using the flaps, but only for minutes, then we would be on the ground and there was nothing I could do to prevent it.

No one said a word. Silence was pervasive, and with the motor no longer functioning, the only sound in the cockpit was that of air rushing against the metal fuselage. We were now essentially a glider and I was not a glider pilot.

But the prospects were not as dismal as the others probably imagined. Part of my flight training years earlier involved landing a Piper Cub after my instructor deliberately, and without warning, cut the power. I had made it down several times, but that was out on the prairies, where one could always find a flat piece of ground. Obviously that was not the case here. The west slope of the Bitterroots, which I could see out the left window, was riddled with rock formations, needle-like spires, massive trees, and lonely boulders.

And there was also the matter of weight. We were well within the weight limits for a 172, but with four passengers we were far heavier than myself and my instructor in a Piper Cub. The Cub itself was considerably lighter, acting at times more like a kite than an airplane. Still this was now, and I had my work cut out for me. My heart was thumping in my chest like a trip hammer and, suddenly my entire body was covered with perspiration. The insides of my hands were clammy, and my knuckles had turned red against the controls. No one was saying a word but, without looking up, I knew their eyes were locked on me. For me to show fear was to increase their's.

I think they knew I had to concentrate on what I was doing and should not be distracted. It was my own voice that finally broke the silence. "Here is what I am going to do," I said. "We have no power, but I am hoping to maintain enough speed to let us glide on to and set down on the largest and longest north-south snow field I can find. Once I decide, there is no turning back. And it could be hairy. To succeed, I have to do everything just right. I'll be skimming the top of the trees when we reach the snow. If I try to set down too far out into the snow, we run the risk of crashing into the trees at the other end.

"You need to know what is happening," I went on. "When we reach within a few feet of the snow, I'll try to lift our nose up slightly, and attempt a belly-flop landing. The snow is deep, and unless the wind has built up hardened snow banks, the surface should be soft and fluffy."

"Can we do anything, Dad.?" Mike asked.

"Try praying guys," I said, making eye contact only with Megan, "and while you're at it, ask for fluffy, powdery snow. We are going to do this. I promise you we will. Hang on, and stay calm if you can."

We had clear skies, and there was a miniscule chance, I thought, that someone, a cross-country skier, a back-country winter camper, or even a Forest Service ranger, might witness our going down. If we were lucky in that regard, help might not be long in coming. I was not a total pilgrim where it came to the section of the Selway-Bitterroot Wilderness we were crossing, though my experience went back three decades, sufficient time to erode anyone's memory. I guessed we were now no more than 15 miles east-south-east of Lolo Pass, and we were no more than a couple miles or so west of the Bitterroot Spine. I knew too that leading away from Lolo pass like tentacles of an octopus were a seasonally maintained east-west road and at least a couple of even more primitive roads, but they too were strictly seasonal roads. All of them would be buried under several feet of snow. Still, treeless paths leading to the north and west seemed a way out if we managed to land without being killed.

Frantically, I surveyed both sides of the north-south aligned spine of the mountains. With seconds to spare, I spotted an oval-shaped patch of snow to my right, on the Idaho side of the border, and I knew immediately that it was in this open space that we would set down.

"Here we go, guys," I said. "That patch of snow on our right is our landing strip. I don't believe I can maintain enough altitude to reach much beyond that. As far as I can see, if I can skim the tops of the trees on this end of the snow field, there are no trees in the patch of snow we could slam into. So, I am going to give it a try. Under that snow could be a frozen lake. If I am right, we can do no better."

We skimmed the tree tops on the north end of the opening, as I had hoped we would, and the plane smoothly floated over the half-mile long patch of snow. I knew we were not going to fly out of the snow. We were committed, but my greatest worry was our landing gear. If the snow had been hardened by wind, making it impossible for our wheels to cut through it, I could see our front end dipping down, forcing us into a very short-lived nose drive. I lifted the nose as much as I could, thinking that if I could drop the tail into the snow, and keep the wheels from biting into drifts before the tail bit in, we could still make it.

The mountain sides were covered with snow ghosts, trees filled by the wind with snow and looking very much like ghosts on their way to a Halloween party in broad daylight. But the surface of the snow we touch down into was soft and fluffy. When we began to cut through it, clouds of snow flew up and over our front windshield, completely snuffing out our visibility, and before we came to a stop we were encased in snow and darkness.

"Everybody okay?" I heard Megan ask. A chorus of yeas filled the cockpit, and I knew we had met the first test. We were alive, and none of us seemed seriously injured. But another problem now facing us was the matter of digging ourselves out of the snow that enveloped us. I pushed against my door, but it opened a couple of inches at the most. Megan tried the same on the passenger side.

"My God," she shouted. "We are trapped in here!"

"Stay cool, boys and girls, " I uttered, "I think if we keep pushing and gradually force the snow away, one of the doors may open enough to let me get out. Outside, I can shovel snow away with my hands."

"Are we going to suffocate in here?" Taylor called out.

"Could we?" Megan echoed.

"Let's just stay calm and keep trying to push back the snow," I said. "I doubt if we are actually buried in the snow. Our windshield is covered with some, yes, but it is mostly what flew up at us when we pushed against it with our nose.

"Let's see if we can build up a side-to-side rocking motion," I suggested. "That might gain us a few inches each time. It is bound to push some snow away from the doors and fuselage."

Together, we rocked the cabin from side to side. When we stopped and I tried again to open the door, we had gained only a few inches, not enough give us an exit. I told the others to sit tight while I tried to reach down and push handfuls away from the crack at the bottom of my door. When I had pushed and pulled away several handfuls, I pulled the door shut then slammed it against the snow with all my might. It worked, and after several repetitions, I was able to push my left leg out enough for me to tell that the snow beneath my foot was more compacted than what I could reach with my hand.

Rocked some more. Stepped out further. Fifteen minutes later both of my feet were planted outside the plane, and I was feverishly scooping and pushing snow away. The snow beneath our wheels was solid compared to the fluffy stuff piled up over us, and it was that hardness, I believe, that slowed us down and kept us from burrowing in deeper. One by one we worked our way out the door on my side, and soon we were outside, standing knee deep in the fluffy stuff.

"Now what?" Michael asked.

"The trees," I said. "We need to try for those spruce trees straight ahead. We're going to sink in two or three feet, so it is going to be tough going. Tougher than anything any of us have ever faced. We are a football field length from the first trees, and we'll be exhausted by the time we get there."

"Dad, why don't you and I make our way over there the first time without carrying anything," Michael suggested. "We can strike a path that will be easier for Megan and Taylor to follow. Maybe we'll have to cover it a couple times before the girls try."

I told Mike it was an excellent idea, and we set out immediately. I was right. Moving forward, involved lifting each leg as high as possible then planting it as hard as we could before trying the other leg. By the time we reached to within the thick stand of spruce my legs felt like they had died. I had no feeling, and with every step I took, I wanted to scream. Nobody had to tell me that several "empty" trips would be needed. Were it not for the fact that the girls were standing outside the plane and trying to haul out our gear, the plane itself would have been lost from our sight. The wings were no more than a foot or two above the flat expanse of snow we had dropped into and, at that, they were covered with several inches of snow.

Nearly two hours were needed to empty the plane. Mike and I brought out anything and everything, because it was likely we would make use of the smallest items, including scraps of paper, maps, and a thick, maintenance manual, before we were rescued. The latter had little value at the moment other than in starting fires. By the time everything, including Mike's saddle was piled near the base of a large tree, we were so exhausted we simply slumped to the ground and fought to catch our breath. The sun was slowly dropping in the west, a few flakes of snow were falling, and I knew we must be settled for the night before dark.

Our haven was the underside of a large spruce tree. It was covered completely with snow, but we were able to burrow through and drop down to the ground beneath and its carpet of needles. My mental calculations said that the snow outside was over 12 feet deep.

Before morning, we would need heat, so while Megan and Taylor sorted through everything, Mike and I scoured the immediate area for firewood. I worked outside while Mike broke away dead branches from below the living, lower fronds of the tree itself. The small fire I built was warming, but our cavern in the snow was quickly filling with smoke. The girls rushed outside, coughing. Using one of the large branches I had brought in from outside, I punched numerous holes through the snow clinging to the large bottom branches. It worked but, even at that, several minutes were needed to dissipate the clouds of smoke that had collected on the underside of the tree. Live and learn, I guess.

My confidence was high that we could survive for several days without eating, and we were not totally bereft of food. It wasn't much, consisting of two Hershey bars and four high-energy Sweet and Salty Almond Nut bars. They, together with a jar of peanut butter and a large bag of trail mix, were the sum and substance of our foodstuff. Not much for variety but loaded with calories. Rationing what we had from the outset was the prudent thing to do. We really had no idea how long we might be there. The variables at work included temperature, wind, and how soon the rescue people could be marshaled. I'm sure there were others, but they were unknown to us.

Water for drinking could be manufactured over the fire in a pot filled with snow. My camping gear, always stowed in the plane's luggage compartment, unless I was riding my horse up into the mountains, proved a to be a veritable treasure trove as far as items that would help us survive and meet our basic needs for a few days. One that could prove invaluable or utterly useless over the days ahead was my .30-.30 Winchester lever action rifle, the same one I used to bring down the cougar up on the permit. Strapped near its butt was a leather case with more than a dozen shells. I saw the rifle as way of alerting chance passers by or searchers to our location. Three shots in the air was the universal signal that someone was in need of aid. And though it seemed highly unlikely, because of our elevation, a deer or some other edible animal might be roaming about in this high country. Should one venture too close, we could put him down and eat like kings.

But there was more, including a 10-inch Swedish cross-cut saw, a light-weight hatchet, an ultra-light, two-person back-packing tent, matches imbedded in melted wax, two butane cigarette lighters, a 10' x 10' blue, plastic ground tarp, two yellow rain slickers, two sleeping bags and, believe it or not, one twin-sized Coleman air mattress. The sleeping bags were rated as protecting down to 28 degrees. It was far colder than that already, and the sun hadn't even dipped below the western horizon yet, but those bags were certainly more inviting than a stiff plastic tarp alone.

In the last flickering minutes of daylight Mike and I trudged through the snow one final time back to the Cessna. The heavy snow that was falling, together with a gusty wind, almost guaranteed the the plane would be buried again under several inches of snow, maybe even several feet, by morning. And by morning it would surely be invisible from anyone flying over.

That we would have to deal with tomorrow. We wanted the top outline of the plane free from snow but, because it was completely white in color except for a dark blue hood cowling, blue stripes on its sides and on the rudder, we would have to enhance the outline by covering the wings, rear fuselage and tail with spruce branches. Someone might notice such an outline. As far as we knew, though, no one knew what had happened to us or where we were.

When we returned to the trees and were back within our comparatively cozy spruce home for the night, Megan was boiling coffee. All of us sipped the warm liquid from my chipped coffee cups, though neither Michael nor Taylor were coffee drinkers. The hot liquid warmed our innards and our hands. We had been so caught up in our chores, that until now none of us had thought to express the relief that was there within each of us.

"We made it guys," I said, looking up from the fire. "We made it!"

"Thanks mostly to you, I think, Jim" Megan said as she slipped away from the fire and crawled over to me. I squeezed her tightly.

She hugged me back, and then she was crying , probably not because she was saddened by our plight, but because we were all alive. Taylor was in Michael's arms, but their words were soft and beyond my hearing.

"We need to talk," I said abruptly, hoping to steer them away from despondency or out-and-out fear. "We need to be sure we're all on the same page as far as our predicament is concerned. I think we would agree that we *are* smack dab in the middle of a sure enough, genuine dilemma. But dilemmas are one thing, being dead is quite another. We don't, in case you haven't noticed, fall into the latter category. Dilemmas we can work our way through. For starters, let me say that I am proud of all three of you. You kept your cool, when it was so hard to do. And you helped me keep mine. In any case, you all know that I filed a flight plan before we departed Missoula, and it will be an essential bit of guidance to anyone involved in searching for us.

"But, I'll be honest with you. I don't think anyone knows where we are other than that we are probably somewhere near the path outlined in our flight plan. Its probably too early for anyone to be sure that we are down. I tried to contact the Missoula airport, but my radio was filled with static, and I doubt anyone heard my mayday message. But Claire and Jennifer are going to start wondering. They may think we simply got a late start or went straight to our own places without a stop at the main ranch. But, in time, perhaps even tomorrow morning, when they discover we never made it home, they'll begin making inquires. When the authorities get around to organizing a search, my flight plan alone should point them in our direction."

"Do you really think so, Jim?" Megan asked, pleadingly. "Do you think they might be looking for us as early as tomorrow morning?"

"Maybe. But I kind of doubt it. Mostly because of the fog. Until it lifts, they are essentially grounded. Later in the day, if the fog lifts down in the valley, there might be some fly-overs. The control tower at Missoula may have heard my mayday call even if all I heard was static. We aren't going to be easy to locate. What I think is more likely is that by morning we will be in the clutches of a blizzard. The temperature is dropping with a thud, and the wind is blowing harder by the minute."

"Should one of us be trying to hike out?" Mike asked.

"Later, maybe. But it is too soon to think along those lines. I want everyone to understand that our situation could be much worse. None of us is seriously injured. We have cover and we have a fire. Inconvenient, yes, but something we can deal with. The main thing is don't let yourself get down. Compared to what it might have been, we are sitting pretty good. We can last here for several days if need be, but rations are going to be very short. Hope it doesn't come to that. I'd much prefer spending Christmas Eve and Christmas on the east side of the Tobacco Roots."

"That makes about four of us," Mike offered. "Who knows, by morning things might be looking up, and we can still make it."

"That makes four of us, again," Megan said.

"Let's hope that's how tomorrow plays out," I said, "but in the morning we'll know better. Right now, it's pitch dark out there, and we're stuck here for the time being. Like I said, if the wind picks up and that fluffy snow starts to drift, we could be here several days. The bright side is that we have at least a small amount of food, we've gathered enough wood to keep our fire going through tonight and beyond, and we've enough bedding to keep us relatively warm."

Almost before I finished, Michael was up and walking around under the canopy of green that covered us, harvesting anything that looked like it might burn. We had already piled several large branches I had hacked away at and separated from a nearby dead tree. They would need sawing, but they were looking mighty attractive to me about now, particularly if it continued snowy and windy.

The bed of spruce needles beneath *our* tree, as I had come to think of it, was soft enough but, with all of our coming and going, we had dragged in considerable snow that had by now melted and left large patches of wetness everywhere. My waterproof tent and an airless twin mattress together solved the moisture problem. Spread out beneath us, they would be an effective barrier. The two unzipped sleeping bags were our blanket, and they shielded us from the cold with the help of the tarpaulin and a thick layer of spruce boughs.

We tucked ourselves between the slices of this strange looking sandwich and, brushing modesty aside, we pressed against each other for the sake of reaping body heat. I positioned myself nearest the fire and, for a time, I was able to keep it burning nicely by simply reaching out and pushing short branches into the flames or coals.

We went to sleep that first night not knowing what the future held, but our fatigue had us sleeping soundly most of the night. Each time either Mike or I awakened to find the fire burned down to a bed of coals, we fed it with kindling and progressively larger branches.

Long before I ever lifted myself out from under my covers, I had grown more fearful that we would find no respite from wind and snow or blowing snow anytime soon. In spite of the insulation given by the blanket of snow held by the spruce boughs, I could still faintly hear the wind. We were using one of the saddle blankets to seal the opening to the outside. Pushing it aside revealed near white-out conditions. We were going nowhere soon. We were trapped!

For two full days and part of a third we were, to put it bluntly, tree-bound. Fine snow sifted through our smoke holes, which was aggravating because it covered our bed, but those same holes kept us with a supply of fresh air for ourselves and our fire, so no one complained. We ate one meal that first day; each of us playing with our one-fourth portion of a granola bar and a bit of trail mix. I can't explain, even now, where our appetites had gone. Was it, I wondered, because each of us intuitively knew we would need nourishment more when our strength began to fail? Or was it a matter of stress?

For better than two days our outhouse was in-house. Other choices: none. But we did take care to cover and bury everything beneath the needles away from our entrance. We talked. We contemplated. We wondered. We slept those days away, and late on the third day, I ventured out beyond our entrance and sank into better than two feet of new snow.

The few bruises and scratches we had suffered seemed to be of small consequence. Megan examined each of us, cleaned visible abrasions and minor cuts and administered four or five Band Aids between us, before proclaiming that none of us could submit any insurance claims.

Taylor was a borderline exception in that she was coping with a sizeable bruise on her leg directly over the break she had dealt with last summer. Of the four of us, she was the only one with a gimpy leg, but it did not seem to be a serious injury. It did mean she would not be walking out of our tree-house and away from the crash site anytime soon. But none of the rest of us would either as far as that went...unless it was me. By no means was I ready to strike out toward the north or west through 14 or more feet of snow.

But if we had not been found in a few more days, I would. We were almost out of food and what little we had left was trail mix and a bit of peanut butter. On our fourth day, all of us ventured out of our hole in the snow and walked to the plane. Once again, Mike and I tried to make it easier for the girls by making the trip three or four times before we let them tackle the snow. By then, we were exhausted. We were hardly more than the length of a football field away, yet making it out and back, even a single time, had me breathing with difficulty once again. When I was breathing easier, we tackled the trail again. With our bare hands, Mike and I shoveled and pushed snow away from the wings and top of the fuselage. Megan and Taylor had light-weight gloves, and they pitched in to help.

In truth our mission was a failure. We could no longer muster enough strength to fully uncover even the wings. But it was a lesson learned. By the time we were back in our tree cave, our feet and hands were wet and freezing.

"We have to figure out some way to keep our hands and feet warm," Megan proclaimed. "I think the tarp is the answer. It's waterproof, and that's what we need. We can make cut-out patterns with your jackknife, Jim, that will cover our feet and reach well above the calf. Taylor and I can sew them together with strands of your rope, then we can steal the latigo leather from Michael's saddle and use it to cinch them on just below the knee."

She was right. We could not survive outside with frozen feet. Michael dragged his saddle close to the fire and began untying the leather straps. I pushed the spruce boughs from the tarp, and Megan began cutting. For the rest of that day, we cut and sewed and brain-stormed how we could fashion mittens out of something.

This time it was Taylor who provided the answer. "We could cut the seam in Michael's heavy saddle blanket," she said, "open it up to twice its size, and cut patterns from that. Each of us can place both of our hands on the open-faced blanket and I can use Jim's knife to cut our way around each."

"Wonderful idea, Taylor," I said. "We can do it." Michael was already slicing through the seam that held the blanket together. Once again we fell back on what was left of my soft, cotton rope as a means of stitching together the pattern. Before they finished, each of us had waterproof covers for our feet, mittens, and crudely sewn skull caps. My contribution to all of this was two needles crafted with my Swiss army knife from Spruce twigs.

One need not be a psychiatrist to see that the task of making the foot booties, mittens and skull caps was uplifting for all of us. But not, from my perspective, enough to wash away the sense of sinking spirits I saw in them. We had been cooped up in what was little more than crawl space beneath the spruce tree for almost a week, and our prolonged sedentary condition was starting to take its toll. Conversation and laughter were tapering off and being replaced with quiet, solitude and what were clearly the early stages of resignation and gloom. No starkly discernible changes in behavior had yet to surface, but we were talking less, spending longer periods mentally and spiritually off by ourselves, and impatience with each other was surfacing now and again.

The time had come or was rapidly approaching when routines must be altered, if only to create new sets of routines. We were physically intact but, involuntary incarceration, and that it what we were contending with, had pushed us nearer an insidious lethargy that grew more profound each day. It was growing more apparent with each passing day that inaction must be replaced with action, that introspection had to move over and make room for dialogue even if, at times, it grew heated. Leaving our sanctuary, even if only for short times each day, had now become a necessity. We had to bundle up, push our way through the small entrance, no matter how uninviting it might be outside, and fight the snow instead of fighting with ourselves or the others.

Over a period of several hours, I turned over in my mind, how best to approach what I saw as a burgeoning problem. In the end, I deliberately said nothing but did insist that there were tasks to be done outside that were best undertaken with a team approach. Engaging them in something, anything, other than sitting around would at least temporarily spare them from brooding over their plight. Since it was no longer blowing and snowing, I suggested we go back and try again to free the upper part of the Cessna from its snowy prison. It was as much an inmate, if not more so, than were the four of us.

Chapter 13

If the truth were known, freeing the plane from its snowy dungeon wasn't, by any stretch of the imagination, only a make-work initiative. My hope that it would help lift the spirits of my companions was real, of course, but my head had been preoccupied with the plane almost since the moment we touched down. I had fallen in love with the flowing, artistic lines, and proportions of that blue and white aluminum sculpture. It was a thing of beauty and, in flight, it endowed me with a degree of power and omnipotence never felt by the earth bound. Perspectives are honed by flight, and almost anyone who has ever flown will attest to that. Somehow, flight lifts the burden of physical or mental weight in a way that enhances and frees one's creativity and perceptions.

Thinking as I do about flight, no one should be surprised that I was bouncing ideas off my brain about the plane's fate shortly after it came to rest in the snow. Doing so may have accounted for my not falling into the same torpor that besieged the others. How could I be sure? I couldn't, of course, but if doing so had kept me away from the early stages of depression, well, that was a favorable outcome.

Whatever the reasons, my thoughts had been quietly and secretly focused on the plane, and I was still sifting through a host of connected ideas. One of my thoughts focused on the plane's landing gears. They might have been sheered off on impact, though I thought it more likely they had merely folded back against the plane's under-body as we pushed against the snow in landing. But otherwise, based on the small amount of the fuselage I could see, I was unable to detect any damage, not so much as a scratch. If there were none other, the plane was salvageable, provided the fuselage had not somehow been twisted enough to lose the balance needed to fly properly.

But to salvage it, I reminded myself, one must wrest it from its snowy prison. To do that, the snow that trapped it where it sat had to be pushed or pulled away. Only then could I inspect the fuselage and fully assess its condition, and only then could strong nylon straps be fitted beneath its underside to lift it into the air.

So that was my justification for the lot of us getting involved in what had to be one of the most unusual snow removal projects ever. Before we could do that, though, we had to figure a better way to move snow than with our hands. Our mittens were warming but certainly not totally waterproof. We needed a tool of sorts that moved the snow away but kept our canvas-covered hands out of the snow. The nearest shovel outlet was miles away, so it seemed imagination and a good bit of fabrication were in order. My first thought was to pry a section of aluminum from the plane itself, but I wasn't at all sure that I could. I couldn't help laughing at myself for even thinking along those lines since it would require a tool even harder to fashion than a shovel.

"I think there's a way we might build ourselves crude shovels," Michael volunteered, "but it's a long-shot for sure."

"Tell us, Mike," I said.

"Well, if you peek your head out through the opening and turn your eyes to the east, you may have noticed, as I have, a bunch of blow-down trees. Probably an acre or more of them. They're better than a city block away, and it's up hill all the way. It would be a struggle to reach them, but it occurred to me some time ago that many are broken off above the snow, and that they might be a source of dry firewood if we ran out here."

"The connection, Michael?" I asked, impatiently, and then felt immediately sorry for doing so. But I pressed for an answer nevertheless. "What's the connection?"

"Well, the more or less uniform absence of bark tells me they were blown down by a fierce wind long ago, maybe many years ago. If we took the time to make our way over there, I think we might find a few large branches hollowed out by rot, with one side intact, the other rotted away by years of melting snow and rain. Take that Swedish saw of yours, saw them into manageable lengths, and use them to scoop snow away from the plane. Not as good as a scoop shovel...but better than our hands. In fact, if we are careful, our hands need never touch the snow."

"But why is it so important to clean snow away from the plane, anyway?" Megan asked, before I could comment on Mike's idea. "It's not going anywhere. Spring will melt the snow around it long after we are back on the ranch."

"I'd agree," I said, "but aside from not being sure that we haven't landed on a snow-covered, frozen lake, we still need to make the plane's outline more visible from above."

"I get the part about making it more visible, but can't we just sweep the snow from the wings and pile on the spruce boughs. Where does the frozen lake come into all this?"

"Well," I replied, "like I said, I'm not sure, but the Selway-Bitterroot map I took from the plane shows a Moose Lake located smack dab in the middle of where I think we and the plane are located. It's oval-shaped and, probably about a half mile long. No, smaller than that, I think. Look out at the snowfield we landed in. Go ahead, one of you, take a look. Oval shaped, right, and with enough length to serve as an emergency landing strip."

Nodding heads told me they thought I might be right, so I reminded them that if the plane were to be saved, it would have to be lifted out by a helicopter before the ice went out. Come spring, the plane would simply slip down into the water, destroying the navigation equipment and ruining the engine. If it is to be saved it must be accomplished before that happens. Pulling it out of what amounts to a huge snow bank, part of which is very hard, I offered, would damage the fuselage. I can replace a motor or a strut, I said, but not a damaged fuselage, twisted out of line. That's another matter all together.

"Mike, do you remember the big helicopter we saw parked just below Lolo Pass on the Montana side? It was here when we drove up here to ski during the Christmas holidays last year. Last year, we watched them lift logs from an area they were harvesting and pile them up next to the highway just east of the pass. They might be using it again this winter. If they are, it could be the ticket to wrenching the plane from beneath the snow."

"Yes. I do. I do remember it, and it was huge. It could lift the plane out without even trying."

None of them wanted to see the plane slip below the surface of Moose Lake or any other lake for that matter. It was a Macintosh family treasure that kept the memory of a lost son alive. Megan understood that far better than Taylor, but even she had heard a good deal from her grandparents about how her uncle had died in the crash of a friend's plane just out of Rawlins, Wyoming.

My own attachment flowed more from the satisfaction I gained by restoring the plane to flying condition. Megan and I had flown to the Mayo Clinic for one of her periodic check-ups and to several places where we just wanted to be alone. We had also used it to establish the location of the Macintosh cattle on the grazing permit. Jennifer and Claire had said the Cessna was mine, gave it to me, I guess, and that they wanted it off their place, because it conjured up hurtful memories, but I knew it would always be theirs even if it was parked at my place.

Unless I was reading the sign altogether incorrectly, the two of them were beginning to see it as a symbol of all of the good things their boy had brought into their lives rather than a constant reminder that he had died. My hope was to one day fly them over the Tobacco Roots, let them look down and see their cattle grazing the permit, and to treat them to a commanding and revealing view of the beauty that surrounded them. No, I would salvage the plane and it would fly again, even if I had to do it all by myself.

Mike's guess that the blow-down area might have rotted log sections that might be fashioned into crude scoops was a good one. The four of us made the trip over. Half the time, we were laughing at each other as we struggled, at times, to even stand up. But in the process we found what we were looking for and were soon on our way back to our tree, dragging dry firewood and a few selected branches to be fashioned into snow removal tools far more efficient than our hands. Efficient? Well, I think that may be an overstatement. In any case, by mid-afternoon, when we grew too tired to shovel any more, we trudged back to the tree for the day. But the Cessna would now be clearly visible to anyone flying over.

Leave it to Mike to ask the tough question: wouldn't our work be for nothing if it stormed again? I hastily admitted it might be, but I deliberately stayed away from pointing out that we were laughing together again, patting each other on the back, both literally and figuratively and seemingly restored to some semblance of our former selves.

"You know what I saw over there today?" Taylor offered more as a declarative statement than a question.

"Bunch of blow-down trees, lots of snow," Michael responded, laughingly.

"Well that, yes, but something else, wise guy."

"What?"

"A rabbit. He stood for a long time staring at us, never moving a hair, never blinking his eyes."

"Really?" I asked. "Where was it. How far away? I didn't see anything."

"Wasn't that far. Michael could throw a football that far, I suppose."

"White, I take it," Megan offered.

"Grayish, I'd say. With black eyes."

"Snowshoe, probably," I said. "Their winter uniform is a kind of off-white. Tame rabbits taste a lot like chicken. Snowshoes may be another story...but they are meat. Tomorrow I will spend the day over there, and if that rabbit shows his face, we'll have the best supper we've had in a long time. Some rabbits, I cautioned, particularly the Jackrabbits that occupy the prairies in eastern Montana, are sometimes diseased. They are hunted for their fur, when pelt prices are decent, but eating them, no, I don't think so."

But, I reminded them, we weren't in eastern Montana, and if by chance I got one, we would cook him until he was very, very well done, and I would personally eat several bites before asking anyone else to do so. A moose or big elk would better suit my fancy, I admitted, but one cannot be choosy when the larder is empty.

Mike and I went over the next morning as soon as we had decent light. We carried the .30-.30 and two of our newly-fashioned snow scoops. With the later we burrowed ourselves into a snowdrift and waited...and waited...and waited. But our patience eventually paid off. I caught one in my sights and sent him flying in the air.

Mike had barely retrieved it, when I saw another dart from tree to tree over to my left. That second shot, I would brag about it for a long time to come. We could have skinned him for his pelt, for it was untouched by my bullet. Can't say the same for the head. It was gone. A .30-.30 cartridge raises havoc with anything as small as a rabbit. Twenty-two caliber rifles are more than sufficient for even a large, mature rabbit. Hit in the right spot, even an air rifle can get the job done.

While it is true that we walked back to our dugout with sizeable chunks of two rabbits, we dispensed with carefully skinning either of them for their pelts, dedicating them instead to rabbit-on-a stick. As I had promised, they made by far the best meal we'd eaten since our breakfast n Missoula.

I think it was while we sat around the fire, slowly nibbling small, but succulent chunks of rabbit, that I decided to make a run for help. We had been rigidly cautious in husbanding our rabbit meat just as we had our power bars and peanut butter, which meant those remaining behind would have something to allay their hunger pangs for a few more days, but not much. The blow-down area had plenty of seasoned firewood, and each of us had dragged back a fair-sized chunk when we returned to our tree the afternoon before.

Dabbing a rope over even one good reason not to tell them of my plan to go for help was impossible. In retrospect, I think it was because there simply were no good reasons. We were a family caught up in a struggle to stay alive. It was not the time for either coddling or deception. In the end I told them of my plan. It would probably take me at least two days, I said. The country between here and the Lolo Pass warming hut, which was my destination, was anything but smooth and I would be plowing snow all the way.

"Been camping over west of here on the Lochsa River in one of the Forest Service campgrounds," I said, "and I've been up to the pass to cross-country ski several times, but I've never hiked this particular area in summer or winter. Years ago my sister and I hiked up Kootenai and Bass Creeks over on the Montana side of the mountains and spent at least one night out each time. Those two creeks flow east almost in a straight line from the peaks of the Bitterroots toward the Bitterroot Valley. From the trail head to the spine of the mountains is about 9 miles. That is about the distance we are now from Lolo Pass. Maybe a bit more, but not much.

"My thinking," I went on, "is that the country between here and Lolo Pass is going to be very much the same as what you'd find east of the mountains. And I point that out so you all understand that, though it is gradually downhill for most of the way, it is likely nothing more than a bunch of ups and downs all the way. I don't even want to think about what its going to be like."

"Maybe it should be me who makes a run for it," Michael ventured. "I'm...well, I'm younger and...what the heck, I'm probably stronger."

"You are younger and stronger, Mike," I agreed, "but I would like you to stay with Megan and Taylor."

"Wouldn't it be better, if we all tried to walk out?" Megan queried. "We could lean on each other. Maybe it would be easier if the all four of us left."

"Thought about that, Honey," I replied, "but it's warm here under the tree. There's a bit of food left and...well, I don't think either of you beautiful ladies is strong enough to make it. Sorry, but I think it would be a mistake."

"But what if you get hurt...or lost? You'd have no one to help you, no one would know we are here. I think we should all leave together."

Surprisingly, it was Taylor who came to my rescue. She admitted that she did not believe she had the strength and stamina to walk

10 miles, much less fight her way through powdery snow up to her waist. "And I don't think you do either, Mom," she added. "Our best chance is to give Jim most of the food and warm clothing. There's only the one pair of snow shoes. Jim can make it, I think. We can't, I'm sure."

The temperature had moderated slightly that night by the time Megan and I walked away from the tree for a few minutes. She was still very apprehensive about what I had proposed and wanted to talk about it privately.

"Jim," she said, imploringly, "is your leaving the right thing to do? I have this dreadful feeling I may never see you again. Can't we just wait it out? We can live for weeks without food if we must, and surely they will find us before that."

She was right, of course. I had agonized over those and other questions, time and again, and nowhere could I uncover an imperative for my leaving. We weren't starving, we were warm, we had water, we weren't shouting at each other yet, no one was hiding in a corner, talking to themselves, and our prospects were actually quite good.

"But what would we do, how would we feel, if one of us suddenly became seriously ill and needed immediate medical attention? Or if in a fit of anger and heightened emotions, one of us were to make a break for what we perceived to be safety during a storm? I can think of any number of unlikely yet plausible scenarios capable of producing tragic results for one or all of us. I hope we never have to face such a thing, but what if we did? What would we do? What could we do? I don't think I could live with knowing that I hadn't tried to reach help."

Megan was not the type to scoff at another's concerns, no matter how notional they might seem, and she didn't now. Instead, she acknowledged that my concerns were hers, for the most part, and that there just might be some merit in my making a run for help.

"I won't ask you not to go, Jim," she said. "I know you feel you must, but if you insist, let's all go together. As a group we can't move as rapidly as you would without us, but we have talked, and we do not wish to be left behind."

"You guys been ganging up on me?" I asked with a smile on my face. "Not fair."

"No ganging up, Jim, but we have talked some. Now we need to talk with the kids. I'll stay out of it."

And talk we did. I began by telling them that leaving them behind never had been nor was it now what I wanted, but that I honestly believed I could make better time alone, that I could bring help sooner.

"The challenge here," I said, "is plowing through snow, and much of it will be on slippery, steep slopes instead of atop a frozen lake. And if you want to know the truth, making it back to Lolo Pass in powdery snow like we've got up here is going to be harder than anything any of us, including me, has ever done. But I think you know that. Still, I'm going to cave in on this one if the consensus is that we go together.

"But, what about you Taylor?" I quickly added, remembering her saying that her mother and her could probably not hack it. "Didn't you say to all of us not long ago that you didn't believe you were up to walking out? Have you changed your mind, or are you just falling in behind what seems to be the majority opinion?"

"No, Jim," she replied in a cutting voice, "I'm not falling in behind anything or anybody. I'm a part of the majority now. Did I change my mind? Yes. Why? Not sure, but when I thought about it, it struck me that if Mom and I get tired along the way or if it storms or whatever, there must be other trees we can hide under. At the very least we should make it part way, which means you'd not have to come back so far to bring us in."

"Good point, Taylor. A very good point that I hadn't thought about. Thanks. You okay with this, Michael?"

"I'm fine, Dad. I want to get home for Christmas even if we are a day or two late."

"All right, then. It's a go," I said with yet some reluctance. "Mother Nature has given us a window of opportunity weather-wise. We should take advantage. We'll leave before noon tomorrow. Between now and then we need to do several things."

The decision to break away from our snow camp as a group was again manifestly transforming. Suddenly, everyone was busily engaged in one facet or another of our preparations. Taylor whistled. Michael hummed. Megan and I smiled.

We were up half the night packing and packing again and again our meager but treasured possessions. When we departed earlier than expected the following morning, we came away with virtually everything except Michael's saddle. Even that was stripped of every inch of latigo leather. The remainder of his tack, which amounted to two bridles, their braided reins, both cinch straps, and even the saddle's silver conchos once held in place with the latigo strips we had seized. With their sharp, rounded edges, we saw them serving as crude knives should I lose mine. We left with the saddle itself wedged more than six feet off the ground between two stout lower branches. It would be reclaimed when we returned with a helicopter to rescue the Cessna.

Bringing our things from the plane to the underside of our tree had required several trips back and forth. There would be no back and forth on this trip, so it had fallen to us to somehow solve the transport problem. Stuffing smaller items into a pack was not an option, for we had none. Michael's book bag came the closest, but its capacity was meager. When we had lashed what we could to our backs using remnants of rope, we were still left with a pile of goods on the ground that did not lend itself to easy transit.

My twin-size air mattress, though hardly designed to serve such a purpose, came to the rescue. The mattress and yet another ingenious idea from Michael's inventive mind did the trick. The kid had a prodigious capacity for spawning ideas that bridged the gap between non-functional and unusable. Inflating the mattress was something I had never considered, because we had used it, not as a bed, but as a moisture barrier between us and our sleeping pad. Michael came up with the idea of making a sled out of it by tying ropes to dog-ears formed at corners of one end. I knew that I had stashed its battery-powered air pump in the pocket on the backside of the pilot's seat, but hadn't thought to bring it in. I had forgotten about it until Michael came up with the sled idea and, even then, I dismissed its utility. The batteries were old, and by now their age combined with sub-zero temperatures had probably robbed them of any juice.

Michael wasn't sure. We should make sure they aren't shot, he said. "I think getting any significant air into this mattress with our mouths is going to be a challenge."

A trip to the plane over a path that was now quite nicely compacted because of use, and the pump was soon cradled in Michael's hands. The long and short of it is, the batteries had just enough power to inflate the mattress to about one-third of its fully-inflated thickness before it ground down to nothing.

"It wouldn't work if it held all the air it could," Mike argued. "Where could I build dog-ears that would hold if it were plumb full? With again as much air, it would have floated easier over the bed of snow, but it's going to be better than no air at all." And time proved that Michael's assessment was right on target. He was going to make one hell of a diagnostician.

Speaking for myself, I have to say that it was a grungy and haggard crew that walked away from our tree home. I was breaking trail, and I mean breaking. The snow we ploughed through...it would be incorrect to say over...gave way beneath my snowshoes to a depth of almost three feet. A sleeping bag was strapped to my back, a length of cotton rope held my .30-.30 against my breast, and that was all I could handle.

Michael followed directly behind me, struggling to inch the sled forward. But the weight of our gear on the fabric sled helped compact the powdery snow, making it easier going for the women. Immediately behind Michael and his sled were Taylor and Megan, both sporting quickly fashioned bear paw type snow shoes. We had used all of the latigo leather from Michael's saddle along with un-braided lengths of one bridle, to lash sturdy branches to their odd-shaped frames. They were not pretty, as they say, but they worked. We knew it was just a matter of time before they came apart, but while they lasted, travel was made easier.

How often we halted to catch our breath or to better secure some object to the sled or to one of us, I could not say. It was often, but between stops we slowly crept forward until one of us called for a stop. Sometimes it was because we were exhausted. Other times it was because we knew the dangers inherent in labor that brought on perspiration our clothes could not quickly wick away. To be cold was one thing. To be cold and wet was quite another.

If my hunch that we had dropped down into the snow-covered surface of Moose Lake proved correct, we had managed to cover only a bit more than a mile before we began looking for a place to spend the night. I didn't need the folded map I carried in my back pocket to know that ahead of us was the junction of two seasonal roads. Both were clearly outlined by the treeless void they left as they cut through the immediate horizon to our right or straight ahead of us. The longer of the two I judged to be, with a zig here and a zag there, 15 or 16 miles almost straight north. It lead directly to Highway 12, the asphalt-covered road that followed Lolo Creek from the town of Lolo to Lolo Pass.

So our route options were limited unless we foolishly tried to bushwhack cross-country through the rough terrain on each side of the road. We turned our backs on bushwhacking and the north-pointing road and fixed our eyes on the opening directly to the west. It was the shorter of the two roads, and I was fairly sure it led to the nearest permanent, warm shelter.

Fixed in my mind was the warming building at the Pass and, in my mind's eye, I could still see those brats and hotdogs browning on the rollers that manually turned them over. My memory was better in recalling the odor and look of those browning dogs than it was for December's calendar. I could no longer fix in my mind the exact day of the month, but I knew my plan to host all of us on Christmas Eve and Christmas day would never be implemented. Not this Christmas, at least, for I was sure we had already missed my chance to display my hosting skills. Still, the span of two weeks that encompassed the Christmas and New Year's holidays would have cross-country skiing enthusiasts out in mass. The tandem tracks would be brimming with the ski people. Were we nearer help than I thought? Time would tell.

We had traveled in relative silence, and though our reticence may have been spurred by a host of factors, including insufficient lung capacity, it fell away like a cascading water fall when we finally came to stand on the road. Over a span of about five hours, we had struggled to traverse a distance of less than two miles. The time had arrived. Yes, we must find refuge before dark.

Our home away from home was yet another soft cushion of needles beneath the lower branches of yet another spruce tree. Burrowing into the space below did not take long, but it soon became apparent, based on the incline leading to the needles below, that we were not out of the deep snow country by any means. Once again, we smoothed a bed of needles and stretched my tent out over it. Megan and I scrambled for firewood in the semi-darkness, and we soon had coffee bubbling over our fire. The small flashlight I kept stashed in my camping gear was in Megan's pocket, but we agreed to save the few remaining, dull rays of light it held for total darkness.

We were out of food except for a dab of peanut butter and one piece of rabbit each. Megan ran a pointed branch through them, taking care not to burn or overcook. It was her attempt to serve hot food. We finished eating quickly, but stayed by the fire, loath to leave its warmth.

I took a minute to glance out through the opening to our cave, which faced north, and I smiled inwardly when I saw that the area was bathed in brightness, compliments of a full moon. Clear skies I took as a good sign, and the outside temperature felt almost balmy, though a soft breeze did make it feel colder as it brushed against my cheek.

Back at the fire, I found my three trail partners staring into it, lost in private thoughts. No one spoke, but Megan looked up to me with a smile as I seated myself at her side. I sensed that while all of us were physically tired, we were not yet sleepy tired, and that we all harbored a need to talk about our day's progress, problems, and possible solutions.

"How's everyone doing?" I asked to no one in particular. "Wore out I suppose."

"Today took the measure of all of us, Jim, I'm afraid to say," Megan offered, "and I'm beginning to wonder if Taylor wasn't correct earlier. How did you know how hard it was going to be? When I think..."

"When you think about the miles yet before us," I offered, as her voice trailed off to silence, "you're wondering if we can make it. Heck, Megan, we are all wondering about that, but don't you worry.

We will. All we need do now is rest and sleep. Tomorrow when we get back on the trail our heads will be saying, 'yes, we can,' and if I'm right, our bodies will be singing the same tune."

"Hope you are right, Dad," Michael ventured. "I know my shoulders and belly are rubbed raw from pulling on the thing...the sled."

"Tomorrow, the sled is mine," I said. "Tomorrow will be easier."

"How about you, Taylor," I continued. "How are you doing?"

"Been better, yes, but when tomorrow comes, I'm going to try and be ready."

"You will be, honey," I said. "We all will be. Besides, tomorrow we are going to slow the pace. And our stops will be more frequent. We're getting closer, you know. Keep that in mind."

Megan and I sat by the fire, holding hands, long after Taylor and Michael sought the comfort and warmth of our foot thick mattress of needles. For Megan and me, words were not needed. We were headed home. We were together. We were in love. Whatever happened in the days that followed, we would face it as a couple. Her lips brushing against my stubbled face were her signal that we should seek the warmth of our bed. I felt her body press close to mine and then, in a matter of minutes, she was sleeping. Our fire burned down to coals twice before I finally found sleep.

Morning brought the reawakened resolve I hoped for, thought might be there, but with it came greater appreciation of how stiff and sore we all were. Words were not needed to reflect the shared feeling that staying put one more day would be therapeutic. It was still there, I'm sure, as we clambered up the snowy stairs leading to the outside world. But no prodding on my part was needed, for they all knew we had to keep moving while the weather cooperated.

The terrain we traveled through was pretty much as I thought it would be, but some of the severity was blunted by the fact that we were following a road. Well, about 14 feet *above* an up and down, switchback road, to be precise. Heavy stands of spruce, intermingled with a few Ponderosa pine, and fewer Cottonwood, Aspen, and adolescent Cedar poked their crowns through the snow. For all of our second day away from our shelter near the plane, the road followed the south fork of Spruce Creek.

Our spruce tree near the crash site sat on the west slope of the Bitterroot Mountains, a couple thousand feet lower than the range's north-south spine. We were slowly dropping further away from those mountains as we moved to the northwest. But I knew our downward hike was only temporary. The warming hut near the cross-country skiing trail head was situated in Idaho just west of Lolo Pass itself, which meant that we must soon begin climbing back up to that spine at Lolo Pass. When we reached our destination atop Lolo Pass, we would actually be about 2,000 feet higher than when we started. Where, I asked myself, was the profit in telling my trail partners that roughly the last half of our hike would be up hill? There was none so far as I could see, so I kept it to myself. Besides, I wasn't at all sure, given the severity of the topography, that any of us would ever know if we were gaining or losing altitude.

Explaining how four snow-plowing hikers, all of whom teetered on the edge of starvation and exhaustion, managed to cover nearly three miles our second day is not easy. Sleep and rest could claim most of the credit, I'm sure, but an early start coupled with the frequent stops also played into the equation.

When we finished our only meal for the day, the peanut butter jar was tossed aside...there was no more. Now we were without any food of any kind. I think we all understood that we could live for several weeks without food as long as our level of exertion was in keeping with our body's ability to claim energy from our core. No matter how I sliced it, the physical demands of exertion were whittling away at our endurance. We were, in and odd way, like long distance runners who constantly guarded against building up an oxygen debt that only rest and a slower pace could pay back. Pressing too hard, our heads would falter first, to be slowly followed by our bodies. If we allowed that to happen, our chances of success would tumble like loose rocks from the mountain side.

Whatever hope I might have had that the four of us could continue as a team fell away like leaves floating on the waters of a rushing creek when Taylor dropped to the ground, screaming.

"Taylor, Taylor," Megan cried out. "What happened? Did you trip on something?"

"My leg!" she shouted. "It hurts so much!"

"Can you stand" I asked, "if I lift you up?"

"I'll try," she said in a sobbing voice, "but the pain is killing me."

Michael and I hoisted her to her feet and held her steady. She tried to step on her right leg, at my urging, but the moment her foot touched the bed of needles, she screamed again. To me it sounded like a very severe charley horse, probably brought on by a combination of strenuous physical activity and insufficient nutrition. Each time she put pressure on the ball of her foot, she shrieked with pain. But she kept trying and, in time, she was standing by herself. The pain subsided, but it did not go away.

I'll give her credit for trying. With some help from Mike, she slowly worked her way about under the canopy of branches that often brushed the top of her head. Her pretty facial features were locked in a grimace she could not conceal and in pain she could not hide. Megan gently massaged her calf muscles and hamstring and, in doing so, brought a degree of visible relaxation.

Dropping down into the bed was clearly painful for her. For a few minutes she worked her leg muscles herself then pulled the covers up to her chin.

"It's better, Mom," were the last words I heard her speak before she slipped into a troubled sleep. Megan turned to me with the look of an alarmed mother, and I think we both thought it unlikely Taylor could go on further. That suspicion proved correct when, during the night, another scream from Taylor pierced the darkness. This time it was her other leg, and once again we managed to allay most of her pain but, I think we suddenly all knew she could go no further without considerable rest. "I can do it, Mom," she asserted, with tears streaming down her cheeks again. "I can do it, Jim."

By now she could no longer stand without assistance. She certainly was not fit to continue traveling. Maybe with a couple of day's rest, she might recover enough for us to try again. But the luxury of waiting was no longer ours. We were out of food, we were exhausted, one of our crew was suddenly an invalid. The others might still be hanging on to a thread of hope for our continuing, but none of them protested when I said the time had come for me to go on alone.

"We can wait out the day here," I said, "but come morning, unless Taylor's legs are dramatically improved, I am going for help on my own. She may need medical attention and none of us is qualified."

Not a single word of protest did I hear. They knew that our best chance of surviving rested in my reaching help. Taylor felt as if she were to blame for our not moving on together, but I tried to reassure her that she was not. I told her it was more my fault than hers. I had asked too much of her, of them all. She deserved a medal for trying. She hobbled about our small enclosure several times, biting her lip and with small tears clouding her vision but, in the end, she gave in to her injuries.

Part of our evening was spent talking about what I would take with me, what I would leave behind. The others were to stay holed-up three full days before they attempted to continue on, and then only if Taylor's condition had improved dramatically. It would take me two days to reach the warming hut. They should allow one full day after that for help to arrive.

During the day, at least one of them was to be posted outside the entrance to their tree haven to enhance the chances of being spotted. Forming a pattern resembling a cross in the snow, using Spruce boughs, was their second responsibility.

We were well within the boundaries of the Selway-Bitterroot Wilderness Area. This was high country, deep snow country, and most of the elk and deer had departed to lower elevations and, in any case, it was now illegal to hunt within the Area.

During most of the year the Wilderness was alive with big game, including bear, elk, moose, whitetail and mule deer, and, among the rocks in the high country, cougars and bob cats. Where there were stands of Ponderosa Pine, Douglas Fir, or even in some of the open, logged stretches with brush, thickets, or new growth, stumbling upon small groups of wild turkeys was not impossible.

They seemed unafraid of man, particularly where they were not hunted for sport. They were not native to the area, but a few forward-looking hunters had, over the years before it became a Wilderness Area, planted Wild Turkeys.

On the other hand, the likelihood of spotting turkeys or, for that matter, any of the big game that seasonally occupied the area was exceedingly small. Still Michael was to take the rifle with him, when it came his turn to be the lookout, and to scout the nearby terrain looking for wildlife. His chances of spotting anything he could draw a bead on, legally or illegally, were slim to nothing. But if supper showed itself in his front sight, my instructions were that he put his finger to the trigger.

My mental outlook the next morning when I said goodbye to the three of them was one of optimism. The sun had already poked its head over the Bitterroots, and the temperature was the warmest it had been since the Cessna belly-flopped in the snow.

I had taken care to repair my crude snowshoes the night before, and I was wearing sufficient clothing to keep me warm and protect me from the wind; my pockets were empty except for my Swedish Army knife and the almost powerless, pocket-flashlight; my feet were dry, and I had fashioned, two relatively straight spruce limb poles to help me keep my balance. Slung across my back with one of Michael's bridle reins was half of one of the sleeping bags. The one item I was missing was the map I had carefully studied the evening before, and my discovery came too late for me to think of turning back. But I had a mind's-eye picture of the lay-of-the-land, and I was confident I could live without it.

What I saw as realistic expectations had me basking in the warming house adjacent to the cross-country ski parking lot at Lolo Pass no more than two days hence. The straight line distance was about five miles. Following the crooks and curves in the road added a couple of miles, but my thoughts were fixed on a spot directly ahead of me where I could cut off a mile or more by climbing to the top of a ridge before dropping down onto the road again.

Before the morning was half over, I had piled one mistake upon a second which, instead of subtracting from the total distance I needed to cover, added to it. The first mistake, now when I look back on it, I'll blame on my forgetting my Wilderness Area map with the others. What I did was leave the road by turning into a small creek I mistook for Brush Creek. It was nearly two miles long but came to an abrupt dead end, and it was not until then that I began to realize what I had done.

My next mistake came about when I tried to bushwhack my way up and over the ridge on my right, thinking it would take me to the length of road I should have taken in the first place. And it would have had I been able to climb it. I burned another two hours of my time trying. When I finally gave up and turned to head back to the north, my body was wet beneath my clothes, and I felt wet snow flakes against my face. The sun was still shining brightly in the south, and I was not overly concerned with what I guessed was a squall line that would quickly pass and take its large snow flakes with it. What I missed seeing, because of the steep ridge that was now off my left shoulder, was a mass of dark, almost black clouds building in the west.

My lack of a map and incredibly poor judgment joined to cost me dearly. As the crow flies I was actually further from Lolo Pass than I would have been had I stayed with Megan, Taylor and Michael. Not only that, I was facing into a wind that seemed to be picking up speed by the minute. Surrounded on every side with loose snow, I knew what the result would be if it began blowing even harder.

While I made my run to the dead end rock wall and tried to climb the ridge, the sun had reached the middle of its arc, so I still had some daylight. What could I do but press on back to the point where I had made a wrong turn? The temperature was holding on the warm side, I was properly dressed, and I had plenty of time before darkness to seek shelter. Nonetheless, I kept my eyes peeled for a likely spot.

By now I knew full well how I had come to make my first mistake, and my hope was to reach the spot where I had made that wrong turn. But I was growing more concerned by the minute, as heavy snow and a gusty wind blotted out the countryside, except when a break in the cloud cover allowed sunlight to penetrate. At times, as if by magic, the wind tapered off dramatically, and I could see my immediate surroundings clearly. The beauty I beheld, in spite of everything, was simply awesome. I was caught up in a wilderness area preserved in a pristine state so visitors can experience it's rugged beauty. New country it surely was to me. I had been in the Selway-Bitterroot Wilderness Area, but I had never laid eyes on the country I now plowed through. It was rugged beyond description, and it was bathed in a snow-white winter beauty. Snow ghosts dominated some of the slopes in grotesque shapes that spoke to the high winds and storms the area sometimes experiences. I guess one could argue that I was experienced with regard to storms. Experience I had earned in the past few days.

Moving slowly and carefully to avoid missing my turn a second time, I edged forward with my skull cap pulled down over my ears as far as I could. Then as if the magician had tossed his wand into a snowbank, the winds rejoined me in earnest. The rough scarf Megan had fashioned for me, I held across my face to blunt the sting of wind-driven snowflakes that bombarded my skin. And without consciously thinking to do so, I was suddenly flailing my arms about and slapping my body to help maintain circulation. The temperature had made a nose dive, driving home to me how urgent it was to find shelter.

My progress toward Lolo Pass was too small to measure even with the delicate calibration of my mind's-eye. I had fooled away an entire day. But suddenly that was less important than finding shelter. Moving slowly to the north, my eyes darted from one side of the steep-sided draw to the other, searching, always searching for cover. Though I barely recognized it because of poor visibility, I managed to reach the junction of the trail where I had made a wrong turn, and I swung to the left and moved slowly on a section of the road heading west.

The wind was blowing hard out of the northwest now, which caused me to focus on the slope to the right. I wanted to find something where the snow drifted over me rather than into my shelter. I found it just as the road made a sharp turn to the south. Finding space under another spruce tree probably saved my life. Beneath the branches I found respite from the wind, warmth and utter darkness. Even on a sunny winter day, darkness ruled beneath the branches.

The pocket flashlight gave just enough light to reveal a few dead branches resting on the bed of pine needles. Combined with the kindling I carried in my jacket pocket they gave me time to find and break away more dead branches from the underside of the tree. I found enough to build a bigger fire that lasted long enough to collect more dry wood and boil two cups of coffee. I had no food. Only the clothes on my back and half of my sleeping bag. A long night it was going to be.

Chapter 14

For a long time, my small fire gave me both company and warmth. My watch said it was late afternoon, and I had already devoted a fair amount of time blaming myself for the blunders that had taken me better than two miles away from the trail back to Lolo Pass. Caught up in my own feelings of guilt, I had hardly thought of the others. But now, in my solitude, I thought only of them. I missed them terribly, and I upbraided myself for being so stupid as to leave them alone.

Like me, they were held captive beneath a tree by the cold and wind. They were safe for now, I was sure, and their privations were no greater than my own. But I missed them. Mix Morgan into the equation and they were the sum of my life. Others there were, of course. My own life had inexorably distanced me from my parents and my children's grandparents and from friends of an earlier time. They now occupied a rung beneath Jennifer and Claire Macintosh, Benny Tovar, and Odin Norgaard, all of whom managed to touch my life every day. It was not that I cared less for my mother and father or the others. They were dear to me. My love went out to them all, without reservation, but they were no longer an every-day feature on my personal landscape.

BACK TO NEVER BEEN

I had returned to Montana, feeling unloved, empty, and forlorn, an existence and state of being easily traced to my ineptitude in love, my preoccupation with self, and a disregard for the needs and feelings of my wife, my children, and a host of others. In spite of that, each of them had in their own way filled my heart again with love. I deserved none of it, but they gave and they gave and they gave.

Michele had been the catalyst for change. At the starting gate, she felt as I did that she could not love again, dare not love again. She had lost the love of her life to an accident. I had thoughtlessly thrown away my own. But we had given in to love again, and we were ready to put our hearts at risk one more time. Her untimely death brought me to my knees, and I retreated once more into myself, pledging never to risk anything again when it came to matters of the heart. Michele's death was for me, at the time, a resounding reminder that love is like a mine field just waiting to detonate. On must tread with care. My marriage to Rebecca fell victim to the mines I, myself, had planted. As I watched and felt my life crumbling around me, I came to believe that without love one could never truly be complete. But too late I had learned it.

My children saved me. Both of them had suffered their own heartbreak and disenchantment, largely because of me, but they ultimately taught me that forgiveness heals wounds that the mere passage of time seems unable to accomplish. Michael never condoned how I had treated his mother, but he understood why we had drifted apart and fallen out of love. He understood how it could happen and he forgave. Morgan, who in the beginning had said she hated me more than she had ever hated anyone or anything in her life, came to understand that her parents were *both* guilty of breaking their marriage vows and that they were both unhappy. She had struggled to understand, mostly because she believed that what had happened was beyond understanding and unforgivably unfair. Still she came to see that in spite of everything, both her mother and I loved her. In the end it was Morgan, my bright and lovely 16 year-old, who showed me it was okay to love again.

And love found me once more in Megan Macintosh. When one finds that one person, that partner for life, there is no turning back. Megan and I had found each other, and nothing could ever pry us apart again, not even a mountain blizzard. I wondered how she and the children were doing, but I knew Michael would have made certain that they had enough firewood to carry them through the night. He would have taken over my duties as the group's fire tender. He might even have brought down another rabbit, but the report of a rifle had never reached my ears.

They were starving just as I was, but we had all gradually grown accustomed to the gnawing discomfort that rumbled through our bellies. They would be talking and speculating as to how much progress I had made and if I had found comfortable lodging. Michael would tend to the smoke holes, and he would see to it that the three of them stayed put until it was safe to go outside again. I hoped they would sleep well this night.

For the first time since the Cessna plopped into the snow, I could not stay warm. My instincts told me that the temperature outside had dropped again to well below zero. I burrowed myself into the needles and pulled my cropped sleeping bag up to my chin. Briefly I slept, but the cold soon wrenched me from my slumber. The fire had slumped to a bed embers, yet it harbored a small cluster of hot coals that burst into flame as I carefully piled on a handful of small branches. Several hours later, surprised at how long I had slept, cold once again drove me back to my fire. This time, I had to start from scratch, but with the help of my butane cigarette lighter I soon had both heat and light. Until the fire's light began to falter again, I stayed up and harvested as many of the dead branches on the tree's underside as I could reach.

Returning to my sleeping bag, I tried again for sleep, but it was like a circling, chicken hawk, dipping and diving and soaring, to avoid being caught. Finally, I got to my hands and knees and crawled toward the opening that allowed me in and out. Black as the underside of a coffin it was, and I could see nothing. A blizzard still raged and to venture into it was to commit suicide.

Within me raged a fierce battle between rushing back to them and staying where I was. My advice to them had been to hunker down beneath their tree if it began storming again. Wait until you know it is safe, I remember telling them. Suddenly I wanted to be with them. I wanted us to be together. I wanted to protect them, and I knew why. I was afraid. For the first time since our crash landing, my confidence was ebbing, and I was genuinely fearful of the outcome for all of us. I wanted to be strong for them, but being so grew harder and harder. They needed me now as much as they ever had, and I was not with them.

The irony of it all was that I wasn't sure I could find them even if I tried. Poking my head out through the entrance again killed my inclination to make a try for their home in the snow, but it persisted throughout the remainder of the day. The promise I made to myself before I crawled into my sleeping bag that night was that even if it was still storming in the morning, I would turn back and try to find them. I couldn't leave them alone any longer.

Finally, I found sleep and, several hours later, I began pulling myself from my bed. Sometime during the night, my brain had made an end-around trip back to reason. What had seemed the proper, sensible thing to do during the night flew away like thistles bounding across a dry prairie during a wind storm. My returning would not help them. It would help nothing. All it could do was delay reaching real help. We needed help from others, anybody. They were hungry and cold like me. They would still be hungry and cold if I returned.

We would all be hungry and cold and not one single inch closer to being rescued.

My first glimpse out through the entrance revealed yesterday all over again, the only difference being that the wind followed a horizontal path and was swirling snow across the ground rather than creating white-out conditions that reached far above the surrounding trees. It was into that blowing snow that I would go, and I would face it head on, for the wind was now racing from the northwest to the southeast.

The trees were shrouded in white, with snow clinging to branches like frosting on the side of a wedding cake, but the path through them was no longer lost in the swirling whiteness of yesterday that washed away sharpness and definition. The opening in the trees, which defined the course of the road, was discernible to me except when savage gusts momentarily blotted my visibility. It was into that maelstrom of Mother Nature I trekked, but I was determined to match it with my own resolve, heightened sense of purpose, and an instinctive trust in myself.

I told myself I was smarter than this wind or any other wind, and I began preparing myself as best I could to face the next twenty-four hours of the greatest test of my life. Twenty-four hours is the time I allotted myself to reach Lolo Pass. To improve the odds of that happening, I strengthened my snowshoes and reinforced the binding with rope. Draping them over a limber length of spruce, I dried my stockings then pulled tight the stitches that held my tarpaulin booties together.

One final cup of coffee trickled down my throat as I pulled the scarf Megan had made over my skull cap and around my collar. Instead of hanging my sleeping bag in a role over my shoulders, I fashioned it into a shawl and lashed it over and around my shoulders and mid-section for added warmth. When I pushed away the snow from the entrance and climbed out into the wind, everything I wore was dry. It was not pretty, but it was dry.

The wind bit into my exposed forehead in a matter of seconds, so the skull cap came forward over my brow. Moments later the rest of my face was stinging from the frost, so I halted long enough to push my scarf up over my nose and away from my face. My breath was condensing against the scarf's fabric and freezing instantly. Pushing it an inch from my face kept my lips and nose away from the sheet of ice that was quickly forming behind my scarf.

Surprisingly, I found that the snow beneath my crude snowshoes was not as deep as it had been yesterday. The explanation, I was sure, rested with the wind. Ground blizzard conditions, which move great quantities of snow along near the surface had, I believed, actually removed some of the snow, depositing it elsewhere. Make no mistake, it was still a massive challenge to move forward. The poles I had fashioned from spruce branches to steady myself when I was pulling the mattress-tent, helped me now to stand as the snow and wind gusts pommeled me savagely. How many times they failed to keep me from toppling one way or another into the snow, I couldn't say. Each time I struggled to find my feet and lift myself to an upright position. Add to that the times I halted to catch my breath or to survey the path ahead, I immediately grasped how slow my progress was. Tortoises were slower but not by much. Every step was a test.

Less than a mile from where I began, I stopped to carefully absorb what my eyes beheld and, then, to consider the best strategy for moving on. On my left the opening in the trees led to the south. I remembered as I stood there that it ran on to the south for about a mile, passed through a notch in a ridge then doubled back on itself a mile or so before it turned again and headed west. Traversing those two miles would reduce the distance to the warming hut by less than one-fourth of a mile. That was not good enough. Before me stood a ridge which, if I could match my strength against its height and ruggedness, I could gain that one-fourth mile without plowing snow for two miles...and I could gain precious time.

My hesitation stemmed from my experience of the day before when I had wasted two hours in a failed attempt to climb such a ridge. Still it was clear to me that my energy was better spent attempting to climb the ridge than trekking the two miles. With every step I could feel that my energy reserves were quickly shrinking, and I knew that conserving as much as possible could be the key to reaching help. I decided to take the chance. If I made it I would be within three miles of the Pass and the warming shed.

My inclination was to turn my back to a wind that seemed determined to put me down. Without the scarf as a buffer, I had the frightening feeling that the wind would suck my breath from my lungs. It was that strong. Now and again, I turned about, but only long enough to catch my breath and rub my face with my homely mittens. Skin, exposed for more than a few minutes turned red and smarted to the touch. When I began to experience a tingling sensation in my arms or legs, I stopped. Incessant movement helped maintain circulation in my lower extremities, but it also robbed my legs of strength to a point where they seemed detached from the rest of my body.

When I reached the base of the ridge I was determined to climb, I halted again. Making my way to a good-sized Aspen, I turned myself side-ways to the wind and, leaning against its smooth bark, I began exploring the ridge's face with my eyes, looking for two things. The first was a narrow, tree-lined corridor affording me hand-holds almost every step of the way. Snow that gave way under one's foot need not be a deterrent so long as a branch or tree trunk was within easy reach.

The second worrisome concern was the stability of snow hanging over the ridge line itself. Given the ridge's eastern face and the area's prevailing northwest winds, I assumed that heavy drifts had built near its tops, particularly on its lee side. Even if they were stable and unlikely to crumble under a climber's weight, it was essential to locate slots between leading edges which were large enough to pass through without triggering a rush of snow capable of burying or seriously injuring a climber.

I soon found the corridor I sought, and I was confident I had also found a slot that would permit me to pass on over the top without dislodging the cap of snow perched on the lip of the ridge. My first steps away from the tree seemed almost effortless, but I knew it was only because I had rested. Those that followed grew progressively more demanding, but I made decent progress...until, until the snow gave way below my left foot and I lost my hand hold on a tree. When I stopped tumbling and sliding, my face was covered with snow and my mittens were filled as well. I shook the snow from my mittens, brushed it away from my face, took a deep breath and resumed climbing.

My next close call came when I was within 20 feet of the top. I had worked most of my way through a slot between two projecting cornices of hard snow as I watched the drift to my left give way and gain momentum on its downward rush. Instinctively, I jumped to my left and threw myself across the snow. At times, I was sure I was covered by the snow and, at other times, I could look up and see clouds rolling past. When all movement subsided I sat up, dazed and disoriented. Below me a dozen feet or more one of my snowshoes protruded from the snow. The other, inexplicably, was still lashed to my foot.

Before I was through I was feeling very much like Megan's Sisyphus fellow who could never finish pushing a stone...or was it a ball...up the hill. I never knew whether he eventually made it all the way to the top...but I did. After half a dozen attempts I was perched at the top, looking down on an opening in the trees to the west. The road, it was there! I had survived two mini-avalanches, each of which dumped additional chunks of hard snow along the slope. So much of the slope came to be blanketed with such chunks that the going was actually easier, because the fluff had been washed away. Dropping down the west side was infinitely less demanding. Gravity was no longer my enemy; it had become my partner, instead. An hour after I began my descent, I was standing in the middle of the road, straddling the wind-blown tracks left by two sets of skis. But before I could follow them back to Lolo Pass, I had to rest. My physical reserves had been depleted by the exertion I had expended in climbing the ridge. My legs wouldn't work properly, and I found myself sprawled across the ski tracks half a dozen times. I felt faint. At times, the world around me was spinning wildly, even when my eyes were closed.

Suddenly, I knew. I was done. I could go no further. I had been used up. I had failed. But I couldn't quit! Three people I loved were depending on me. Somehow I managed to crawl up next to a tree and sat against it, thinking time might wash away the dizziness and nausea I was feeling. I closed my eyes and waited. Suddenly in the distance, I saw a small but bright light. I knew instantly that it came from Claire and Jennifer's house. The first time I had visited them, I had staggered up to their front door, drunk, wet, and totally disoriented. It had been my beacon in the rain. Now it was shining brightly through the snow. This time, I would crawl instead of stagger, if it came to that, and hope they would hear my knock on their door. Thinking I might yet save Megan and the kids, I watched as the light grew nearer. I called out to them as loudly as I could, hoping against hope that they would see me and come help me into the house.

Then a voice I did not recognize called out, "Mister, for God's sake what are you doing down there on the ground? You'll freeze to death if you don't stand up."

"Here, let me help," another voice cried out.

The next thing I knew, and remember now only fuzzily, someone lifted me from the ground and began rubbing me everywhere with their gloved hands.

"The light over there," I said. "It's Claire and Jennifer's place. The Macintoshes. I work for them. They are probably searching for me. That's why they aren't out here to see me. I'm going to marry their daughter. She so beautiful...her eyes...they... No, please, help me over there. I'll show them where to find Megan and the kids. If you won't help me, stay out of my way."

"There's no light anywhere in sight, mister," one of them uttered. "What you saw was the light on my snowmobile."

"The hell there ain't" I shouted. "Plain as day. I've got to get there. They have a phone. They can call for help. Maybe call a wrecker."

One of them said *they* were my help, and I have a fuzzy recollection of the other saying he was going to run back to the pass and get more help. Arguing was pointless. They weren't listening. I tried to stand on my own but fell instantly. The person who stayed and who turned out to be a pretty young girl, kneeled at my side, rubbed me with her heavy mittens, and plied me with questions. I remember saying our plane had crashed.

"My God!" the girl screamed. "Are you one of those people they have been searching for all week long? Where have you been?"

To weak, and to confused to answer, I closed my eyes and leaned back against my tree, feeling lost and defeated...feeling like I was dead. I knew I would never reach Jenny and Claire's house. I had failed again just as I had failed in love.

The loud roar of a motor brought me back from my sleepy journey to never been, and I looked up to see the bright lights of a vehicle of some sort racing toward the two of us. Minutes later, a huge, yellow contraption pulled up beside me. The doors flew open, and before I could grasp what was happening, they had me loaded inside and we were on our way, I hoped, to Claire and Jennifer's place.

"I should call them and tell them I will be there shortly and that they should get their jackets on," I said.

By the time we stopped, I had collected myself enough to see that we had stopped before a small, lighted building. The warming shed! I had made it!

They carried me inside and began interrogating me like I might have been an escapee from Deer Lodge. There questions all had to do with the location of the others.

"They are just short of where the road turns to the south," I said. "Under a tree. In the needles. We have to find them before dark. I'll show you."

"In a few minutes," someone said. "We've called the country search and rescue people. They'll be here shortly. But in the meantime, we have to warm you up and get you out of those wet clothes."

"They're wet?" I stammered. "Don't feel wet."

Attired in a pair of blue, insulated pants, with a wide stripe going down the side, and a goose-down jacket, I later found myself sitting on a chair in the middle of the room sipping on a cup of steaming hot chocolate. The place was crowded with people now, all of whom were, I gathered, part of a large group of searchers who had apparently come to see the bedraggled oddity that I must have seemed. No one said much. I guess they realized my mental state was one of confusion and that straight answers were unlikely. I didn't care. When that helicopter arrived, I would show them the way.

The roar that wiped out all other sounds within the shack was that of the helicopter. I lifted myself from the wooden chair, and began staggering toward the door. Strong hands and arms grabbed me and, I guess, kept me from falling. In no time I was lifted into a side door and someone began strapping me in."

"We've a good idea where the others are," a deep voice said. "We'll head up there in a couple of Snow Cats and our trail grooming snowmobile. We'll find them. Better get this guy to St. Pat and get back here on the double."

"No!" I screamed as I fumbled with my seat belt. "I can show you."

"We'll find them," a tall man said in a soft voice. "We'll bring them down to Missoula in a couple of hours. You need medical attention, and you need it now. You are suffering from frost bite, and the sooner we get you down to the valley, the better chance there is your fingers and toes can be saved."

My words of protest fell on empty ears, and before I knew it we were lifting off the asphalt parking area. I watched as someone hung a clear plastic bag over my head, felt the needle prick my skin, and that was it. The next thing I remember was someone squeezing my hand so hard it hurt.

Looking up, I saw Megan, Michael and Taylor standing next to me. I sensed others were in the room but they were hidden in the shadows. I fought back tears but I lost. Somehow, I knew that my tears were tears of happiness, not sadness. I had been found! They had been found! How long I lay there, with my face soaking in tears, I could not say, but if it reflected my joy and relief at seeing the three of them, it was for a long time. I stammered something about how much I missed them, then started crying again. What the hell kind of a Montana cowboy was I any way? Crying like a baby without a sliver of shame.

Part of the time, Megan and I were crying a duet, you could say, but neither of us could stop. When she cried, I cried.

"It's okay, Mom," Taylor said. "He is going to be all right."

"I'm not *gonna* be all right, Miss Taylor," I said. "I *am* all right. But what about you guys? You okay?"

"We're fine," Megan replied, "and so are you, in case you're not sure."

"Have I been here long?"

"Days."

"Did I loose anything?" I asked cautiously.

"Not a thing, Dad," Michael's voice ventured. "Jack Frost nipped some of your toes and fingers, but the doctors are saying they can save them. They're probably going to turn black temporarily, and they're going burn like all get out for a while, but that's all. You are very lucky. We are all lucky, thanks to you."

"Well, what about me?" a soft voice called out. "When am I ever going to hug my dad?"

I knew instantly that the voice I heard was Morgan's. I watched as she slipped in between Michael and Taylor and reached for my hand. Tears were streaming down her face now. Michael was brushing his eyes too, and I knew it was tears he was trying to hide.

"Everybody is feeling sorry for you, Dad," she said, squeezing down hard on my hands above the gauze, "but I'm a little put out, if you must know. I'm wondering what could have been so important to you, that you couldn't at least be home when your daughter travels all the way from Baltimore to spend Christmas with you."

"Come here, child," I cried. "Plant a big one on your dad's cheek. I love you. Can't believe you are here."

She did as I asked and then told me I had other company. I looked up to see Claire and Jennifer edge up next to my bed. Claire touched my shoulder with his calloused hand, and Jennifer touched her lips to my cheek. No one needed tell me they had worried about me, and the others, and that this was one of the happiest days of their lives, and mine. I could see it in their eyes and feel it in my heart.

Next in line were a washed and scrubbed Benny Tovar and Odin Norgaard.

"Good to see both of you," I said, meaning it. "Benny, have you ever been so far from home?"

"Nope. This is the most farest I been," he answered. "Brought your Christmas present, a pair of good leather gloves. Me and Odin we figure, you'll need them when you get home. Lots of work been piling up while you been gone."

"Brought you my present too," Odin interjected, in his bashful voice. "Tackle box. Told Benny it's time I teach you how to fish."

We told Benny and Odin they should stay back and watch the stock" Jennifer said, "but they both said if they couldn't come along, they'd quit."

There were other surprises in store for me, not the least of which were my parents and Rebecca's mother and father. They said they'd been sitting on the edge of their chairs for over a week, watching the news and waiting for word about me and the others. They said they wanted to be here when we were found, and I said I was more than happy to oblige them.

Yes, I was glad. I knew my mom and dad would settle for nothing less than being there when we were found. The Hales need not have, but I sensed they had not stopped caring for their former son-in-law. There were others: Jason Carmack and his mother, Ellen, Daniel and Flynn Hegary, Jim Madsen, and Marty Larson, Michele's hulking brother. The Carmacks were quiet, but Daniel and Flynn joked with me about needing more flying lessons and neglecting their calves. Jim Madsen brought with him the best wishes of his partners and staff, in what I saw as a thoughtful but unnecessary gesture.

Marty Larson was the last to leave the room other than for my spruce tree companions and Morgan.

"Good to see you are okay, Jim," he said. "I'm going to say goodbye, but I wanted you to know that a lot of people were praying for your safe return. You have a lot of friends out there, and I hope you can call me one of them. My wife and I would like to drop in some time with the kids. Like to spend a little time at Michele's grave. We all miss her. She would be proud of you."

What could I say. Michele and I had shared so much, and I still missed her, I would always remember her. But I had found a new love, and she was sitting in a chair next to my bed, holding my hand. She looked up when Marty walked out the door, but said nothing. We held hands for a long time without saying a word. Then suddenly, we both began speaking at once. Megan held her hand in the air signaling that she wanted to be first.

"Jim," she began, "I need to tell you, right now, that you will always be my go-to guy. You saved my life. You saved all of us. None of us will ever forget, none of us can ever find words to tell you how thankful we are, so I'm not going to try.

"I know it has been hard for us both to love again," she continued, in a soft voice, as I tried to lift myself to a sitting position, "but we have drifted in that direction, ever so slowly since, maybe, the first day we met. We both fought it at first, I think, but maybe that's the best way. I owe you for saving my life, but I owe you more for letting me fall in love again."

"You owe me..."

"Let me say what I must say, Jim. I'm never going to let you go. You are a part of me already. You have made me complete. Promise me we'll fill the rest of our lives with each other. Let's fix that plane so we can travel. More calves. We need more calves. I want more calves. Let's add on to your place and let Earl and Ellen live in my house. Let's show my mom and dad what its like to soar above the clouds on our way to places we've never been. Let's watch our kids grow, and lets stick around to see our grandchildren make their way in the world. I want a covered porch surrounding our home that gives us a view in every direction. Mornings I want to look out at the Roots and remember our first night together. Afternoons, I want to feast my eyes on the Madisons as the sun casts its shadow into its corners and defines its ridges and peaks. Evenings, I want to sit there with you and make plans for living. I don't want to waste a minute. I owe you so much. You gave me back my life."

"*Nothing* is what you owe me, Meg," I was able to say, finally. "Nothing at all. It's me who owes. Listen to me, please. My mother tells the story that once when I was about three years old she scolded me for misbehaving in some way and that I looked up to her and said, 'If you're not going to let me do what I want to do, they why'd you born me?'"

"And...?"

"Well, I've asked myself that question again and again over the years, never certain what my role in life was to be. Now I know. It hit me while I was ploughing through that snow on the way to Lolo Pass. She born me for you and for our kids. Think about it. We couldn't possibly know, but we've been following the same path from the beginning, and it led us to each other. The things that happened were supposed to happen. I understand now why your folks took me in and treated me like a son. They were just holding me for you. We were supposed to be together. Everything that has pointed us straight at each other. You're *my* reason for being here today, not the other way around. Destiny planned for us to be together. We are each other's reason for living. I would have plopped down in a snow bank and slept my life away, if it weren't for you. It was *you* who saved *me*. Any questions?"

"Nope."

"Well I've got a few..."

"Let's hear 'em."

"The plane? We need to get it out of that snowbank."

"It's out. Benny and Odin are hauling it back home in the morning.

Some people from the airport removed the wings and fastened them in place against the fuselage. We're going to ride in it a thousand times, if I have my way. Any other questions?"

"There's a ton of work waiting for me back home. When am I getting out of here?"

"When I say so."

"Who's watching our calves?"

"Earl."

"When are we getting married?"

"When I'm ready."

"Can you be more specific?"

"Soon. Morgan wants to know what we are waiting for."

"Pick a date and a place, then."

"A week from today, at your...no, at our place."

"Good! I'll bring the salad."

Montana
Montana Montana
Montana Montana Montana
Montana Montana
Montana

LaVergne, TN USA
17 September 2009
158290LV00001B/6/P

9 781432 739171